THE OTHER NAME:
SEPTOLOGY I-II

THE OTHER NAME:
SEPTOLOGY I-II

Jon Fosse

Translated from the Norwegian by
Damion Searls

**TRANSIT
BOOKS**

Published by Transit Books
2301 Telegraph Avenue, Oakland, California 94612
www.transitbooks.org

LIBRARY OF CONGRESS CATALOGING INFORMATION AVAILABLE UPON REQUEST

DESIGN & TYPESETTING
Justin Carder

DISTRIBUTED BY
Consortium Book Sales & Distribution
(800) 283-3572 | cbsd.com

Printed in the United States of America

9 8 7 6 5 4 3 2 1

The translation has been published
with the financial support of NORLA.

To Anna

'And I will give him a white stone, and on the stone a new name written, which no one knows except him who receives it.'
Revelation

'Dona nobis pacem.'
Agnus Dei

I

AND I SEE MYSELF STANDING and looking at the picture with the two lines that cross in the middle, one purple line, one brown line, it's a painting wider than it is high and I see that I've painted the lines slowly, the paint is thick, two long wide lines, and they've dripped, where the brown line and purple line cross the colours blend beautifully and drip and I'm thinking this isn't a picture but suddenly the picture is the way it's supposed to be, it's done, there's nothing more to do on it, I think, it's time to put it away, I don't want to stand here at the easel any more, I don't want to look at it any more, I think, and I think today's Monday and I think I have to put this picture away with the other ones I'm working on but am not done with, the canvases on stretchers leaning against the wall between the bedroom door and the hall door under the hook with the brown leather shoulderbag on it, the bag where I keep my sketch-pad and pencil, and then I look at the two stacks of finished paintings propped against the wall next to the kitchen door, I already have ten or so big paintings finished plus four or five small ones, something like that, fourteen paintings in all in two stacks next to each other by the kitchen door, since I'm about to have a show, most of the paintings are approximately square, as they put it, I think, but sometimes I also paint long narrow ones and the one with the two lines crossing is noticeably oblong, as they put it, but I don't want to put this one into the show because I don't like it much, maybe all things considered it's not really a painting, just two lines, or maybe I want to keep it for myself and not sell it? I like to keep my best pictures, not sell them, and maybe this is one of them, even though I don't like it? yes, maybe I do want to hold onto it even if you might say it's a failed painting? I don't know why I'd want to keep it, with the bunch of other pictures I have up in the attic, in a storage room, instead of getting rid of it, or maybe, anyway, maybe Åsleik wants the picture? yes, to give Sister as a Christmas present? because every year during Advent I give him a painting that he gives to Sister as a Christmas present and I get meat and fish and firewood and other things from him, yes, and I mustn't forget, as Åsleik always says, that he shovels the snow from my driveway in the winter too, yes, he says things like that too, and when I say what a painting like that can sell for in Bjørgvin Åsleik says he can't believe people would pay so much for a painting, anyway whoever does pay that much money must have a lot of it, he says, and I say I know what you mean about it being a lot of money, I think so too, and Åsleik says well in that case he's getting a really good deal, in that case it's a very expensive Christmas present he's giving Sister every year, he says, and I say yes, yes, and then we both fall silent, and then I say that I do give him a little money for the salt-cured lamb ribs for Christmas, dry-cured mutton, salt cod, firewood, and for shovelling the snow, maybe a bag with some groceries that I bought in Bjørgvin when I've gone there to run an errand, I say, and he says, a little embarassed, yes I do do that, fair's fair, he says, and I think I shouldn't have said that, Åsleik doesn't want to accept money or anything else from me, but when I think about how I have enough money to get by and he has almost none, yes, well, I slip him a few more bills, quickly, furtively, as if neither of us knows it's happening, and when I go run errands in Bjørgvin I always buy something for Åsleik, I think, because I may not make much money but he makes almost nothing compared to me, I think, and I look at the stack of finished paintings with the homemade stretchers they're on facing out and every painting has a title painted in thick black oil paint on the top board of the stretcher, and the painting I'm looking at the back of, at the front of the stack, is called *And the Waves Beat Their Message,* titles are very important to me, they're part of the picture itself, and I always paint the title in black on the top of the stretcher, I make my stretchers myself, I always have and I always will as long as I paint pictures, I think, and I think that there may actually be too many paintings here for a show but I'll take them all to The Beyer Gallery anyway, Beyer can put some of them in the side room of the gallery, in The Bank, as he calls the room where he stores pictures that aren't in the show, I think, and then I take another look at the picture with the two lines crossing, both in impasto as they put it, and the paint has run a little and where the lines cross the colours have turned such a strange colour, a beautiful colour, with no name, they usually don't have names because obviously there can't be names for all the countless colours in the world, I think and I step a few feet back from the picture and stop and look at it and then turn off the light and stand there looking at the picture in the dark, because it's dark outside, at this time of year it's dark, or almost dark, all day long, I think and I look at the picture and my eyes get used to the darkness and I see the lines, see them cross, and I see that there's a soft light in the painting, yes, a soft invisible light, well then yes so it probably is a good painting, maybe, I think, and I don't want to look at the picture any more, I think, but still I'm standing and looking at it, I have to stop looking at it now, I think, and then I look at the round table over by the window, there are two chairs next to it and one of them, the one on the left, that's where I sat and sit, and the right-hand one was where Ales always sat, when she was still alive, but then she died, too young, and I don't want to think about that, and my sister Alida, she died too young too, and I don't want to think about that either, I think, and I see myself sitting there in my chair looking out at the fixed point in the waters of the Sygne Sea that I always look at, my landmark, with the tops of the pines that grow below my house in the middle of the centre pane in the bisected window, in the right-hand part, because the window is divided in two and both parts can be opened and each side is divided into three rows and the tops of the pines will be in the middle row of the right side and I can make out the pines and I've found the mark, right at the midline I can see waves out there in the darkness and I see myself sitting there looking at the waves and I see myself walking over to my car where it's parked in front of The Beyer Gallery, I'm there in my long black coat with my brown leather bag over my shoulder, I've just been to The Coffeehouse, I didn't have much of an appetite, I often don't, and just skip dinner, but today I've had a simple open-faced ground-beef sandwich with onions and now the day's over and I've bought everything I wanted to buy in Bjørgvin so now it's time for me to drive home to Dylgja, after all it's a long drive, I think, and I get into the car, I put the brown shoulderbag down on the passenger seat and start the car and then leave Bjørgvin the way Beyer taught me, one day he showed me the way, showed me how to drive into Bjørgvin and out of Bjørgvin, how to get to The Beyer Gallery and then leave The Beyer Gallery the same way going in the opposite direction, I think, and I'm driving out of Bjørgvin and I fall into the nice stupor you can get into while you're driving and I realize I'm driving right past the apartment building where Asle lives, in Sailor's Cove, right at the edge of the sea, there's a little wharf in front of it, I think, and I see Asle lying there on his sofa and he's shaking, his whole body's shivering, and Asle thinks can't this shaking stop? and he's thinking he slept on the couch last night because he couldn't get up and get undressed and go lie down in bed, and the dog, he couldn't even, Bragi, the dog, couldn't go outside, and he's still drunk, he thinks, really drunk, and he needs to stop shaking so badly, his whole body's shaking, not just his hands, Asle thinks and he thinks that now he really has to get up and go to the kitchen and get a little something to drink to stop the shaking, because last night he didn't get undressed and go to bed, no, he just stayed where he was and passed out on the sofa, he thinks, and now he's lying here staring into space while his body keeps shaking, he thinks, and everything is, yes, what is it? an emptiness? a nothingness? a distance? yes, maybe yes, yes maybe it's a distance, he thinks, and now he has to go pour himself a little drink so that the worst of the shaking will go away, Asle thinks, and then, then, he'll go outside and go out to sea, that's what he'll do, Asle thinks, that's the only thing he wants, the only thing he longs to do is go away, disappear, the way his sister Alida went away back when she was a child, she just lay there, dead in her bed, Sister, Asle thinks, and the way the neighbour boy went away, Bård was his name, he fell off his father's rowboat into the sea and he couldn't swim and he didn't make it back on board the boat or back to land, Asle thinks and he thinks now he'll make an effort and get up and then go to the kitchen and pour himself a stiff drink so the shaking stops a little and then he'll walk around the apartment and turn off the lights, walk around the whole apartment and make sure everything is neat and organized, and then leave, lock the door, go down to the sea and then go out to sea and just keep going out into the sea, Asle thinks, and he thinks that thought again and again, it's the only thought he can think, the thought that he's going to go out to sea, he thinks, that he's going to disappear into the sea, into the nothingness of the waves, Asle thinks and the thought goes around and around in his head, it won't stop, it just keeps on circling around, this one thought is all that's real, everything else is empty distance, empty closeness, no, nothing is empty, but it's something like empty, there in this darkness, and every other thought he tries to think he can't think, the other thoughts are too hard, even the idea that he should raise his arm seems too hard, and he realizes he's shaking, even though he's not moving his whole body's shaking and why can't he manage the thought of getting up? of lifting his hand? why is the only thought he can think that he wants to go out to sea? that he wants to drink enough to make the shaking stop and then turn off the lights in the apartment, maybe straighten up the apartment if it needs it, because everything needs to be neat and tidy before he goes away, Asle thinks, and he thinks that maybe he should've written something to The Boy, but The Boy is a grown man now, isn't he, he hasn't been a child for a long time, he lives in Oslo, or maybe he could call him? but he doesn't like talking on the phone and neither does The Boy, Asle thinks, or maybe he should write to Liv? after all they were married for many years, but they were divorced so long ago that there are no hard feelings between them, because he can't go away just like that without saying goodbye to someone, that feels wrong, but the other woman he was married to, Siv, he can't even bear to think about her, she just left and took The Son and The Daughter away and moved far away from him, she'd left before he knew it, he hadn't thought about getting divorced at all and she told him she'd had enough and took The Son and The Daughter and left, she had already found a new place for herself and them, she said, and he never noticed anything, Asle thinks, and then for a while The Son and The Daughter came to spend every weekend with him, he thinks, but then Siv found a new husband and she took The Son and The Daughter and moved to a place somewhere in Trøndelag to be with this new man, she took the children and went away and then he was alone again and then Siv wrote and said he had to pay for this and that and as soon as she asked him he paid her, whenever he had money, he thinks, and why think about that? Asle thinks, it's just something that happened, now everything's been taken care of, everything's ready, all the painting supplies are in their proper place there on the table and the pictures are leaning against the wall, stretchers facing out, the brushes are in a neat row, all cleaned, big to small, all wiped clean with turpentine, and the tubes of paint are also arranged properly, next to each other, full to empty, every cap screwed on tight, and there's nothing on the easel, everything's clean and taken care of and in its proper place and he's just lying there shaking, not thinking anything, just shaking and then he again thinks he should get up and leave and lock the door and then go out and then go down to the sea and out into the sea, go out into the sea, go out until the waves crash over him and he disappears into the sea, he thinks it again and again, otherwise nothing, otherwise the darkness of nothingness, the way it sometimes sweeps through him in quick glimpses like an illumination and yes, yes, then he's filled with a kind of happiness and he thinks that there might be a place somewhere that's an empty noth-ingness, an empty light, and just think, what if everything could be like that? he thinks, could be empty light? imagine a place like that? in its emptiness, in its shining emptiness? in its noth-ingness? Asle thinks and while he thinks about a place like that, which is obviously no place, he thinks, he falls into a kind of sleep that isn't like sleep but more a bodily movement where he's not moving, despite all his shaking, yes, he's been shaking the whole time, everything's heavy and hard and there's a place in the big heaviness that's an unbelievably gentle shining light, like faith, yes, like a promise, Asle thinks and I see him lying there in the living room, or studio, whatever it's called, I think, he's lying on the sofa next to the window looking out over the sea and there's a table by the sofa and a couple of closed sketch-pads on the table and some pencils, all in a neat row, it's his room, Asle's room, just that, I think, and everything in his room is neat and tidy and hanging on one wall is a large canvas with the stretcher facing out, the picture turned to the wall, and I see that Asle has painted *A Shining Darkness* on the stretcher in black paint, so that must be the title of the painting, I think, and there's a roll of canvas in a corner of the room, there are pieces of wood for making stretchers in another corner, I see, and I see Asle lying there on the sofa and his body is shaking and he's thinking that he has to go get a drink so he can stop shaking and he sits up and then he's sitting on the sofa and he's thinking that now he really needs a cigarette but he's shaking so much he can't even roll a cigarette so he takes one out of the pack lying on the coffee table, he gets a cigarette out of the pack and gets it into his mouth and gets his matches out of his pocket and strikes a match and manages to light the cigarette and he takes a good drag and thinks he won't take this cigarette out of his mouth, the ashes can just fall wherever they fall, and now he definitely needs a glass of something, Asle thinks, and he keeps shaking and he manages to put the matches back in his pocket and he bends over the ashtray on the coffee table and spits the cigarette down into the ashtray and I'm driving north and I think I should stop by and see Asle, I shouldn't just drive past his house here in Sailor's Cove, but I can't stop him from going out to sea and going out into the sea if he wants to, if that's what he really wants to do he'll do it, I think and I'm driving north and I see myself standing and looking at the picture with the two lines that cross and I see myself go to the kitchen in my old house, because it is an old house, and an old kitchen, and I see that everything's in its proper place and the sink and the kitchen table have been dried off, I see, everything is clean and nice, the way it should be, and I see myself go into the bath-room, turn on the light, and there too everything's neat and organized, the sink is clean, the toilet's clean, and I see myself stop in front of the mirror and I see my thin grey hair, my grey stubble, and I run my hands through my hair and then take off the black hairband holding my hair back and my hair falls long and thin and grey down over my shoulders, down onto my chest, and I push my fingers through my hair, pull my hair back behind my ears, then I take the black hairband and gather my hair and tie it back with it and then I go out into the hall and I see my black coat hanging there, how many years have I had that coat now? I think, no one could ever accuse me of buying lots of clothes I don't need, I think, and I see some scarves hanging on a hook and I think that I have a lot of scarves be-cause Ales used to give me scarves for Christmas or as a birthday present, since that's what I wanted, she asked what I wanted and I usually said I wanted a scarf and then that's what I got, I think and I go into the living room, or studio, whatever it's called, really it's both, but I call it the main room or the living room and I see the brown leather shoulderbag hanging on the hook above the paintings I've put aside, the ones I'm not totally satisfied with, the ones leaning against the wall between the bedroom door and the hall door, and when I go out I always take the brown shoulderbag with me and I keep a sketch-pad and pencil in it, I think, and I see the shoulderbag there on the passenger seat next to me and I'm driving north and I think how I'm looking forward to getting back home to my good old house in Dylgja and I see myself standing and looking at the round table by the window and the two empty chairs next to the table, there's a black velvet jacket hanging over the back of one of the chairs, yes, the jacket I'm wearing, there on the chair closest to the bench, the chair where I always used to sit, and Ales used to sit in the chair next to it, that was her chair, I think, and I see myself stand back up and look at the picture with the two lines that cross, I don't like looking at the picture but I sort of have to, I think, and I'm driving north in the dark and I see Asle sitting there on the sofa and he's looking at something and he's not looking at anything, he's shaking, trembling, he's shaking the whole time, he's trembling, and he's dressed just like I'm dressed, black pants and pullover, and over the back of the chair next to the coffee table is a black velvet jacket just like the one I have and usually hang on the back of the chair by the round table, and his hair is grey, it's pulled back to his neck in a black hairband the way my hair is, and his grey stubble, I have grey stubble too that I trim once a week or so, I think, and I see Asle sitting there on the sofa and his whole body's shaking and he lifts a hand slightly, in front of him, a bit to the side, and his hands shake and he thinks that it seems better now, easier, for some reason, and he thinks he needs to eat a little something but he's shaking so much that the first thing he needs to do is get up and go get something to drink, he thinks, sitting there on the sofa, and I think I can't just leave Asle alone when he's like that, I shouldn't have just driven past his building in Sailor's Cove, I should go see him, he needs me now, I think, but I've already driven a long way past the building where Asle lives, and I shouldn't have done that, and maybe I should turn around and drive back? but I'm so tired, I think, and I drive north and I see an old brown house at the side of the road and it's falling down, I see that a few roof tiles are missing, and that's where Ales and I used to live, I think, and it seems like such a long time ago, almost in a different life, I think and I drive past the house and after I've driven a bit farther I see a turnoff and steer into it and pull over and stop the car and then I'm sitting in the car, just sitting, not thinking anything, not doing anything, just sitting there, then I think why on earth did I stop at this turnoff? I've never stopped here before, even though I've driven past it so many times, no really I need to get home now, I should've gone to see Asle but now it's too late, I think, and I keep sitting in the car and I think that maybe I'll say a prayer and then I think about the people who call themselves Christians and who think, or in any case used to think, that a child needs to be baptized to be saved, and at the same time they think that God is all-powerful, and so why is baptism necessary for salvation? can't God do whatever he wants? if he's all-powerful then mustn't it be his will whether or not someone's baptized? no, it's crazy to believe that baptism is necessary for salvation, no it's too much, I think and I notice that the thought makes me happy, the thought of the folly of the Christians who think that salvation requires baptism, how could they ever have come to think that, the idea is so stupid, so obviously stupid that you can't even laugh, such obvious stupidity is nothing to laugh at, nor is the foolishness of the people who

call themselves Christians, many of them, not all of them, obviously, I think and I think that people who think like that can't
have big thoughts about God, and I think about Jesus, how
much he loved children, how he said that children were of the
kingdom of God, that they belonged to the kingdom of God,
and that is a beautiful and true thought, I think, so why would
they need baptism to become that? since they belong to the
kingdom of God already? I think, and I think that baptism,
child baptism, is all well and good but it's for mankind's sake,
not for God, it's important for people or at least it can be important, or maybe it's just for the church, yes really it's mostly
for the church, but it can't be for God, or for the children who
are part of the kingdom of God already, and we must be as they
are, we must become as little children to enter into the kingdom of Heaven, that's what the Bible says, I think and I think
no, now I need to stop, now I'm thinking foolishly myself,
thinking about other people's folly while my own thoughts
don't make sense, they're never clear enough, they don't fit together, of course you don't need to be dipped in water to be
baptized, you can also be baptized in yourself, by the spirit you
have inside yourself, the other person you have and are, the
other person you get when you're born as a human being, I
think, and all of them, all the different people, both the ones
who lived in earlier times and the ones who are still alive, are
just baptized inside themselves, not with water in a church, not
by a priest, they're baptized by the other person they've been
given and have inside them, and maybe through their connection with other people, the connection of common
understanding, of shared meaning, yes, what language also has
and is, I think and I think that some people are baptized, as children or as adults, yes, some are washed clean with water, with
holy water, I think, and that's all well and good in its own terms

but no more than that, and every single baptism of this or that person is a baptism of everyone, that's what I think, a baptism for all mankind, because everyone's connected, the living and the dead, those who haven't been born yet, and what one person does can in a way not be separated from what another person does, I think, yes, just as Christ lived, died, and was resurrected and was one with God as a human being that's how all people are, just by virtue of being men and women in Christ, whether they want to be or not, bound to God in and through Jesus Christ, the Son of Man, whether they know it or not, whether they believe it or not, that's how it is, it's true either way, I think, Christianity knows a thing or two too, and sure enough I converted to the Catholic Church myself, something I probably never would've done if it hadn't been for Ales since I didn't even agree with the Catholic Church about child baptism, but I never regretted converting, I think, because the Catholic faith has given me a lot, and I consider myself a Christian, yes, a little like the way I consider myself a Communist or at least a Socialist, and I pray with my rosary every single day, yes, I pray several times a day and I go to mass as often as I can, for it too, yes, mass too has its truth, the way baptism has its truth, yes, baptism is also a part of the truth, it too can also lead to, yes, lead to God, I think, or at least to God insofar as I can imagine Him, but there are also other ways of thinking and believing that are true, other ways of honestly turning to God, maybe you use the word God or maybe you know too much to do that, or are too shy when confronted with the unknown divinity, but everything leads to God, so that all religions are one, I think, and that's how religion and art go together, because the Bible and the liturgy are fiction and poetry and painting, are literature and drama and visual art, and they all have truth in them, because of course the arts have their truth,

I think, but now I can't just keep sitting and frittering away my time thinking confused thoughts like this, I think, I need to keep driving north and get back home to Dylgja, to my good old house, I have to stop sitting here freezing in my car, I have to start the engine and then drive to Dylgja, because I like driving, it gives me a certain peace, I fall into a kind of stupor, yes, to be honest it gives me a kind of happiness, and the thought of getting back home to Dylgja and back to my good old house makes me happy too, I think, even if I'm sorry I'm going back to an empty house now that Ales has died, no, that's not true, because even if Ales has been dead a long time she's still there in the house, I think, and I think that I should've found myself a dog because I've always liked dogs, and cats too, but I'd rather have a dog, there can be a greater friendship with a dog, I think and I've thought it so many times but I've never gone ahead and done it, got a dog, I don't really know why, maybe it's because I'd still rather be alone with Ales? because even though she's dead she's still there in a way, I think, or maybe I should just go ahead and get a dog? I think, but Asle has a dog, yes, he's had a dog for all these years, I think, and I think I shouldn't have just driven past Asle's building, someone like him the way he is now can't just be left alone, weighed down as he is now, so weighed down by his own stone, a trembling stone, a weight so heavy that it's pushing him down into the ground, I think, so I should turn around and drive back towards Bjørgvin, I think, and I should go see Asle, I think, I have to help pull him out of himself, I think and I see Asle sitting there on the sofa and he's shaking and shaking, I should have driven back, he needs me, but I'm tired and I want to get home, I want to keep driving north, driving home, because I've been to Bjørgvin and I've gone shopping for canvases at The Art Supply Shop and I bought wood for the stretchers at The Hardware Store, and I bought a lot of groceries, and now I want to drive back home to Dylgja right now, I think, and actually it did cross my mind to stay in Bjørgvin and go to evening mass at St Paul's Church but I was too tired, maybe I'll just drive back to Bjørgvin next Sunday to go to morning mass, I haven't been to mass in a long time so it'd be good to take communion, and then I can go see Asle, I think and I see him sitting there on the sofa and he's shaking and shaking, but doesn't he need to go walk his dog now? I think and I see Bragi lying there by the hall door wait-ing to be let out and I see Bragi get up and pad over to the sofa and then jump up on the sofa and lie in Asle's lap and then he's just lying there and the dog is shaking too and Asle can't move, he can't even lift his hand, can't say a word, just to say one sin-gle word feels like too much for him, it's as though he'd have to force himself to do it, he thinks, but now, yes, now for some reason his thoughts aren't so fixed any more, they're not going around and around in the same circle now, not any more, his thoughts have begun to calm down now that the dog has come and lay in his lap, he thinks

Good dog, Asle says

Good boy, Bragi, good boy, he says

and Asle strokes Bragi's fur with his shaking hand and kneads his fur and Asle thinks how can he have thought about going into the sea, because who would take care of the dog? there's no way he could decide to leave the dog, Asle thinks, and now he's shaking less, but he's still shaking, his body is trembling, I think and no I don't want to think about Asle any more, I don't want to see him before my eyes any more, his long grey hair, his grey stubble, I don't want to think about him any more, there's no point in thinking more about him because he's just one person among many like that, he's alone, he's one of the many solitary people, he's just one artist among many, one painter among many, just one of the many painters almost no one knows about except some close family members and a few friends from school days, and maybe a few fellow artists, he's one of thousands, no I don't want to think about him any more, I think, and then I think again that I should have dropped by to see him, alone as he is, falling apart as he is, I should have dropped by and asked him to come get a drink with me, yes, he could have a pint of beer with a glass of something stronger and I could have a cup of coffee with milk since I don't drink beer any more, no beer or wine or anything stronger since I stopped drinking, that's what I should've done, because if Asle had something to drink it would be easier for him, he'd stop shaking, then he'd calm back down, just getting something to drink would make things easier, the stone would get lighter, yes, his stone might shift off him a little bit so that he could get a little light and a little air, I should have taken him with me someplace where there are other people, where other people are having drinks, where people are together, comforting their souls, that's what I should have done, I shouldn't have just driven past his building, I should've stopped and then taken him with me out into life, yes, so he could live a little, yes, but instead I kept driving north like I wasn't worried about him, like I was in such a hurry to get away from him, because I couldn't do it, I couldn't see Asle lying there, I think and so I just kept driving past the building in Sailor's Cove where his apartment is, as if Asle was too hard, as if his pain, or his suffering, maybe that's the better word, made me want to keep driving, not because I didn't want to see him or spend time with him but because, no, I don't know, but I wanted to get away, and maybe I thought I could drag his pain with me in a way, pull it behind me, that I could pull his suffering off of him and away from him if I kept driving? anyway that's an excuse I can think of now for not having stopped and visited his apartment but instead having just kept driving, because why didn't I go see him? was it because I was scared to? not prepared to share his pain with him? share his suffering, but what do I mean by that? that's just a manner of speaking, *share his pain, share his suffering,* it's a manner of speaking, as if you could share someone's pain, or suffering, I think and I see myself sitting there in the car and I'm looking out the window and looking at the playground down below the turnoff, there are no children in it, but there, yes, there's a young woman with long black hair sitting on the swing and there on a bench next to the swing is a young man, he has medium-length brown hair, he's in a black coat, wearing a scarf, it's late afternoon or early evening and he sits there and looks at the woman sitting on the swing, and there's a brown leather bag hanging over his shoulder, and she's staring straight ahead, it's autumn, some leaves have already started changing colour, this is the best time of year, the most beautiful, I think, and maybe most beautiful of all in the evening when the light is right at the point of disappearing, when some darkness has entered the light but it's still light enough to see clearly that some of the leaves have lost their green colour, I think, this is my time of year, it always has been, for as long as I can remember autumn has been my favourite, I think and I look at the young man sitting on the bench not moving and staring straight ahead as if not seeing anything and I look at the young woman sitting on the swing, she too is staring straight ahead, as if at nothing, and why are they sitting so still? why aren't they moving? I think, he on the bench, she on the swing, both just sitting there, why are they just sitting there? why aren't they talking to each other? why are they completely still, motionless, like a picture? I think, yes, yes, they're exactly like a picture, like a picture I might paint, I think and I know that precisely this moment, precisely this picture, has already lodged itself in my mind and will never go away, I have lots of pictures like that in my mind, thousands of them, and from just one thought, from seeing just one thing that it looks like, or for no reason at all, a picture can turn up, often at the strangest times and places, a picture, a motionless picture that still has something like a kind of motion in it, it's as if every picture like that, every last one of the thousands of pictures I have in my head or wherever I have them, is saying something, saying something almost unique and irreplaceable, but it's practically impossible to grasp what the picture is saying, of course I might think that the picture is saying this or that, obviously I can think that, and obviously I do think it, and I manage to think some of what the picture is saying but never what it's actually saying because you can't fully understand a picture, it's as if it's not entirely of this world, as they put it, and yes, it's strange, it's weird, he and she in that picture I see inside me that's so inexpressible, I'm really seeing them, he's sitting on the bench there, she's sitting on the swing there, they're sitting like they can't move, like something invisible is holding them in place, and like they've been sitting there a long time, that's how it seems, yes, it's as if they've been sitting there like that always, forever, for always, and she's wearing a skirt, a purple skirt, and the skirt has turned a bit dark in the early evening darkness, yes, the purple is moving towards black, and he's sitting in his long black coat, with the brown bag hanging over his shoulder, and his hair is brown and medium length, and I don't see any beard on his face, but I can't just sit here like this, I think and I think that they, he and she, are sitting without moving and that's what I'm doing too, just like them, I'm sitting without moving, and I can't very well just stay sitting in my car like this because anyone driving by will wonder why I'm just sitting in my car, why I'm not driving any farther, but there's no one driving by and if anyone did drive by they wouldn't find it unusual that I was spending a moment in the turnoff, and anyway so what if they did, the people in the playground would certainly think that if they noticed me but clearly they haven't noticed me, at least neither of them has looked up at me sitting in my car while it's slowly starting to get dark out, it's still light but darkness has come into the air, slowly, slowly the darkness comes into the air, I think, sitting there looking at the young man in the black coat on a bench with a brown leather bag on his shoulder and the young woman in a purple skirt on a swing, because they're still just sitting there, without moving, yes, like part of a painting, yes that too, but when I paint it's always as if I'm trying to paint away the pictures stuck inside me, yes, the ones like this picture, of him and her sitting there, to get rid of them in a way, be done with them, I've sometimes thought that that's why I became a painter, because I have all these pictures inside me, yes, so many pictures that they're a kind of agony, yes, it hurts me when they keep popping up again and again, like visions almost, and in all kinds of contexts, and I can't do anything about it, the only thing I can do is paint, yes, try to paint away these pictures that are lodged inside me, there's nothing to do but paint them away, one by one, not by painting exactly what I've seen or what's stuck inside me, no, I used to do that too much, paint just what I saw and nothing more, just duplicate the picture you might say, and that always turned out as a bad painting and I didn't get rid of the picture inside me either, the one I was trying to paint away, no, I have to paint a picture in a way that dissolves the picture lodged inside me and makes it go away, so that it becomes an invisible forgotten part of myself, of my own innermost picture, the picture I am and have, because there's one thing I know for sure, I have only one picture, one single picture, and all the other pictures, both the ones I see and the ones I can't forget that get stuck in me, have something about them that resembles the one picture I have inside me and that isn't something anyone can see but I do see some of what's in it, some of what's lodged inside me, yes, that's what it's like now in what I'm seeing while I sit in my car and look at a young man and a young woman just sitting and staring into space and not looking at each other, they're not saying anything to each other, but it's like they're listening together, like they're one, because it's like he can't be seen without her and she can't be seen without him, her black hair, his brown hair, her long hair, his medium-length hair, they are inseparable from each other as they sit there, and the fact that they're not moving is probably no odder than the fact that I'm not moving, I'm just sitting quietly in my car for no particular reason, just sitting, and why? I think and then I realize I could go down to them, get out of the car and just go right down to the two of them there in the playground, but it wouldn't be right to do that, would it? they should be left alone, the two of them are sitting there in such a big slow calm fragile peace that I can't go bother them, it would disturb them if I went down to them, they're so calm there, so peaceful, I think, but still, am I going to stay sitting in my car like this as if I can't do anything, can't manage anything any more, as if I'm exhausted from having seen Asle in his apartment by the sea in Sailor's Cove and seeing all the shaking in his body, as if I'm too tired after all the errands I ran in Bjørgvin, I think, now I need to get home, drive back home to my old house in Dylgja, my good old house, because enough is enough already, I think and I look at the young woman sitting on the swing and the young man sitting on the bench and he's thinking that when he was young they used to spend a few weeks every year in the summer with his grandparents, his mother's parents, and their house was next to a playground exactly like this one, a little playground with a swing, a bench, a seesaw, and a sandpit, it was a grey brick house, not too big, and the flagstone floor in the hall comes into his mind, and there was a little outbuilding half-hidden behind the grey brick house, surrounded by some bushes, and then, next to the house, a little beyond it, was a small playground, and he spent a lot of time in that playground, he thinks, and maybe he should tell her that, but she's probably not interested in hearing things like that and now they've been sitting there for such a long time without saying anything, he should break the silence by saying that when he was little he sometimes stayed in a grey brick house next to a playground like this one, he thinks, because they can't just stay sitting like this forever, can they, not even saying anything, he thinks

When I was young, he says

and he looks at her

Yes, she says

and she looks at him and it's like there's a lightness and expectation in her voice and yet he's still sitting there without saying anything else and she asks him what he was about to say

Yes? When you were young? she says

Yes, I sometimes stayed next to a playground just like this one, he says

You did, she says

It's almost like it's the exact same playground, he says

It's kind of strange, he says

It seems like it's the exact same playground, he says

But there's not a grey brick house here, is there? she says

No, no, it's not actually the same playground, of course, of course not, he says

It just seems that way? she says

Yes, he says

and then neither of them says anything, and again she stares straight ahead, and he stares straight ahead

It was a little house, a little grey brick house, he says

and she sits there on the swing, he sits there on the bench, they sit like that without moving and they're not saying anything and then she says that he grew up on a small farm, on a small farm on Horda Fjord, with fruit trees, she says, and he says yes, that's right, and he says that he stayed in the little brick house only sometimes, it was when they were staying with his mother's parents, his grandparents, that they lived in a brick house like that next to a playground like this, he says and I know that I need to paint this picture away, the next picture I start will be of these two people, I'll paint them away, I'll paint them in towards my innermost picture, because when I do that, if I can do that, then the picture will disappear and go away and the uneasiness inside me will stop and it'll bring me peace, I won't be haunted any more, and if I don't I'm sure that this picture will keep coming from inside me again and again, but I've probably always been painting this picture, or one like it, almost exactly like the one I'm seeing now, but in any case I need to paint it away yet again, I need to paint it away again and again, I think, but now I need to start the car again, I can't just sit here like this in my car watching two people who don't know I'm sitting here looking at them, I think and suddenly I feel miserable, I feel grief, yes, it's like grief is bursting from inside me, from nowhere, from everywhere, and it feels like this sorrow is about to choke me, like I'm breathing the sorrow in and I can't breathe it out and I fold my hands and I breathe in deeply and I say to myself inside myself Kyrie and I breathe out slowly and I say eleison and I breathe in deeply and say Christe and I breathe out slowly and say eleison and I say these words

again and again and the breaths and the words make it so that
I'm not filled with sorrow any more, with fear, with sudden
fear, with this sorrow in the fear so strong that's suddenly come
over me and that overpowers me and it's like it's made what's
I in me very small, turned it into nothing, but a nothing that's
nonetheless there, lodged firm, unshakable, even clearer in its
motionless movement, and I breathe in deeply and I say to myself Kyrie and I breathe out slowly and say eleison, I breathe
from the innermost part of me, I try to breathe from the thing
that's most inside me, and I breathe in deeply and I say Christe
inside myself and I breathe out slowly and I say eleison and I try
to breathe from the thing that's there in my innermost place,
from the picture that's there that I can't say anything about, I
try to breathe from what I am inside, to keep the sorrow away,
or in any case keep it under control so the fear doesn't take
over, so the terrors don't overwhelm me, and I know that this
sudden sorrow, these sudden terrors that have welled up inside me will get smaller and I will get bigger and I think that
that's really ridiculous, if someone saw me now they'd laugh
and laugh, if they saw me thinking I could sit in a parked car in
a turnoff saying Kyrie eleison Christe eleison, it's absurd, they'd
have to laugh, but let them laugh, let them, let them, because
it helps! it helps! yes, now I feel calmer again and I look back
down at the man and woman in the playground and I think that
it's time to drive home to my wife and our child now, they're
at home waiting for me, but I'm here on the road to Dylgja,
this is the way to Dylgja, isn't it? yes now I need to keep driving to Dylgja, obviously, where else would I be driving to? and
I'm driving back to my wife and our child, in a way, to wife
and child, no, how could I think that? no, I have to drive back
to the old house in Dylgja where I live, just me, alone, I live
there alone, that's how it is, how could I think I was going

home to my wife and our child, maybe it's because I wish I was? because I wish that that's what I was doing? going home to my wife and our child? not having to go home to an empty house, my cold and empty house? not having to go home to my own loneliness? and that's why I think I'm going to drive home to my wife and our child when actually I'm going to go home to an empty house, a cold house, although actually I left the heater on didn't I? and it'll be good to get home anyway, it will, to get home to my good old house, and really I can't stay sitting here like this, in my car, on this turnoff, I think and I look at the playground and it's already almost dark and I see that the young man has stood up and moved and is standing in his long black coat behind the young woman and he takes the ropes holding the grey wooden board she's sitting on and he gently pulls her back

No, she says

I don't want to swing, she says

I'm not a little kid, she says

and he lets go of the rope and she swings forwards

No stop it, she says

and she swings backwards

Stop it, stop it, she cries

and he goes on pulling her back towards him and then pushing her away, pushing harder each time, he makes her go faster and faster and she's swinging back and forth and he thinks that if she doesn't want to swing she can just put her foot on the ground and stop the movement of the swing, simple as that, she has shoes on, but she doesn't stop the swing

I don't want to swing, she says

Why are you pushing the swing when I don't want you to? she says

I didn't ask you to, she says

I didn't say I wanted to, she says

I don't want to, she says

You just started pushing me like it didn't matter whether I wanted to or not, she says

and he keeps pulling her back towards him and then pushing her away and he thinks now why is he doing this? also, why is he pushing her away from him harder and harder each time? and pulling harder each time, and she steadily soars ahead, away from him, and comes steadily back, towards him, and then he pushes her again, back and forth, away and back

It's just a game, he says

and he gives a push with all his strength and the swing flies away and she screams and her skirt flutters and her black hair is sticking straight out behind her, yes, that was a scream, she screams that he needs to stop, she doesn't like it, he really has to stop now, she's scared, she's really scared, she could fall off the swing, she cries, he needs to stop, enough, she doesn't want to any more

Stop, she cries

But you like it? he says

No stop, she says

You like it, he says

No, no, she says

You do too, he says

and she says no, she says what if she falls off when she's at the highest point, and he gives another push, pushing as hard as he can, and she flies away, her black hair sticks straight out behind her when she's on her way up, skirt flapping, and she screams, a kind of squealing shriek comes out of her when she's at the top of the swing, even louder than before, and on her way back down her dark hair flies to the side and forwards and she shrieks no, no, stop it, I don't like it, I'm scared, stop, I mean it, stop

You do too like it, he says

and when she comes back he makes her go faster again, he pulls the swing and gives her a good push and she flies forwards, up, and now she's not yelling, now she's starting to help, now when she's at the top she bends her knees back and as it were throws her upper body forwards and the swing comes back stronger and when she's come all the way back she raises her feet forward and at the moment he pushes on her back she as it were flings herself forward and amplifies the swings, she goes farther forward, higher up, every time it's farther forward, higher and higher

Faster, she cries

Push harder, she cries

As hard as you can, she cries

and she is out of breath and a little hoarse almost, and he pushes as hard as he can

Aahhh, she screams

Yeahhh, she screams

Like that, as hard as you can, she screams

and he thinks he can't push any harder, he's already using all his strength, he's already pushed the swing as hard as he can, he's starting to get tired, he thinks

Push harder, she cries

and he doesn't push as hard but he gives regular pushes, almost the same strength every time, even, regular, they are now in an even rhythm, up and down, she swings evenly back and forth and she shouts this is great, it's wonderful, she feels a tickling in her stomach, he can't stop, he needs to grab tight and pull her and push her away, perfect, so evenly back and forth, she says, a little faster now but still evenly, she says and now he has to pull as hard as he can once or twice, push her as hard as he can a few times, she shouts but she's shouting in a way softly, she keeps shouting softly that it's tickling, it's tickling so nicely in her stomach, all over her, but it's scary, awful, horribly scary, but good too, incredibly great, she shouts softly, breathlessly

Pull, push, as hard as you can, she cries

Do it, she cries

Do it a few more times and then we'll stop, she cries

and he thinks all right that's enough, you get tired of just standing and pushing a swing, and it's getting darker and darker, and at first she didn't want him to push her, now she doesn't want him to stop, that's the way it goes isn't it, he thinks and he steps back a little and the swing comes towards him

Push, push my back, she cries

and he backs slowly away

Can't you do any more? she says

and he pushes and she pumps her legs and swings by herself as well as she can, she pulls the ropes with all her strength and throws herself forward as hard as she can and when she's at the hightest point she shouts Aaahh, aaahh, aaahh, before she comes back down and back

This is great, she cries

More, she cries

and he looks at her and takes a running jump with the swing and hurls it forward with all his might

Yeahhhhh, she screams

and she draws it out, shrieks yeahh again, and then shouts yeahh more slowly

At first you didn't want to, he says

I was scared, she says

And now you don't want to stop, he says

No, no I like it, she says

But you've been swinging long enough now, he says

It's so good, it's great, she says

and the swing moves back and forth less and less, up and down, back and forth

It was scary in the beginning, but then I wasn't scared any more, she says

That's often how it is, he says

It was fun though, she says

and the swing has almost stopped moving, it's moving back and forth only a little and she says that when she was young she never dared swing, it was so scary, she felt, or else she did dare but only barely, a little bit forward and a little bit back, and he says maybe he shouldn't have pushed her so hard and she says it was great that he did, she liked it, even when she was saying she didn't like it she was actually liking it, she says and he says yes well that's how it often is, people often say one thing and mean something else, even the exact opposite, he says and she says she's not sure that it happens all that often but anyway it did just now with her on the swing, she says, and the swing is now moving back and forth by no more than its own width and he grabs the ropes and stops the swing and stops her and he stays behind the swing holding onto it until it stops moving altogether, and then he's just standing there and she's just sitting there and then she looks up at him

That was fun, she says

Yeah, even if we're grown-ups, he says

Or at least almost grown-up, she says

Kind of grown-up at least, he says

Kind of, yeah, she says

and he carefully pushes the swing again, pulls the rope

Kind of grown-up, she says

Kind of kind of, she says

and the swing is moving back and forth by itself, not very far each way now, but still up and down, gently now, gently back and forth

We'll be grown-up soon anyway, she says

Yeah, he says

and he takes the ropes again and the swing stops

But it's dark, he says

It's still a little light, she says

One last time? she says

and he grabs the ropes again and takes a step back pulling her with him, he goes as far back as he can go, he pulls her back as high as he can, and then lets go of the swing and she howls no, no, no more, not so hard, not so strong, I can't, no more, she shouts, aaahh, no, no, she shrieks and he moves away from the swing

Not so much, she cries

That's too much, she cries

Aaahh, she cries

and he stands and looks at her and he sees her swinging back and forth, up and down, but more and more gently, and then she pumps the swing herself a little, back and forth, up and down, and then it gets slower and the swing just drifts back and forth and he moves a bit farther away from the swing

Where are you going? she says

Nowhere, he says

But you're going to the gate, are you leaving? she says

No, no, he says

I'm not leaving you here, but it'll be dark soon, maybe we should go home? he says

Just wait till the swing stops, she says

and she puts her feet on the ground and stops the swing and she looks at him and smiles and says that was really fun, she hasn't been on a swing since she was a little kid, she says, and back then she didn't like it very much, she was such a scaredy-cat, she was scared of everything when she was little, when she was a little girl, she says

You were too scared to go on the swings? he says

To go that high, she says

Yes, he says

No, I really didn't dare, and when I did swing a little it was only to show I could do it, sort of, she says

and she says that that's what she was like as a child, yes, and then neither of them says anything, and then she asks if he was brave enough to go on the swings when he was little

Were you brave enough? she says

and he nods and she steps off the swing and she goes over to him and he looks at her long dark hair hanging straight down now and then she raises her face to his with half-open lips and he puts his mouth on her mouth and their mouths meet, open wide

That was a cautious kiss, she says

and he puts his hand over her hair, but off it, so to speak, without touching her hair, and then they put their arms around each other and hold each other tight and he puts his hand on her hair and starts to stroke her long dark hair, up and down, and she rests her head on his shoulder and I see them standing there, not moving, they're like a picture, like one of those pictures I'll never forget, a picture I'll paint, I need to paint them close to me and paint them away, I need to paint them close and paint them away just the way they're standing there now, I think, because now it's like a light is coming from them, standing there so close together, as if they were one, standing as if two people were one, yes they're so close as it gets dark and the darkness falls over them like snow, a darkness somehow like snowflake after snowflake yet also like one darkness, one undivided darkness, not bits of darkness but one snowing darkness, and the darker it gets the more light is coming from them, yes, a kind of light is coming off them, I can see it, even if the light is maybe invisible it's still visible, because light can come from people too, especially from eyes, mostly in glimmers, an invisible shining light, but from these two comes a silent even light always the same and never changing, it's like the two of them standing there are one light, yes, that's what the light coming from them is like, one light, I think and he realizes that she's almost all light, at least that's how she seems to him right now, he thinks, standing there, but how stupid is that? he's standing here holding a flesh and blood woman and he's thinking that she's light, it's not a good idea to think things like that, he thinks, and sure he's never been all that smart but that's how it feels, like he's holding a light in his arms, that's strange, he thinks, and the fact that he's thinking something like that as they stand here with their arms around each other, she holding him, he holding her, no, it's too stupid, thinking that, he thinks, it's downright unmanly, he thinks, because she's not pure light, she's a flesh and blood woman and shaped like a flesh and blood woman, she's not light, no, she's a woman, she's his girlfriend, not made of light, he thinks and I see them let go of each other and then they move a little ways apart and I see the darkness move a little ways off from them and now they're standing there as if cut out of the darkness, they're standing a little apart from each other, and they look a bit tired and he thinks he can't think she's light, what a stupid thing to think, he thinks, thoughts like that are big and empty, he thinks and he takes her hand and then they go over to the see-saw and they let go of each other's hand and she sits on one side, sits almost all the way on the ground, the ground with its tufts of grass on the grey dirt, and then he goes and pulls the see-saw down a little and she helps with her feet and he raises one foot over the board and puts it down on the ground and then sits on the see-saw and then the see-saw starts to sink down to the ground on his side and she pulls in her feet and then she's up in the air

It was nice being up on that swing, it's been a long time, she says

I feel like we're children again, he says

We're making each other like children again, she says

I'm like a little girl again, either I'm soaring and moving on the swing, or hanging in the air, like now, she says

Every child likes being up in the air, she says

And every grown-up child, he says

Yes maybe, she says

We do anyway, he says

We do now, anyway, he says

But now we're saying such dumb things, she says

I'm almost embarrassed, she says

and then he kicks off and goes up in the air and she sinks to the ground and then she kicks off and goes up in the air and he sinks down to the ground

Everyone likes being up in the air, he says

and he reaches the ground and kicks off

Regular movements, he says

and she sinks to the ground and reaches the ground and then kicks off

Like breathing, he says

and he sinks to the ground and he kicks off

And like heartbeats, she says

and she sinks to the ground and she kicks off

Being in the same movement, he says

and he sinks to the ground and he kicks off

Being together in the movement, she says

and she sinks to the ground and she kicks off

Being the same movement, he says

and he sinks to the ground and he kicks off

Like waves, she says

and she sinks to the ground and she kicks off

Like waves in the same sea, she says

and he sinks to the ground and he kicks off

Like us together, she says

and she sinks to the ground and she kicks off

Like you and me, he says

and he sinks to the ground and he kicks off

Like us, she says

and she sinks to the ground and she kicks off and he lets it happen and lets his weight tilt the see-saw down and he's sitting astride the seat with his feet on the ground while she and her feet are hanging free in the air

That's how it'll be, she says

Like this, he says

and then he kicks off with his feet and she sinks down and her feet touch the ground

And like that too, she says

and she kicks off

Like that too, he says

and they stay like that, he on the ground, she up in the air

When you were little, she says

Yes, he says

When you lived there, over the summer, on summer holidays, in a little brick house, grey brick, she says

You just told me about that, she says

Yes, he says

But you grew up on the little farm, and you had a boathouse and a rowboat there? she says

Yes, he says

And your parents still live there? she says

Yes, he says

And an orchard? she says

Yes, yes I told you, he says

You did, she says

Yes, several times, he says

and then they're sitting and not saying anything

Why are you asking about that again? he says

I don't know, she says

No, he says

Couldn't we go there sometime soon? she says

and he doesn't say anything

Visit your parents? she says

Don't you want to? she says

Yeah, he says

and he hesitates as if he doesn't want to talk about it

You don't want to? she says

But we can go anyway, he says

It's nice there in Barmen, he says

And the farm is nice, it's on Horda Fjord, and it's nice being out on the boat in the fjord, he says

Yes you've told me that, she says

That you really like being out on the water, she says

Yes, I've always liked that, he says

and then it's quiet, they're just sitting there

But we have to go there at least once, she says

And it'd be nice to see your parents, she says

I don't see them much any more, he says

No, you and your mother, she says

and she breaks off

We won't talk about that, he says

and again neither one says anything, and they sit like that for a long time and I think why are they just sitting there? it's like they're frozen in place, it looks like they're both looking away from each other, keeping their eyes fixed on something next to them, and for them to just sit quietly like that, for so long, yes, how can they do that, I think and then she looks at him

Do you think we should leave? she says

and he doesn't say anything and she asks if he's going to be painting again tomorrow and he says he probably will, yes, tomorrow the same as every other day, yes, since he was maybe twelve years old, somewhere around there anyway, there hasn't been a single day when he didn't either paint or draw, it just happens by itself, that's how it is, like it's him in a way, painting is like a continuation of himself, he says, and he stops himself and says no that's too much, way too much, really painting is just something he does, every day, true, it's an old habit you might say, he says, and she says well then that's how it is and she sounds a little sulky I think, her voice makes it seem like she doesn't entirely like what he's saying, and he says that the painting he's in the middle of at the moment might turn out to be really good but it's so hard to get it right, he has to be so careful, it only takes the tiniest thing to have done too much on it and then the whole picture can be ruined and it'll be impossible to find his way back to what was good in the picture, to what the picture was trying to say, or however you'd describe it, actually it can't be described, because a picture says something and doesn't say it at the same time, it speaks silently, yes, or more like it shows something that can't be said, he says and I think no, I've really got to be getting home now, it's late now and it's time to get moving, keep driving, I think and then she says it's even darker now, maybe they should go home soon? she says and he says yes they really should and he asks if she liked flying through the air and she says yes, she had a great view, even though it was so dark by then, a better view than the one she has sitting down anyway, she says, and that, the fact that she sees better than him, is an old story, let him paint as much as he wants yes she sees better than he does whether it's light out or dark out, she sees especially well, as for him he doesn't see anything but this or that picture, this or that thing right in front of his nose, she says, and then suddenly he pushes off, as if he's angry or something, I think, and she sinks down to the ground and she screams, a long low scream, and he lifts one foot off the ground and stands up and gets off the see-saw while slowly lowering the see-saw with his hand and then she's sitting safe on the ground and he walks around to her and holds out his hand to her and she takes his hand and she gets up and then they just stand there and I think now I've really got to be getting home, it'll be totally dark soon, and then I sit and look at the playground where a young woman and a young man are hanging around playing, like children, and by now it's so dark that I can only just make them out, or is all of this just me seeing things? this isn't all in my mind, is it? am I just imagining that they're there? no, of course not, I saw them, I'm seeing them now, I think, definitely, and maybe I should get out and stretch my legs? get a little fresh air? go down to the playground too? I think, but a person can't just do something like that, can he? if I do do it I have to do it before it gets too dark, I think, and it's probably not all that strange for a person to get out of his car and take a little walk? go down a little path to a playground and walk past it, leave the road and go down past a playground and up a hill on the other side, I see the hill, and obviously I don't need to go into the playground, just walk past it, yes, right now either I need to drive home or I need to get out of the car and stretch my legs, I think and I get out of the car and I look around, the mountain rises up gently on the other side of the road before getting steeper and rising up sharply, and there, up at the top, I see the sky, and the stars are out, shining weakly, and then there's the road, a narrow country road running along the base of the mountain, and then a hill leads gently down towards the playground and there's a little path down the hill from the turnoff to the playground and it goes past the playground and continues uphill to the top of another hill behind the playground and that's strange, I've never noticed that before, this path down to the playground and then continuing up a hill behind the playground, I think, and then I'm standing there looking down at the playground and I see him and her standing there in the darkness, they're barely visible, but I can see that they're standing without moving, holding hands, and it was a good idea to get out of the car and get a little fresh air, I think and I feel how nice the cool air is, I sort of revive a little and of course I'm as free as anyone else to take an ordinary little stroll, I think, yes, of course, but I always tend to think I'm not allowed to do things, that's why I always do the same things over and over, I think and I start walking towards the path and I start down it past the playground and I look at the two people there in the playground and they must not have noticed me as they stand there holding each other, they're standing there like they are one, he holding her, she holding him, and neither can be separated from the other, and then they let go of each other and I walk carefully down the path

It's already dark, she says

Yes, it's autumn now, he says

Almost winter, she says

But not quite yet, he says

Yeah, she says

Now we've done everything but play in the sandpit, he says

Are you saying we should play in the sandpit? she says

and her voice sounds a little surprised almost

Yes, well, why not? she says

But we'll get sandy and dirty, he says

Maybe we shouldn't? she says

No, maybe not, he says

Our clothes'll get dirty, he says

and she says they could always take some clothes off and she takes off her jacket and pulls her pullover up over her head and now she's standing there in just a bra and her purple skirt, can you believe it, standing there almost naked like that, in this cold, I think and then she pulls him over to the sandpit and I walk slowly, step by step, down the path and I think this is unbelievable, I should quietly walk past the playground and up the hill over there, I should see what's on the other side of the hill, and then I should turn around, it's time to be getting back home, it won't be long before it's totally dark, I think and I try to stop looking at them but I see them bring each other over to the sandpit and then they're standing next to the sandpit and then she lays out her jacket and pullover on the sand

Now we're kids again, she says

Now we're doing whatever we want, she says

Yes, we're kids, he says

Naughty kids doing whatever they want, she says

and she lies down in the sand on her jacket and pullover, she's lying there in just her bra and purple skirt and her dark hair spreads out and then she says that he needs to take his clothes off too

No we can't do this, he says

Yes we can, she says

Someone might see us, he says

It's almost totally dark, she says

Come on, she says

and then she pulls up her purple skirt and tells him to come over, he needs to come over to her now, because it's cold and he needs to warm her up, she says and he says that's what he said, it's too cold to take off any of their clothes, and she says come on, come on, and he says no, no we can't do this, someone might see us, he says, she needs to put her clothes back on right away, he says and she says that it's almost totally dark, no one's coming, no one might see them, come on, come on, just come over here, she says and then he takes off his brown shoulderbag and puts it down next to the sandpit and takes off his long black coat and lays it over her and then he covers the both of them with the coat so that only his coat is visible and, and, no, I have no right to look, to watch this, I think, and is it really happening? or is it all just something I'm dreaming? or is it something that actually happened to me once? isn't that me, lying there in the sandpit on top of her with my long black coat covering us both? isn't that exactly what happened to me once? I think, but even so I have no right to watch what's happening, I think, and I keep walking, quietly, as quietly as I can, I continue slowly down the path and I don't want them to notice me, I don't want to bother them, I want them to stay alone in their own world, and now I can just barely see the coat there in the sandpit, or maybe I can't see the coat? maybe it's all just something I'm picturing in my mind? no, I think, and I can't watch, I have no desire to see this and now I need to turn around, now, I think, I need to turn around now and go back to my car, because all of this, is it even really happening? or do I just think it's happening? or remember it happening? is it something that happened to me once? it must have been a long long time ago because I can't remember it, but isn't that me lying there in the sandpit under my long black coat? and isn't that the same coat I wear all the time? my good old long black overcoat? and she, lying under me and under my long black coat that's covering us? isn't that me? isn't that us? I think, isn't that me sometime in the past? or is this happening now in reality, before my eyes, right there in the playground? I think and I stop and now it's dark, totally dark, and with a kind of clear-sightedness that lets me see in the darkness I see the two of them lying there in the sandpit and the clear sounds of breathing are coming from the sandpit and I hear them moving with the same regularity, like waves striking land, I hear the regular movements like waves, back and forth, again and again, and everything is one movement, one breath, out and in, hearts beating, two hearts beating against each other in the sandpit, and my own heart is beating, beating, and in a steady movement, like waves against the shore, I walk up to the road and my car, and I hear from the playground movements, waves against the shore, back and forth, and I'm walking in the same movement, step by step, and now I mustn't turn around and look at them, I think, and I keep going and then I don't hear the sound of any more movements coming from the sandpit and I look at the young man and now he's standing in the sandpit with his pants down below his knees but his black coat is still draped over her and he has a bucket in his hand and he fills it up with sand and then pours the sand out all over his coat, over her, he refills and empties the bucket, covering her and the coat with sand, no, impossible, incredible, he really is pouring sand over her as she lies under his coat with a little bucket some kid left behind in the sandpit and, no, I mustn't watch, now I need to get home to Dylgja because I can't walk in the dark like this and watch a young man stand next to a young woman lying under his long black coat and empty bucket after bucket of sand over the coat and her, I think, but I can't take my eyes off the two people in the sandpit and can't stop seeing him empty bucket after bucket of sand over her and then he finally pulls his pants up and buttons them and then he takes his coat off her and sand sprinkles off his coat and she stands up and tugs at her skirt, picks up her pullover and jacket, shakes out her skirt, brushes the sand off them and he shakes the sand off the long black coat and he puts it on and then drapes the brown leather bag over his shoulder and it looks like he's ready to leave

Come back here, she says

and she looks at him

Don't go, she says

Don't just leave like that, so suddenly, she says

Come to me, she says

and she holds out her hand to him and he goes over to her and takes her hand and they stand still for a moment

Time to go? he says

Yes, she says

and then she opens her arms and puts them around him and holds him close and I turn around and I keep walking, up to the road, and she says sweetheart, my darling boy, you, I, she says and he says sweetheart, my darling girl, my darling darling girl, my darling darling girl, you, he says and then she says it's pretty cold and he says yes it's really cold, he says he's freezing even though he has his coat on and I walk carefully and as quietly as I can and I look back at the playground and see her long dark hair, hanging straight down over her back, almost down to her hips, and he is just standing there, not doing anything, and his medium-length brown hair is tousled and sticking out in every direction like it's confused while her hair hangs straight down, and then she brings her face to his, her mouth to his, and she kisses him on the mouth and then she says that there's really a lot of sand on his coat

Yeah, he says

and he gives a little laugh

It's all over us, he says

It's 'cause you poured all those buckets of sand on me, she says

Yes, he says

You almost buried me, she says

Almost, not quite, he says

and they stand there and it's like they don't exactly know what to do or say

Now it's really dark, she says

And cold, too, she says

Like you said, she says

Yes, he says

We should go home, he says

and she nods, and then they move a little bit apart from each other and she looks at him, he looks at her

Because you're Asle, she says

And you're Ales, he says

and they smile at each other, they shyly smile at each other and she says can you believe we took our clothes off in the dark, when it's so cold out too, she says, we took our clothes off outside, so late in the autumn, when it's so dark, and so cold, and then to lie down in a sandpit, naked, she says and she laughs, but anyway it's somewhere to live, she says, yes even if the house is falling down, he says, practically a shack, she says, yes it's going to be almost impossible to heat that house, he says, but it's somewhere to live anyway, she says, and he says that when they get home he'll have to thoroughly brush all the sand out of their clothes and then they just stand there holding hands

And then we'll need to wash them, she says

Or at least brush and wipe all the sand off, she says

We're pretty wild, she says

No, what we did wasn't totally crazy, he says

Imagine what people would say, she says

Yeah, he says

I think there's a car up there in the turnoff, he says

No, she says

Yup, he says

It's cold and we need to get home, she says

To our new place, yes, he says

It'll be at least a little warmer there, she says

A little, maybe, he says

But anyway, that's the home we have, she says

And it's good we have somewhere to live, he says

And that we have each other, she says

We do, he says

and she turns her face towards him and they give each other
a short kiss

We have each other, she says

In deepest darkness we have each other, he says

And we stick together, she says

Through thick and thin, he says

There will always be us, she says

There will always be you and me, he says

Asle and Ales, she says

Ales and Asle, he says

The two of us forever, just us, you and me, she says

That's right, he says

and now it's completely dark and I've made it back to the
car and I get in and sit down and stay sitting there looking
straight ahead and I lean back in the seat and put my head on
the headrest and look straight ahead and now I see nothing but
darkness in front of me, just the black darkness, nothing but
black, and I think that I'm parked in the turnoff by the brown
house where Ales and I used to live, I stopped here to take a
break because I was tired, I think, and because I wanted to pray,
since I pray three times a day almost every day, I say a prayer

that I've put together myself, in the morning and once in the
middle of the day and then in the evening, yes, laudes or mat-
ins, as they call it, and then sextus, and then vespers, and I use
a rosary with brown wooden beads to pray with, there's a loop
with five decades, as they call them, five groups of ten beads
each, with a gap between each group and then there's a string
hanging off the loop with a gap and a bead and then a gap and
then three beads and then a gap and then a bead and then a gap
and then a cross at the end, and I always have my rosary with
me, around my neck, it was Ales who gave it to me, it was she
who taught me about rosaries, I had barely heard the word rosary before I met her, I think, yes, I remember that I heard the
word once and wondered what it meant, I think, but now I always wear a rosary around my neck like a necklace and I always
silently say to myself the Pater Noster or Our Father, two or
three times, and I see every prayer before me, yes, like a picture, I've never learned any of the prayers by heart but I recall
them by seeing them in front of me, since I can also easily see
things written in front of me, but I try not to do that, so there
are only a few things I see before my eyes in writing, and unlike
with pictures I can decide whether or not I want to remember
something written, I think and I think that I also like to pray
three Ave Marias and one Gloria Patri each time, and I pray either in Latin or in my own translation into Norwegian,
Nynorsk, and after that what I pray varies a little, it's often the
creed, the short Apostolic Creed, that they say the apostles
spoke, or anyway something like that, and in any case I say the
whole thing silently, before the Pater Noster, the long creed,
the Nicene Creed, I see just pieces of that before my eyes, yes,
light from light, Lumen de Lumine, visible and invisible things,
visibilium omnium et invisibilium, and then I sometimes say
something from Salve Regina right to the end and sometimes I

try to stay silent, not think about anything while I'm praying
and just let there be a silence inside me, and then I can pray for
something, but I almost always pray for intercessions, I pray for
other people, almost never for something I'm planning to do
myself, and if it is then it has to be something I can do to help
God's kingdom to come, for example paint pictures so that
they might have something to do with God's kingdom, and I
always make the sign of the cross, both before I start praying
and after I'm done, and I say In the name of the Father and the
Son and the Holy Ghost Amen or else In nomine Patris et Filii
et Spiritus Sancti Amen, and in the mornings it's a short prayer,
often just the sign of the cross, and in the middle of the day I
pray the longest, and in the evening I usually pray myself to
sleep with something from the Jesus prayer and saying to myself
Lord Jesus Christ, and I say each syllable while either breathing
deeply in or breathing slowly out, the same when I say Have
mercy on me a sinner, again and again I say these words, or else
I say to myself Domine Iesu Christe Fili Dei Miserere mei pec-
catoris again and again, breathing deeply in, breathing slowly
out, but I almost always say this prayer in Norwegian, for whatever reason, and then I disappear into sleep, I think, I fall asleep
either to that prayer or to the Ave Maria, I think, and what I'm
looking for in all my prayers is silence and humility, I think,
yes, God's peace, I think, and I take the rosary in both hands
and lift it from under my pullover and pull it up over my head
and then sit with the rosary in my hands and I hold the cross
between my thumb and forefinger and I think that I must have
fallen asleep and dreamed, but I wasn't asleep, and I wasn't
dreaming, I think and it was all unreal and at the same time real,
yes, all of that happened both in a dream and in reality and I sit
there staring straight ahead into the darkness, now the darkness
is blackness, it's not just dark any more, and I just look into the

blackness and I think that now I have to start making my way home, but I've thought that so many times already and now as if it's the middle of a sunny day I see the two of them walking towards me, a young man with medium-length brown hair and a young woman with long dark hair, they stand out in the darkness, it's as if a light coming from them stands out in the darkness, yes, they're walking straight at me like they're illuminated, and their faces are peaceful and still, and they're holding hands, and they are like one, like one shape walking, and they might have noticed me or my car but they're much too involved with each other, they are in each other, they are present to each other, in their own world, and they walk past the car and I turn to follow them with my eyes in the darkness and I see his medium-length brown hair so clearly and I see her long dark hair hanging straight down her back and I see them slowly disappear into the darkness and go away and I let go of the cross and put the rosary back around my neck and tuck it under my pullover and then I make the sign of the cross and I say to myself In the name of the Father and the Son and the Holy Ghost Amen and then I start the car and I think no, that, that didn't happen, I think, and now I really need to get home, I think, now I need to drive home to my wife and our child, I think and I drive out of the turnoff and onto the country road and I think I should have gone to see Asle, he was so worn down, half-dead, I should have asked him to come out with me, I should have driven him into town to The Alehouse, like I've done so many times, and he could've had his beer and his something stronger and I could've had a cup of coffee with milk, and food, yes we could've bought dinner there, food and beer for him and food and water for me, yes I've totally stopped drinking, because I used to drink much too much and Ales didn't like it, she didn't like me when I was drunk or at least she liked me more when I was sober and that's why I totally stopped drinking, but I also stopped because by the end I was drinking way too much, yes, by the end I was never sober, to tell the truth, and I paint so badly when I'm drunk, and I've never missed it, not the beer, not the wine, not the stronger stuff, but that's because of her too, because of Ales, without her I never would have been able to stop needing to drink, I think, and now Ales is waiting for me, she and our child, and I need to get home to them, to my wife, to our child, but what am I thinking? I live alone there, I'm going home to my old house in Dylgja where I used to live with Ales but she's gone now, she's with God now, in a way I can feel so clearly inside me, because she's there inside me too, she isn't walking around on earth any more but I can still talk to her whenever I want to, yes, it's strange, there's no big difference or distance between life and death, between the living and the dead, even though the difference can seem insurmountable it isn't, because, it's true, I talk with Ales every single day, yes, most of the time that's what I'm doing, and we most often talk to each other without words, almost always, just wordlessly, and of course I miss her but since we're still so close and since it won't be long before the time comes when I myself will go over to where she is, yes, I manage just fine, but it's painful, yes, being without her was like being without everything in life, it almost finished me off, and we never had children, there were just the two of us, so why am I thinking that I'm driving home to my wife and child? it's probably just that I fall into a kind of stupor when I'm driving and when that happens thoughts can come to you, but I know perfectly well, I'm not crazy, that I'm going home to my old house, home to Dylgja, to my house in the little farming and fishing village of Dylgja, I think, the house where I've lived alone for all these years, yes, I wasn't such an old man when we moved there, and

Ales was even younger, that was where we lived, first the years when I lived there with Ales and then afterwards all those years when I lived alone in the good old house, and it is good, it's good that I have my house, that I have a safe place to live, a house where I feel safe, because it's a well-built old house and I've taken good care of it, whenever any of it started falling apart I replaced the wood, I replaced all the windows, but I made the new ones as much like the old ones as I could, I put the windows into the same frames just with an extra pane of glass so that there'd be less of a draught, now there are two panes of glass instead of one in every window, one pane that opens out, one that opens in, and it was so much easier to keep the house warm after the new windows were put in, I ordered the windows from a carpenter who made them to measure, by hand, the same way they used to make windows, so that the new windows were just like the old ones, and then I put the windows in myself, but not alone, Åsleik helped me, without his help I'd never have been able to put them in, that's for sure, we had to work together, but together we could do it, even if the first window ended up being put in crooked and we had to redo it, take the window out and put it back in, but the other windows went in the way they were supposed to, the other windows were easy, I think, yes, Åsleik's helped me a lot, and I've helped him too for that matter, I think and now it'll be good to get home, light the stove, make some food, I'm really hungry, yes it'll definitely be nice to get back home to my good old house in the little village of Dylgja, where just a few people still live, good people, none of them lock their doors when they leave the house, or go on a trip, not that they do that very often, and most of the people who live there have lived there their whole life, and then I moved there, or we did, my wife and I, yes, Ales and I moved there and it was because Ales got her aunt's house when she died, her father's sister, old Alise, because her aunt was childless and there were no other heirs and since we didn't own a place to live anywhere and just lived in the rundown brown house that I just drove past we moved into the old house in Dylgja, yes, that was many years ago now, I think, and then we lived there, Ales and I, and then, no I don't want to think about that, not now, I think and I drive north and I think that I like driving, as long as I don't have to drive in cities, I don't like that at all, I get anxious and confused and I avoid city driving as much as I can, in fact I never do it, but Beyer, my gallerist, he told me how to get to and from The Beyer Gallery which is in the middle of Bjørgvin, and outside the gallery there's a big car park and that's where I always park my car, so I can manage in the city of Bjørgvin, I think and I get to Instefjord and then I start driving out along Sygnefjord and I'm so tired but I'm almost home now, I think, it won't be long before I see Åsleik at the door, yes, Åsleik, actually I've never liked him much but in a strange way that's why I like him, I think, you can't always understand things like that, I think, and now it'll be good to get home, but I shouldn't have just driven past Asle's apartment in Bjørgvin, in Sailor's Cove, he's always shaking, before I drove home to Dylgja I should have driven him into town to The Alehouse like I've done so many times, of course he would've been fine there in The Alehouse alone, surely someone he knew would be there or would get there soon, I wouldn't have had to stay there with him, actually what I really should have done was drive him to The Clinic, but he'd never have gone along with that so we'd have ended up at The Alehouse anyway, he with his long grey hair and grey stubble, me with my long grey hair and grey stubble, in our long black coats, each with our hair tied back in a pony tail, I think

You look like a little girl, Åsleik says

Actually more like an old woman, he says

and I don't know what to say

I'm not an old woman, I say then

You almost are, Åsleik says

or maybe I am a little like an old woman, I don't know, I think, maybe a little? it's not entirely wrong to say that I am, I think, anyway Åsleik likes to say so, either that or he says I look like a Russian monk

You're like a Russian monk, he says

Why's that? I say

Because you are, you're like a Russian monk, he says

and how can he have come up with that? I think, and now I'm driving back to my house and the headlights light up the road and I can see the road in front of me and I see Asle sitting on the sofa with Bragi in his lap and he's thinking he wants to get up and go outside and then go out into the sea and he's thinking that all the paintings he's putting into his next show at The Beyer Gallery are bad paintings anyway, Asle thinks, and he thinks that he can't just stay sitting like this, he needs to go to the kitchen and get something to drink, to make this shaking stop, Asle thinks and he looks at Bragi lying on his lap and he thinks he needs to walk the dog, it's been a long time since the dog has been out, he thinks and I think I need to concentrate on my driving now, because the road to Dylgja is so narrow and winding, even though I've driven it countless times I still need to pay attention, I think, and it'll be good to get back to my house again, because it's my home, that's what it's become, and Ales lived there too for many years, yes, but then, yes, she died, with no warning, and now she's gone, that's all there is to say about that, I think, and now I need to just drive, slowly, just keep my eyes on the patch of light that the headlights make reaching forward on the road, they light up a bit of the landscape alongside the road too, and I'm driving carefully out along Sygnefjord, and I think that there's so many times one or more deer have been crossing the road or just suddenly standing in the middle of the road, or else bounding across the road, it's like the deer can't hear the noise of the engines or see the light from the headlights, like they just don't notice it, they've become used to the engine sounds and headlights and no longer pay any attention to them but at the same time they've never realized how bad it would be if a car hit them, I think and I turn off the country road onto the driveway leading up to my house, good, good, I think, now I'm home, that's good, and the driveway up to the house is one I had built myself, not so many years ago either, it was very expensive but it was certainly nice to have a driveway up to the house and no longer need to park the car a long way off down on the country road, I think, and even if the driveway is steep it's easy enough to drive on it, I think and I don't want to think about what it used to be like coming home when she was there, when Ales was there, when she was in the house with her long dark hair, it was so good to come home then, wasn't it, I think, but I don't want to think about that, and I can't complain, I think and I steer the car around the little hill and there, there in front of the house, is that Åsleik standing there? yes it's none other than Åsleik himself, my neighbour and friend, standing there in front of the house, as if waiting to welcome me home, and now that was a stroke of luck, that he should be looking in on me just when I got home, I think and I stop the car by the front door and I realize I'm happy to see Åsleik in front of the house but it wasn't exactly luck, because this isn't the first time he's been standing in front of the house when I get home from Bjørgvin, Åsleik must have been standing and waiting for me in front of the house for a long time, that's for sure, he sat down for a bit on the bench near the door, got up and stamped his feet a bit and then sat back down on the bench, because after all I bought a few things for him down in Bjørgvin the way I usually do and he's waiting for me to get back, keeping a lookout, even though he always acts like he never wants to accept what I've bought him but then he does anyway, as if without seeing it, I think, and since I always ask him before I go into Bjørgvin whether I should buy him anything there, since it's cheaper to buy things in Bjørgvin than at The Country Store in Vik, he says every time that it's not necessary, that what little he needed, as he liked to say, he could buy at The Country Store in Vik, in the little shop, if you can call it that, that we have closest to Dylgja, but it's certainly a good thing that we have the little shop at all or else we'd have to drive a long way just to buy the least little thing, and not everyone here has their own car either, or is able to drive it, some people are too old, some never got a driving licence, some don't want to drive because they're never sober enough to drive so they don't do it, but not everyone who drinks avoids driving, some drive no matter how much they've drunk, they just drive slowly and carefully, I think, and I think that Åsleik is about to say well that was a long trip to Bjørgvin, I spent a while there but when I got there, yes, there was probably so much to do that you'd have to expect it to take some time before I got back home, since if I didn't have anything special to do in Bjørgvin I could always just take the opportunity to hang around there, or go running around after the ladies for all he knew, that's what he's about to say, and then he'll give a good laugh I think and I open the car door

Welcome! Åsleik says

Glad you could drop by, he says

Isn't it me who should be saying that? I say

Or have you taken over my house too? I say

Sure did! Åsleik says

You did? I say

Yes, you said that it's mine now, he says

What are you talking about? I say

There's yours and there's mine, I say

Yes you have yours and I have mine, I say

That's how it needs to be, I say

I have my own place, even a farm, so there's nothing to argue about, he says

Yes that's what I meant, I say

But why did you say you're glad I could drop by? I say

Why not? Åsleik says

Is there something wrong with saying that? he says

Isn't that something you're supposed to say? he says

Something people always say? he says

It's something you say when it's your own place, that's when you thank someone for dropping by, I say

Especially when it's your own farm, he says

and in a way I probably have something like a farm too, even though it's just an old house with a few rocky hills and a little boggy soil and some heather and a couple of small pine trees around the edges

And it's not like this is a farm, Åsleik says

It's a house anyway, it's my house, I say

Your house, yes, Åsleik says

Of course it's your house, who would say it wasn't, he says

That's for sure, he says

In a way, yes, I say

and we fall silent and then Åsleik says of course it's my house, whose else could it be? even if I wasn't born and raised in this house it was still my house, no one can deny that, even if he does remember very well old Alise who used to live here, he says

Yes, I say

and we fall silent

She was a good woman, old Alise, Åsleik says then

Yes she sure was, he says

and we fall silent again and then I say that my wife, Ales, was named after her, and maybe that's why old Alise wanted Ales to inherit her house, I say

Yes, no, I know, Åsleik says

There weren't any closer relatives, after her husband died so long ago, and then her brother, Ales's father, was dead too, he says

and again we fall silent and then Åsleik says that he can just barely remember old Alise's parents, he's certainly getting on in years himself, he says, but they were truly old, as far as he remembers, yes, from an ancient time you might say, and it was a pretty bare house, but the father, old and bent, he sure was old, didn't he row to The Country Store in Vik to his dying day, he would go down to the water as long as he had the legs for it and then row to The Country Store, and that wasn't something for a frail old guy like him to do, no, Åsleik says

Yes, I say

They sure were made of strong stuff back then, Åsleik says

Of course it was hard work, a real chore for him, but how else could he get food into the house? he says

So he had to, he says

and then silence sort of spreads out and settles in

Yes, yes, I remember it well, Åsleik says then

Back then there were no cars around here, you know, it was a long way to walk, but just in the countryside, between the country farms, there weren't roads out of the country, no, he says and he says he was quite old when they built a road out, yes, he remembers it well, and the old people in the country, isolated, religious folks, they thought it would've been just as well if that road never did get built because of all the evil and sinfulness that could come into the countryside now, and who wanted to drive out to the countryside anyway? some of them felt, so the best thing would have been if the road never got built at all but the road was built, and because of that Dylgja became part of the world too and because of that someone like me could move to the country, that's what it meant to have a road out, so actually maybe the pious old people had a point about what they said, despite everything? since now that a road had been built all kinds of people could come driving along and then before you know it one of them might want to move out here? Åsleik says and I think that Åsleik will always, always be like this, starting to talk about one thing and then ending up somewhere else, and he just keeps on talking, without stopping, maybe it's because he's alone so much and doesn't have anyone to talk to that he can sometimes just launch into talking nonstop, about this and that, past present and future all jumbled together, and it's all things I've heard before, many times over, I think

Yes now you've got a bad memory, he says

I have a bad memory? I say

and I don't understand why he'd say that all of a sudden, as if my memory was something we needed to start talking about of all things, Åsleik bringing up my supposedly bad memory just like that, out of nowhere, no, I don't know how I've been able to stand him all these years, how can I stay living here in this godforsaken place that time forgot, almost no one else lives here of their own free will do they? I think, and Åsleik says besides, maybe it's not really my house, in a way, don't I remember what I said, that time, yeah, that if he could move that boat I'd give him my house? he says

But that's just something people say, I say

Just something people say? Åsleik says

Did I manage to move that boat or didn't I? he says

I helped you move it, I say

You helped! he says

Yes, I helped! I say

I moved that boat by myself, he says

No, the boat was stuck until I grabbed it too and helped, I say

So you were lying, and now you'll break your promise, he says

I'm not lying about anything, I never lie, I always tell the truth, I say

You always tell the truth, he says

Nothing but the truth, he says

What I say is true, I say

and then it's suddenly quiet, we both stop talking and stand there a moment without saying anything

Nice weather we've had today, calm too, Åsleik says then

Yes, I say

It was dead calm all through the morning but then in the late afternoon yes then the wind picked up a little like always, he says

And what else would you expect, here we are in late autumn already, Advent's here, we should expect to see some storms, he says

and then he says we won't have to wait long, the first storms of the year'll be here before you know it, it's strange that they haven't started already, he says, and then we stay standing there some more, not saying anything

And everything in Bjørgvin was the same as usual? he says

Yes, I say

and again it's quiet

It's nice to drive into town now and then, I say

Yes, I suppose so, Åsleik says

and I think now I should ask him about the last time he was in Bjørgvin, but I've done that so many times before and it always bothers him a little, he always squirms a little, shakes his head a little, because the truth is he's probably almost never been to Bjørgvin, maybe a few times long ago, that's it, so I shouldn't bring it up, not now, that wouldn't be nice, I think and again we're standing there not saying anything

I'm glad I can go fishing, have something to do during the day, Åsleik says then

Me too, I make the days go by in my own way, I say

Yes, you and those paintings of yours, he says

Yes, right, I say

You spend whole days painting, he says

and I think that Åsleik has said that so many times before, he's repeated it over and over, time after time, but then again I've said the same things over and over again myself, I've asked Åsleik again and again if he's caught anything today and again and again he'd say that his net came up empty, or else that it was so full he could barely heave it up on board The Boat, or else that there wasn't much, something like that, and if I showed him a picture I'd painted he'd say something, too, or else not say anything, but when he did say something what he said was always amazingly smart, he always saw something I hadn't seen myself, and then these stupid little arguments of ours, as if we always had to have a little fight over some tiny thing before we could really talk to each other, I think and I hear Åsleik ask me again, the same as he's done countless times before, why I paint, won't I ever stop painting these pictures of mine? I've spent almost my whole life painting these pictures and now I'm supposed to stop? no, he doesn't understand me, for him it's simply incomprehensible, he's never drawn even the simplest thing himself, not once, and he's always had someone else paint the house too, he's never even tried to paint the house, he can wax a boat no problem of course but that doesn't count, that's not like painting anything, no, he says and I say, the same as I say every time, that I don't know why I paint these pictures I just do it, it's a living, I say, and Åsleik says I've kept on painting since I was a little boy, and now I know he wants me to tell him about how I couldn't do maths when I went to school and so I sat there and drew in my maths books instead of doing maths, I drew The Schoolmaster and drew the boy sitting next to me, I drew my classmates one after the other, and why did I do that? I did it just to do it! simple as that! I did it so I wouldn't have to think about numbers, only about drawing, yes, I could add, and subtract, I could do that in my head if none of the numbers was too big or too hard, but when it came to multiplying or dividing or percents or anything like that, no, I just didn't understand it, pure and simple, I understood the difference between big and small numbers, and how to add more or take away, and that's all I needed to get through life, there was no need for more, but other than that I understood nothing, I couldn't do it in my head, and the poor Schoolmaster, he tried and tried, he was so patient, and he was confident too, again and again he tried to explain multiplication to me, and when I didn't understand he said surely I had to understand it, everyone had to learn how to multiply, he said, to get through life you needed to know how to multiply, and he said take two and multiply it by two and you'll have four, he said, two twos are four, he said, and I said I understood that, and he said so two plus two is four and two times two is four, he said, and if you take seven and multiply it by seven how much is that? The Schoolmaster said, and he said I could figure it out by adding seven plus seven and then seven more until I'd added seven plus seven seven times in all and I did it and got the wrong number every time, it was always wrong, but I should have just memorized what the number was, seven times seven, but I couldn't do it, no, I never ever saw the sevens before my eyes the way I could see pictures so easily, even that was practically impossible, and to this day I can't do the seven times tables, I can't, and I don't understand why it was always so hard for me, it was like the numbers shifted after I memorized them and turned a little too big or a little too small, there was just no way I could do it and that's why I'd draw, because I could do that, yes, I could draw anyone no matter who, either just their face or, preferably, someone in motion in some way or another, what I liked best was drawing the movement, drawing someone or something moving, drawing the line you might say, yes, it's hard to understand, and I didn't understand it either, I didn't understand why I liked it or how and why I could do it, but I thought about it a lot and I'll probably never figure it out, I think, but I know that Åsleik wants me to tell him the whole story again, he likes it when I tell it, when I talk about how I couldn't do maths but I did know how to draw, nobody in my class could draw like me, absolutely no one, but I don't feel like telling Åsleik that story again, not now, and the truth is I don't think he wants to hear it either, not now, he just wants us to be talking about something, anything, and it's been a long time since we've had anything especially new to say to each other, we've known each other so long and chatted together so many times, so I say just that I don't know why I paint and that I don't know why I've done it since I was young, and I think that at some point I'll tell him the whole story again, about drawing in my maths notebooks instead of doing maths in them, but not now, and then Åsleik will say that he wasn't good at much of anything in school, not maths, not reading, not writing, and definitely not drawing, but actually, he'll say, it wasn't because he couldn't have done it, done all those things well, it was because he was so scared of his teachers, he was so scared that he didn't do anything, whenever he saw a teacher it was like he was paralysed and not a single thought stirred inside him and he froze up and he couldn't do anything, that's what he'll say, the same as he always says, I think and then I say well I probably paint for the same reason he fishes

To pass the time, he says

Yes, and to bring in a little money, I say

Yes that too, he says

and there's another long silence

They're pretty much the same thing really, Åsleik says then

Yes, I say

and I ask Åsleik if he'd like to step inside and he says yes, maybe he'll do that, why not? he says and I go and open the door at the back of the car and Åsleik says, the same as he always does, that I have a big, practical car now don't I, you can fit a lot more into that back area than it looks like from the outside, he says, and I pull a roll of canvas out of the back of the car and he takes the roll under his arm and goes over to the front door of the house and opens it, since I never lock the door, it's never locked, no one in Dylgja leaves their door locked, that's how it's always been and that's how it'll always be, and I untie a thick bundle of pinewood boards ten feet long from the rack on the roof of the car, boards I'll use to make stretchers, and I take them inside and Åsleik has turned on the hall light and put the roll of canvas down in the corner by the door to The Parlour and I put the boards down next to the canvas, and later I'll carry the canvas and boards up to the attic, I think, because

I have my storage space in a room upstairs, with all the stuff I need for painting, and I go into the main room and I turn on the light there and the cold hits me

It's cold in here, I say

and Åsleik comes into the room

It sure is, he says

Should I light the stove? he says

and I say yes, that'd be good, and I can bring in what I've bought, I say and I see Åsleik go over to the stove and crouch down and with wood chips in his fist he looks up and says do I know where these wood chips come from? and I say yes, yes, I know perfectly well, and I thank him very much for the wood chips and for all the wood he's brought me, I say and I see Åsleik put the chips and some kindling into the stove with the firewood, and yes, it's from Åsleik that I got all the wood chips, the firewood, all the wood, because he likes working with wood, as he says, gathering wood, and then I pay him for the wood, he always says that he doesn't want anything for the wood but he needs the kroner that I give him, I always have to give him the money kind of furtively, even though I'm doing well, as they say, strangely enough there are still plenty of people who want to buy the pictures I paint, I don't know why but that's how it is, ever since I was young I've made money from my paintings, the first pictures I painted were of the building next door in the farming village where I grew up, in Barmen, and in the pictures it was always a day of beautiful weather with the fruit trees in bloom and the sun shining over the house and the farm, the fjord blue, actually it was the light I was painting, not the buildings, they were pretty enough as far as that goes, it wasn't that, but painting the buildings as such was too boring, that was why I tried to paint the light, but in the sharp bright light of the sun what looks brightest are the shadows, in a way, yes, the darker they are the more light there is, and what I like painting the most is the autumn light but people always wanted to see their house painted in brilliant sunshine, and I wanted to sell my pictures, of course that's what I wanted, yes, after all that's why I painted them, so I had to paint them the way people wanted them, but none of them saw what I actually painted, nobody saw that, just me, and maybe a few other people, because what I painted were the shadows, what I painted was the darkness in all that light, I painted the real light, the invisible light, but did anyone see that? did they notice that? no, probably not, or maybe some people did? yes, well, I know there were some people who saw it, Åsleik too for that matter, he has a real understanding of pictures, I have to admit, but I painted buildings and houses, and people bought the pictures I painted, and that's how I could buy more canvas and tubes of oil paint, because oil paint on canvas has always been what I've liked, nothing else, oil on canvas, always, it was like that from the very first time I saw a picture painted in oil on canvas, and the first picture painted in oil on canvas I ever saw was in the local schoolhouse where a painting hanging crooked on the wall in one of the classrooms was meant to show Jesus walking on water, and to tell the truth it was a terrible painting but the colours, the individual colours in themselves, colours in certain places, colours the way they were on that canvas, yes, they were fixed on that canvas, they clung tight to it, went together with it, were one with it and at the same time different from it, yes, it was unbelievable and I looked and looked at that painting, not at the picture itself, it was so badly painted, but it was oil paint on canvas and that, oil paint on canvas, lodged inside me from the very first moment and stayed there to this day, yes, that's the truth, yes it somehow lodged itself in me for life, the same way oil paint fuses with the canvas I was fused with oil

on canvas, I don't know why but I guess I needed something
or another to cling to? get attached to? and The Schoolmaster
noticed, he noticed that I was always staring at that painting,
and he told my parents that I had a gift for drawing, and probably for painting too, if I could just try it, and that way if I
couldn't do maths I could at least paint pictures, yes, that's how
it was, and then my parents got hold of some kind of kit with
tubes of paint and brushes and a palette, and a tool for mix-
ing colours and scraping the paint off if the paint was wrong, a
palette knife they call it, one of those was included too, and I
was astounded, I was beside myself, I knew what I wanted to
paint because at home there was a picture hanging in the living
room that Mother and Father had been given as a gift, I think
it was Father who'd been given it when he turned forty, and
the picture was called *Bridal Procession on the Hardangerfjord*, by
Tidemand and Gude, it was what they called a reproduction, a
word I liked a lot, what I didn't like as much was that both the
paint and the canvas were missing, the picture was flat with no
oil paint stuck to any canvas, but anyway I decided to paint a
copy of this picture, none other, as well as I could, yes, I'd told
my parents that this was the first picture I wanted to paint and
both my mother and my father said I'd never be able to, and
I told The Schoolmaster too and he too was sure I'd never be
able to do it, but I'd decided to do it, I wouldn't touch a brush
until I got a canvas in a frame exactly the same size as *Bridal
Procession on the Hardangerfjord* so my father bought me a canvas
and frame in that size, I was given that too, I remember, it was
a Christmas present, I think I must have been about twelve, yes,
somewhere around there, yes, and then they took down the
picture and I put both *Bridal Procession on the Hardangerfjord* and
the empty white canvas on the floor, up in the attic at home,
and I started to paint, carefully, slowly, because the colours had

to be exactly right and had to go in exactly the right places, I painted carefully, almost point by point but at the same time they were supposed to turn into brushstrokes somehow, it went slowly and took days, the whole week between Christmas and New Year's I was up in the attic busy with my painting and my parents were more and more beside themselves with amazement because miracle of miracles my picture looked like it, yes, to a T! it was almost better than the picture I was copying! they had to admit that they would never have believed it, they said it was exceptional, unbelievable, and Father couldn't restrain himself and he went and told The Schoolmaster and then The Schoolmaster came by to see the picture for himself and then he asked if he could buy the picture from me, and Father hummed and hawed, he'd probably be willing to let go of the picture I'd copied, how about that, Father said, but The Schoolmaster wasn't interested in buying that, and I said I needed money, both for tubes of oil paint and more canvas, so I wanted to sell the picture, and since after all it was me who'd painted it Father had to go along with what I wanted and The Schoolmaster bought the painting from me and paid good money and I can still see The Schoolmaster before my eyes, one Sunday not far into the new year, walking down the driveway away from the house with my painting under his arm and I stood there with the notes in my hand, I can't remember how much it was but I can remember that one day I took the bus from Barmen to Stranda, because that's where the shops were, most of the shops were there, and at The Paint Shop in Stranda they sold both house paint and art paint, and that's where I went and I bought tubes of oil paint, and a roll of canvas, and wood for stretchers, and ever since then it's been oil on canvas, I have lived on nothing but oil paint on canvas, I've never made money doing anything else, yes, since I was a boy, because already as a boy I made enough money from my paintings and that is what Åsleik likes me to talk about most of all, yes, how I could paint pictures of houses on the neighbouring farms and sell them to the neighbours and use the money to buy tubes of oil paint and more canvas, but I don't feel like talking about that now

You've sure got it good, spending your whole life painting, Åsleik says

That's true, I do, I say

Really good, I say

You get by anyway, Åsleik says

Yes, I get by, I say

You could always get by, he says

and I don't want to talk yet again about when I was young and painted pictures that I sold, because actually they were terrible pictures, beautiful lies, about as bad as pictures can be, only the shadows were painted well, and the copy I painted of *Bridal Procession on the Hardangerfjord* was even worse, that's why I don't want to talk about it, not now, it can wait, some time later I'll tell Åsleik about it again, I think, and I think that I'm ashamed of those pictures I painted in my youth, but why? well, the fact is I was violating something, degrading something, those sunny pictures I painted back then were pure lies, except in the shadows, the darkness, the light, yes, sometimes I was close to something but then I tried to sort of hide it in the picture, I would paint over it, yes, I painted over the best things in the picture! and it's awful to think about, but the picture looked real, it looked so real, and the fruit trees were in bloom and the sun was shining on the pretty white house and the water in the fjord was blue, and the only thing I needed to paint a painting like that was a photograph of a house, or farm, or whatever they wanted me to paint, and then I'd find out roughly how big they wanted the picture to be, and once they'd told me that I got started, and oh they looked so real and oh how ashamed I was of those pictures I painted, but really it wasn't anything to be ashamed of, I should've been proud of myself, actually, it's not the worst thing in the world for a kid to be able to paint like that, it looks so real! they said, and they paid me and I painted and that's still true today, it wasn't the worst thing in the world for a kid to paint pictures like that, and yet I'm so ashamed of them, it was like I was disrespecting, yes, desecrating something by painting them, and I wish all those paintings would just disappear! let them vanish for all time! if I could've burnt every last one of them I would have, and that's what I thought even well before I started at The Academic High School, and I really didn't like painting pictures like that, and luckily I never wrote my name on those pictures, sometimes someone would ask me to and when they did I wrote my first name in the right corner but just my first name, no more than that, and however upset they got about that I didn't write any more than that, it would have to do, but sometimes people would write on the back of the picture that I'd painted it, and in what year, and those ugly portraits I painted of my parents! I really wish they would just disappear from the face of the earth! they were total lies, they looked so realistic, just like my parents, and they looked so nice and pretty, it was all disrespecting, yes, desecrating art, pure and simple, to tell the truth, and those pictures, those pictures were what Åsleik liked to hear me talk about, and he just couldn't understand why I was so ashamed of those pictures, he'd seen some of them himself, he had relatives in Barmen, his mother was from Barmen and he'd been there a few times and he'd seen those pictures of mine, they were the best and finest pictures I'd ever painted, that's what he thinks, there was nothing I painted later that he liked as much as what I painted back then, he said and I thought he didn't know what

made a good painting any more than a horse's arse, that's who
I was dealing with here, a fool, yes, this person I constantly saw
was just an idiot, I think and I look at Åsleik making the stove
burn well and he puts a birchwood log in and I go outside and
get two shopping bags out of the back of the car and I go back
inside and into the hall and open the kitchen door and turn
on the light and then go in with the bags and put them down
on the kitchen table and then go into the main room and I see
Åsleik standing in front of the stove with the hatch open and
he says that it's burning nicely now so he can help me bring the
rest in and then he shuts the stove door and we go outside together and I hand him two bags and he takes them and I say he
can put them on the kitchen table and then I take out the last
two shopping bags and put them down and I take the door to
the back of the car and shut it and it clicks shut and I see Åsleik
go up to the door of my house and I say it's good we live somewhere where no one needs to lock the door

That's for sure, Åsleik says

There's never been talk of locking front doors here in
Dylgja, he says

Never, he says

and he emphasizes the word as if he's now said something
that really means a lot, and he has, too, he really has, there
aren't too many places left where people can leave their front
doors unlocked when they aren't home

It's good we can count on each other here in Dylgja, I say

Everyone in Dylgja can count on everyone else, yes, Åsleik
says

and I see Åsleik from behind, standing in the doorway with
the two bags and I know deep inside that I will never forget
this exact moment, this exact flash, yes, a flash is what it is, because there's a light in it, coming to it, or coming from it, there

where I see Åsleik in the doorway with his back to me, his bent
shoulders, that almost bald head with a ring of long grey hair
below the bald spot, and I can see his long grey beard, I think
he's hardly ever cut his beard since he started growing one as
a teenager, I think, and then those two plastic shopping bags
weighing him down, one on each side, making his shoulders
round, it's like he's framed by the doorway, and even though
it's dark and there's no outside light on and there's just a little
light coming out from the light in the hall I can see him as a
shape, as a shape with its own light, that's how I see him, and
it's probably the light of his angel, I think, but if I were ever
dumb enough to say something like that to him he'd have a
good laugh and say I was like those old wandering fiddlers who
learned to play from the Devil, that's what I was like, but in
a Christian way, something like that is what he'd say, and it's
always been this way, these glimpses of this or that thing that
lodge inside me and never leave my head again, never, they
lodge there as pictures and stay there and I can never get rid
of them, so they have to be painted away, yes, that's how it is,
that's how I am, I think, but this light, this flash is part of Åsleik
the person too, I think, but why isn't he going into the house?
why is he just standing there in the doorway? or is it only for
me that time has stopped? I think

You need to take those to the kitchen, I say

I am, Åsleik says

But I don't understand, why did you stop in the doorway?
I say

I didn't stop in the doorway, he says

You need to go inside, I say

Yes that's what I'm doing, Åsleik says

and he goes inside and I pick up the two bags next to me
and I go inside and I see Åsleik walk through the open door

into the kitchen and I go in after him and he puts his bags down on the kitchen table and then I go and put my bags down there

You sure bought a lot, Åsleik says

Six bags, he says

Yes, that's a lot, it always turns out to be more than you think it'll be, I say

and I go out into the hall and shut the front door and then go back into the kitchen and shut the kitchen door behind me

Do you need all that, a man living alone? Åsleik says

Not really, I say

You did buy a lot, Åsleik says

Anything to drink in there? he says

and he winks at me

No, I say

and I knew he was going to say that, it's like he always wants to remind me that I don't drink any more, I've stopped drinking, yes, it's been many years, since, no I don't want to think about that

No beer, nothing stronger either, he says

And Christmas coming soon and all, you know it's a common custom, right, people usually have some beer in the house, or something stronger, Åsleik says

But you didn't buy anything? he says

No, no, let's not talk about it, I say

With Christmas coming? he says

No, I say

Don't you like Christmas? Åsleik says

No, or, how should I put it, I say

You don't like being alone on Christmas? he says

No I can't say that I do, I say

I can imagine, Åsleik says

and we stand there in the kitchen not saying anything

And on Christmas you're going to your sister's house in Instefjord, same as usual, I say

Yes, Åsleik says

and then he says, the same as always, the same as he's done for years, that ever since Sister, yes well of course her name's Guro but he always calls her Sister, has lived alone, ever since her man ran off and never came back, that loser, yes, she's always asked him, Åsleik, to come over for Christmas, she's practically begged him, she has, and he has no reason not to, nothing against going to Sister's house for Christmas, because she serves the best Christmas lamb ribs you can find anywhere, how does she get them to taste like that, you know he has no idea how she always manages to give those lamb ribs of hers that exact special flavour, and she, Sister, won't tell him, but he can guess, he says, and anyway Sister is just joking around, or maybe more like trying to annoy him, when she refuses to tell him how she gets that flavour, it must have to do with how the lamb is smoked, but it can't be that because she has a smoking room in the cellar not a special smokehouse like he has, Åsleik says, so that means it must be about what she uses to smoke the lamb with, yes, he's figured out that much, he says

She gets the lamb from you? I say

Yes, Åsleik says

I kill and clean and carve it myself, you know that, he says

Sure, he says

Every year she gets a ewe lamb from me, he says

and he says that every autumn he takes a newly slaughtered and carved lamb with him and takes The Boat up through Sygnefjord to Øygna, where Sister lives, there by Instefjord, and I've seen her house lots of times, every time I drive to or from Bjørgvin I drive right by it, he says, a little grey house, it could use some repainting, anyway a lot of the paint has flaked off, he says, but yes, well, she salts and smokes the lamb herself, the old way, no one knows how old, Åsleik says, I know how he does it of course, I get lamb from him every single year, and if you ask him he makes a pretty good smoked Christmas lamb himself, good dry-cured lamb too, or mutton, they call it, but Sister always insists on salting and smoking hers on her own, he could easily do it for her but she's right to want to do it herself because it gives her lamb a totally special and exceptionally good flavour and whether or not he wants to admit it Sister's Christmas lamb ribs taste better than his, it's not easy to accept that, not easy to admit it, but that's the truth, and what's true is true, Åsleik says, yes, Sister's lamb ribs taste incredible, you've never tasted anything like it, he says, and anyway now that the man she used to live with, The Fiddler, skipped out, he, Åsleik, has taken The Boat and rowed across Sygnefjord to Sister's every Christmas, because Sygnefjord never ices up, the currents are too strong for that, so even though she lives way up in Sygnefjord, by Instefjord, in Øygna, where there's the inlet, and he lives as far out as you can, where Sygnefjord opens out into the Sygne Sea, out into the ocean, yes, it's not without good reason that the place a bit farther in at the end of Sygnefjord where Sister lives is called 'Inste' Fjord, it's the farthest in, yes of course I know that already, he's just saying whatever comes into his head, Åsleik says, but still, well, every year during Christmas week he takes The Boat over to Sister's, and the crossing takes some time, most of the whole short day, right, and up to now it's always been good or at least pretty good weather but still, the weather can be rough at this time of year, the sea can get so choppy that only a fool would set out on it, only someone not used to the water, a landlubber, but he was no landlubber, not him, he knew when he should stay ashore and when he should set out, but, there's no way around it, the

weather does sometimes change all of a sudden and it's practically impossible to predict even with all his long experience, no
one can ever be completely sure about it, still if the wind picks
up he just needs to reach land as quick as he can, and if he's far
from shore then it can be a hard job, it can, but up until now
he's always made it safe back to harbour, and that isn't true of
everyone now, there's many a fisherman who never made it
back to land, many a boat lying on the bottom of the Sygne
Sea, yes, in Sygnefjord too, that's for sure, everyone knows
that, many a man's found his grave there, yes, when all is said
and done the sea is the biggest graveyard there is in these parts,
that's a fact, but it's better nowadays, now people have motors
on their boats, but before, when people rowed, or sailed, well
that wasn't the same at all, nowadays as long as your motor
doesn't stall, and that didn't happen as long as you remembered
to change the filter every so often, ideally once a year, and per-
sonally he always keeps a spare filter on board, in case the
engine goes out, yes, truth be told he always has two filters with
him in case there's a problem with the first one or he damages
it while putting it in, you never know when that might happen,
because isn't that always the way, filters almost always get
clogged just when the water's bad, yes, when it's at its worst in
fact, plus it's not always so easy to get down there on all fours
and take out the old filter, even if you've got needlenose pliers,
which of course you do, and even if he's changed the filters lots
of times he's had to do it in bad weather only once, yes, the
motor stopped and a medium-strong gale was blowing, if not a
storm, and the weather'd turned bad all of a sudden, the way it
can sometimes do you know, and bam the motor cut out and
he couldn't get it started again and then he realized that the filter was clogged and he cursed himself for having been lazy and
not having changed the filter, how long had it been since he'd

changed it, no, he didn't even know, but however long it'd been there it was and now while The Boat rocked from side to side and bobbed up and down and the water crashed over the sides he had to open the engine hatch and keep it open and, no, Åsleik says and he shakes his head, but it turned out all right, yes, the fact that he's standing here chatting and complaining right now is proof of that, he says, but he'd had a tough time of it, he can't remember exactly how he got through it but luckily he did, the motor started back up and he steered The Boat well in the choppy water, he could do that, whenever the motor was working he could always manage that, well, almost always, he says, but just almost, and Åsleik falls silent for a moment, yes, well, he says then, but there's one thing he knows for sure and that's that it's not too fun being out on the water in rough weather, in a strong wind, in a storm, no, that's for sure, he definitely avoids that whenever he can, of course he doesn't go out when the weather is bad, he's not that big a fool, but, yes, well, as he said before, you can never be sure, the sea changes so suddenly, it's fickle, you never entirely know what you're going to get, but there's one thing you can know, if the weather's good and the sky's clear then you can assume the sea won't get too rough, Åsleik says, and I say in English, Red sky at morning Sailor's warning Red sky at night Sailor's delight and Åsleik says let's have none of that now, stop it, he remembers hardly any of the English they taught him in school, and his teachers weren't good at English either, Åsleik says, and that's why, since it's so hard to know in advance how the water's going to be, it's really not a totally good idea that he waits until Christmas Eve every year before taking The Boat in to see Sister, the way he's always done, Åsleik says, what he really ought to do of course is sail in during Advent on a day with good weather, then the weather most likely won't turn around and get too bad, yes, when Christmas is approaching and the Sygne Sea is more or less calm or at least calm enough that it's not too bad to go there, and there's no hint that it'll suddenly get rough, yes, that's when he should go, even if it's several days before Christmas, but he'd rather get to Sister's house as close to Christmas as he can, then go home again as soon as Christmas Eve is done with, on Christmas Day, yes, that's what he's always done and strangely enough the sea has always stayed calm even on the first day of Christmas, yes, it's almost enough to make you superstitious, those exact days, Christmas Eve and Christmas Day, have had good weather every single year for as long as he can remember, but to tell the truth he likes it best at home, yes, this is where he belongs, where he's comfortable, he says, but these visits to see Sister in Øygna have turned into a kind of habit by now, and if he's going to be totally honest about it he doesn't really like being all alone on Christmas, there are so many memories, about when he was a boy, when he and Sister lived at home, and about their parents, about Father and Mother, now long since passed, but they were good people, Father and Mother, and at Father's funeral the pastor said he's gone to a good place, and at Mother's funeral he said the same thing, she's gone to a good place, he said, and that's the kind of thing he sits around thinking about when he's alone on Christmas Eve, about Father's funeral, Mother's funeral, and the food doesn't taste as good, however good the lamb ribs are they don't taste good to him then, plus he just likes it at Sister's, she doesn't like being alone on Christmas Eve either, but when Sister was living with The Fiddler, well that's what he calls him, never called him anything else, yes, then it wasn't so festive being there with them for Christmas, the fact is he didn't like it one bit, of course Sister still asked him to come spend it with her then too, with them, and one year he did go but it wasn't an especially merry Christmas that year, yes, the fight they had that night, he's never told me about what happened has he, he will at some point, yes, someday he'll tell me about it but it's got to wait, he'll tell me that another time, because it's not a secret or anything, far from it, still it's not so nice to think about, The Fiddler sure liked his drink, yes, well, yes, well, as long as Sister lived with The Fiddler he preferred to spend Christmas alone, but every year since The Fiddler skipped out, and couldn't she have found a better man? he did like to hit the bottle, The Fiddler, that's for sure, to tell the truth, whenever he had one drink he couldn't stop, he never really understood why she hadn't found a better man, she wasn't bad looking, Sister, she wore her years well, she'd had her hair in the same style for as long as he could remember, medium-length blonde hair with not a grey hair in it while the little he had left had turned all grey, not to mention his beard, that was all grey, no one would think they were brother and sister to look at them, and there wasn't even much of an age difference between them, him and Sister, even though he was older, but yes, as long as Sister was living with The Fiddler, except once, he spent Christmas Eve alone, since their parents had died of course, and no, that's probably not something he should think about, or talk about, it's terrible how he talks, just talks and talks, Åsleik says, he spends too much time alone and that's why he always talks so much whenever we see each other, he says, but anyway in any case he's going to spend Christmas with Sister again this year, same as usual, he adds, she got the house in Øygna from her uncle and his wife, who died childless, while he, as the old-est son, got the farm in Dylgja, he says, she got the house cheap, practically free, yes, for little or nothing, to tell the truth, but then he didn't have to pay too much to buy out Sister when he got the farm either, he says, and it's not like she had money to pay him with, she doesn't earn much sitting there sewing her Hardanger embroidery, tablecloth after tablecloth, big and small, table runner after table runner, short and long, and then the colourful embroidered bodices for folk costumes, there's a little money in that but not much, just barely enough to live on, and some years, like after she finished school, she worked at a shop in Bjørgvin, called Hardanger Regional Products or something like that, but then the shop went under and she came back home and the house in Øygna was standing empty so she ended up there, and she did her best to take care of the house, when it needed a new coat of paint she painted it, once anyway, and then it was The Fiddler who painted the house, you have to give him that, before he skipped out, and actually it was Sister who got tired of him and sort of said he should go, she hinted at it and said she was sorry but he should go away and proud as he was that's what he did, he left on the spot, but as long as he was living with Sister he did look after the house, and he made a little money from his music gigs, he'd come home with a few kroner, not drink it all up before he got home, plus he almost always had a few bottles of booze with him, Sister had told him, but anyway he painted the house, once, he did do that, Åsleik says, and he doesn't drop by to check in on Sister too often, he says, except on Christmas Eve, since Sister's been alone, it's better to spend it at her house than to be alone anyway, and Sister's lamb ribs, as he's said, are unbelievably good, Åsleik says, and he stops for a second as if thinking something over and then he looks right at me and asks me couldn't I come with him this year, just once, he says, and spend Christmas with him and Sister, it's always been nice with just him and Sister together, it goes well, but it wouldn't hurt to have someone else sitting around the table, there are always so many memories, about Mother and Father, and for Sister about

her man The Fiddler, who skipped out and settled down somewhere in East Norway with another woman, people say, so
why can't you come along? Åsleik says, but he doesn't have
high hopes, he says, because he's asked me about this plenty of
times before, he might as well give up, he says, because I've
never ever come with him, he says, and hasn't he given Sister
one of my paintings every single Christmas? a small one, always
one of the little paintings, and every single Christmas since she's
been alone Sister has said that he needs to ask me to come spend
Christmas with them next year, in fact he has to admit he won-
ders why she hasn't given up asking him because I've never
come, and Åsleik says he tells Sister he's asked me to come lots
of times, he says, and yes, yes he's sometimes thought that Sister
might have ulterior motives, because she and I are the same age
more or less, and we're both single, and some people, well, especially women, well, no, there's no difference between men
and women when it comes to that, some people don't like to
live alone, and after The Fiddler ran off, yes, he just left and
never came back, that loser, he never even said goodbye to
Sister, and now he's probably, people say, gone off to East
Norway or some other place, with some woman or another
too, yes, it's probably way out east in Telemark he's gone, but
he was a really good fiddle player, no one could deny that, and
if he's being honest he'd have to say that he thinks that's why
Sister wanted to be with him, because he played so well, he really was a virtuoso, you have to say, Åsleik says

    Yes you've told me that before, I say

    Yes well is there anything I haven't told you before? he says

    Good point, I say

    and it's quiet and we both stand there looking down

    Won't you come this year either? Åsleik says

    No I'd rather stay home, I say

You're going to paint on Christmas this year too? Åsleik says

Yes, I say

and it's quiet again

Even on Christmas Eve? Åsleik says

Yes, I say

But you'll at least eat some Christmas lamb ribs on Christmas Eve? Åsleik says

and I say no and hum and haw a bit and Åsleik says yes well since you get lamb ribs and lutefisk and wood and other things in exchange for the painting I get to give Sister, mutton too, now Sister has a whole collection, almost a whole wall of her living room is covered with pictures you've painted, yes, and then there're the three pictures hanging above the sofa, and more in the hall, they're everywhere, so actually it's a good thing that you've always given me small pictures in exchange for everything, Åsleik says, even if it's just out of stinginess that you've only given me small pictures, he says

You can have one of the big ones this year, I say

Well thank you, Åsleik says

and then he says that what makes it better is if, after I've eaten all the mutton from the lamb bones he's given me, I add potato dumplings and cook them with the bones and then have him over for dinner, he says, yes, he always looks forward to these meals, he has to admit, yes, and add a little Voss smoked sausage, some bacon, carrots, turnips, it makes him hungry just thinking about it, Åsleik says and I say yes I eat lamb ribs and lutefisk too over Christmas but not on Christmas Eve itself, you know that Åsleik, I've told you that before, I say, and of course I'll have him over for the potato dumplings that you cook when there's not enough meat left on the bones to have on its own and you cut the bones into pieces and cook them, I say, and

Åsleik says yes of course he knows that, and besides he comes over every Advent to have some lamb ribs or lutefisk, we take turns, this year I'll serve the lamb ribs and he'll serve lutefisk at his place, and the food I serve him is always really good, because food always tastes so much better when you're not eating alone, he says, that's probably why the two of us always have no less than three meals together around Christmastime, two of them during Advent and then we always spend New Year's Eve together too, either over at his place or here at my place, one year at one place, the next at the other, and we always have lamb ribs, Åsleik says, but he, Åsleik, has provided both the lamb ribs and the lutefisk, of course, Åsleik says, he's caught the fish and cleaned it and dried it and soaked it in lye and raised the ewe and slaughtered it and skinned it and salted and smoked the lamb, he says, and I say I never liked Christmas, it's a bad time, the worst part of the year, and Christmas Eve day is the very worst day, I say, and I go into the main room and Åsleik follows me and then we're standing in the middle of the room and I think that the only thing I want to do on Christmas Eve is make the day disappear, paint it away, and that's what I do, and I'd rather not eat anything on Christmas Eve either, I just fast, as they call it, and paint, I paint from early in the morning through the whole time I'm awake until night, except for when I nap for an hour in the middle of the day, and fortunately I get tired early, I usually go to bed early, by nine o'clock, and yes, however stupid it is to think so, and whether or not it's true, but there's some truth in it too, the one thing that makes Christmas bearable, other than going to mass on Christmas Day at St Paul's Church in Bjørgvin, and other than painting of course, yes, the one thing that makes Christmas bearable is thinking about a young man and a young woman in love, yes, a little like Ales and I once were, it's just that we never had children, it just never worked out, no, I can't think about Ales, I think, it's too terrible, I'd rather think about a young woman with child and a young man in love with her even though he's not the father of her child, the two of them are the only ones in the world, and he, the young man, is thinking that the young woman makes him so happy that even though he isn't the father of the child she's carrying he has to help her, they have to find a place where she can give birth, the young man thinks, and then the two of them, the man and the woman, go off to find a place somewhere and someone who can help, but as they're walking it starts to rip and tear inside the young woman's body and then they're at a farm, they go up and knock on the door but no one opens up, so either there's no one home or else no one wants to open the door for them, but the house is dark so probably there's no one there, so they go into the hay barn, there are some cows in the stalls, some sheep walking around in the main part of the barn, and it's probably the heat that the animals are giving off that makes it less cold in the barn than it is outside, so the girl lies down in the straw and there she gives birth to a baby and she says that an angel has told her she would give birth to a baby boy so it must be a boy, she says, and she says that the angel told her not to be scared because God was with her and the young man sees that a light is coming from the child, an incomprehensibly beautiful light, and then the young woman takes her breast and she gives it to the baby and the boy falls silent, and he sucks, he sucks, the young man thinks, and everything about it is unbelievable because there's such a strange light shining from the baby lying there at the young woman's breast, then she looks up at the young man and she smiles at him and the young man thinks that this, this light, no, he can't understand it, because this light from the child in the darkness, in the dark barn, no, it's impossible to understand, he thinks, and he goes outside, because even though it's cold at this time of year he's covered in sweat now, so he stands out there in the wind, in the cooling wind, and he lets the cool air brush his face and he looks up and sees a star shining bright in the sky, yes, so much brighter and stronger than all the other stars, and it's shining straight down at the barn, the light from the star is just like the light that's coming from the child, he thinks, and he sees the star send a beam of light right into the barn, such a sharp clear line of light, and the light coming from the star is precisely the same light as the light coming from the child, he can't understand what's happening, the young man thinks as he stands there looking at the beam of light, following with his eyes the line of clear strong light down from the star through the sky until it goes straight into the barn, no, he can't understand it, he thinks and now he has to go back inside and help the young woman, he thinks and then he hears footsteps and then he sees three strange men, three men he's never seen before, three men unlike anyone he's ever seen, come walking up, they have long hair, and long beards, and are wearing very colourful dishevelled clothing and they come walking up to him and he sees that their hands are full of beautiful blankets and clothes and food and jewellery and wine and who knows what else they're carrying and when they see the young man they say that every night they sit and look at the stars and try to figure out what meaning the stars might have and tonight they saw something they'd never seen before and something they're never going to see again, they saw a star start to shine so much clearer and brighter than any other star and then they saw a beam of light come down from the star, a mysterious, incomprehensible light, it was beautiful and warm and there to look at and disappear into, they say, and the beam of light was pointing somewhere, and then they knew, they said, that this light meant that God had now sent his Human Son to earth, they were sure of it, it had finally happened, so they followed the light from the star and set out and then miraculously arrived at the place the star was shining at, and now here they were, outside a barn, and the light from the star is shining straight into the barn, they say and now they want to go give their gifts to the newborn child, they say and I think that it's this light, yes, this exact light, yes, that this light is what I think about to get through Christmas Eve day and to stop thinking about all the other things that it's so awful to think about, I think, and also I paint, on Christmas Eve day the same as every other day, and there has to be a light in everything I paint, an invisible light, I think, and maybe the light I try to paint has something to do with the light coming from the child in the barn? and from the star? I think, but no, it's not like that, and what's strange is that the easiest way to get pictures to shine is if they're dark, yes, black, the darker and blacker the colours are the more they shine and the best way I can tell if a picture is shining, and how strong or weak the light is in it, and where, is to turn out all the other lights, when it's dark as blackest night, of course it's easiest to tell when it's as dark as possible outside, like now, during Advent season, but in summer too I try to cover the windows and make it as dark as possible before looking at where and how much a picture is shining, yes, to tell the truth I always wait until after I've seen a picture in pitch blackness to be sure I'm done with it, because the eyes get used to the dark in a way and I can see the picture as light and darkness, and see if there's a light shining from the picture, and where, and how much, and it's always, always the darkest part of the picture that shines the most, and I think that that might be because it's in the hopelessness and despair, in the darkness, that God is closest to us, but how it happens, how the light I get clearly into the

picture gets there, that I don't know, and how it comes to be at
all, that I don't understand, but I do think that it's nice to think
that maybe it came about like this, that it came to be when an
illegitimate child, as they put it, was born in a barn on a winter's
day, on Christmas in fact, and a star up above sent its strong
clear light down to earth, a light from God, yes, it's a beautiful
thought, I think, because the very word God says that God is
real, I think, the mere fact that we have the word and idea *God*
means that God is real, I think, whatever the truth of it is it's at
least a thought that it's possible to think, it's that too, even if it's
no more than that, but it's definitely true that it's just when
things are darkest, blackest, that you see the light, that's when
this light can be seen, when the darkness is shining, yes, and it
has always been like that in my life at least, when it's darkest is
when the light appears, when the darkness starts to shine, and
maybe it's the same way in the pictures I paint, anyway I hope
it is and I've tried to tell Åsleik that but I've never been able to
make Åsleik understand anything about that, that's why I don't
say anything about it to him any more, because he'd just say
that he, Åsleik, is not a believer, someone lives and then he dies
and that's that, no more no less, and he doesn't want to hear
anything about any invisible light, that's exactly what Åsleik
would say and that's why I don't want to say anything to him
about it, someone lives and then he dies and that's that, no
more no less, Åsleik says and he's probably right about that too,
but then again maybe it isn't so simple, because life isn't
something you can understand, and death isn't either, actually
to put it in other words it's like in a weird way both life and
death are things you can understand but not with thoughts, this
light understands it in a way, and life, and paintings, I think, get
their meaning from their connection to this light, yes, when
I'm painting it's actually about an invisible light, even if no one

else can see it, and they definitely can't, or don't, I don't think anyone does, I think, they think it's about something else, it's about if a painting is good or bad, something like that, and that's why I can't stand thinking about the pictures I painted to make money when I was young, they were just pictures, they didn't have any light in them, they were just pretty and that's why they were bad, they looked so real and the sun was shining and there was light everywhere in the picture and that's why there was none of this light, because this light is only in the shadows, maybe, I think and suddenly I hear Åsleik say that even if he's just a fisherman he knows a thing or two about how everything goes together, everything fits into a big unbreakable whole, people catch fish, for food, and for the fish to be caught this and that has to happen and for someone to successfully catch the fish this and that has to happen and so everything goes together in a mysterious way, everything is one big whole, but you believe in God and I don't, he says, and I say what I always say, that no one can really say anything about God and that's why it's meaningless to say that someone does or doesn't believe in God, because God just is, he doesn't exist the way Åsleik imagines, I say and I think that Åsleik and I have talked about this so many times, it's something that's nice to talk about again and again, and also boring to talk about again and again

Yes, well, I say

You won't come to Sister's for Christmas this year either? Åsleik says

No, I'll just stay home, I say

Yes, well, Åsleik says

But you believe in God and I don't, he says

and I say what I always say, that no one can say anything about God, but it is possible to think that without God nothing would exist, but because God isn't anything He is separate from the world of created things, where everything has a limit, He is outside time and space, He is something we can't think, He doesn't exist, He's not a thing, in other words He's nothing, I say, and I say that no thing, no person, creates itself because it's God who makes it possible for things to exist at all, without God there's nothing, I say and Åsleik says what's the point of thinking like that? that's not something a person can believe in, is it? there's no point in believing in nothing, is there? and I say that he's right about that, we agree on that point, we do, but it's also wrong to say that God is nothing because at the same time He is all, everything all together, because what I think, I say, is that since nothing can exist without God sustaining it, without God having made it exist, given it being, as they put it, then it's He who is, it's He that everything has in common, yes, God says about Himself, about what we should call Him, that His name is I AM, I say

Now that I don't understand, Åsleik says

No, I don't really understand it either, I say

It's just something you think? Åsleik says

Yes, I say

and then neither of us says anything and we stand there and look at the floor

You and this faith of yours, Åsleik says

I don't always understand you, he says

But no one can think their way to God, I say

Because either they can feel that God is near or they can't, I say

Because God is both a very faraway absence, yes well, being itself, yes, and a very close presence, I say

Maybe it's like that for you, Åsleik says

But it doesn't really make sense, he says

and I say no it doesn't, that's for sure, it's a paradox, as they call it, but then again aren't both he and I paradoxes too just standing here, because how do the soul and the body go together, I say, and Åsleik says yes who can say and then we stand there and neither of us says anything and then I say that the cross is already a paradox, with those two lines that cross, the vertical and the horizontal, as they say, and that Christ, yes, God himself, died and then rose again to conquer death, he who came down to earth when people were separate from God because of what they call original sin, when evil, yes, devils took control of this world, as it says in the Bible, yes, it's impossible to understand that, I say, and I say that evil, sin, death, all of it came into the world, yes, into the universe, it all exists because God said yes but there was also someone who said no, if you can put it that way, I say, because otherwise there would be neither time nor space, yes, everything that exists in time and space has its opposite, like good and evil, I say, and everything that's in time and space will someday pass away, in fact most things, almost everything that there's ever been in time and space is already gone, almost every last thing is outside of time and space, it isn't anywhere, it just is, the way God isn't anywhere but just is, so it's not at all strange that someone can want to leave this earth, get away from what can be found and rest in what just is, in God, as Paul said, yes, something like that, I say and Åsleik says that we've talked about this a lot before and we'll probably talk about it a lot more and I say you're right and I see Åsleik go over to the picture I have standing on the easel, which is set up in the middle of the room, and unusually for me it's a rather big canvas and rectangular, and first I painted one line diagonally across almost the whole surface of the picture, a brown line, in very thick drippy oil paint, and then I painted a matching line in purple from the other corner and it crossed the first line in the middle, forming a kind of cross, a St. Andrew's

Cross, I think they call it, and I see Åsleik stand there and look at the picture and I go over to it too and look at it and I see Asle sitting there on his sofa, and he's shaking and shaking, he's thinking he can't even lift his hands, he feels too heavy even to say a word, Asle thinks, and he thinks that the only thought he can think is that he should disappear, go away, he'll leave and go out and then go out to sea and then he thinks it's been a long time since he's walked the dog and I see that the thick oil paint has dripped a bit more, and where the lines cross a totally new colour has formed, more shining than it was when I looked at the picture earlier today, I think and I stand there and look at the painting and I think that really it was because of Asle that I decided so suddenly to drive into Bjørgvin today, I just didn't realize it, I realized it only when I drove past the building where his apartment is, in Sailor's Cove, but then I didn't stop to see him even so, didn't stop to help him, not when I was driving into Bjørgvin and not when I was driving back out of Bjørgvin either, I think and I think that all my pictures are like that and I think I don't know what I mean by that, all my pictures are like that? like what? what do I mean by that? because this isn't a picture yet, it's just a picture I've started on, but in all the pictures I paint there is something this picture reminds me of, however different this one is from all the others I've painted, this is what I'm always trying to paint, and when I get a light into the picture, when I get a light to come from the picture, it's by doing this, I have to go into myself, as deep in as I can, so that I can come back out and go into the picture, I think and I hear Åsleik say now this here looks like something real, I've painted a picture that looks like something for once, it looks like some kind of cross, he says and I say that this is something I just started painting today, before I drove into Bjørgvin, and he says why did I start a picture and just paint two lines and then rinse the brushes and put them away and drive into Bjørgvin instead of painting more? he says and I say that it just felt like the right thing to do and Åsleik doesn't say anything and then he says it just felt right, yes well then it probably was, he says, and I think that now Åsleik's probably thinking that I'm talking nonsense, I think, but he probably always thinks that about me anyway, I think and then Åsleik says again that he doesn't understand why I would paint just two lines and then stop, why didn't I paint anything except those two lines? he says and I say that it's not so easy to explain and Åsleik says no of course it isn't, the truth is he's never really totally understood me, or my pictures, he says and I think that Åsleik has said this so many times and well it's something nice to talk about over and over, and it's also boring to talk about it over and over, the same as talking about how God, or in any case some divine force, came down to humankind to give them help in all their despair and need when Jesus Christ came to earth and died and rose again, yes, this unbelievable story, this foolishness that there's really no way to believe, and I think what I really believe in is the force of this foolishness, the power of thinking this way, I think, and I believe in this and Åsleik doesn't, but what's the difference really whether someone believes it or not? there's no difference, in the strict sense, I think, and I don't always believe in Jesus Christ as a saviour either, just in God, in God's presence, yes, in his absence too, yes, I can never doubt that, because it's reality, not belief

So, you won't come to Sister's for Christmas this year either then? Åsleik says

No, I'll stay home, I say

and I think he keeps asking this over and over, can't he just stop already, I think

Yes, well, he says

and Åsleik stands there, it's like he doesn't want to leave, and he looks at the picture where I've painted two lines that cross

You don't get sick of all this painting? he says

And you, you're always fishing, you don't get sick of all that fishing? I say

That's different, he says

Yes, you're right, painting and fishing aren't the same, I say

How stupid do you think I am, Åsleik says

and we look at each other

No, you're not stupid, I say

Well then, he says

Fishing a lot doesn't make a person stupid, I say

It looks like it's upside down, he says

Painting a lot is what makes a person stupid, more like, he says

and I can't argue with that, fishing gives a person a lot more wisdom and understanding than painting does, yes, fishing contains a beautiful truth, I say, because you never know what's going to happen, whether you'll catch a fish or not, I say, it all comes down to luck, just like life, I say and Åsleik says I may be right about that but the important thing you need to do to catch fish is go fishing and it's not blind luck that decides whether or not you go fishing, it's something you decide to do, fishing is, it's something you do, a task, a mission, see he can use big words like that too, he says, and when someone undertakes this mission, namely fishing, when he does it for the first time, because one of those times is going to be the first time, there's always a first time, and later if he does it again and again, yes, you have to admit that too, he'll end up really knowing how to fish, and where the fish are, and if they're biting, and he'll learn the various landmarks and seamarks for various fishing grounds, each has its own qualities, some grounds are good when the tide is rising and some when the tide is falling, not to mention the currents! and how much it depends on the season, the month, the moon, even the week! how much fish you'll catch, yes, of course that's not something you can talk about, because it's obvious, it's self-evident, Åsleik says, but he emphasizes the word self-evident, and then repeats it, *self-evident,* yes, it's *self-evident,* he says and I say yes it certainly is

So no it's not all just blind luck, it isn't, he says

No but in life it's not all just blind luck either, that's obvious too, I say

Of course, Åsleik says

and then he looks down at the floor in that way he has and when Åsleik looks down in that way it's like he isn't looking down, it's like he's looking up, like he's looking at everything all together, like he's seeing a big context without being clear about it and then something comes over his face, yes, it's like he is suddenly falling out of this evil world and into a still and peaceful clearing or clarity, an area of stillness, of light, yes, of shining darkness, because it's like he's fallen out of himself, out of where he usually is, like he no longer knows himself, like he's gone, away from himself, as he stands there looking down with a light that's like what the sky can give off, together with the clouds, when that's what the light wants to do, yes, a light like that comes from him, the kind of light that can come from a dog too, from a dog's eyes, yes, that happens a lot, when I think about it I've often seen that strange light coming from a dog's eyes

So that's why you drove down to Bjørgvin today? he says

To check in on that friend of yours, the one with your Name? he says

It just suddenly came over you that you should do that? he says and Åsleik looks down again and I think I didn't tell him anything about Asle and also I didn't drive to Bjørgvin to see Asle, it was just something I decided to do, I wasn't thinking about Asle at all until I drove past the building where his apartment is, but then again maybe I was thinking about him in a way, without realizing it? and I say that that happens sometimes, a picture makes me suddenly decide to do something, but that's rare, very rare, while most of the time, in fact every time, a picture has something to do with something I've seen, something that's stuck inside me in a way, and that I suddenly see again, yes, it's like a vision, it's like I have a huge collection of pictures stored in my head, of pictures I can't forget, and like I'm trying to get rid of them by painting them, I say and Åsleik says that makes sense and he stays there looking down at the floor and I too bend my head, look down, and we stay standing like that for quite a long time

No, I've never amounted to anything, Åsleik says

and he's saying it as if to himself

Nothing, he says

I was born in Dylgja and I lived in Dylgja and I'm going to die in Dylgja and be buried in the ground and turn into the ground myself, he says

I've never made anything of myself, he says

I was baptized in Vik Church and confirmed there and that's where my funeral will be, I'll be buried in the churchyard of Vik Church and that's where I'll rot away, Åsleik says

and I think now he's about to start saying what he usually says about how he's remained a bachelor and Åsleik says that there's no woman in the world who'd want someone like him, that's easy enough to understand, why would anyone want a ridiculous guy like him? and so, getting married like a respectable man, he gave up on that when he was young, yes, he wasn't

yet old when he knew he'd be spending his life alone, in sol-
itude, there wasn't going to be any wedding in Vik Church
for him, or any baptism of a child of his either, he said, and
then there's the farm, or piece of land really, it was more like
a steep hill with stones as big as boathouses scattered across the
fields, if you can call them fields, beneath steep cliffsides, and
it happened pretty often that a stone came loose and tumbled
down the rock face and came to a stop in the fields, almost
every night he'd lie there before he fell asleep in fear and think
now, now, soon, it's coming, the big stone, or the big avalanche, that'll take his house and farm and field and sweep it
all together into Sygnefjord, yes, he's seen it in his head so
many times, he's seen in his mind's eye how a stone as big as a
house would come loose, or maybe the whole rock face would
come loose and turn into stones hurtling down faster and faster
and picking up grass and dirt and smashing houses into boards
and splinters and sweeping away everything he owned and the
sheep, and him in the middle of it all, inexorably sliding down
the mountain until it was all gone, until it disappeared into the
water, he along with his whole farm, he along with everything
he had, all disappeared into the water, yes, he would lie there
like that and see it all in his mind before he fell asleep, it was
like these thoughts were never satisfied, and lots of times this
or that small avalanche had woken him up, and he'd inherited
this fear of avalanches from his parents, especially Mother, but
also Father, they used to talk constantly about the avalanche
that was going to come one day, yes, it wasn't just maybe going
to come, it had to come, it was only a question of time, today,
this morning, in a year, in twenty years, in a hundred years, or
even longer, but eventually the avalanche would come, that
was certain, they knew that, they just didn't know when it
would come, that's the kind of thing Father and Mother would

say to each other, while he and Sister were still little kids too, and listening, they'd talk like that, because did grown-ups ever think about how such talk would enter into a child? no, not back then, never once in all that time did they think that, and he and Sister, who were nearly the same age, he was two years older, and the heir, that word was always spoken as if there was something especially splendid about it, yes, the word *heir* was always given its own special emphasis, spoken with special respect, *son and heir,* he was the *son and heir,* it was he who would one day take over the whole small farm along with everything on it, the same way Father had taken it over from his father one day, and he from his own father, yes, no one knew how long people from his line had lived on this farm but it was a long time, yes, that much was known for certain, a very long time, yes, the farm had passed from father to son and obviously all the men before him had found a wife, since the farm had passed from father to son all the way down to him, which meant he was the first one to stay unmarried, a bachelor, yes, well, he'd tried, more than once, put himself forward a few times, but no, he'd had no luck, not a single old spinster wanted to have him, so he never got a wife, he stayed a bachelor and looked after things and puttered around, now he had these sheep, they brought in a few kroner, for the meat, and a little for the wool, not much, but then again he didn't need much, and when he had a good catch fishing he'd dock at The Wharf in Vik, go from The Wharf to The Country Store in Vik, and that's how he'd sell a little fish, yes, there were lots of people who didn't fish themselves who bought fresh fish from him, and dried fish from him too, because he hung up pretty much all the cod he caught to dry, either in the attic of his house in the winters, or, in the summers, outside under the eaves, and it was always easy to sell the dried fish, and then there were crabs and lobsters, they were usually pretty easy to sell too, that's for sure, he'd made quite a few kroner from those, it had added up to a tidy little sum over the years, that's the truth, yes, and then there's the woods, it was quite a number of cords of wood he'd cleared and sold over the years, at first to country people but after the country road got built it was mainly people from Bjørgvin who wanted to buy wood from him, there were knocks on his door so often, on weekends and holidays, that to tell the truth he'd started locking his front door, no, he'd never done that before, but recently he'd actually started locking his front door and not opening it when people knocked, so he'd always managed to get by, and other than that? yes well he'd always liked to read, and he went into The Library in Vik almost every time he was in Vik, it wasn't so far away from The Wharf, it was in The Town Hall, yes, I knew that perfectly well, I'd been there many a time myself, now why would he tell me where it is? so almost every single time when he was there doing business at The Country Store he went into The Library and he's read almost everything they have, on any and every topic, or else poetry, yes, he even liked reading poetry, he enjoyed it, especially poems by the younger poets, what wouldn't they think of next? those poems rarely meant much or had much connection with anything but there were sudden turns of phrase, quick bursts of wind, that were said in a new way, put in a new way, often in ways impossible to predict beforehand, and he liked most of them, but when one of them was too much like the others, when there was one you could hardly tell apart from the others, then it was hard to read it, a poem had to have some kind of quality of its own in it to be worthwhile, yes, that's what he thought about that, it was just his opinion, nothing more than that now, yes, well, Åsleik said and then he fell silent

And so there's a lot to do on a farm, the buildings need a lot of work, Åsleik says and he says that he's tried to the best of his ability to take good care of the buildings, the house, the barn, the outbuilding, the smokehouse, the boathouse, but in recent years he'd let things go a bit, so the house needed painting, well in fact all the buildings did, yes, they've needed it for a while, but the avalanche might still come, he was sure about that, and the time was approaching, the time was always coming closer and closer, and so that's why he'd let things go a bit, since there wasn't much reason to paint the house, or the other buildings, yes, or maintain them in other ways either, when the avalanche was going to come any day now, that's how he saw it, but now thoughts like that weren't exactly pearls of wisdom, no, really they were more like an excuse not to do anything, a kind of cover for his own laziness, it was crazy really, everyone before him had done so much to keep up the farm, and the buildings had stood there all that time and they were still there, the same as they'd always been, yes, the house, the barn, the shed, the smokehouse, the boathouse, and a lot of work had gone into all of them, done by both of his parents, his grandparents, his great-grandparents, his great-great-grandparents, however far back in time you wanted to go, but there wasn't much point in going back too much farther than the grandparents, that's what he thought, the rest was part of the great silence, he said, that's more or less how he thought of it, and there's not really anything that you can think about what's part of the great silence, there's no point, it's just there, it just is what it is, yes, he says

Yes, I say

The great silence, he says

and I think I should say that God is in the great silence, and that it's in the silence that you can hear God, but then I think that it's probably better if I don't say that, and we stand there and I think that this too, like everything else, is something I've heard Åsleik say so many times before, because once he gets started he can go on and on about stuff like this, and it's probably because he spends so much time alone, I think, and I think that even if he's said it before it's in a way new every time he tells me, I think, something about it is new, something's different in how he tells it, how he looks at it, every time, I think and Åsleik says that the only thing that bothers him, yes, the only thing is, no, not that he never got married, not that, a female would've been a nuisance and a burden, when you came right down to it he was a born recluse, a hermit, as they say, but, he says and then he says nothing for a long time

Yes? I say

Yes, that, he says

Yes that what, I say

That there's no one to take over the farm after I'm gone, Åsleik says

and again he looks down at the floor and then he looks up and looks at the stove and he says that it probably needs another log, a good dry birchwood log, he says and I see Åsleik go over to the stove and open the hatch and put a log in and he closes the hatch and I think I really should have gone to get a glass of something with Asle at The Alehouse in Bjørgvin, and even if where he really should've been taken was The Clinic he'd never have gone along with that, he wasn't doing well these days, Asle, when he wasn't drinking he was thinking all the time about putting an end to himself, it just felt like he couldn't go on, so I should have dropped by, and so why did I just keep driving? I think, was it because I dreaded seeing him? because I didn't feel like going to The Alehouse? I think and now Asle is just sitting there on the sofa, with his long grey hair pulled back behind his ears and tied in the back with a black hairband, and his grey beard too, and he's shaking and shaking, I think and I see Åsleik go over to the easel and stop and look at the picture I'm in the middle of painting and I go over to the stove and I open the hatch and even though Åsleik has just put a log in I put another log in anyway and I stand there with the hatch open and I look at the firewood and I see Asle sitting there on the sofa and he's thinking that food no longer tastes good to him, he knows he needs to eat but he doesn't want any food, it disgusts him, to tell the truth, he tries to eat but it makes him want to throw up and he spits out the food and goes looking for something to drink, but he can't drink without eating, that is one rule he's always stuck to, and it's already long since daylight and he needs to stand up, no matter how hard it is to get to his feet, no matter how hard it is to put one foot on the floor in front of the other he has to do it, yes, even while he's shaking all over, and his hands are shaking most of all, but even so he needs to get himself something to drink, a little glass of something, Asle thinks and he gets up and puts one foot down on the floor and then the other and he feels himself shaking all over and he thinks he has to get to the kitchen and pour himself a drink, and he leaves the main room and goes to the kitchen and unscrews the cap from a bottle that's on the kitchen table next to a glass and he holds the round bottle in both hands and sticks the opening into the glass and manages to pour a glassful without spilling any and with both his shaking hands he holds the glass tight and raises it to his mouth and empties it in one gulp and he puts it back down on the table with trembling hands and then supports himself on the edge of the table and shuts his eyes and he breathes in deeply and then breathes out slowly, he does that many times, and then he puts both his shaking hands around the bottle again and even though he's shaking all over he fills his glass and he feels a gentle warmth spread through him, and he feels his hands shaking less, and immediately he feels the warm gentleness inside, Asle thinks, and then he thinks he should roll himself a proper cigarette now, and he takes the tobacco pouch out of his pocket and now he can roll a cigarette and then he lights it and it's so good to feel the smoke spread through his body, he thinks, there is such a big difference between hand-rolled cigarettes and packaged cigarettes, Asle thinks, and he thinks he should drop by The Alehouse and he sees himself sitting there in The Alehouse alone and reading a newspaper, and there aren't many people at The Alehouse, and then the street door opens and a woman about his age, somewhere around forty or fifty, something like that, walks in and she has medium-length blonde hair and Asle sees her as it were come to life when she sees him and she comes over to his table and he looks up and he too as it were comes to life, his eyes sparkle

No, is it really you, Asle says

Yes, she says

and she's a little shy

Are you waiting for someone? she says

No, no, he says

and it's quiet for a brief moment and then Asle says she should just sit down, if she wants to, if she's not doing anything, he's here alone, as she can see, yes, just with his glass, he says and he raises the shot glass and she says it's sure been a long time and that it's great, really great, to see him again, she says

Have a seat, if you want, he says

You and me, we're old friends, he says

You and me, Guro and Asle, he says

and she doesn't say anything and they're quiet and Asle thinks that Guro's hair is the same medium-length blonde hair it's always been and she's still standing there and she turns a little, slowly, and Asle looks at her and he feels like they're right back where they've always been, they're exactly the same as they used to be, they're in the same place, they are the same place, their place, they are still each other's secret, they are still each other's own beautiful world

It's so great to see you again, she says

You too, he says

And things are still the same with you? she says

Yes, not much new with me, he says

But I'm so happy to see you here, she says

It's great for me too, that you saw me, he says

and I see her sit down at his table and I see Asle standing there next to his kitchen table pouring himself another glass of something strong and I think he's going to make it, he's about to stop shaking now, I think and then I see the dog come walking up to him

Here you are, Asle says

Good boy, good Bragi, he says

and he says the dog must be hungry and thirsty too and he fills the dog's water dish and takes a handful of pellets of dog food from a bag on the floor next to the kitchen table and puts them down in the dish on the floor and Bragi goes over to the dishes at once and starts eating and then there's a knock on his front door and he just stands there, he stands with his glass in his hand, there's another knock, and he puts his glass down and puts the cigarette in the ashtray on the kitchen table and goes and opens the door with Bragi at his heels and two little girls are standing there and looking at him with their eyes wide in surprise and one of them asks him if he'll give them some money for this or that cause and he says he'll see what he has and then he goes back into the main room and over to the black velvet jacket that's on the chair by the coffee table and he finds his wallet in the inner pocket and finds a few coins there and with the coins clutched in one hand and the wallet in the other he goes back to the two girls and one girl holds out a box with a slot in the lid and he puts the coins in, one by one, and the girls say thank you at almost the same time and then he sees them turn around and go to the door across the hall, to the neighbour's apartment, and Asle shuts the door, locks it, checks to see that the door is locked, and then thinks about Bård, the neighbour boy who drowned, he and Bård were the same age, they hadn't even started school yet, he thinks and then he goes back to the kitchen and he thinks he'll just drop by The Alehouse, or maybe he'll go knock at Guro's door? or maybe she's even at The Alehouse? Asle thinks and he sits down at the kitchen table and stares emptily into space and he picks up his glass and drinks and looks, yes, what is he looking at? he's looking at something or other, but it doesn't matter what because it's like he doesn't see anything, he just feels the warm intoxication fill him up and he pours himself another glass, and drinks it all down, but not as fast as before, more gently, sip by sip, and with more time between the sips, then he pours himself another glass and watches the level of liquid in the bottle go down and he needs to save a little for tomorrow, he thinks, because how else will he be able to stop the shaking? he thinks, so maybe he really should go out for a bit, to The Alehouse, buy himself something to drink there, since he has to leave some of what he has here until tomorrow, and maybe he'll drop by Guro's in The Lane and knock on her door on the way to The Alehouse? or maybe it'd be better on the way back? he thinks, it's been a long time now, he thinks, and maybe he can spend the night at Guro's at her apartment in The Lane? yes, like so many times before, the first time he did it was many years ago when he was living with Liv, but then a man moved in with her, a fiddler, in any case Guro always called him The Fiddler,

and then of course he had to stay away, and Guro and The
Fiddler lived together for many years, but then The Fiddler just
disappeared one day, just went away, he moved to somewhere
or other in East Norway, it was certainly somewhere a long
way east of Telemark, Asle thinks, and since then he's often
thought he should go drop by Guro's place, but it's never happened, he thinks, and he thinks that he needs to go buy some
more to drink tomorrow, the quarter bottle he has left will be
enough to last him till tomorrow morning, he thinks, so he'll
just put on his warm clothes, because it's cold out, it's snowing,
and go to The Alehouse, or maybe he should stop by Guro's
place in The Lane? like he used to do so often, no, she probably
doesn't want him to come by so he'd better just go to The
Alehouse and then he'll need to buy himself more to drink tomorrow morning, because sitting in his kitchen drinking beer
until the shaking goes away, no, he can't do that, his hands'll be
shaking so much that it'll be all he can do to get a shot glass up
to his mouth, but now that he's managed to get a couple of
glasses down yes he's calmed down little by little, the shaking's
gone away, it took a little while but he's stopped shaking, and
now he won't need that much to drink for the next several
hours, just a little beer, yes, there were lots of times, before he
needed to drink something strong to get the shaking to stop,
Asle thinks, and he thinks that he's alone, and that it's good to
be alone, if only he were better, if only he didn't have to drink
all the time, he thinks, this horrible shaking, he thinks, and
aside from those two girls in the hall he probably hasn't talked
to anyone in a week, for sure, barely a word or two when he
went to buy something to drink or a little food when it wasn't
like it was today, before, when he wasn't lying there heavy and
unable to move and shaking all day, yes, on days when there
wasn't that weight and things were easy and one day disappeared

into the next and neither day existed on its own then everything was good, floating along, then it was good to be alone, yes, everything was a floating picture then, in a way, Asle thinks, and then he painted, and when he started on a picture he could totally disappear into the picture, but that was before, now he can't paint any more, he can't do anything, it's all too big and heavy for him, and he shakes all the time, and he's tried to call The Boy, who lives in Oslo, but The Boy didn't answer, and The Son and The Daughter live somewhere in Trøndelag, and he hasn't seen Liv even once in many years, or Siv either, and these weights inside him, his stone, and these shakes, because if he doesn't get something strong to drink he shakes, and sometimes he shakes even if he has drunk quite a bit, he thinks, the only thing he can do now is have a little drink when he wakes up, and then a few more times throughout the day, but he often can't get rid of the shakes even then, or else he needs a lot to drink before he can stop shaking, which means he'll need more to drink by tomorrow morning, Asle thinks, so he'll go buy some more tomorrow morning and by evening he might feel so much lighter that he can think about going out, the same as to-day, yes, drop by The Alehouse, the same as now, because it's like he's feeling a little stronger again, yes, and if he doesn't have the strength for anything else then at least he has the strength to pour himself another drink, at least he feels that, he thinks, and that's something, he thinks, but thinking things like that, yes, drinking's helped him a lot, he thinks, but now the drinking is taking over, after it got to the point when he was so heavy that everything felt too heavy, even speaking a single word, drinking was the only thing that could make things a little lighter, so that he could move his hands, get up, say anything, and he takes another big sip, and again he feels the warmth spread through his body, because on these days when there's nothing moving inside him, when he's just heavy, yes, he has always been heavy, heavy of spirit as they say, melancholy, as they put it, but never before has he been so heavy that it was hard to say a single word and the only thing he wanted to do was go outside and down to the water and go out to sea and disappear into the sea and do it in the light that shines now and then from the darkness, when the darkness is most impenetrable in a way, he thinks, but now he doesn't want to be alone, he wants to go out, and he wants to go to The Alehouse, and maybe he'll run into someone he knows there, someone or other, someone he can talk to? maybe Guro's there? it's been so long since she's gone there, but maybe he could meet someone he's never talked to before? someone he didn't know before today? and tomorrow he has to go buy more to drink and since he has to save what he still has at home to drink in the morning he needs to go out, go drop by The Alehouse, or The Last Boat as it's called, Asle thinks and I see him put his wallet back in his inside pocket and put on the black velvet jacket that's hanging on the back of a chair by the coffee table and then he goes out into the hall and puts his long black overcoat on, then he puts on a scarf that's hanging on a hook there, then he feels his coat to make sure he has his wallet in his jacket pocket, and it's where it should be, and he has money in it, he knows that, and he's been carrying in his wallet for all these years a little reproduction of *Bridal Procession on the Hardangerfjord,* of all things, he saw the painting in a schoolbook back when he was a boy, in a school textbook, and he thought it was so beautiful, so beautiful, he knows some people look down on this painting but he still thinks it's wonderfully fine, yes, people can say whatever they want, it's an exceptionally good painting, he's never painted anything like it himself, far from it, yes, what he's painted himself can't compare to that painting in the least, but ever since he was a boy he has always kept the little picture he tore out of the school textbook in his wallet, yes, he tore out the page with the picture from the textbook they used in his school and then cut out the picture and then put it in the wallet he had at the time, because he already had a wallet then, even if he rarely or never had any money in it, anyway he had this little reproduction of *Bridal Procession on the Hardangerfjord* in his wallet, and since then he has always kept this picture in his wallet, yes, he's changed wallets many times of course but he always transferred the picture of *Bridal Procession on the Hardangerfjord* from the old one to the new one, and now the picture was so worn that you could barely see that it used to be *Bridal Procession on the Hardangerfjord* but in a way that just made the picture even more beautiful, not that he looked at it very often, but still he did take it out sometimes and to make more room in his wallet he'd folded it in quarters, folded it once and then again, and so over time the picture had obviously come apart into four pieces, the folds had torn of course, but he'd taped them back together on the back once a long time ago and the tape had lasted well so that's why the picture was still in one piece, more or less anyway, and so he went around with this picture in his wallet, the same as before, and even if it was basically impossible to see what the picture showed any more he still sometimes took it out and looked at it, never at home, but sometimes when he was sitting alone at The Alehouse or somewhere else and had nothing else to do, it wasn't all that often that he looked at the picture but sometimes he'd look at this old photograph of *Bridal Procession on the Hardangerfjord,* torn out of the textbook from his schooldays, yes, cut out on one side and torn out on the other, Asle thinks and then he thinks that now he needs to pick up his keys from the bureau in the hall and then go out to the front door, and now he just has to not run into anyone, any of the neighbours, as long as no one comes up to him on the stairs, Asle thinks and he sees Bragi standing there looking at him and Asle thinks that he needs to take the dog out but he can't do it now, he'd rather do it when he gets back home, it won't be too many hours till he's back and then he says to Bragi now be a good boy and watch the apartment and the dog just looks at him and then Asle unlocks the apartment door and then he goes down the stairs and he walks past the bicycles and pushchairs down in the hall and he thinks that as long as he doesn't run into some neighbour or another, he thinks, and he goes to the street door and he opens it and he sees someone walking towards him

Good evening, the man walking towards him says

and Asle stands there and holds the door open for the man and he says Good evening and the man Asle is holding the door open for asks if he's going out for a walk

Yes you have to every now and then, Asle says

Some fresh air, that's a good thing, the man says

Yes, Asle says

and the man walking up to him says that it's so nice out now that the new snow is falling and Asle says yes, yes, it's so white, it's like it's shining, he says and Asle sees the man go into the lobby and he shuts the door behind him and it slams shut and I stand there and look at the firewood in the stove and I hear Åsleik say it's burning nicely in the stove now isn't it? should I shut the hatch? he says and I say I'll do it and I shut the hatch and I think I should have gone to see Asle, I shouldn't have just kept driving, going right past, because his drinking is going to finish him off before long if someone doesn't do something, if someone doesn't help him, I think, but I, I, I just looked at the building in Sailor's Cove where his apartment is and drove right past it and then I think I need to drive back into Bjørgvin, because I need to go see Asle, I just have to, I think, yes, a mute voice inside me tells me I have to drive back into Bjørgvin and go see him, and that must be the voice people call conscience, I think, yes, even though it'll take a couple of hours to drive to Bjørgvin I'll just make that drive, I'm not too tired, I think, and then I'll just spend the night at The Country Inn where I like to spend the night, in Room 407, the smallest room they have, as long as it's empty I'll stay there and not just because it's one of the least expensive rooms, I also like it best, the room has windows looking out onto the back yard, although something, I think it must be the lift shaft, blocks half the view from the room where I stay if it's available, and I usually book the room well in advance but even if I haven't booked it ahead of time I've never once had it happen that there wasn't room for me somewhere at The Country Inn, true there was one time when it was full and I had to sleep on a spare bed in the attic, they put up an extra bed for me there, I think, anyway now it's decided, I'm going to drive into Bjørgvin and look in on Asle, I think and I hear Åsleik say well it's time to get going home and I look at him and I say that I stupidly forgot the most important thing I needed to do in Bjørgvin so I need to drive back there right away, I say

Now, tonight? Åsleik says

and he seems both surprised and a little alarmed, as if I've gone a little crazy, as if he's suddenly become a little nervous about me, I think

Yes, right now, I say

You've already done a lot of driving today, Åsleik says

and he says do I really want to do this? now, so late? and it might snow too, he says, yes, a few snowflakes started coming down this afternoon and the weather seems like it might well start snowing and I say I've already put the snow tyres on and

Åsleik says well that's good, yes, if there was one thing he regretted in life it was that he never got a driving licence, he said, even though it would've been nice to have a car, especially given where he lives, instead he has to either walk or drive the tractor, it's a good thing he has that, and he's had the same tractor for probably thirty years now, yes, must be that long at least, he says, yes if he needs to drive somewhere he has to either take the tractor or ride with someone else or else take The Boat, no, mustn't forget that, it's good he has that as a means of transportation, yes indeed, he says and I say yes, well, I have to go to Bjørgvin, I can tell him about why some other time, I say and I say that I can give Åsleik a ride, and he says thanks for the offer but he'd rather walk, it's fine, it's not far, just a mile or two, of course he'd have nothing against getting a ride, he says and then he asks me again if I really need to drive back to Bjørgvin, I just got home, and right after coming back into the house after being in Bjørgvin I'm going to drive back again, dark as it is, and night is falling, and it might start snowing, as he said, and I say I just have to, I'll tell him why later, I say and Åsleik says all right then that's how it is, I'm going to just do what I want to do, he says and then he says well I guess I'll just go out front then and Åsleik goes outside and I see that the wood's still burning in the stove and I turn off the light in the main room and go to the kitchen and turn the light off there and go out to the hall and turn the light off and then I go outside and shut the front door behind me and I see Åsleik standing out front and I tell him he can have a ride, since I'm going in his direction, but I could have driven him home anyway, the way I've done so many times before, I say and Åsleik says well thanks for that, since I'm driving in that direction he could always ride with me but he's used to walking, walking's fine with him, he does it all the time, it's no problem for him to get home, not at all, but well he could also ride with me since I'm driving down the same road, he says, since it is pretty cold out, yes, now that it's late autumn, well, more than that, we're already in Advent, it won't be long before it's Christmas, and winter, yes, Åsleik says and it's going to start snowing tonight too, Åsleik says and he gets into the car and I get in and start the engine

Yes it's definitely going to start snowing, I say

The first snow of the year, it is, Åsleik says

But it won't stick, I say

No, but still a lot might come down, Åsleik says

Yes, I say

And I'll clear your driveway while you're down in Bjørgvin, yes, that'll need to be done, Åsleik says

So that you can come back to a cleared road, he says

Thank you, thanks very much, I say

'Cause I can drive a tractor anyway, even if I can't drive a car, Åsleik says

It sure comes in handy, I say

And it's old but it works great, I can get it to start every time, after a minute or two anyway, he says

Anyway you've had that tractor for as long as I can remember, I say

It was my father who bought it, old as he was, Åsleik says

But it's still running, I say

and I drive down the driveway and turn right, onto the country road, because Åsleik's farm is a mile or so farther in along Sygnefjord and Åsleik says that that was an odd picture, yes, a strange picture, the one I'd started painting, with the two lines, one purple and one brown, he says and I feel myself not wanting to talk about it, I've never liked talking about a picture I'm working on, or about any picture I've finished either for that matter, never, once a picture is finished the picture says whatever it can say, no more no less, the picture says in its silent way whatever can be said, and if it's not finished yet then how it's going to turn out and what it's going to say isn't something that can be said in words, I think, and after all these years Åsleik must have realized that I don't like talking about my pictures, about what they represent, about what they mean, I can't stand any of that kind of talk, not in the slightest, and now Åsleik's going to start going on and on about those two lines as if they were just two lines and then he says that it's a St Andrew's Cross I painted and he says the words with such emphasis that I almost jump and I notice how proud he is of having those words at his disposal, St Andrew's Cross he says again, very proud of himself, *St Andrew's Cross,* he is genuinely proud of knowing such a term and what it means, and now, after Åsleik has said this term that way, sort of haughty and proud about knowing it, I think that I simply don't get how I can stand him, year after year, day after day, he's such a fool, and probably the only reason I put up with him is that I don't have anyone else to talk to, or be with, no that's not true, he's no fool, he's not stupid, Åsleik, he's pretty wise in his way, I think, so it was bad to think that, disgraceful really, I think and then we're at the bottom of the driveway to Åsleik's house and I stop and Åsleik asks when I'll be back and I say I'll be back tomorrow and maybe he can come by again then, tomorrow evening, I say and Åsleik says that he'll do that because then maybe he can pick out a picture that he can give Sister for Christmas, he says, and I say sure we can do that and then Åsleik says thanks for the ride and he gets out of the car and I raise my right hand and wave goodbye and Åsleik raises his hand and waves too and then I keep driving slowly in along Sygnefjord and I think this is madness, I think, sheer madness, driving back into Bjørgvin now after I've already driven both there and back earlier today, and I'm tired,

I realize, so maybe I should turn back? I think, no, no, I have to go and see Asle now, I think, I should never have driven by his building in the first place, that was practically cowardly, I think, so now I need to drive back into Bjørgvin, I think, and why did Åsleik have to start talking about the picture I started painting earlier today, haven't I told him time and time again that I don't like talking about a picture I'm in the middle of working on, and don't like talking about pictures I've finished either, done is done, painted is painted, it turns out however it turns out, both pictures and life too, I think, and then his bringing up the St. Andrew's Cross over and over, I think, and I think that Asle is just lying on the sofa in his apartment almost all the time now, under the window that looks out onto the snow, and that's why I painted those two lines that cross in the middle, it's probably in some strange way a picture of Asle lying there that I've painted, I think, and in another way it's not him and of course I shouldn't have driven home without looking in on Asle, because he's in such despair, but it is a long way to drive to Bjørgvin, I'm tired after being out all day, after driving to Bjørgvin and back, and now I'm driving to Bjørgvin a second time today since I feel such uneasiness inside me that I just have to drive back again, I think and I drive and I fall into a kind of peaceful unthinking stupor and I see a few snowflakes land on the windshield and I drive farther in along Sygnefjord and I see more and more snowflakes land on the windshield and I turn on the wipers and they make semicircles for me to see through, and it's white around them from the snow, and I think that Asle probably isn't home, he's probably gone out, to The Alehouse, I think, so I shouldn't go ring his doorbell, I should drive into Bjørgvin and park the car in front of The Beyer Gallery and then go to The Country Inn and get a room for the night and then go to The Alehouse, because Asle's probably sitting there

alone at a table, I think, and if he's not there I can drive back
to his place and ring the bell, but maybe I should go by his
place first, probably? maybe he is home? but anyway he probably won't answer even if he is? I think and it's snowing and it
stops snowing and I drive south and I get closer to the turnoff
I stopped at earlier today, by the playground, and I think that
this time I should just keep driving, and I'm really not sure
whether what I saw in the playground today was something I
really saw or something I just imagined, yes, dreamt, in a way,
I think, but it was real, I'd be lying if I said otherwise, I think,
and I think that anyway it wouldn't hurt to take a little break
from driving, I did drive for a long time today and I'm probably
more tired than I realize, so maybe I should stop in the turnoff
I'm coming up to and take a little break there again, yes, get
out, stretch my legs, get a little fresh air, yes, I'll do that, I think,
and I keep driving south and I'm at the bend that the turnoff is
just past and I drive around the bend and I see the turnoff and
I pull into it and stop the car and now it's so dark out and the
snow is falling so thick that I can't see the playground, I think,
and there's no one here now, I think, and I think that I'll just
rest here for a minute, get out of the car and get a little fresh air,
and stretch my legs a little, I think, and I stop the engine and
step out into the snow, there's already a good layer of it on the
ground, everything is white, the benches, there's snow on the
trees and I stand there and look at the snow coming down and
then there are just isolated snowflakes falling and then it stops,
and goodness it's so much brighter when the landscape is white,
yes, the white snow gives light to the night, and there, on the
path down to the playground that's covered in new snow, I see
a couple walking hand in hand, and it's the same two people I
saw earlier today, yes, definitely, so it wasn't something I just
imagined then, was it, I think, because now I see a young man

with medium-length brown hair almost covered in snow walking next to a young woman with her own long dark thick hair, and her hair too is almost totally covered in snow, and I hear her say it's so unbelievably beautiful here with all the new snow

Yes, it's beautiful, he says

Beautiful and white, he says

Everything's turning white, the trees, the benches, everything, he says

And we're turning white, she says

We're turning white too, he says

and then they let go of each other's hands and he puts his arm around her shoulders and she puts her arm around his back

It just so sad when the snow turns to slush, he says

We have to enjoy it while we can, she says

Yes, while it's bright and white and lovely, she says

Since it'll probably rain tomorrow, like usual, he says

and they look at each other and they give each other a kiss

But let's not think about that, he says

What shouldn't we think about? she says

About the snow being washed away by the rain tomorrow, he says

And that it'll turn to slush, she says

That's how it goes, he says

Yes, she says

and then they go into the playground and he picks up a bit of snow and makes a soft snowball and throws it at her, but misses, and then she picks up some snow and makes a snowball and packs it tight between her mittens and she throws it at him as hard as she can and he ducks and the snowball flies over his head and I stand there in the snow looking at them but they don't notice me, and I feel how good it is to have stepped out of the car into the fresh air, and then I just stand there and then

I see their footprints in the snow, how clear they are in the snow, going along the country road and then turning and going down the path to the playground, and then I start walking the same way and I follow their footprints when they turn and go down the path, the same path I went down earlier today, and I look at the playground and I see the two of them holding each other and it's like they're totally swallowed up by each other and I carefully follow their footprints and I see that they've let go of each other and she lies down in the snow with her arms at her sides and her legs pointing straight down and then she brings her arms and her feet up, and then she moves her arms and legs down, and then again, several times, and then she's lying with her feet sticking out and her arms straight at her sides, like she's frozen stiff, with an open mouth and wide-open eyes, and then I hear him say with fear in his voice that she mustn't lie there like that, it almost looks like she's lying there dead, she needs to stand up, he says and she stands up and she says she didn't mean to look dead and then he says she didn't really and she says yes well, and she goes over to him and takes his hand

Look how beautiful snow angels are, she says

Yes, he says

Can't you lie down and make one too? she says

I could, he says

and I walk past the playground and start up the hill on the other side, carefully, step by step, up to the hilltop, and there are no footprints on the path there, I am leaving my own new footprints in the new snow, and then I stop, turn around, and look at them still standing there holding hands and I think it's strange that they're so occupied with each other that they don't notice me, they only have eyes for each other, but if they did see me, did notice me, wouldn't they be scared, or maybe they'd feel embarrassed? or maybe they wouldn't care about

me being here at all? I think and I see them let go of each other's hand and he lies down in the snow and does what she did,
just faster, with sharper movements, like he's rushing to get it
done almost, and she says no not like that and he stops and she
says now it's her turn, she wants to make a third snow angel,
because it's better with three angels than two, she says, and
then he too lies stiff in his snow angel, with feet together, arms
at his sides, with wide-open eyes and an open mouth, and she
says he mustn't lie like that, she doesn't like it, it looks like he's
dead, she says, and just like he didn't like how she was lying she
doesn't like how he's doing it, lying there so that he looks dead,
she says, so he needs to get up, she says and he stands up and
then she again says she wants to make another snow angel, she
says, and he goes over to her and they are standing there looking at the two snow angels lying there so pretty, next to each
other, one of the angels practically touching the other with one
of its wings, but just practically, just almost, or maybe not just
almost, yes, the wings are touching each other and she says the
snow angels are so beautiful like that that they should just leave
them the way they are, she doesn't want to make a third angel
after all, she says and he says that's what he thinks too, that the
two snow angels are so nice that it's better just to stop with two,
that feels right, sort of, he says

Until they get covered in more snow, he says

Or rained away, she says

Yeah, or both, he says

and they take each other's hands again and walk out of the
playground and up the path to the road and I stand there and
look at them and he says look, there's a car there, in the turnoff,
it wasn't there when we walked by earlier, was it, he says and
she says she can't remember if there was a car there before or
not, in any case she didn't particularly notice a car, she says and

I stop and stand stock-still for a moment because I don't want them to notice me, I'm not sure why but for whatever reason I don't want them to, I think, and then I start down the path again, carefully, taking short steps since it might be slippery, and I go down in my own footsteps that I left there when I went up and I'm looking down and I stop and look up and I see them, she and he are crossing the country road and I see them walk past the turnoff where my car is parked and then I look at the two beautiful snow angels in the playground and then I go into the playground and stop and stand there and look at the snow angels and they are so beautiful, so beautiful that if I tried to paint them it would turn out to be a bad painting, compared to the sight of the snow angels, I think, because that's how it is, that's how it almost always is, what's beautiful in life turns out bad in a painting because it's like there's too much beauty, a good picture needs something bad in it in order to shine the way it should, it needs darkness in it, but maybe, can I maybe paint a picture of two snow angels dissolving as they melt away? could I make a picture like that shine? I think and I know at the same moment, at this very instant, right now, that another picture has lodged inside me, it will be there forever, another picture has entered into me that I'll have to try to paint away, I think, and I notice at the same time that it's extremely cold now, I really need to get back into my car and then make it to Bjørgvin before it gets too late, so I really ought to get driving now, I think and I see the footprints in the snow, four of them going down, right next to one another, two bigger and two smaller, and four of them going up, right next to one another, two bigger and two smaller, and then mine going down after the four, and my footprints look so lonely, so alone, and so un-even, so erratic, as if I wasn't entirely steady on my feet, as if I was drunk, or staggering a little, I think, but I'm not drunk, it's been many years since the last time I had anything to drink, so maybe it's just my gait that's become a little unsteady, I think, but anyway it feels like I'm walking steadily and evenly like I used to, or maybe I didn't use to, I think and I go straight to the car, stamp the snow off my feet, brush snow off my trouser legs, sit down in the car and start it and pull out onto the road and in a kind of stupor I start driving south towards Bjørgvin, but I need to be sharper, because there are no tyre tracks on the road, everything's white, and I need to stay on the road and not drive into the ditch, I think, and then I see in the light from the headlights the two people I saw making snow angels walking hand in hand and he says it'll sure be nice to get home now and she says they'll be home soon

Ales and Asle, he says

Asle and Ales, she says

and I drive carefully past them and I drive farther south and I think that it was so beautiful seeing those two snow angels in the playground, and I'm absolutely sure that I saw what I just saw, it's not just something I saw in a dream or imagined, what I saw earlier today wasn't and the two of them lying under the black overcoat wasn't because that was the same long black coat he was wearing just now, I think and it's a coat like the one I'm sitting in now, I think and I fall back into a kind of stupor without any thoughts, I just drive south and a little farther along I catch up to a car that leaves tyre tracks on the road and then it gets easier to drive, I can follow its tracks, I think and it's really something, what I'm doing, I think, driving from Dylgja to Bjørgvin and back home and then back to Bjørgvin again on the same day, late, in snowy weather, but, yes, it feels like the only answer, I think, and I fall into that stupor again and I think that the reason I like driving so much is that my thoughts go away, I'm just concentrating on driving and so no thoughts bother me, no sorrows come over me, I'm just driving, no more no less, and time passes and I drive south and I get closer to Bjørgvin and not far up ahead I can take a right and drive down a road and then get to the block where Asle's building is, in Sailor's Cove, and I think it hasn't snowed any more since it stopped snowing at the playground but it was snowing in Bjørgvin too, everything is white and beautiful in Bjørgvin too, even if there are tracks, of both tyres and footsteps, and I think I should ring Asle's doorbell just in case, even though he's probably not home, or in any case won't open the door for anyone, and I turn off the main road and drive down to the building where Asle lives and park on that block and then go over to the front door of the building and press the doorbell button next to his name, and I stand there and wait, but of course no one comes to open the door, and I ring Asle's bell again and this time I hold the button down for a long time, and then I let go, I stand there, wait, but no one comes, and of course Asle's not home, I didn't think he was, he's probably at The Alehouse, at The Last Boat as it's called, he's probably sitting alone at a table there, I think, because he always goes to The Alehouse with all the retired old sailors, everything's cheap there, and sometimes he buys dinner there too, dinners are cheap and the beer is cheap plus you can get a shot of something stronger for a reasonable price, I think, yes, I don't believe he ever goes to any other restaurants or bars, not any more, he always goes to The Alehouse, to The Last Boat, so that's where I'll go and look for him, I think, and I have my regular parking place not far from there, the car park at The Beyer Gallery, and I get back into my car and start it and think now I'll drive straight to The Beyer Gallery and it's almost unbelievable how much Beyer has helped me, I think, not only did he give me my first show in The Beyer Gallery back when I was still going to The

Art School, and it rarely or ever happened that anyone debuted there while they were still at The Art School, yes, to tell the truth I was the first artist he ever showed before that artist had graduated from The Art School, yes, that's what Beyer said, and even more unbelievable was that all the paintings in my debut show sold, and since then it's been Beyer who's sold my pictures, yes, I don't know what I would have done without Beyer, and I remember very well the first time I saw him, it was the first time I set foot in The Beyer Gallery too, it was Ales who brought me there, she'd been in The Beyer Gallery many times, ever since she was a girl, even when she was little her parents used to take her along to exhibitions, and the first exhibition I saw in The Beyer Gallery was of paintings by Eiliv Pedersen, who would later be my painting teacher at The Art School, I think, and ever since my first show at The Beyer Gallery it was Beyer who's sold my paintings, I think, and he always manages to sell almost all of them, but sometimes, in the first couple of years, I have to admit, they sold for a terrible price, to tell the truth, but most of the pictures sell for a good price now, and there are always a few that don't sell, the best pictures too a lot of the time, and Beyer doesn't sell those ones cheap any more, he stopped doing that a long time ago, he'd rather put them in what he calls The Bank, the side room of the same gallery, where he keeps in storage the pictures that aren't in the show, and Beyer has the idea that the pictures that don't sell in Bjørgvin might sell in Oslo, because his good friend Kleinheinrich, who runs The Kleinheinrich Gallery in Oslo, likes having a show of my pictures as soon as there are enough of them, so when Beyer has enough unsold pictures sitting in The Bank The Kleinheinrich Gallery shows them in Oslo, eventually there's enough for a show in Oslo, about every four years, and since then I've sold almost all of my paintings, and then Beyer puts aside the paintings that didn't sell in Olso either because sooner or later he'll show them in Nidaros, at The Huysmann Gallery, because Beyer knew Huysmann well, he said, Huysmann ran the best gallery in Nidaros, Beyer said, yes, that's what he thought, Beyer said, and sooner or later there'll be a show in Nidaros too, I think, and Beyer himself also owns a large collection of my pictures, he's bought a picture for his collection from every one of my shows, and a few years ago when it was hard to sell my pictures for a good price he bought lots of them himself, and then other people copied him and bought pictures too, Beyer said, no I truly have no idea where I'd be without Beyer, I think, and now I'm going to have another new show at The Beyer Gallery soon, every year I have a show there before Christmas, a kind of Christmas show, yes, that sounds bad but the annual show I have there is just before Christmas, during Advent, because that's the best time to sell pictures, or in any case my pictures, Beyer says, and by now I have enough pictures waiting in Dylgja for the show this year, because I paint and paint, day in and day out, so now I just have to drive my paintings to Bjørgvin and if I'd thought about it I could have brought them with me earlier today, of course, but that would have been too much, I think and I drive to The Beyer Gallery where I always park my car when I'm in Bjørgvin

You can park in front of the gallery whenever you want, Beyer told me

and I said thank you and then Beyer taught me how to drive out of Bjørgvin from The Beyer Gallery and into Bjørgvin to park in front of The Beyer Gallery, which is located more or less in the centre of Bjørgvin, so that's where I've parked my car all these years, and other than that I never drive into Bjørgvin or any other city, I like driving but not in cities, in cities I get confused and anxious and feel lost and can never find where I'm going and sometimes I've gone down one-way streets the wrong way and everything's a mess, but I did learn how to drive to The Beyer Gallery and how to drive away from it, Beyer met me in Sailor's Cove once and sat in my car next to me and he told me everything I needed to do to drive in and then we drove into Bjørgvin, to The Beyer Gallery, and then we turned around and drove out of Bjørgvin, and at Sailor's Cove we turned around and drove back in to The Beyer Gallery again, and then we drove out of Bjørgvin again, to Sailor's Cove, and then in to The Beyer Gallery again, we took many trips in and out and eventually Beyer said now I should be able to remember the way, and I said that I thought I could, and I could, I think, and having learned how to drive to and from The Beyer Gallery has come in very handy, that's for sure, and without Beyer's help I'd probably never have dared to drive into the centre of Bjørgvin, most likely not, but now I simply drive straight to The Beyer Gallery at 1 High Street and park in front of the Gallery, as long as there's an empty space there, and there almost always is, if not I just sit and wait a little in the car and then a space always opens up, I think, and if it takes too long then I drive out to Sailor's Cove and turn around and then drive back, and it's never happened that there wasn't a space in front of The Beyer Gallery then, I think, and I know the quickest way to walk from The Beyer Gallery to The Alehouse, you just go down High Street for a bit and then down one of the little narrow passages, The Lane, which at its narrowest is honestly no more than three or four feet wide, and when you go down The Lane and out onto the street you see The Fishmarket just a few yards to the left, and then you cross that and take the street to the right along The Bay to get to The Alehouse, and next to The Fishmarket there's also The Prison, but if you take a street to the right after you get to The Lane and go to the first crossing, then go down the side street a little way, you'll get to The Country Inn, it's on The Wharf itself, with The Coffeehouse on the ground floor, yes, and I've taken these streets so many times that on the whole I have no trouble finding my way even when it's totally dark, I think, now, at night, all the snow that's fallen is shining, and the streets are partly lit by the light coming from the windows of all the buildings, I think, and I park my car in front of The Beyer Gallery and then go down High Street and then the snow starts falling and it's not just a flurry, the snow's really coming down, big wet snowflakes, and I stop, I squint, I run my hands through my hair and brush some snow from my eyes with the back of my hand and it's unbelievable how hard the snow is falling, now I just want to get indoors, and well it's not that far a walk to The Alehouse, to The Last Boat as it's called, and Asle will probably be sitting there, I think and I feel how tired I am, so tired, so if Asle isn't there I'll go straight to The Country Inn and ask if they have a room for me, I think and I brush snow off of my hair and eyes again and I walk on and I think that I'm tired, I'm truly exhausted, so maybe I should go to The Country Inn first and reserve a room right away and then go look for Asle in The Alehouse, and if he's not there I'll go straight to The Country Inn and lie down, in a warm room, on clean sheets, I think and I keep walking and I start down The Lane and that's not someone lying in the snow up there, is it? yes it definitely is, it's a person, that's what it looks like, I think, yes someone's there in the snow, covered with snow, with his head up on a little step, facing a building's front door, a person is lying in the snow that's falling and coming down on the person lying there and I hurry over to him and it's him! it's Asle! yes, Asle's lying there in the snow! how is that possible? Asle is just lying there in the snow and he seems lifeless, it's like he's lying there asleep, it's like he just fell, toppled forward, and he's lying there and the snow is falling and covering him and I hurry over and grab his shoulder and shake him from side to side and he says hello, well then, how lucky, yes he's alive but he wasn't conscious when I got here and I think what, what happened?

Did you slip? I say

I must have, Asle says

and Asle thinks he must have slipped, he's slipped for some reason, he thinks

But I don't remember slipping, he says

No, I say

and then I stand there and look at Asle and hold his shoulder

I don't understand what's happening, Asle says

and I keep my hand on his shoulder and then I put my hand under his arm and I try to lift him up off of the ground and he stays kneeling and his whole body is shaking and I say he must be freezing and he says no, no it's not that, and he breaks off, but you don't happen to have anything to drink on you? he says, yes, that's why I'm shaking, I need a drink, he says, you need to get me a little something to drink, something strong, he says and I say we need to catch a taxi and go to The Clinic

No, Asle says

and he's thinking he's not going to any damn Clinic, all he needs is a little something to drink and then everything'll be fine, everything'll be all right again, he thinks

I don't want to go to any Clinic, Asle says

I don't need to, he says

and again Asle says that all he needs is a little drink, he says and he kneels up and I stand back up and then take him under both his arms and pull and he helps as best he can and then Asle is standing and it's stopped snowing now and Asle shakes himself off, brushes the snow off himself

Well I'll be damned, I must have slipped, he says

and he says that now we need to get over to The Alehouse, to The Last Boat, yes, it's not far, it's just over there, he says, we just have to go the rest of the way down The Lane, he says and I see that we're standing in front of building number 5 in The Lane and he says yes and then we just need to take a left and we'll see The Fishmarket and there, on the other side of The Bay, there's The Alehouse, with a view onto The Bay, Asle says, and it was really great to run into me again after all this time, he says and I think well then we'll go over to The Alehouse and I'll buy him a little something to drink so he stops shaking and then I'll drive him home, I think

It's really been too long since we've seen each other, I say

Yes, Asle says

But now we'll have a glass of something and talk, he says

Yes, I say

and I think that this was an act of God, it was God's doing that I drove into Bjørgvin again, just think if I hadn't done that, think if Asle had stayed lying there in front of 5, The Lane, he'd have frozen to death, if no one had found him in time he'd have frozen to death right there in the snow, I think, so I absolutely did the right thing by driving into Bjørgvin, but why did I do it? when I was so tired? it turned out to be the right thing to do but what made me do it at all? I think and I hold Asle's arm and we walk down The Lane and now he's walking steadily, I think

I'm not drunk, Asle says

You don't need to hold my arm, he says

and I let go of his arm and Asle thinks that things are all right now, he's almost not shaking any more, but what a damn shame that he passed out, yes, he must have thought that he should ring the bell at Guro's house, and now why would he do that? what kind of a notion was that? he thinks, and then he passed out in front of the door and why was he lying on the steps of the building where Guro's apartment is, he thinks

I never get drunk any more, Asle says

I wish I did, he says

and I ask him in that case why does he drink, and he says that he drinks to get back to normal, to not shake, yes, to be normal the way other people are, he says and I say yes, yes, if that's how it is then that's how it is and by now we've come out from The Lane and we take a left and walk down the pavement and I see Asle start shaking again and I think that the way Asle's shaking now he needs something to drink in a hurry, to be normal again, I think

I only need a shot or two to be all right again, Asle says

and I think he mustn't drink so much, he needs to cut down on his drinking, he needs to get rid of this horrible shaking of his, I think, but can he do it? does he want to do it? I think and I say now we'll go to The Alehouse, to The Last Boat, and he can get a shot there and warm himself up a little, I say, and I say that after that I can drive him home

I'll buy you a shot or two and a glass of beer, I say

This round's on me, I say

No I can get this one, Asle says

I'm positive it's my turn, I say

Yes all right thanks, he says

No way are you buying, I say

and Asle says thanks, thanks, that's nice of you, he says and now we've reached The Fishmarket and I see Asle stagger a little and I grab his arm and he says thank you and then I hold Asle's arm and I say we'll be there soon, it's not far, no, I say

Yes, yes, he says

and it seems like he's shaking a little less, but now and then

I notice that it seems to come in waves, the shaking moves through him like a wave and then he's still again

We can already see the sign from here, The Alehouse, he says

and then suddenly, totally unexpectedly, he crumples next to me, and I grab him and try to hold him up but I can't do it, Asle just collapses and stays lying on his side and I bend down and I shake him and he doesn't wake up and I hold my hand in front of his mouth and he's breathing, no, impossible, I can't take him to The Alehouse, we need to go to The Clinic, I think, and Asle sort of wakes up and he thinks damn it, he must have passed out again, he thinks and he looks up at me

I seem to have slipped again, he says

and I think it's good that I'm here, it's good that Asle isn't alone because what would happen to him then? he's totally weak and helpless now, isn't he? he's not exactly in good shape, I think, and anyway he couldn't be, I think, and I say again that we really ought to go to The Clinic and Asle says no, we're almost at The Alehouse and if he just gets a little something to drink he'll feel better, he says

I haven't had much to eat in a while, he says

I've hardly eaten in the past couple of days, that's why I'm so weak, he says

and he says that first he'll just have a drink, then he'll get himself a little food, they have good food at The Alehouse, first something to drink and then something to eat

All right, I say

But you just collapsed, I say

You're not okay, something's wrong, I say

and Asle thinks he's okay, it's just this shaking, and he does need to start drinking less, cut down, wean his body off drinking, he thinks

It's just that I need a drink, he says

We need to go to The Clinic, I say

No we'll go to The Last Boat, Asle says

and he tries to sit up and I grab him under his arms and help him get to his knees

No, you're not well, I say

and Asle says that he doesn't want to go to any Clinic, he'll be fine if he just has a drink, he says and I hold out my hand to him and he gathers his strength and I pull and he pushes off from the snow with his other hand and struggles up and gets up and then he's standing steady on his feet and I hold his arm and I think yes, well, then we'll just go to The Alehouse, but Asle isn't well and I should have taken him to The Clinic, I think, but I won't refuse him anything, he has to do for himself whatever he thinks is best, I think and then we walk carefully onward, step by step, and now he's steady on his feet, I can see that, and it's stopped snowing now, and I think that we'll make it, it's just up ahead, he'll get something to drink soon, and then something to eat, I think and I open the door to The Alehouse and Asle goes in and he says thanks and now he's perfectly steady, except that he's shaking, his whole body's shaking, especially his hands, and he stops right inside the door and brushes the snow off himself with shaking hands and I say he should sit down and I'll go buy him a drink, I say, and Asle walks over to the nearest table and sits down with his black overcoat still on and he puts his brown leather shoulderbag down on the chair next to him

It must feel good to sit down, I say

Yes, Asle says

and he's thinking that it's nice and warm in The Alehouse and if he just gets a drink then the shaking will stop and he sits nice and straight on the chair and I see that his whole body is shaking, and he needs some food, I think, but he probably can't manage to eat anything, I think

I'm having trouble getting food down, Asle says

As soon as a bite comes near my mouth I feel like I want to throw up, he says

Have you eaten anything today? I say

No, he says

Yesterday? I say

I don't think so, he says

and he looks at me and I say then I'll just go buy some beer and a shot for him, as for me I just want a cup of coffee, with a little milk, nothing else, I say and Asle nods and I go over to the counter and say what I want and the bartender goes to fetch it and I pay and then go over to the table where Asle's sitting and put a pint of beer and a shot glass down in front of him and then I go back and get the mug of coffee, which I add a little milk to, and then the second shot glass, and I go put it down next to Asle and I put the mug of coffee down on the table by the chair across from Asle and he puts his hands around the first shot glass and tries to pick it up but his hands are shaking too much and a little splashes out and I take his glass

I'll help you, I say

Thanks, he says

and I raise the glass to his mouth and Asle swallows it all in one gulp and then he breathes deeply in and out and he says now he'll feel better soon, everything'll be better in a minute, he says and he's thinking that if he just has that second drink then he'll be fine again, he thinks

I'll just have that too, Asle says

and he points at the full second glass and I ask him if I should help and Asle says he'll try to do it on his own

Yes, you do what you want, I say

and Asle raises the glass to his mouth with both hands and empties half of it and he thinks that was sure good, he already feels himself starting to calm down, he feels himself shaking less

That went well, I say

Yes, um, he says

and there's silence

You're not drinking any more? he says

and I say that I stopped drinking many years ago, I drank way too much, to tell the truth I was always drunk, and I needed to be sober in order to paint, I say, and Ales, my wife, well, of course she didn't like that I drank so much so I decided to stop, and it was hard at the beginning and I had to change a lot of what I was used to but I managed it, I finally managed to stop drinking, but I needed help, I say, and I think that I've already told Asle this so many times and still he always asks me if I've stopped drinking, I think

That's good, Asle says

That you were able to stop, he says

No, well, I say

It wasn't that hard, I say

and I think that I shouldn't say how I was able to do it, the fact is that I prayed and prayed to God every time the great thirst came over me, and also that if it hadn't been for Ales, and for my faith, I never would've been able to do it, I think, but since Asle's alone, and isn't a believer, I can't tell him that

I need to stop too, Asle says

But I can't, he says

It's impossible, he says

You need to get help, I say

Yes, he says

and then he puts his hands around the pint glass and tries to pick it up and he's shaking but not as much as before and with both hands he manages to bring the pint to his lips and he takes a good gulp of beer

That went all right, then, he says

I'm fine and dandy if I just have a drink, Asle says

and he thinks that he wants to live, so he needs to stop drinking, but often, yes, most of the time, he doesn't want to live any more, he's always thinking he should go out to sea, disappear under the waves, Asle thinks and he says as soon as he has a little something to drink he stops shaking, yes, it's like he gets all his strength back, he says and then there's a long silence

But you were lying there, in the snow, I say

Yeah, Asle says

Do you remember falling down? I say

No, he says

I just remember that you were there, that you woke me up, he says

and I sit down on the chair across from Asle and I see that there aren't many customers in The Last Boat at night, there are a few men scattered around the place sitting alone, each one by himself, each at his own table, one here and one there, with a pint of beer in front of him and a tobacco pouch on his side of the table, they roll themselves a cigarette, light it, take a good long drag of it, exhale the smoke, pick up the pint and take a sip of beer, sitting there alone, one here and one there, they sit there all alone in the world, each one at a different table, and it's like they never notice that anyone else is even there, I think and Asle takes out his tobacco pouch and box of matches and then rolls himself a cigarette and he says he often shakes so badly that he's had to start buying packs of cigarettes, but nothing tastes as good as a hand-rolled cigarette and beer and he's left the pack of cigarettes at home, Asle says and he lights his cigarette

You stopped smoking a long time ago too, right? he says

Yes, I say

and there's a pause

It's been years and years, I say

I switched to snuff and that's enough for me, I say

and I take out my snuffbox and take a good pinch

Maybe snuff would work for me too? Asle says

and again there's a pause

But the most important thing is to start drinking less, he says

Yes, I say

and I think that it's good he wants to drink less, but he won't be able to do it without help, I think

It was hard to break the habit of drinking, the thirst was still there, but after the beginning the thirst did go away and then it was easy to leave it alone, I say

and I say that I didn't actually want to stop smoking, but I was smoking so much that I'd wake up in the middle of the night to have a cigarette or two, and I was so tired of that that I started taking a pinch of snuff and then I would sleep through the night, and before that I always had to get out of bed to smoke as soon as I woke up, but when I started taking a pinch of snuff the need for a morning cigarette went away and I could lie in bed and relax without needing to get up to smoke, I say, and there's a pause and I take off my shoulderbag too and put in down on the chair next to me and I look around at the other people in The Alehouse, sitting with their beer and tobacco in front of them like a fragile line of defence against the world, clinging to their cigarettes, their pints, as they sit there, and the sea inside them is large, whether stormy or calm, as they sit there and wait for the next and last crossing they'll set out on, the one that will never end, that they'll never come back from, and they don't feel fear, it'll be how it is and how it has to be, it must have a meaning, yes, Our Lord must have given it meaning, they think, he writes straight on crooked lines, they think, or anyway the good Lord is part of it all somehow, and it's the devil who made the lines crooked, they think and they hold onto their cigarettes and pints and then they pray a silent prayer, a prayer more like a look out over the sea inside them, wordless, but as far as the eye can reach over that sea the prayer extends, entirely wordless, because the words will be left behind, definitely, but there must be a port for people like them too, they're probably thinking, and then they feel a prick of something like fear so they raise their pint and have a taste of beer, the good old taste, it gives them a sense of security, I think and I see Asle raise his pint and take a gulp of beer

Delicious, he says

and I raise my mug of coffee and milk and clink his pint with it

Cheers, I say

Yes, cheers, he says

You're allowed to toast with this too, I say

Now we'll have some more to drink and then we'll take a taxi to The Clinic, I say

No, Asle says

and there's silence

You should just drive me home like you said, he says

and I think that whatever happens I can't leave him, because he's not well, just think if I hadn't driven back to Bjørgvin tonight, if I'd let myself think that I was too tired to drive, that a tired driver is a dangerous driver, if I hadn't made myself drive back to Bjørgvin or had been afraid to, I think and I don't understand why it felt so important that I do it, I think

That would be best, Asle says

Okay, I say

and I think that if Asle had fallen in The Lane, on the little steps outside number 5, and had lain there, covered in snow, had just stayed there under the snow, who knows how it would have ended? because people rarely walk by there, not in weather like this at any rate, he could have frozen to death, he definitely would have frozen to death in the snow, I think and I raise my coffee and milk again and Asle raises his pint

We've known each other a long time, you and me, I say

Almost our whole lives, he says

That's what it feels like anyway, he says

and he takes a sip of beer and puts the pint back down and he says he needs to piss and now that he's recovered it'll be fine, Asle says, and he gets up and I stay in my seat, looking straight ahead, at his pint, at the golden yellow beer, and then I hear a crash and I look up and I see Asle lying on the floor in his black overcoat and I get up and go over to him and The Bartender comes over to us and stands there with his hands hanging down and I look at Asle and the men sitting alone each at his own table get up and come over to us and one of them bends down and takes Asle's hands and holds it for a long moment, then looks diagonally up at us

His pulse is weak, he says

and he looks at me and I just nod and I hear Asle softly say help me up then, he says, and the men who came over are just standing there and I say it's no good, you're not well, this is the third time you've collapsed, I say and the man standing there says yes that happens sometimes, that happened to him too, I've probably heard of the shakes? he says, or delirium tremens, as they call it, the DT's, he says and he says that twice he's been on boats where people died of it, but that was a long time ago, he's not a young man any more, not by a long shot, no, he says, and he says that they took both of the men who died and wrapped them up real well and tied a weight to their feet and then they were carefully lifted overboard and then when the captain said

rest in peace they dropped the body into the sea while one of
the religious people onboard, because there are always one or
two believers onboard a boat, said the Our Father and then anyone who knew a little of the psalm tried to sing Nearer My
God To Thee and then it was over and everyone felt relieved
and then, especially then, you felt better after a drink or three
and someone else says yes, you sure did, and a third says yes that
used to happen a lot before, that someone would die far from
shore and be dropped into the sea, he says, what else were you
supposed to do with the body? so far from shore? in the heat?
in the boiling hot sun? the only thing you could do was wrap
the dead man up well and tie a weight to his feet and then drop
the body into the sea as soon as you could, he says, and the sea
took him in, he says, and someone else says yes, yes, that's true,
for the sea has God in it, he says and a third person says that the
sea is the biggest graveyard in the world, and maybe the best
one too, someone says, yes, there's more of God in the sea than
in the earth on land, someone says and then it's quiet and then
someone says

Sea and sky, he says

Sea and sky, yes, someone else says

and two other people say that they'd also been there when
people had the DT's and died from it and were buried at sea,
but that was a long time ago, it's not like that any more, that's
just how it used to be, before, a long time ago, now boats have
freezer rooms of course, and they've had them for a long time,
someone says, and thank goodness for that says the third man,
and someone says that he used to have the DT's himself, he
says, yes, well, who hasn't, someone else says, but he's shaking so badly, I say, yes the best thing would be for you to take
him to The Clinic, The Bartender says and someone else says
that's right, someone there'll probably admit him, and he'll get

medicine that'll maybe make him stop shaking, he says and Asle
says they need to help him up and he thinks dammit what happened? what's wrong with him? he's fallen down again, and
he's on a boat? yes, he is, and since he's so wobbly on his feet
they must be on some some really rough seas, he thinks and his
drink, where's his drink? he thinks, because if he just has a little
more of something strong, and a little more beer, he'll be fine
again, Asle thinks and I hold him by the arm and The Bartender
takes his other arm and then we pull and Asle helps as much as
he can and we get him to his feet and then Asle is standing and
I'm holding his arm

Little to drink and I'll be fine, Asle says

No I don't think so, The Bartender says

You need to go to The Clinic, I say

and Asle says what the hell, he doesn't need to go to any
Clinic, he's not sick, he just needs a drink, a lot to drink, he says
and I say it's time for us to go to The Clinic now and the men
standng around us say yes he's right, and one says he knows too
many people who died from the shakes and The Bartender says
he can call a taxi and I say yes and Asle says what the hell, but
what can he do? there's no place for him here on this boat, Asle
says and I see that The Bartender has gone over to the bar and
picked up a phone and he's saying something into it and then
he comes back and says he's called a taxi and it'll be here in a
couple of minutes and he says maybe I need a drink for strength
and I'm about to tell him that I don't drink, I had to stop,
but The Bartender has already gone and he comes back with a
generous pour in a glass and he holds it out to me and I say I
don't drink any more, I've had my share and that's enough, I
say and The Bartender says he understands and he lifts the glass
to his own mouth and empties it in one go and then he says
we can go outside now, the taxi'll be here any minute, he says

and I see Asle standing there in his black coat and I go and put on my shoulderbag and pick up Asle's and put it on him and then I take Asle by the arm and steer him across the room and one of the other men takes Asle's other arm and a third goes to open the door for us and we go out and then one of the men who's come outside with us gives Asle's shoulder a shake and says it'll be fine, he'll get through this, he himself has been through what Asle is going through now, even if it was a long time ago, and he got through it, just barely, he says, but he was on a boat, far out to sea, and Asle is on land, and there's good medicine you can take now, medicine that reduces the shaking and helps you get to sleep, he says and the taxi comes and The Taxi Driver gets out and opens the rear door and Asle gets in and I go around the car, open the door, and get in next to Asle and I say we're going to The Clinic and The Taxi Driver starts driving without saying anything and I don't say anything either and when we're in front of The Clinic I pay for the ride and I say no when The Taxi Driver asks me if I want a receipt and then I open the door and get out and The Taxi Driver gets out too and opens the door on Asle's side and I take Asle's arm and get him out of the taxi and The Taxi Driver asks if I can handle the rest on my own and I say yes it'll be fine, I say and then Asle says where the hell is he? wasn't he just on a boat? in rough weather, the weather was bad as hell! he says and I hold Asle's arm tight

I can walk fine by myself, he says

But you kept collapsing, I say

Yes I know that, he says

That's just because the weather's so rotten today, he says

and then Asle says he just needs a little more to drink and everything'll be fine, a drink is all he needs, he says and I say yes yes and I open the door to The Clinic with one hand and

we go inside and I see that no one else is there and Asle says I
need a drink, he says that several times, and then he asks where
he is, and I say we're in The Clinic, because he's not well, I say
and while I keep hold of Asle's arm we go over to the reception desk and the woman sitting behind the desk slides open
the window she's sitting behind and I say he's not doing too
well and I nod at Asle and she asks me his name and date of
birth and I've never been able to remember birthdays and I ask
Asle when he was born and he answers who do I think he is,
do I really think he's someone who goes around remembering things like that? he says and she asks for his relations, yes,
that's what she says, and I say I'm just a friend but I know that
his parents are dead, and he also had a sister but she's dead too,
Alida was her name, and now why am I saying that? I think,
and then I say that he was married twice and he has three children, one grown son and two younger children, a boy and a
girl, and she asks if I have their names and addresses and I say
I don't even know their first names, he always just talks about
The Boy, who's grown-up now and lives in Oslo, and The Son
and The Daughter, who live with their mother somewhere in
Trøndelag, and I say that the only thing I know is that his first
wife was named Liv and the second was Siv, I don't know their
last names or addresses or anything like that, I say and then I
say where he lives and I give her my name and my address
and phone number and she says that a nurse will come get us
in a moment and then a doctor will examine Asle and I thank
her and then Asle and I go sit down on a sofa and I say now
we'll just wait a little and then a doctor will examine him and
he says he doesn't want anyone to examine him, not a doctor
and not anyone else, he doesn't need any doctor, that's the first
thing, he says, and the second thing is that there isn't any doctor here on this boat, so the only thing he needs is a drink, and

this boat? why is he on board this boat? and where is he? and
what's the name of this boat he's on? is he on The Last Boat?
Asle asks and he says he doesn't think we're in Bjørgvin, this
is some other city, so where are we now? Asle says and I say
that we're in Bjørgvin and Asle says no, no goddamn way, he's
been in Bjørgvin long enough to know what it's like there so
where are we? we're not on a boat, have we landed on Sartor?
he says, are we in Flora? where are we? he says, now, yes, now
he's got it, we're on Sartor, no doubt about it, he says, yes,
that's where we are, Asle says and then I see a nurse holding
a door open and I take Asle over to the door and The Nurse
says welcome and then we go through the door and The Nurse
points across a corridor and she opens the door to an office and
we go in and a man is sitting behind a desk inside and that must
be a doctor and The Doctor says yes and I say he's shaking like
this and he collapsed a few times, he was unconscious for a bit,
and he's started saying things that don't make sense, and well he
doesn't entirely know where he is and stuff like that, I say and
Asle again says can't I find him anything to drink, he needs a
drink, if he could just get a little drink everything would be fine
again, he says, and why are we on Sartor? what are we doing on
Sartor? he says, when did he get here? he says and I look at The
Doctor and I look at Asle and The Doctor says Asle needs rest
and The Nurse says I can leave now, they'll take care of him
now, Asle needs his rest now, just rest, he needs to sleep and
rest as much as he can, she says, but I can call tomorrow and
then maybe I can come see him, or maybe the best thing would
be to let him rest more and I won't be able to see him, she says
and I say Asle might need some things and I can come by and
bring him whatever he wants at least, I say and she says I can
call tomorrow and they'll know more, she says and I say thank
you for all your help and then I tell Asle take care

You're leaving? he says

You don't have to go, he says

I do have to go, I say

But you can't, we're too far out to sea, he says

I have to go, I say

And you need to take good care of yourself, I say

and then I leave and cross the corridor and go out to the reception area and I see that some more people have come to The Clinic now, they're sitting and waiting their turn, and then I leave The Clinic and stop outside the door and I breathe in deeply and breathe out slowly and I see that it's started snowing again, big white snowflakes are falling and falling and I think now I'll go to The Country Inn and get a room there and then maybe I'll see Asle tomorrow morning, and then I'll drive back to Dylgja, as early as I can, I think and it's snowing, not heavily, not lightly, but evenly, quietly, the snow is coming down in big snowflakes evenly and quietly over Bjørgvin and I think now I really need something warm to drink, yes, a cup of coffee, a cup of coffee with milk would hit the spot, I think and I walk away from The Clinic and I think that I was only able to take a couple of sips of coffee back at The Alehouse before we had to go to The Clinic, and it would have been nice with something to eat too, just something light, I think, so now I need to go somewhere you can get food and drink, anywhere's fine, I'll get a cup of coffee with milk, definitely, I think and I think that if only I had a phone number for one of Asle's children I could have called them, the best would be The Boy, the eldest, who lives in Oslo now, but I don't even know his name, and I've heard about The Son and The Daughter and I know that Asle's first wife was named Liv and the second wife was Siv but I don't know where they live or anything like that, I think and then I see the lights from a sign above a door and the glowing sign says Food and Drink in a blue swoop of letters, that's where I'll go, I think, and then I'll go to The Country Inn, and I'm sure I'll be able to get a room there even though I haven't reserved one, sure, there are lots of times I've just showed up at The Country Inn and asked for a room and they've always had space for me, even if I had to sleep on a spare bed in some kind of store room in the attic that one time, so I'm sure it'll be fine, they're so helpful and nice at The Country Inn, I think and I open the door beneath the shining blue sign that has Food and Drink on it and I go in and right inside the door I stop and look around and I see that there's a bar in the middle of the place, it's not an especially big place, there's some kind of rectangle in the middle of the room and then some tables by the walls, but no customers, yes actually there's one woman sitting alone at one of the tables, with medium-length blonde hair, she's sitting and rolling herself a cigarette and there's a glass of red wine on the table in front of her, and she looks familiar, doesn't she? no, I've never seen her before, that's just something I'm imagining, since people look like other people, I think and I wait and I watch for a bit to see if I can just go sit down or if I'm supposed to go over to the counter and then The Bartender nods towards me and I go over to the bar and The Bartender looks at me and holds out his open hand towards me

A glass of beer for the gentleman? he says

No thanks, I say

What can I get for the gentleman? he says

Just a cup of coffee, I say

I can do that, he says

and then The Bartender is already filling a white mug with coffee from the percolator and Food and Drink is printed on the mug and then he asks if I'd like a little something to eat with that and I say yes, maybe, a bite to eat with that would be nice, I think and The Bartender hands me a menu and I glance at it quickly and I see that I can get an open-faced ground-beef sandwich with onions and I say I'd like an open-faced sandwich, ground beef, anyway I always get that, I think, and The Bartender says he can take care of that, I can just take my coffee and sit down and he'll bring me the sandwich, he says, and I say thanks very much, and then I ask him if he has any milk for my coffee and he apologizes and says he should have asked me about that himself of course, he says, and yes of course he has milk, he says and then he puts a little pitcher of milk down on the kitchen table next to the mug and he hands me a little coffee spoon and I take the spoon and pour a little milk into the coffee and stir it and then I look for an empty table, and I see the woman with the medium-length blonde hair sitting alone and there's an empty table behind her and I go over to the table and put the mug down and at the exact moment I sit down the thought comes to me, Asle's dog! Bragi, his dog, he's alone in Asle's apartment! and it may be a while before Asle gets out of The Clinic in the worst case, yes, it might take a long time before he gets back home to his apartment and his dog, so I need to get into the apartment and get his dog, Bragi, and walk him, and then it'd probably be best to take him with me back to Dylgja, I think, because I need to take care of the dog until Asle is better, until he's back home, I think and I take a sip of the coffee and it's very hot but good, coffee really warms you up, and I take another sip, yes, that's good, I haven't had anything to eat or drink for most of the day, I think, almost nothing, so this'll be good with a little food, and at the same moment a feeling of happiness comes over me, I'm glad I can just be sitting here together with other people, so to speak, even if it's just the woman with the blonde hair sitting in front of me drinking red wine and smoking, and people should drink as much as they want, I mean except for people who can't stop when they need to, no that's not what I want to think about any more right now, I think and I wonder if I've seen her before, the woman sitting in front of me with her back to me, some time or another? maybe we've even spoken to each other? or met somehow? it's definitely possible, and anyway it's good that there's somebody else at this café too and I didn't end up sitting alone, it's always a little sad to sit all by yourself in a café, it's like something that should be there is missing, not like when I'm at home, then it feels like something's wrong if I'm not alone, but not when Åsleik's there, but anyway there's no one who ever comes to see me besides him, I think, so how can I even think about it? about how I get sort of uncomfortable when people come visit me, I think, and I think that Asle's dog can't be left by himself, so I need to go get the keys to his apartment and then get the dog, I need to go back to The Clinic and get the apartment keys and then I need to drive and get the dog, yes, Bragi, yes, and then I'll need to look after him until Asle is better again, I think and I see The Bartender coming towards me carrying a white plate with a ground-beef sandwich on it in one hand and a knife and fork in a white napkin in the other hand and he puts the plate down in front of me and he puts the knife and fork in the napkin next to the plate and then he says he hopes the food tastes good and I think it looks absolutely great, I'm so hungry, and I start eating right away and I eat the food and drink my coffee and it tastes incredible, I was really hungry, I think and I see the woman with the medium-length blonde hair sitting at the table in front of me stub out her cigarette and stand up, and I see that she's pretty drunk and I think now she's going to come talk to me, and I look down and I take another mouthful of ground beef, onions, and bread

It's you, it can't be, she says

and I look up and see the woman with the mediumlength blonde hair standing in front of me holding the edge of the table and I know that I've seen her before, but I can't quite remember when it was, where it was

Don't you remember me? she says

and I try as hard as I can to recall who she is

Silje, she says

and she laughs

You really don't remember me? she says

Not even my name? she says

and the woman who says her name is Silje looks at me almost amazed, and then she says that she thinks about me a lot, she's often hoped we'd run into each other, it's been so long, but I was married then, wasn't I? and she didn't know where I lived, all she knew was that my name was Asle, she says

And now here you are, sitting right in front of me, she says

At last, she says

I almost can't believe it, she says

It's been so long since I've seen you, she says

You remember me, right? she says

You weren't that drunk, were you? she says

And you came to my place a bunch of times, she says

and I start to see before my eyes a small apartment, a sofa, a bookshelf, some photos on the walls, and, no I don't want to think about that

You must remember me, don't you remember? she says

My place in The Lane? she says

Ground floor, she says

and I don't say anything and I see that I've finished eating my open-faced sandwich, I sure was hungry, that went down quick, I think and I put the knife and fork down on the plate next to each other

Anyway it's great to see you again, she says

and I nod, I drink my coffee, empty the mug, and then I say I'm afraid I have to go, there's something I need to do, I say and I wave to The Bartender and scribble in the air with my hand and he nods to me and then she says I really should come and see her, she still lives where she did before, number 5, The Lane, ground floor, she says, and she says surely I remember her? I can't have been that drunk all the time? and I must remember that she was with me at The Country Inn too? she, Silje, or whatever her name was, maybe it was something else? was it maybe Guro? yes, she'd even slept in the same bed with me at The Country Inn, she says, and she remembers it, yes, even though it was a long time ago, even though I had medium-length brown hair back then worn loose and not the grey hair tied back with a hairband I have now, she says and she laughs and she says she even remembers my birthday, because I told her my birthday so she could calculate my lucky number, she says and she asks if I remember what my number was and I say I need to go and she says it was eight, or four times two, and then she says she'd be happy to see me if I came by sometime and The Bartender comes over and I take the bill he's handing me and I take out my wallet and take a note out and hand it to him and I say that's fine and he says thank you and I get up and then I push my chair in and she lets go of the edge of the table and I see that she's not too steady on her feet and I say I need to go, I'm actually in a real hurry, I say and she says she knows my name is Asle and that I'm an artist, and she knows more than that, she says, because every single year during Advent she goes to the show I have up at The Beyer Gallery, she says and she falls silent and suddenly she gets a kind of dreamy look in her face and then she says that it was so long ago but ever since the first time we met she's seen all of my shows in Bjørgvin, and she's often wanted to buy a picture, but she couldn't afford it, yes, she thinks my pictures are really great, she says and I say have a good night and she says she'd be happy if I dropped by sometime, number 5, The Lane, that's where she lives, surely I remember? I was never that drunk, she says

Silje, she says

and she laughs and puts a hand on my back

Or maybe it was Guro? she says

But The Lane, number 5, you remember that much? she says

And so my name is Guro, she says

and I say I have to go now but it was nice to see her and I hear her say something but I can't quite catch what it is and then she says good night and I say thanks same to you and then I leave and I think now I need to go back to The Clinic and get the keys to Asle's apartment, because his dog can't be left there by himself, and I can take care of the dog while Asle's sick, I need to tell Asle that, I think, and I think I'll find my way to The Clinic, it'll be fine, I wasn't walking for long before I came to Food and Drink so it'll be easy to just go the same way in the opposite direction, I think, standing there in the snow on the pavement outside Food and Drink and I think I should go straight, in one direction or another, so now it's only a matter of picking the right direction, I think, and when I was coming here I was on the other side of the street, and when I saw the sign saying Food and Drink I crossed the street, that's what happened, I think, so now I obviously just need to cross the street and go straight, that must be right? I think and I think that it's good it's stopped snowing, it's easier to find your way when you can see where you're going, obviously, I think and I cross the street and I go straight and it's not snowing now but for some reason or another I almost always go the wrong way, I think, I don't know why, even if I know the way very well I somehow always manage to get it wrong, it's like with numbers, whatever I'm supposed to do with them goes wrong, I don't know why, I always add wrong and I always walk the wrong way, so the best thing to do would be to take a taxi, if one comes, I think, because I need to go to The Clinic and get the keys to Asle's apartment because his dog is still there, and he, Bragi, can't stay there alone so I need to go get the dog, I think and once they give me Asle's keys I need to get back to my car in front of The Beyer Gallery and then drive out to the building in Sailor's Cove where Asle's apartment is and get the dog, Bragi, and then I need to drive back and park the car in front of The Beyer Gallery and then I need to go to The Country Inn and check into a room, I think, so first things first I need to get back to The Clinic, I think and the moment I think it I see a taxi and I stick out my hand and it stops and I open the door and get in and I say I'm going to The Clinic and The Taxi Driver says yes, that'll be no problem, it's not far, he can get me there no problem, he says and I say don't know my way around Bjørgvin too well and The Taxi Driver says that's all right, if I don't he does, he says and then neither of us says anything and he drives and practically as soon as he starts driving I see the sign that says Clinic and The Taxi Driver stops by the entrance and I pay and I say that wasn't a long way and he says well a ride is a ride, he says and I get out of the taxi and I'm a little embarrassed, I didn't think we were that close to The Clinic, it was maybe a block away and I took a taxi, which is almost crazy, I think, and I go into The Clinic and now the entrance is empty again and I go over to the reception and the woman there is the same woman as before and I go straight to the window and the woman sitting there recognizes me and she slides the window open and I ask about him, yes, Asle, yes, and she says they transferred him to The Hospital almost immediately, she says, so if I want to see him I have to go to The Hospital, she says and I ask, I don't know quite why, if she's been on duty a long time and she looks at me and smiles a slightly tired smile and says it's been a long shift, yes, because the woman who was supposed to relieve her couldn't come because of a sick child and they didn't find anyone else to substitute and so she said she could stay on duty until they found someone else and the woman who's supposed to relieve her is on her way now, she says, and gosh it'll be good to get some sleep, she needs to go to sleep, and sleep well, when she gets home she's going to sleep, just sleep, she says and I look outside and I see the taxi I came in still parked by the entrance to The Clinic and I say if I hurry I can maybe take the taxi that's there to The Hospital and she says yes it's still there, the taxi, and I say goodbye and she says thank you at the same time and then I hurry outside and open the rear door of the taxi and I ask if it's still available

Yes, sure, The Taxi Driver says

That was a quick visit, he says

Everything's quick with you isn't it, he says

and I ask him to take me to The Hospital, because the man I wanted to see has been transferred there, I say

It must be serious then, The Taxi Driver says

Serious? I say

Yes, the only people who get transferred to The Hospital are the ones in really bad shape, he says

and then I get into the taxi and I think yes, he truly was in bad shape, yes, Asle collapsed several times and I found him lying in the snow, covered in snow, there in The Lane, there in front of number 5, and wasn't that where Silje or Guro or whatever her name was said she lived? or was that number 3, The Lane? yes I think it probably was, and what a strange coincidence, I think, and Asle was shaking so badly, his whole body was shivering, I think and it was so lucky, so lucky that I drove back to Bjørgvin, and actually it's a total mystery why I did it, I think, since I'd already driven to Bjørgvin and back earlier, but this uneasiness or whatever you want to call it just came over me, and if I hadn't found Asle he might still be lying under the snow and shaking, no, no, that's not true, someone else would probably have found him, there are plenty of people in Bjørgvin, someone or another is always out and about, I think and I hear The Taxi Driver say he hopes there's no more snow tonight, but at least the people who're supposed to keep the streets clean have done their job for once, both the main roads and the side streets have been ploughed well, he says, they don't usually get it done so fast, he says and I don't say anything and then The Taxi Driver stops talking too and we start driving and there's not much traffic and the taxi pulls over in front of The Hospital and stops by the entrance and I pay and say thanks for the ride and I go into The Hospital and I see the reception desk and I go over to it and the woman sitting there looks up at me drowsily and I tell her my name and say that I'm here to see Asle and she says we have the same name and she says yes well she'll see where he is and she flips through her papers a little and then she looks me, she looks long and hard at me, and she asks what I said his name was and then she says ah yes Asle yes and then she pages through the pile of papers sitting in front of her

Asle, yes, I say

Asle, that's right, she says

and she turns more pages

Yes your Namesake was admitted, tonight in fact, she says

Can I see him? I say

No, not now, she says

and she looks down and I felt something give a little start

inside me, because his dog, Bragi, his dog can't be left alone, I
have to go get his dog

Is he seriously ill? I say

Yes I should say so, she says

and then she says he was admitted tonight, not long ago,
and that he's seriously ill, yes, she says, and she says that I'm list-
ed as a relative and I say we're old friends but I'm just a friend,
but it was me who brought him to The Clinic, I say

But does he have a family? she says

Yes but he lives alone, I say

and I say that he's divorced, he was married twice, and
that neither of his ex-wives and none of his children live in
Bjørgvin any more, but he has a dog, and his dog is alone in his
apartment, and the dog can't be left alone there and she nods
and says so he's divorced and he has three children

Divorced twice, I say

Three children, I say

and I say that I know he doesn't have much contact with
either ex-wife or any of the children, but still, it's his dog I'm
thinking of, he, the dog, Bragi's his name, can't be left alone in
the apartment, someone has to go get him and take care of him

Someone needs to look after his dog, I say

Of course, she says

Can I have the keys so I can get the dog, walk him, and take
care of him until Asle's able to do it himself? I say

I can't give you the keys to his apartment, she says

and then she says that he has children, and I'm just a friend

But the children don't live in Bjørgvin, I say

The oldest son lives in Oslo and the two others live somewhere in Trøndelag, I say

and I say that he's not in contact with either of his ex-wives
and he's barely in contact with his children, just a little with the

oldest son, The Boy he calls him, but The Boy lives in Oslo, I say and I think there's no way she's going to give me the apartment keys and I think what in the world am I going to do then? will I have to break into his apartment? because the dog, Bragi, can't stay there alone, I think, and now she doesn't want to give me the keys, I think and I see her pick up a telephone and she dials a number and then she says something about seriously ill and someone who's asking about him and he says there's a dog alone in the apartment of the man who was admitted and then she looks at me and asks if there isn't some super or custodian there and I say that there isn't, not that I know of, I say and she nods and then she says into the phone that there isn't a custodian where he lives and that I really want to go look after the dog, and there aren't any close relatives in Bjørgvin who could do it, she says

The dog can't just be left alone, I say

and she listens more and then says thank you, good, yes, she says and then she says that they've taken all his clothes, his sketch-pad, his keys, everything he had with him, and put them in a closet in the room where he is now but someone will go get the keys and then that person will drive me to the apartment and go in with me so I can get the dog, since she can't give me the keys, because the rules are that she can only give the keys to a family member and I'm just a friend

Yes, I'm just a friend, I say

Right, she says

and she sighs and she says I can sit and wait for as long as it takes but it shouldn't take too long, because someone'll get the keys and then take me to the apartment to get the dog, yes, this isn't the first time something like this has happened of course, she says, in fact they have a strict procedure for what to do, she says, and look, here he is already, she says and I see an older

man come walking towards me and he says he'll take me to
pick up the dog, he says

Thanks, I say

and then I say thank you for your help to the woman sitting
at the reception desk and then I go over to the older man and he
doesn't say anything and then we go out and get into a car and
then the older man says that there's been a lot of snow but he's
already brushed the snow off the car, he says, and I can hear that
he's from Bjørgvin and I say yes it certainly was coming down
earlier and he says that this happens sometimes, someone's admitted and they have a pet at home that someone needs to look
after, but they're usually not in a position to tell anyone about
it themselves so then it's some neighbour or another who calls
and complains about a dog yapping and says it's been yapping for
days, that happens a lot, he says, and then a lot of the time it's him
who goes to get the pet, that's part of his job, and he takes the pet
to The Animal Rescue, or sometimes it's a relative or neighbour
or friend or someone who takes care of the pet, like I'm planning
to do, the older man says and he says well, he's a kind of handyman at The Hospital, he says, and I explain to The Handyman
where Asle lives and he says he knows where that is, and that it's
not far, he says and then we sit there in silence and drive on and
The Handyman stops and parks the car in front of the building
where Asle's apartment is, almost exactly where I parked earlier, and then we get out of the car and he unlocks the front door
of the building and I say Asle's apartment is on the second floor
on the left and we go there and we hear the dog yapping and I
say the dog is waiting by the door yapping and yapping and The
Handyman says that's quite a voice on that dog and I say that little dogs, and this is a little dog, I say, often have the loudest voices

Yes and of course they often bite people too, The
Handyman says

Are you scared of dogs? I say

No, he says

and then he turns and then he says that he's a little scared of dogs

It must be, well, it must be because a dog bit me once when I had to go get him, The Handyman says

And they often act very threatening, dogs, when I come to get them, he says

And when I'm alone I wear thick protective gloves, he says and he holds out his hands

I can go in first, I say

If you wouldn't mind, he says

I'll unlock the door and then you open it and go in, he says and then The Handyman stands there and fumbles with the keys and then unlocks the door and I open the door and go in and as soon as I'm in the hall the dog starts jumping up and down at my feet and he's yapping and yapping and I feel around on the wall with my hand and find a switch and I turn on the hall light and I look down at the dog yapping and jumping around at my feet and then I bend down and pick up the dog and I hold him in my arms and I pet him on the back, I pet him and pet him and say good boy, good boy, Bragi, good boy Bragi, I say and the dog calms down and The Handyman comes into the hall behind me and I say I think I know where the leash is and The Handyman says we can't stay in the apartment, we're not allowed to, it's not permitted, we have to just pick up the dog and leave, he says and I say I'll just look for the leash and I know that it's usually on the bureau a little way down the hall and I see the leash sitting there and I see that all the doors are shut, the one to the kitchen, the one to the living room, or the studio, and I say I should have used the bathroom earlier and The Handyman says well I can go ahead and do that,

surely there's nothing wrong with that, he says and I go into the
bathroom and I find the light switch and I turn on the light and
I see that everything is clean, everything smells clean and fresh,
so Asle must have washed the floor and scrubbed the toilet
and the sink, I think and I think no, if he's cleaned everything
so nicely maybe I should hold it in until I get to the room in
The Country Inn, but the dog? I can't just take the dog to The
Country Inn with me? are people allowed to bring dogs to The
Country Inn? I think, and no, I hadn't thought of that, but, yes,
well, the dog can probably sleep in my car, simple as that, and
then tomorrow I'll drive to Dylgja and I'll bring the dog home
with me of course, I think, and it'll be nice to have a dog, actually I've always wanted a dog, but when I was little Mother
didn't want me to get one, and Ales didn't want a dog either,
and after Ales was gone, well, I sort of stopped thinking about
how it might be nice to have a dog, but anyway now I'm going
to have a dog for a while at least, I think, yes, when I wake up
tomorrow morning I'll have a little breakfast, I think, and as I
think that I realize I'm hungry and I see in my mind the generous breakfast buffet at The Country Inn, fresh bread, scrambled
eggs, bacon, some of the bacon is crispy and some of it's still
soft, and I have to admit I'm really looking forward to breakfast
because that ground-beef open-faced sandwich, it was good,
but it wasn't exactly filling

You need to come out now, The Handyman says

Yes, right, I say

The rules are that we have to just pick up the house pet and
not stay any longer in the home than we need to, he says

and I say I'm coming, and I turn out the bathroom light
and go out into the hall and I see The Handyman standing in
the front doorway and he's holding the door handle and I think
now I want to look in the main room and I open the door to

that room

No, we need to leave now, The Handyman says

I just thought I should make sure everything's all right, I say

Yes, okay, he says

and I turn on the light and I see that everything's where it belongs, everything's in its place, and pictures are stacked in neat piles, all with their homemade stretchers facing out so that you can't see a single painting, and the brushes and tubes of paint and everything are in their proper places on the table, and a roll of canvas is propped in a corner and there's wood for stretchers in another corner and I hear The Handyman ask if everything's all right in there and I say yes everything's fine, everything's where it should be and he says in that case we need to leave and I say yes all right and turn out the light and shut the door to the living room or studio or whatever it should be called and The Handyman says all right come on then and I think it's horrible how he's fussing about all this and I say I need to just look in the kitchen too, and he says yes, yes, that's probably fine, yes the rules allow for that too now that he comes to think of it, they say a person can look around to make sure everything's in order, that the lights are off, that the burners aren't on, things like that, yes, but he usually doesn't do all that because the most important thing is just to do what you need to do and get out, do it and leave right away, for example get the dog, or the cat, if necessary, and other than that, yes, well, it's the family, the relatives, who should take care of the rest, he says and I say yes yes

But hurry up, The Handyman says

Yes yes, I say

and I open the door to the kitchen and feel my way over to the light switch and turn on the light and of course, yes I think of course, yes, obviously everything here too is as it should be, everything's where it belongs, there's a glass in the sink and a bottle with a little still water in it on the table, there's not a crumb anywhere, and it's almost creepy how neat Asle kept everything, I think, and I don't know why that should be sort of creepy

Now we need to go, The Handyman says

Yes yes, I say

and I turn off the kitchen light and I shut the door and then I pick the leash up off the bureau with one hand while I hold the dog with the other and then I go towards the doorway where The Handyman is standing and he steps aside and I turn off the hall light and he shuts the door and then I stand there with the dog in my arms and I see The Handyman lock the door and then I start down the stairs and I hear The Handyman checking to feel if the door is locked and checking it again and I go to the front door of the building and once we're outside I put the dog down and the second I put him down in the snow he jumps a little to the side and raises his leg and I see him make a yellow hole of piss in the white snow, it's not so nice to look at, and then the dog starts hopping and dancing around in the fine white loose snow and I kick some snow over the yellow piss and everything's white and pretty again and the dog jumps around and around in the snow, burows his muzzle into the snow, rolls around, yes, it's like the dog is taking a bath in the snow and then I hear The Handyman say well then that takes care of that, he says, and he asks me where he should take me now and I say I'm staying at The Country Inn and he asks if guests are allowed to bring dogs into the rooms there and I say I don't know and he asks what I plan to do with the dog if I can't bring him up to the room and I say in that case he can sleep in my car

Yes I suppose he could always do that, The Handyman says

and then we stand there and look at the dog skipping and

jumping around in the snow

Did you know him well? The Handyman says then

Did I? I say

Yes, right, do you, he says

Yes, I say

He's a good friend? he says

Yes, I say

Just a friend? he says

Yes, just a friend, I say

Just a friend, okay, he repeats

and then The Handyman says we should go and I say I'm sure the dog needs to go, and I watch the dog hunch up, with his rear end sort of sticking up over the snow and his tail in the air, and he takes a good long shit

That wasn't nothing, The Handyman says

He really needed to go, didn't he, I say

and The Handyman nods and the dog is finished and then The Handyman asks shouldn't I pick up the shit and I ask him if he has a bag to pick it up with and he says he doesn't and I say I don't either and so I kick some snow, powdery white snow, over the dogshit

Yes it's sure been snowing, The Handyman says

It's not often it snows in Bjørgvin, he says

No, I say

Pretty unusual actually, he says

But it's nice with the new snow, he says

Nice and white, he says

Yes, I say

and then we stand there and look blankly at all the whiteness and neither of us says anything

Even when it's dark out, it glows when there's new white snow, The Handyman says

It's a little like daytime even though it's night, he says

Yes it is nice, I say

But in Bjørgvin the snow never stays long, he says

No, it'll get rained away soon, I say

and The Handyman asks where I live and I say I live in Dylgja

Is it the same there? he says

Yes, yes, one day it snows and the next day it rains, I say

It turns into dirty snow and slush, I say

Right, The Handyman says

Not to mention when it turns icy, he says

Right, the first thing that happens is it ices over, I say

and then we start walking towards his car and I call Bragi and then the dog comes jumping towards me

So the dog's name is Bragi, The Handyman says

Yes, I say

Bragi, right, he says

Yes, Bragi's his name, I say

Tomorrow it'll rain again, The Handyman says

Yes, yes, it will, I say

That's how it always is, he says

There's never a real winter in Bjørgvin, there's maybe two days a year when it's really winter and that's it, he says

That's how it is, he says

Have you ever lived in Bjørgvin? he says

Yes, well, I say

Many years ago, I say

Did you work in Bjørgvin? he says

I went to school here, I say

and I think that The Handyman is so inquisitive he's prob-ably going to ask what kind of school I went to, but if he does I'll just say something to make him think it was just a normal school, I think, but he doesn't ask me anything else and we get to his car and he unlocks it and the dog shakes, shakes the snow off, and I stamp my feet and kick my shoes against each other, to get the snow off, and then I pick up the dog and brush snow off him

You like dogs? The Handyman says

Yes, don't you? I say

No, he says

Because one of them bit you? I say

Probably, he says

But I never did like them really, he says

I like cats though, he says

Me too, I say

I like dogs and cats both, I say

But you like dogs the best? he asks

Well I think more about getting a dog, at least, I say

You want a dog? The Handyman says

Yes, I say

and there's silence

But it's a big responsibility too, having a dog, I say

and it's silent again and we get into the car, and I sit with the dog on my lap and The Handyman asks me where I want him to take me, to The Country Inn, right? he says and I say he can take me to a place near The Lane and he asks if that's near where I parked my car and I say yes it is, so he can drop me off there, but I don't want to tell him where I parked my car because then he'll start asking me if I know Beyer, if I know rich people in Bjørgvin, the high society, or maybe I'm an artist, or maybe an art collector, he'll start asking things like that and he says yes all right and I don't say anything, but no way will I tell him where I parked my car, but I'm lucky to have a regular place to park, it can be really hard to find somewhere to park in Bjørgvin, lots of times the parking space is too small and too narrow for a large car to fit, people always say the spots are itsy-bitsy, I wonder why, you never hear anything called itsy, whatever that is, or bitsy either, whatever that is

I can do that, The Handyman says

Do what? I ask

Drop you near The Lane, he says

Great, I say

and then he starts the car and drives and we sit there in silence and then it starts snowing again a little, one snowflake after another falls down through the air and The Handyman turns on the windshield wipers and then he turns them off again, and again snowflakes land on the windshield one by one and he turns the wipers on again

It's pretty with the new snow, The Handyman says

and then we sit there not saying anything, me with the dog in my lap, and Bragi is lying there totally peacefully and it's nice to feel his warmth, I think and I pet his back again and again and the warmth from the dog does me good, it's good to feel his fur, I think and it snows and snows and the windshield wipers go back and forth, back and forth, and I see The Beyer Gallery and The Handyman says maybe he can stop here and I say that's fine and he stops and he asks a little uncertainly if this is where I wanted to be dropped off and I say yes great thanks and then I ask if I should pay for the ride and The Handyman says I shouldn't and then he says good night and I say yes good night and then I get out and I shut the car door behind me and then I stand there with the dog in my arms and it's snowing and snowing and I see The Handyman turn the car and drive away down the same street he drove here on, and I think now I should just go over to my car and put the dog in the car and then go on foot to The Country Inn, I'm sure I know the way from The Beyer Gallery to The Country Inn, I've learned how to get there, of course I can do that, that was where I was going when I found Asle lying in The Lane, covered with snow, I think, yes, if I can't even manage this then I shouldn't be living alone, I think and I see my car parked outside The Beyer Gallery, covered in snow, and as more snow keeps coming down I go over to it and I think I can't leave the dog in the car, it's suddenly turned wintry, and maybe he's never slept alone in a car before? maybe he'll be scared and spend the whole night yapping or howling and the neighbours will come complain to Beyer and then maybe he won't want anything more to do with me because of it? and what'll I do then? where will I show my paintings then? how will I make enough money to live on? I think, and it's cold out, the dog might be cold, so no, it was not a good idea to think the dog could sleep in the car, but then what can I do with him? I could always drive back to Dylgja now, but I'm so tired, so tired, so it wouldn't be safe to drive back there tonight, but maybe I can keep the dog with me at The Country Inn? maybe he can sleep in my room? I've never had a dog with me there before, and never seen anyone else with one, so bringing your dog probably isn't allowed, but maybe you can? I can ask in any case, I think, and I tie the leash on him and put him down on the ground and then we start walking across High Street and there's so much snow on the ground that the dog's head just barely sticks out above the snow on the pavement, it's a small dog, but he easily pushes his way through the loose powdery snow, with his snout in the air, and I march ahead, and then we start walking down The Lane and I think that's lucky, it may be snowing hard but it's not far to The Country Inn, I think, and now I need to go straight to The Country Inn because I'm tired, so tired I feel like I might collapse too, I think, and it's snowing and snowing, it's not a flurry any more it's really snowing, with a wind too, you might say it's practically a snowstorm, I think and I think that with all the snow coming down being blown by the wind it's hard to see where you are, but I've walked from The Lane to The Country Inn so many times that I could find my way to The Country Inn even if it were pitch black and impossible to see anything, I think, so if it's snowing too hard to see anything that doesn't matter, because it's not far now, we're almost there, I think and I walk and I look at the dog ploughing through the snow and it looks like he's getting a bit tired too, he's puffing and panting hard, since he is just a small dog, and getting on in years, so I stop and pick the dog up and then keep walking with the dog in my arms and I'm not thinking anything and it's snowing and snowing and there's no one in sight and it's snowing and snow-ing, but it's not far to The Country Inn, you just take the first right at the end of The Lane, and I've done that, then you get to an intersection and go down that street, and I've done that, but I don't see it anywhere, The Country Inn with The Coffeehouse on the ground floor, so did I go too far? maybe I walked past the first intersection, which I should've gone down? I think, it feels like I went too far since it's really not far from The Lane to The Country Inn, but I can't have gone the wrong way, can I? it's impossible, it's unbelievable! I've walked from The Lane to The Country Inn so many times, I don't even know how many times, you just walk down The Lane and take a right and go down the first street you get to and you can see The Country Inn down on The Wharf, and I took a left and crossed and went down a street but I can't see The Country Inn, and I've never had to walk this far, I don't think, so I must have gone the wrong way somehow, since I couldn't see where I was going because it was snowing so much, I think and I stop and I try to figure out where I am, but damned if I know, I can't remember ever being on this street before, there is nothing about it I recognize, to the extent that I can see anything at all in this blizzard, but it's just unbelievable that I couldn't manage to get from The Lane to The Country Inn, I did the same thing I've always done, walked the same way I've always walked, or did I do something different? I haven't seen The Country Inn today since it started snowing, have I? but, no, I must have gone the wrong way, so I just need to turn around and go back the same way I came, I think, and I start going back along the same street, and now I'll be at The Country Inn any minute, I think, and I keep walking with Bragi in my arms and it's snowing and snowing and the wind is blowing, that too, yes, it's a real snowstorm now, I think and I think now I better run into someone soon so I can ask them the way to The Country Inn, I think, or else if a taxi drives by I can hail it and take the taxi to The Country Inn, yes, it doesn't matter how short the ride is, I think and I keep walking and I think anyway I'm sure to run across someone soon, I think, or else a taxi is sure to come driving by, but there's no one in sight, no people and no cars, it's snowing so much that people are probably staying indoors and that's why there are no taxis either, I think, but I just have to run across someone or other soon, or a taxi, because I need to get to The Country Inn, on foot or by car, and get a room there, because there's surely a room free at The Country Inn, and some of the people working at the reception there have worked there for so many years and they'll recognize me, and that's also partly why I always stay at The Country Inn, yes, it feels a little bit like coming home when I arrive there, a little like that, I think and I should have gone straight to The Country Inn, but I seem to have gone the wrong way somehow, I think and I'm really tired, anyway I'm definitely too tired to drive home to Dylgja, because even if I like driving

it would be totally reckless to drive now, and I'm a careful driver, at least I try to be, and driving while I'm exhausted is not a
good idea, after having driven a car for many years I know that
you have to be alert, to pay attention, that might be the most
important thing, you have to realize that something unexpected
can happen at any moment, and be prepared for it, yes, you
need to be able to see the future so to speak, since deer can suddenly appear in front of your car, in a flash a deer leaps out onto
the road, and in the dark too usually, or at dusk, or dawn,
something unexpected can always happen, yes, and often does
happen too, I think, you have to know if a car is coming around
a bend and know if it's going to stay on its side of the road, and
if it doesn't you need to be prepared for that, maybe even slow
down to almost a stop and wait for the car to come around the
turn, and the roads that go from Instefjord and to Dylgja, or
from in on Sygnefjord out towards Sygne Sea, I bet one of
them is the most narrow and winding road in all of Norway,
because I've driven a lot in Norway, yes, when Ales was alive
we drove all over the Nordic countries, Sweden and Denmark
too, and Iceland, and the Faroe Islands, and Finland, but I don't
think I've ever driven roads like these anywhere, so narrow,
with so many sharp turns, and when the weather's bad too, as
it often is of course, yes, after a heavy rain that leads to flooding,
rain that comes off the cliffsides and steep hills and floods the
roads, yes, then there're holes in the road it can be real trouble
to drive over, otherwise I like driving, to tell the truth there's
not much that makes me happy any more but driving makes me
happy, I think as I push ahead through the snow on the pavement, with Asle's dog Bragi in my arms, at my breast, and I
think about how lots of times while driving the roads between
Instefjord and Dylgja just for the fun of it I've thought that a car
is just about to come around a bend or else that there's no car,

like I was seeing the future, and every single time my predic-
tion was right, when I thought a car was coming a car came and
when I thought no car was coming no car came, I've tested it
so many times that it got kind of boring since I was right every
single time, or maybe I was wrong once or twice but I was right
so often that eventually testing my predictions was no fun and
I stopped doing it, but obviously I know that being able to predict things is very important for driving safely, and I'm good at
driving safely, but not at finding my way, especially in cities,
but in general, finding the right way to walk or drive when I'm
somewhere unfamiliar is something I'm terrible at, I always
walk or drive the wrong way, it's just as inevitable as my being
able to predict whether or not a car is going to come around a
bend, and now isn't that strange? mysterious? I think, and I
think that even after living in Bjørgvin for several years I didn't
know the city any better, and still couldn't find my way around,
no, I'm almost always wrong but not quite always, I think and
that's why I always go down the same streets and alleys again
and again, I've found my paths through the city so to speak, for
example from where I park my car in front of The Beyer
Gallery, across High Street, down The Lane, and from there to
The Alehouse, or The Country Inn, I think, so I can't have
walked completely the wrong way, I must have made a little
mistake, and if only someone would walk by I could ask them
the way, there has to be someone or another out walking, even
at night, that I could ask? but I don't see anyone and anyway it's
a good thing I'm in a city at least and not out in the middle of
the mountains, not to mention at sea, I think, yes, yes, I think,
today I need to figure it out myself since there's no one anywhere in sight and no taxi either, because what usually happens
is that I run into someone who shows me the way or I hail a
taxi and it takes me where I'm going, that's how it usually

works, I get lost, go in the totally wrong direction, away from where I'm trying to go, I stop people on the street and ask them to tell me how to get where I'm going, and people are nice and helpful and they point and tell me where I should go, go there and then there, but then I get lost again anyway, so I have to ask the next person I meet, it's pretty much the same as it was with numbers when I was going to school, it turned out wrong no matter what I did or didn't do, it came out wrong anyway, and I'm still like that with numbers, it's almost like not being able to do maths and not being able to find my way are related, but they can't be, can they? because a sense of direction and mathematical aptitude are very different, aren't they? but the one thing I know for sure is that I have neither, I have no sense of direction and no mathematical aptitude, yes I think that's the term the The Schoolmaster used, you have no mathematical aptitude, he said, something like that, mathematical aptitude, it was probably a term that The Schoolmaster had come up with himself, mathematical aptitude, but sense of direction is a nor- mal term and I don't have that either, obviously, because now I've already been walking for a long time, much longer than it should take to get from where the car is parked in front of The Beyer Gallery to The Country Inn, that's for sure, for all I know I've been walking in circles and I'm about to be right back at The Beyer Gallery, that would be the best case, actually, and it must be because it's snowing so hard, yes, it's a real bliz- zard, and it's hard to see, and I walked the wrong way, there can't be any other explanation since I've walked this way so many times before, but I've really managed to get lost today, I've been walking so long now, much longer than it usually takes to walk from The Beyer Gallery to The Country Inn, but maybe I can put the dog down and he'll go back to The Beyer Gallery and I can follow him? he might, maybe he can smell the

way we took? I think and I put Bragi down and he just stands
there and looks up at me with his dog eyes and then I shake the
leash a little and I say go Bragi, walk, and then the dog starts
walking and he goes the opposite way from how we were
walking, he goes back and I follow him, because I can't think
of any other way to find out where we're supposed to go, I
think, so I just trust that the dog will go back to The Beyer
Gallery, I think, because anyway we're nowhere near The
Country Inn, that's for sure, I think, but that doesn't mean, as
far as I can tell, that we're getting closer to The Beyer Gallery,
there's nothing I recognize about the buildings I can glimpse
through the snow coming down so hard, but at least the wind
has let up a little so now it's just a heavy snowfall, not a blizzard,
I think, and even though I've been walking for a long time, at
least that's how it feels, I haven't passed a single other person
and I've only seen a couple of cars drive by, no taxis, and if only
a taxi would drive by I could hail it, I think, and what a fool I
was not to have The Handyman drive me to The Country Inn,
why did I ask him to drive me to The Lane? what kind of idea
was that? was it because I didn't want him to know that I was
going to stay at The Country Inn? I think, but I'd already told
him I was going to stay there, I think, yes, I had, but for some
reason or another I asked The Handyman to take me to The
Lane, I think, following the dog, and if the dog is heading
somewhere then it must probably be back to The Beyer Gallery,
right? I think, because he probably can't smell a path anywhere
else? I think, but it's terrible to watch the dog pushing his way
through the snow on the pavement, with his snout up, he's
puffing and wheezing, and I walk along behind him and he's
going uphill and it's pretty steep and I think now surely someone has to turn up soon and I can ask them the way? or a taxi I
can hail will turn up? I'm in Bjørgvin after all, despite everything,

Norway's second biggest city, I think, but it's not an easy city to find your way around, that must be said, and now where am I? no, I have no sense at all of where we are, but anyway I don't think we're heading towards The Beyer Gallery, I think, and then I think that if I just go downhill towards the sea I'll be able to find The Country Inn, because it's on the water, along The Bay, I think, it's even on The Wharf, yes, but now what direction should I go in to get to the water? I think, because now I'm following the dog uphill, but that was a bad idea, I think, because to get to the sea we need to go downhill, so now I'll turn around and go back downhill, despite everything, that must be better than wandering around after a dog uselessly hoping that he's heading back to The Beyer Gallery, I think, because we have to go in one direction or another and if we go downhill we'll eventually get to the water somewhere, I think, and I shake the leash and the dog stops and then I start walking in the opposite direction, downhill, and now I'm walking in the footprints the dog and I have made in the snow, and with the dog at my heels, but it's still snowing and it must be tiring for the dog walking there with his snout in in the cold winter air to keep it above the snow, and I look at the dog and then Bragi walks past me and he keeps going, you have to give him that, Bragi, yes, and now the snow isn't falling so hard and there, there's someone walking towards me, thank goodness, there is finally someone here and I go over to the person walking a little to one side and I say excuse me, excuse me, but I'm from the country and I think I've managed to get lost in the city and a woman looks back at me from under a thick white knit cap covered with snow and she asks me where I'm trying to get to and there's something familiar about her voice and I say I'm going to The Country Inn, the hotel, The Country Inn, yes, I say and she says yes well in that case I'm going in the

exact wrong direction, she says and she laughs and then I see
that it's the woman who was sitting alone at a table at Food and
Drink, who recognized me, and I sort of recognized her too in
a way, yes, it's definitely her, the woman called Guro, or maybe
Silje? and she was sitting drinking wine at Food and Drink the
whole time until now, yes, she must be really drunk by now, I
think and I say I thought I should go downhill because The
Country Inn is on the water, and if I just get to the water I'd
find my way to The Country Inn, I say and she says yes, I might
think that, sure, but it's really not the right way, for all she
knows I could have ended up in Denmark Square as easily as
The Country Inn, she says and it's not easy to go along the water either, it's not so simple, there are too many places where
you can't follow the edge of the water, she says, well anyway,
she says, it wasn't so easy for her to find her way around
Bjørgvin either when she first lived here, it took quite a long
time before she was sure she knew where she was going, but
now, after so many years in Bjørgvin, yes, now it's easy, she
can't claim to know every last nook and cranny, every last itsy-bitsy lane and alley, but still she at least knows what direction
to go in to get to this or that place, and I, yes, I ought to know
better, because I used to lived in Bjørgvin for many years myself, even if it was a long time ago, she says, but anyway I'm not
heading towards The Country Inn now, that's for sure, it's
down on The Wharf and I'm walking in the exact opposite direction, so I should go with her, she's going the same way, she
says, because she's going home, and as I know perfectly well she
lives at 5, The Lane, near The Country Inn, she says and I think
now that's strange, running into Guro or whatever her name is
now, the same woman as was sitting at Food and Drink when I
was there, and I thank her, I say thank you very much and then
I start walking downhill again, walking next to her

You do remember that my name is Guro? she says

and she gives a little laugh and I say yes and we walk downhill and the woman named Guro says it sure came down
suddenly, and so much snow, now we're slogging through it
and no one's shovelled and no one's ploughed a path through
the snow, and what about the dog, it must be really hard for
him to walk? she says, and I pick Bragi up again at once and
brush the snow off him and she says I didn't have a dog with
me at Food and Drink and she asks if I had him tied up outside
Food and Drink, and now is that something to ask a person? I
think, and I won't answer, why would she ask something like
that? I think and then she asks me why I've come to Bjørgvin
and I say that a friend was sick so I wanted to check up on him,
and it was a good thing I drove down because he was in really
bad shape, so I took him to The Clinic and they admitted him,
transferred him to The Hospital in fact, I say, and she says that
in that case I definitely did a good deed, she says, and I have
nothing to say to that and she says so I still live in Dylgja? and I
nod and she says she actually knows that already, since she
knows me, she says and then she says that she can hear in my
voice that I'm originally from Hardanger, yes, even if she didn't
already know I'm from Hardanger she could hear it, she says
and I say yes, she's right about that, I grew up there, in
Hardanger, I say, in Barmen, on a small farm there, an orchard,
I say and she says yes she knows that, I've told her all that, don't
I remember anything? she says, but I was probably too drunk to
remember anything, one time, long ago, I told her that I was
from that region, that I grew up on an orchard in Hardanger,
she says and I say yes that's true that was where I grew up, but
then I lived in Bjørgvin and now I've lived for many years in
Dylgja, I say and she says if I lived in Bjørgvin so long I should
know my way around the city, and I say she's right, she's totally

right, but it's been many years since I lived in Bjørgvin, and when I did live here I didn't walk around the city much, I went to The Art School, in a course of study they called Painting, but I never graduated from The Art School, I say, and she says no then I wasn't here all that long, she says and she says that she knows all that, I've told her that already, I'm an artist, yes, she says and I say yes I guess I am in a way and she says that even if she wouldn't call herself an artist she's good with her hands, she likes doing crafts, in fact that's what she lives on, she's sewn countless tablecloths, big and small, and table runners, short and long, in Hardanger embroidery, she says, and she learned how to make Hardanger embroidery from her Grandmother, so she works firmly in the tradition, she says, and she makes bodices for the national folk costume too, decorative bodices, and she learned that from her Grandmother too, yes, she's lost count of how many bodices she's sewn, but it's a lot, because it seems like everyone wants national folk costumes nowadays, and there can't be many people left who still do Hardanger embroidery and decorative bodices, she says, and so she supplies The Craft Centre and that's how she makes a living, she says, and she ended up in Bjørgvin by chance more than anything, but once she finished school she worked in a shop called Hardanger Regional Products and she worked there until it went out of business and then she just stayed on in Bjørgvin, she'd lived in other places but she's been here for years now, yes, she's lost count of how many, she rents an apartment not far from The Country Inn, at 5, The Lane, on the ground floor, she says, as I know perfectly well, she adds, and today she went to Food and Drink to get a glass of wine before going to a girlfriend's house, but if she'd known winter was coming so suddenly, that the snow would come so suddenly, she would have just stayed home, she says and I think that she likes to talk and talk and I can't take in any more, I think and I think that she wasn't at any friend's house, she just sat at Food and Drink drinking more red wine, because she's very drunk, I think, but maybe she drank red wine at her girlfriend's house? I think, and she says again that she was going to a girlfriend's house and she thought she should have a glass of red wine before she went to her friend's place, she says, so she went into Food and Drink, and I was tempted to drop in there too, while she was there, she says and I think yes, yes, she could have stopped in Food and Drink first and then gone to her girlfriend's house and kept drinking red wine there, I think, yes, and whether it's true or not she does know how to get to The Country Inn, I think and then I say I hope there's a room free at The Country Inn, and she asks didn't I reserve a room already and I say no, I usually do but this trip came up kind of suddenly and I say I often stay at The Country Inn and some of the people who work at the reception have been there for ages and I know them and they know me, some of them, not all, because in the past few years there've been a lot of new people working at the reception, it seems like people have only just started when they're gone again, I say and she says yes, I know, there are so many hotels and other places to spend the night in Bjørgvin, and new ones keep opening up, so whatever happens I'll be able to find a roof over my head, she says, and if for some crazy reason it's full everywhere then I can always spend the night at her place, she says, she'd never refuse to put up someone from the country who's in Bjørgvin and needs a roof over his head for the night, and especially someone who's even slept in her apartment several times before, yes, in her bed even, she says and I don't understand what she's talking about, she must just be chattering away, I've supposedly slept in her bed? I think and I say thank you, thank you, thanks very much, but I don't like intruding on people, I'm shy that way, I say, and I'd rather just stay at The Country Inn as long as there's room there, I say and she says I can do whatever I want, but if The Country Inn is full then, yes, I can always spend the night at her apartment, because she's even slept with me in the same bed at The Country Inn, after all, she says, yes she remembers it well, even if it was a long time ago back when I had medium-length brown hair worn loose not like my grey hair now tied back with a black hairband, she says and I don't understand what she's talking about and she says in this weather it'll be a real pain to go from hotel to hotel looking for a room, even if there are lots of hotels next door to one another on The Wharf, she says and I say again that there's usually always room for me at The Country Inn and she says yes there are rooms free there most of the time but sometimes there are various events in Bjørgvin, classes, conferences, conventions, even gatherings of fiddlers, she doesn't know, but she does know that it might be full at The Country Inn, she says and she starts going on about a confirmation or was it a wedding or maybe a funeral or whatever it was when she tried to reserve a room at The Country Inn for some people who were coming to Bjørgvin and there were no rooms to be had at The Country Inn and I don't answer and then we start walking uphill and before long we've reached The Hill, where The University is in Bjørgvin, I think, and that place, even the name, has always, well, not in- timidated me but filled me with a kind of respect, yes, even awe, and I don't know why, but a university, a place where people read and think and write day and night, and have con- versations, and know all about all kinds of different subjects, yes, I'd have to say I admire a place like that, and the people who work there, I think and my Ales studied there too, she studied art history and specialized in icons, I think and when I was going to The Art School it was someone from The

University in Bjørgvin who gave art history lectures, Christie was his name, a professor from The University, and those lectures might have been what I got the most out of during the years I went to The Art School, yes, more than anything else, to be told about the history of painting from the earliest times to the present, because Professor Christie talked and explained and showed slides, he had slides of drawings and paintings and sculptures from every country and every period, and he talked and talked, and it was absolutely overwhelming all the things he showed us and told us, every work of art was a masterpiece, one after another, to tell the truth, and if I hadn't understood it before I learned then how little I myself had to work with, but not nothing, I had something too, something all my own, because there was something in my pictures that wasn't in any other picture I was shown, I saw that, and even if it wasn't all that much it was something, I could do something, I knew something, I saw something that you couldn't see in anything Professor Christie showed us, something different, with its own light in it, but was that good enough? could someone be an artist and consider himself an artist just because he had something all his own in the pictures he painted? doesn't a person need more than that? yes, that's how I used to think and I started doubting I could paint pictures that were worth anything, maybe I should just give it up, I was just barely what you could call an artist, I knew that, and I had something that no one else had but it was probably too little, so maybe I should just, yes, well, what else should I do? was there anything else I was good at? was there anything else I had a talent for? anything else I had a gift for, as they say? no, what would happen? and was there anything I wanted to do besides paint pictures? I thought, walking along next to this woman apparently named Guro who I've apparently slept with, yes, even slept with at The Country Inn, no, there's no end to what she's making me listen to, I think and I pet the dog's back over and over and he's nice and warm against my chest and then the woman who I think is named Guro says it's not far now, we're getting close, even if it's slow, since it's hard to walk in all this snow, more like trudge really, she says and I think that I gradually came to understand more and more clearly that the pictures that meant the most to me, and the artists I felt closest to, were the ones who most clearly had their own pictures, or however you'd say it, the pictures they'd paint again and again, but their pictures were never similar, no, not that, never, they were always different, but every picture resembled one another too, and they were like a picture that's never been painted, that no one could paint, that was always invisible behind or in the picture that had been painted, and that's why the picture that had been painted was always like the invisible picture, and this picture was in every single one of the individual paintings, I think, and for me there was never any doubt about which paintings mattered, it was oil on canvas, no more no less, nothing else, because sculpture and drawing and prints of various kinds in various techniques can be as beautiful as they want, sure, but for me only oil on canvas matters, and I truly cannot stand acrylic paint, and of course I could draw, and I drew a lot in the years when I was at The Art School, they said it was important to be able to draw, but after I was set free from The Art School, yes, I have to admit that's how I think about it sometimes, so after I was released I rarely or never drew, in the strict sense, but now and then I do scribble a sketch, scribble down a design for a picture, even if it most often looks nothing like the picture I paint later, it's more like it points towards it, or just suggests it, gives you an idea of it, and maybe that's why I always keep a sketch-pad and pencil with me in the shoulderbag I always have with me, I think and

I hear the woman who I think is named Guro ask me, just like everyone else, if I can live off my art, off my pictures, my paintings, and I've been asked this question so many times by now that I don't want to answer it any more and I don't understand how she, of all people, someone who makes a living sewing tablecloths and table runners in Hardanger embroidery and decorative bodices, can ask that and I just say yes well

Yes well you know, she says

That's not the worst thing, she says

You need to be a good painter to do that, she says

Well anyway I already know you are, she says

and she gives a little laugh and she's about to say more but I sort of quickly say painting pictures is what I can do in life, more than anything else at least, I say

Still, she says

And there are people who want to buy your pictures too? she says

Yes, there are, I say

and she says she knows that of course, that people buy my pictures, because she, yes, I didn't know that, but she goes to my shows, and she herself has often wanted to buy a picture, she really admires my pictures, but of course there are some pictures she likes more than others, she says

It's like pictures talk, the same as people, she says

A kind of silent language comes out of a good picture, she says

Yes, it's hard to explain, but a really good picture says something all its own, something you can understand but that can never be said in words, she says

and I say she's exactly right, that's how I think about it too, I say, and she says she's never been able to afford to buy a picture I've painted, and besides, yes, well, now that she thinks

about it, she says, the way I support myself is probably not all
that different from how she supports herself, not really, she just
sits and sews this Hardanger embroidery of hers, these decorative bodices, and that's how she makes a living, well a kind
of living at least, more or less, yes, she's been doing it since
she was a girl, yes, since she was sitting in her Grandmother's
lap, she says, yes, because even back when she was sitting in
her Grandmother's lap she was watching how she was doing
what she was doing, how she was sewing, yes, following along
with her eyes while her Grandmother did it, and when she was
older her Grandmother taught her everything she knew about
Hardanger embroidery, and how to sew bodices, and then she
started doing it herself, yes, when she was still a girl, and she's
kept doing it ever since, to this day, and during all those years
she's sold what she made to The Craft Centre, when she felt she
had sewn enough she went to The Craft Centre with what she
had, and she was paid well, cash on delivery, so that was nice,
but especially after her husband left, yes well she calls him that
even though they weren't actually married, and she says that he
left, yes, he just disappeared even though it was actually more
like she threw him out, and she's really regretted that

It was so stupid to do that, she says

and she says it's painful to talk about it, because he was a
good man, or had been one, she doesn't like big words and
doesn't use them much but still she can say that they loved each
other, but, yes, she says and she stops and we keep walking in
the snow, trudging ahead, because it's still snowing, but less
now, it's more like individual snowflakes, and I keep petting
and petting the dog's back and I'm holding him pressed to my
chest and then she says she's never heard anyone play the fiddle like he did, never, and when they lived together she always
called him The Fiddler, just that, are you coming, Fiddler? it's

time to eat, is The Fiddler hungry? and he was such a talented Hardanger fiddler, and he won lots of national contests, first place, yes he sure could play, but, but, she says, but then there was all that drinking, she says and she stops and then she says that in the end she couldn't take it any more, his drinking, his overdoing it, she threw him out, because it was her apartment, the apartment on The Lane that she'd rented for all these years, and she said she'd been supporting him for a long time, and he should at least pay for his booze himself, even though he actually did she said it anyway, she says, yes, she said one nasty thing after another to him, that she'd had enough, that she wanted him to leave, and then he did leave, The Fiddler, and he wasn't slow to do it either, he just took his fiddle and headed out over the mountains to the east, and there, yes, no, she shouldn't talk about it, but he was from East Norway, so then, well, I probably know what she means, the fiddle had disappeared and the rest too, yes, and he was sleeping away from home a lot, she'd heard it not from him but from other people, yes, I know what she means, she says, and so it was probably some woman or another somewhere in the east, in Telemark, who took pity on him and took him in, let him stay with her, she probably owned a house or some other place to live, and then she's sure he stayed living there for some years and then he died, and he surely drank to the very end, but he was a good man, he was, and she missed him, yes, she really did, every day she missed him, not a day went by without her missing him, she said, and she's often thought it was so stupid to do that, to tell him to leave, she's so often regretted it, yes, she's so often sat and cried over her own stupidity, she says, because he'd never just taken his fiddle and left before so she started to miss him, and that was how she'd felt every day since that terrible day when he skipped out, she says, because she hadn't meant what she said, even though it was true, but she did ask him to leave and then he just looked at her and as drunk as he was he didn't say anything, because in some ways he was never drunk, not in the usual way, just in his own way, he played the fiddle the way only he could play, even when he was totally drunk in his own way, at least he didn't get drunk the way other people did, he was sober from drinking in a way, yes, he wasn't like anyone else, and she had no idea how he got his booze, and how he paid for it, no, but somehow or another he always managed to, and it's probably always like that with people who need to drink, with real drinkers, she says

Will you still be with me when I'm dead? she says

and she looks at me and I feel something give a little start inside me

That's what he used to say to me, she says

Imagine saying that to someone, she says

and she says that he said that exact thing to her so many times, yes, when he'd been drinking, or at least in the last few years he'd said it a lot, because then he was almost never totally sober, she says and she laughs and she says that he played best when he'd drunk a little, but not too much, when he drank too much it was ruined and got confused, yes, one time he was so drunk that he got up and left the stage in the middle of his set and said no, it's no good, and then walked off the stage, or more like staggered off, she was there, she saw it with her own eyes, she says

Right in the middle of a tune he got up and left the stage, she says

It's no good, he said, and then he left, she says

and she says that it's probably partly, at least before he was, well, an alcoholic, you'd probably have to call him that, it's probably partly because he was shy that he drank, yes, it was from shyness, and then also his moodiness and sadness, but it worked out fine for many years, yes, that's the truth, believe it or not, everything was balanced in its way, he earned some money from his playing, gradually more and more, he played at weddings the way fiddlers have always done, and then it got to where he would play almost every week at dances in Gimle, one gig or another would always turn up, but he drank, he was drinking the whole time, and it wasn't too much, at least not until the drinking totally took over and there were lots of times when he wasn't in any shape to actually play and his playing was nothing but a big mess of notes and screeches, yes, you know how people always say the Hardanger fiddle sounds like a cat screeching, now how can people who consider themselves fine upstanding Bjørgvin women bring themselves to say things like that, they know so little, these fine women, they understand so little, she says, yes to tell the truth she regrets with all her heart that she told him to leave, how stupid was that, she says again, because as long as he drank she never had that much trouble with him, he was always nice, and they used to have a drop or two together too, lots of times, because she liked a little something to drink too, it wasn't that, she was no teetotaler, I knew that, I saw her with a glass of red wine in her hands today, she says, and the best moments she can remember, yes, the best moments in her whole life were while she was sitting and drinking red wine and he was playing, it was the most beautiful thing she's ever heard in her life, it almost makes her cry just thinking about it, just hearing his tunes in her mind, she can't think about it any more, she says, because in the end the drinking totally took over, but he was a good man, yes, even then, truly, and we shouldn't speak ill of the dead, she says, anyway, yes, the first time she saw him it was at a competition, it was the first music contest she'd ever been to and he was sitting at the front of the stage and playing like an ordinary fiddler but then he played his way farther and farther into the music and sort of moved away from himself and from the others and it was like both he and the music and everyone listening rose up into the air and then he turned around on his stool and played with his back to the concert hall, his back to everyone listening, and everything kept swinging through the air, it was exactly as if the music he was playing just flew up and sort of disappeared into the air and into nothing and then he stopped and then he got up and walked right off the stage without turning around and the audience was clapping and clapping, yes, the applause wouldn't stop, it was like the people in the concert hall had witnessed something like a miracle, she had never heard any-one play that well before or since, not him or anyone else, and that was, well, since she's told me this much she might as well say the rest, that was the night when they became he and she, became a couple, she says, and then we walk silently on, step by step through snow no one has walked in before us

Yes, alcohol is both good and bad, I say

He used to say that too, she says

and then she asks if I drink and I say yes I used to, quite a bit too, but, well it's a long and difficult story, I say, and in the end it came down to either drinking or painting, yes, drinking or staying alive you might say, and yes, well, somehow I got free of the alcohol's hold on me, but it wasn't easy, I say, and of course Ales, my wife, didn't like that I drank, and if it wasn't for her then no I don't know what would have happened to me, I say

You don't drink any more? she says

No, I say

and there's silence

And Ales, your wife? she says

She died, she's gone, I say

and there's a long silence and then I say that I haven't drunk at all since I stopped drinking and she says good for me that I could do that and I say no, no, it wasn't about me, I just did what had to be done and I had help, and without help from both earthly and heavenly forces, yes, why not say it, it's true, from heaven too, I'd never have been able to do it, but most of all it was thanks to Ales that I could do it and once I'd managed to stop drinking it wasn't hard at all to not start again, but stopping in the first place, weaning myself off drinking, well that was hard, yes, that was a struggle, I say and she says that her husband, yes well as she mentioned she calls him her husband anyway, yes, The Fiddler was never able to stop drinking, and he didn't really try either, she knows that, and then that woman in Telemark took him in to live with her, but she was a big drinker too, yes, she almost had to be, or else she wouldn't have been able to stand him, and so it happened the way it had to happen, he wasn't an old man, no, she doesn't want to think about this sad and unpleasant situation any more right now, she says and she raises her face and look, she says, and she raises her arm, look there, there, on the, on the other side of The Bay, you can see The Country Inn, there it is, you're saved, she says and she chuckles a little and I say thank you so so much for helping me, and she says it's no problem when you know the way, she says, but if you don't know the way that's a different story, she says and she says she didn't mean it in a bad way when she laughed just then, if there was any reason at all for her to laugh it was just that she recognized herself, country folk in Bjørgvin, she says, but yes, well, as she said, if they don't have a room for me at The Country Inn I can always spend the night at her place, she says, anyway there's more than enough room in her apartment, all too much room, she says and I think that

I've never really liked going into other people's homes, I've always been shy about that, yes it was like I was doing something I had no right to do, like I was intruding, forcing myself into other people's lives, like I was getting to know more about their life than I had a right to know, like I was disturbing their life, or at least I felt disturbed by their life, their life intruding on mine, yes, like another life was sort of filling me up, I think, and for someone to come into my house, well that's one of the worst things I know of, yes, I get so nervous and uneasy then that I don't know what to do with myself, no, it doesn't happen when people I know well come over, like Åsleik, nothing happens then, it's just normal, yes, everything's the way it should be, that's how it is with friends, they sort of belong there in a way, and I also don't think it's hard to go into the houses of people I know well, friends' houses, but there aren't many of those people, I think, strictly speaking there's just Åsleik now, I think, yes, Åsleik and no one else, not many, and when he comes over it's almost not like someone else is coming over, and when I go to his house it's not like going to someone else's house, because Åsleik and I have known each other for so long and it's like you no longer have much of anything to hide from a person like that, well of course we have some things, but it's like we both know what we're hiding or like we know it but don't want to know it, and don't dwell on it, don't think about it, it's like we just leave it alone, leave it in peace, let it lie, without waking it up or shaking it, without disturbing it, but it's not like that with people I don't know, and visiting people? earlier in my life? yes, strictly speaking it was only when Ales and I were living in Bjørgvin that we had people come over, after we ran off to Dylgja it was just Ales and me, and then, while she was still alive, yes, the only person who came and visited us in Dylgja, aside from her mother Judit, and Åsleik of course, was Beyer, but only once, no, I can't think about that, about Ales, it's too much, I'd just sink and sink into it and disappear, I think, but the day Beyer came to see us Ales didn't want to stay home, she wanted to be at her mother Judit's house in Bjørgvin instead, so the day before Beyer came I drove her to Bjørgvin, yes, to The Beyer Gallery, and the day after I went to get her from The Beyer Gallery, because if I didn't like getting visits from anyone Ales liked it even less, I think

I think I know you better than you realize, Guro says then

and I don't understand what she means, she knows me better than I realize, what's that supposed to mean? it's true I've been interviewed a few times by *The Bjørgvin Times*, I'm afraid so, but that can't be what she's talking about

My name is Guro, she says then

and she says it emphasizing the name like she's sort of trying to remind me of something and then she says now at least I know her name, in case I'd forgotten it, she says, so if my memory's so bad that I can't remember much more about her at least I'll have to remember her name now, she says, and she says it's about time we said hello properly, she says, and she shakes my hand

So, my name's Guro, she says

and I shake her hand and hold Bragi with just one hand

And my name's Asle, I say

Okay, now we know at least that much about each other, she says

and there's something like mockery in her voice

Our names, she says

Yes, I say

and it's silent for a moment and then she says she'll go to the next show I have at The Beyer Gallery, and that it'll probably be during Advent this year the same as every year, that's always when they have it, she says and she's gone to all my shows, she says, and we get to The Country Inn and I say I'll go in and ask if there's a room free for me, and she says she can wait outside, in case it's full, you never know, and if it is I can always, as she's already told me, spend the night at her place, she says and I thank her and she says she might as well go inside with me and then I open the front door and the woman named Guro goes in ahead of me and I go in after her with the dog in my arms and I see that it's the old guy from Bjørgvin, The Bjørgvin Man, sitting at the reception desk, where he's been for all these years, he's one of the people I know, one of the people who's checked me in and checked me out of The Country Inn before, he's a polite older man from Bjørgvin, and I see that there are a lot of keys hanging on the wall in the reception area behind The Bjørgvin Man, so there must be rooms available, I think

Good afternoon, or good evening I should say, The Bjørgvin Man says

So this is the fellow who's out and about tonight, he says

and he looks at me and then at the woman standing behind me

Or rather the two people, he says

and it seems like he recognizes the person I'm with and he stands up and bows

Ye, yes, I say

You don't have a room for me, do you? I say

You mean for the two of you? he says

No, just for me, I say

and at that same moment I think that maybe he didn't mean me and the woman apparently named Guro but me and the dog

I see, The Bjørgvin Man says

Well for me and my dog, I say

You've got a dog with you? he says

Yes, I say

and I think that I don't want to get into the whole business of why I have a dog with me

It's not actually allowed, having a dog in the room, The Bjørgvin Man says

And you've never had a dog with you before, he says

No, I say

Well, I don't know, The Bjørgvin Man says

and Guro says that she can take the dog with her, and I can get him back tomorrow, she's always liked dogs, and she used to have a dog herself, but that was back when she was a girl, she says

I'm sure we can work something out, The Bjørgvin Man says

Because, he says

and suddenly there's a long silence

Because, well, yes, since it's you, one of our regular guests, yes well I think I can make an exception, I'll hardly lose my job over it, he says

and I stand there and I don't know what to say, because I've never brought a dog to The Country Inn before

As long as the dog doesn't bark, The Bjørgvin Man says

No, he won't as long as I'm with him, I say

That's good to hear, he says

Because even if there aren't that many guests at the hotel tonight, I'm sure they won't exactly want to be woken up by a yapping dog, he says

Of course, I understand, I say

But I can take the dog with me, Guro says

and I think that she said she was called something else when we were talking at Food and Drink, Silje or something like that, I think, but now she's said many times that her name is Guro and now I think of her simply as Guro, I think

Your usual room is free, The Bjørgvin Man says

Room 407, I say

and I say that this trip into Bjørgvin came about a bit unexpectedly, I usually reserve a room in advance and The Bjørgvin Man says yes he knows

Yes, great, that room, same as always, I say

Your room is free and since it's you we'll take the risk and assume everything'll be fine with your dog, he says

and I say thank you, thanks very much, and I say that as long as the dog is with me he won't start barking

That'll be fine, your room is ready and waiting for you, The Bjørgvin Man says

and he takes a key off the hook on the wall behind him and he hands me the key and he says have a nice stay and he's sure I can find my own way and that I know when breakfast is served and all that as well as he does, he says and I say thank you, thanks, everything'll be fine, I say and I turn around and Guro is standing there and I say thank you so much for your help and she says it was no problem, and then she says she hopes we run into each other again, and I say that yes I'm sure we will and then we shake hands and say goodbye and then I walk towards the lift and she walks towards the front door and then she stops and then she says

But what about breakfast? she says

and I turn around and look at her

You'll have to leave the dog alone then, won't you? she says

You have a point there, The Bjørgvin Man says

You can't bring the dog to breakfast with you? she says

and I say I hadn't thought of that and The Bjørgvin Man says he wouldn't recommend it, and why did she have to bring up breakfast? hasn't today been long enough? aren't I exhausted? can't I get a little peace and quiet? I need to go to sleep, and I suddenly realize how totally exhausted I am, I'm so tired I might collapse right here

You have a point, The Bjørgvin Man says

and I don't know what to say and Guro says that she can take the dog with her and I can get him back tomorrow morning, she says and I realize I can't talk about it any more, I'm done, the dog'll sleep wherever it'll sleep, I think and I look at her

I'll come back here at ten o'clock with the dog, she says

Or you can come by and ring the bell around then, or earlier if you want, she says

and I nod and then Guro says that if I want to get the dog then, or earlier, or later, well I know where she lives, it's on The Lane, number 5 The Lane, she says, as she's said before, she says, so she lives right near The Country Inn, you just take a right and then take the first right after that and the first narrow street you get to is The Lane, uphill to the left, she says and she smiles and The Bjørgvin Man looks at me and Guro walks up to me and I hand her the dog and I say his name is Bragi and she takes the dog and the leash and The Bjørgvin Man says that it's probably for the best, all things considered, yes, even for the dog, maybe, he says and I turn around and walk towards the lift and push the button with an up arrow and the lift comes and I turn around

Goodnight, I say

and both the woman apparently named Guro and The Bjørgvin Man say goodnight and I open the lift door and I hear the front door close and I go into the lift and I press the button with 4 on it and then I stand there in the lift and it jolts into motion and I feel so tired, so tired, so unbelievably tired, I think and I think that it was a good thing I drove back to Bjørgvin, because imagine what might have happened to Asle if I hadn't? he was lying there covered in snow, he was sick, he was shaking constantly and kept collapsing, falling down and just lying there, and what would have happened if I hadn't come back to Bjørgvin? I think and the lift moves slowly upwards, it's an old lift and it rises slowly, and with little jolts, and I think that now I don't want to think about Asle any more, or about anything else, now I'm tired, so unbelievably tired, so now I'll just go straight to bed, I think and the lift gets to the fourth floor and it stops with a jolt, and bobs up and down a little, and I look at the lift door and it feels like forever before I can open it and I go out into the hall and suddenly I don't know if I'm supposed to take a right and go down that corridor, or if I'm supposed to take a left and go down that one, even after having stayed in Room 407 so many times I'm still not sure, dammit I'll just go either left or right and then see where I am, I think, and I feel really angry, as I should, I'm angry at myself, I seriously curse myself and I take a right and I see 400 on a door and I go down that corridor and the numbers on the doors get higher and higher so I am going the right way and there, there at last, is 407 on a door and I use the key and I unlock the door on the first try and then I go into the room, turn on the light and then take off my brown leather shoulderbag and put it down on a chair and then I take off my black coat and I hang it on the chair and then I go right to the bed and lie down without taking any of my clothes off, even the black velvet jacket I'm wearing, and my shoes are still on, and then I breathe deeply in and breathe slowly out several times and then I fold my hands and I make the sign of the cross and I say to myself Pater noster Qui es in cælis Sanctificetur nomen tuum Adveniat regnum tuum and I stay lying down and I say to myself Our Father

Who art in heaven Hallowed be thy name Thy kingdom come
and I think God's kingdom does need to come, but it already
has come, I feel it, whenever I feel or realize how close God is,
yes, he is all around me like a field, or maybe it's his angel, my
angel, that I feel? I think and may God protect him, may God
protect Asle, let Asle get better again, I think and then I think
that it won't be long now before I too come to God, to God's
kingdom, I think and then I breathe in deeply and I say inside
myself Kyrie and then I breathe out slowly and I say eleison and
then I breathe in deeply and I say Christe and then I breathe out
slowly and I say eleison and I say that over and over and then I
just lie there quietly and stare straight ahead into empty space
and at first I don't see anything and I just feel how tired I am
and then I see a canvas there on an easel and I see two lines
there that cross each other and then I hear Åsleik say St Andrew's
Cross, he says it with his provincial pride, St Andrew's Cross,
and suddenly I feel an aversion to the whole picture, there's
nothing more to do with that picture, just get rid of it, be done
with it, because it's done, despite it being so unfinished it's
done, it's finished, the way it's painted is just the way it is and
the way it's going to stay, it doesn't need any more, the big
white canvas and then those two lines crossing, the lines forming a cross, and that's it, obviously what I was painting was Asle
but I don't like to think like that, not now, because now I'm at
peace, and I say to myself Pacem relinquo vobis Pacem meam
do vobis and I say Peace I leave with you My peace I give unto
you and I don't know what more I can do with the picture, it's
stiff, it's dead, it's just two lines, two thick lines that cross in the
middle, it doesn't have the light in it that a good picture needs
to have, it's really not a picture at all, it's a St Andrew's Cross,
Åsleik says, and he's right, and then he says it again, *St Andrew's
Cross*, he says and he puts a heavy stress on the words like he's

proud of knowing them, proud that he, Åsleik, knows a term like that, something like that is what he's saying in the way he says the words, and things like that just make him look stupid, putting on that provincial pride makes him worse than he is, I think and I lie there and think that I just need to forget that picture, or try to forget it, but the picture is firmly in my mind, because some of the pictures I paint get lodged inside me but most of the other pictures I have lodged in my mind are pictures from life, not my own paintings, yes, these glimpses of something I've seen that stayed with me and that torment me, actually, because I can never get rid of them, and that I try to paint away, and in a way I do manage to paint them away, or in any case paint them into being something that doesn't just exist in my mind, something that isn't stuck in there, in a way, I think and I think that all the paintings for the show I'm having soon at The Beyer Gallery are already finished, so if I had thought of it I could've brought them with me and delivered them to Beyer today, or maybe tomorrow morning, I think, but I don't always think in such reasonable ways, or plan well, for example this morning I just decided to drive to Bjørgvin to go shopping and then I did, and I think that tomorrow when I get back home I'll put aside that picture with the two lines, the St Andrew's Cross, as Åsleik says, yes the picture should be called *St Andrew's Cross,* and I'll paint the name, the title, in black oil paint on the top edge of the stretcher, the way I always do, and then I'll paint a big A on the picture itself, in the lower righthand corner, the way I also always do, unless I've already done that? haven't I already added the picture's title and signed it with a big A and taken it off the easel and put it aside with the other paintings that also aren't done stacked together with the stretchers out between the bedroom door and the hall door? haven't I done that already? I think, but if I haven't then I'll put

it aside as soon as I get home tomorrow, I think and then I'll
take out another painting I have stacked in that pile of unfinished pictures, of pictures I've almost managed to finish as good
pictures but not quite, pictures that are missing something, that
I can't figure out what to do with and have to let sit for a while,
when I get back home to Dylgja, finally get back home to
Dylgja, I'll take out one of the paintings deep in the stack,
which means one of the unfinished paintings that I set aside a
long time ago because I wasn't entirely happy with it, I wasn't
satisfied it was the picture it needed to be, I think, and then I
think that I need to put the paintings stacked in two piles next
to the kitchen door with the stretchers facing out from the wall
into the back of my car and drive to Bjørgvin and deliver them
to Beyer, because those are the pictures I'm done with, there's
a stack of big ones and a stack of smaller ones, and it's those pictures that I set aside and decided I was done with after I realized
I couldn't do any more with them, I made those pictures as well
as I could make them, I don't know how good they are but I
know that I can't make them any better, so they're ready for
the next show, yes, there are always either too many pictures or
not enough, I think, but if Beyer feels there are too many he
just puts the ones he doesn't want to include in the show in the
side room, The Bank, as he calls it, and I do need to drive the
pictures to The Beyer Gallery soon, it's getting kind of urgent,
so I need to get it done, because Beyer hangs the pictures up
himself, and he puts a lot of thought into the installation, I
think, and it was thanks to Beyer that I could make it as a painter, because for someone to live off painting pictures he's really
got to stick it out, I think, yes well more or less the same thing
is true of probably every profession or craft, even if being an
artist is supposed to be different, not a job like ordinary house
painting but one that's out of the ordinary, noble and special,

there's something affected about the whole thing, to tell the truth, actually I'm ashamed to be an artist, an art painter, but what else could I have been? and now, anyway, now that I'm so old? no, unfortunately I'm not much use for anything else now, besides painting pictures, because I've always been clumsy, in everything, yes, even when I draw or paint, yes, it's hard to believe it, it can't be because I'm physically unable to do something well that I can't do it, no, it must be something else that prevents me, and I don't know what it is, so I would have been a bad tradesman, that's been true ever since I was a kid, and as for anything to do with maths I can't do it, that's for sure, and nothing with writing either, or, well, actually to tell the truth it's pretty easy for me to write, there was nothing wrong with my style in school and I was pretty good at English, yes, I even used to be able to write in English well enough, and German too, and I enjoyed reading books in both English and German back in the day, there were quite a lot of words and idioms I didn't understand but I got the meaning one way or another, and then I read Swedish and Danish books too, of course, it was back when I was going to The Art School that I started reading foreign books in the original languages, because a lot of the literature Professor Christie referred to was written in either English or German, especially German, and occasionally in Swedish or Danish, rarely in Norwegian, and then always written in Bokmål, never in Nynorsk, and for a lot of the books I wanted to read I had to venture into the stately University Library and ask to borrow them, and since I was going to The Art School I was allowed to borrow books from there, and not many of the books Professor Christie mentioned were available at The Public Library, and I read and read and didn't understand even half of what I read, probably much less than that, but it sort of didn't matter much, I understood some of it, and what I did understand gradually helped me learn more and more of the language I was reading, because even though I had dictionaries I didn't like looking things up in them so I'd either guess what a word meant or, most often, I could figure it out from the context, the word had a clear meaning when it was in context with other words, so yes, I was pretty good at languages, it was mathematical aptitude that I always had a problem with, and what I totally don't have is a sense of direction, a sense of place, plus I'm so clumsy, so it's true probably the only thing I could have ended up doing was painting pictures, and if I wanted to make a living I needed to paint, and that's both good and also wrong, but that's what I did and kept doing, I painted picture after picture, I did that at least, and when I wasn't painting I often spent hour after hour just sitting and staring into space, yes, I can sit for a long time and just stare into empty space, at nothing, and it's sort of like something can come from the empty nothingness, like something real can come out of the nothingness, something that says a lot, and what it says can turn into a picture, either that or I can stay sitting there staring into empty space and become completely empty myself, completely still, and it's in that empty stillness that I like to say my deepest truest prayers, yes, that's when God is closest, because it's in the silence that God can be heard, and it's in the invisible that He can be seen, of course I know my Pater Noster and I pray with it every day, to tell the truth, at least three times a day, and often even more in fact, and I've learned it by heart in Latin, and learned it by seeing it before my eyes, I never memorize mechanically because I can remember written things by seeing them, a bit like pictures, yes, but I try to only remember the written things I think are important to remember, and unlike with pictures I'm able to turn off the memory of written things, and then I made my own translation of the Our Father into Nynorsk, and of course I know that by heart, yes, I can see it in my mind, but still it's probably these moments when I'm sitting and staring into empty nothingness, and becoming empty, becoming still, that are my deepest truest prayers, and once I get into the empty stillness I can stay there for a long time, sit like that for a long time, and I don't even realize I'm sitting there, I just sit and stare into the empty nothingness, and probably in a way I am the empty nothingness I'm looking at, I can sit like that for I don't know how long but it's a long, long time, and I believe these silent moments enter into the light in my paintings, the light that is clearest in darkness, yes, the shining darkness, I don't know for sure but that's what I think, or hope, that it might be like that, I think and I lie there and I think now I need to go to sleep soon and I'll pray one of the quick prayers with my rosary, my usual kind, because it's not that often that I pray in my own words, and when I do it's for intercession, I'm embarrassed when it comes to that, if I pray for something that has to do with me then it has to be to let me be good for someone else, and if it specifically has to do with me then I pray that it should be God's will that it happen, yes, Thy will be done Fiat voluntas tua On earth as it is in heaven Sicut in cælo et in terra and I am so tired so tired I need to sleep but I'm probably too agitated to get to sleep, I think and then I sit up on the edge of the bed and stand up and I take my black velvet jacket off and hang it on the back of the chair with the brown shoulderbag lying under the black overcoat and then I push my heels against the floor and kick off my shoes and I take off my trousers and I leave them on the floor and then I take off my black pullover and drop it on top of the trousers and the room feels cold and then I turn off the light and get into the bed and I tuck the duvet tight around me and I gather my thoughts and then I think may God be good and help my friend, Asle, to get better, he's too young to die, he paints pictures that are too good for him to have to die now, yes, I don't presume to know what's best for Asle better than God but that's what I want, and I think that I can hope that in all humility, and as meekly as I can I pray to God to please let Asle live, let him regain his health, yes, yes, I pray to you, dear God, that you will make Asle better, I think and then I stay lying there and looking into the emptiness before me, into the dark nothingness, and I must be tired, tired, so tired, but maybe I'm too worked up to get to sleep? I think and I think that maybe I paint better when I'm under pressure, when I need to finish a few more paintings for my show? because even though I like painting, yes, there's often a lot of pain in what I paint, and in me too in a way, because these pictures lodged inside me, yes, they're almost all connected to something bad that I remember, the light is linked to the darkness, yes, that's how it is, and there are painters who don't like getting rid of their pictures, who'd rather keep them, not sell them, but I'm happy every single time I sell a picture, happy to be free of it, almost, and maybe that goes back to when I was a boy and made a few kroner by painting pictures of neighbours' houses and farms, back when I was still a kid, but it made me happy to do that, yes, to paint pictures and then get rid of them and get money for them, and it still makes me happy to this day when I sell a picture, yes, selling the picture in itself makes me happy but then also, yes, I have to admit that I think this way too, when I sell a picture I'm also giving away, almost like a gift, the light that the picture has to have in it, yes, it's like I'm passing on to someone else a gift that I myself have been given, I think I've been paid for the picture itself but not for the light that's in the picture, because that's something I was given and as a result I have to give it away again, and that light, yes, it's most often connected to something bad, to pain, and suffering, I might say, if that's not too big a word, and I'm paid for the painting itself, for the picture, but not for the light, and the person who buys the painting is also given some of the light, and the suffering too, the despair, the pain that's in the light, I think, and if there isn't any light in the picture well then I keep it, a picture's not done until there's light in it, even if that light is invisible, I think, yes, even if no one else can see the light, just me, it has to be there, see the light, yes that's what they say, he's seen the light, they say, and if they only knew how right they were, even if they always say it about someone they consider more or less lacking in wisdom and intelligence, someone not entirely of this world, as they also say, with a certain mockery, but what difference does it make? because I see what I see, I've seen what I've seen, I've lived what I've lived and I paint what I paint, so they can say whatever they want, I think, yes actually that's another reason I'm happy to sell pictures, because I'm passing along the light, I think, and since I also make my living from the pictures I paint, since I've never made my living from anything else, I obviously need to sell the pictures! how could I live off my painting if I didn't sell my pictures? no, I'd have been in a bad way, destitute, there are plenty of painters who live in the most dire poverty, even if most of them try to hide it and peacock around and scatter money to the winds once they manage to make a few kroner, but I've never been someone like that, I've never spent more money than I needed to, I think, usually less in fact, if you want to put it that way, yes, I've lived modestly, they say, and I've always managed to get by, I think, and one of the reasons was my being so modest, even thrifty, probably to the point of stinginess, even penny-pinching as the old folks say, the fact is I just don't like to spend money, and I've never liked to spend money, but I need it just like everyone else, even if all I like buying is canvas and tubes of oil paint, yes, all kinds of painting supplies, but I like buying those things so much that I have so much canvas and turpentine and so many tubes of oil paint and boards for stretchers and brushes and rags and whatever else that I basically don't need to buy any more of any of it for the rest of my life, almost, and I've stored most of it up in a room in the attic, it's all up there, well organized, everything where it belongs, I think, and still I keep buying more new supplies rather than using what I have up in the attic, like how I bought a roll of canvas at The Art Store today and a good amount of boards for stretchers at The Hardware Store, but it feels like that was so long ago, yes, like it was ages ago that I was in The Art Store and The Hardware Store, even though it was earlier today, but yes well when it comes to buying what I need to paint with I never think about saving money, and that probably goes back to my childhood too when I sold a picture and with the money I made I bought canvas and tubes of oil paint and turpentine, I think, lying in bed at The Country Inn, in Room 407, in the bed I've slept in so many times before, and I am so tired so tired and I can't sleep, because how is Asle doing? what's happening to him at The Hospital? because Asle needs rest, they said he needs to get his rest now and that's why I couldn't go see him, and of course I didn't argue, I just left, and it's only to stop thinking about Asle that I'm thinking about all these other things, all the things I usually think about, because Asle needs to get some rest, that's the best thing for him, The Nurse said, and that's why it was best that I come back again tomorrow and ask if I can see him then, she said and I said I could do that, but if he's asleep when I come by he'll need to keep sleeping, because he needs to rest now, what's important now is that he sleep as much as possible, she said and I said I'd come back tomorrow and ask if I can get anything for him, if he isn't asleep

then, and if he is asleep then that's great, I won't get him anything, I'll just come back another day, because I live a long way
north of Bjørgvin, in Dylgja, if she knows where that is, I said
and The Nurse said that she didn't know and I said well no it's
such a small place that almost no one has heard of it, I said and
she said well then that's what we'll do, I should come back tomorrow or some other day, and I can call first to see if I can
come and we'll tell you how it's going, she said, that's how it
went, or is that just something I'm imagining? that it went like
that? that The Nurse and I had a conversation like that? I think
and anyway now I'm lying in bed at The Country Inn, in my
regular room, Room 407, and I can't get to sleep and I think
that a lot of the people who are supposed to know what's good
and what's bad, what's good art and what's bad art, don't think
much of my pictures, yes, for several years now painting pictures wasn't something you should do if you wanted to be a real
artist, paintings as such weren't real art, and during that time the
people who painted pictures were obviously said to be less
worthwhile, they weren't considered artists at all, just illustra-
tors past their expiration date or something like that, and the
worst of all were the people who painted pictures and then sold
them, who put pictures they'd painted on sale, yes, the people
who painted pictures someone actually wanted to buy were the
worst, because where was the art in that? weren't such pictures
mere entertainment? purely commercial? nothing but something to put on a wall? something to hang above the sofa since
after all something has to hang there? maybe yes maybe no, but
in any case it's not art, they would say or think, but I know
what I'm doing, I know the difference between a good picture
and a bad picture, and I know I can paint pictures that only I
can paint, because I have my very own inner picture that all the
other pictures come from, so to speak, or that they all try to get

to, or get close to, but that one innermost picture can't be painted, and the closer I am to that inner picture when I paint the better I paint, and the more light there is in the picture, yes, that's how it is, I think, and what I've seen and lived, and know deep inside, in my innermost picture, is also something I want to tell the world, something I want other people to know, or to have hanging over their sofa for that matter, because I want to, yes, share what I know, show it, yes of course it can't be said but maybe it can be shown? at least a little of it? and insofar as it can be shown I want to show it to someone else, since it's true, I'm sure of it and I know it's good, it's good for me and it's good for other people too, and what I want to show to other people has to do with light, or with darkness, it has to do with the shining darkness full as it is of nothingness, yes, it's possible to think that way, to use such words, and it's also something that comes from the picture I have inside me that I see when I see something that lodges itself inside me and that I can never get rid of again, these flashes of pictures, clear pictures, that I have in my mind and that torment me, yes, it's true, and it's been like that since I was a boy, there are so many pictures like that, there are countless such pictures, like those black boots of Grandfather's on the road in the rain, one dark night, or Grandfather's hands, shining, glowing, in a flash, and some pictures come to me again and again while others just lay there in a group sort of resting, and emerge only rarely, but one that comes to me again and again is Ales's face in the rain, in the darkness, the rain running down over her despairing face, but in all the pain, all the suffering, there's her light, that black light, yes, I should be ashamed of myself but my eyes are starting to get teary as I lie here, the light, the black light in her despairing face, the invisible light, those desperate eyes, twisted, her mouth half-open, and the rain running down her face in the dark night, or the opposite, yes, glittering on Ales's thoughtful peaceful face when she disappears into herself and in this movement becomes like part of an incomprehensible light that streams invisibly from her face, yes, there are so many faces in my mind, some in pain, some resting, and most of all faces that are just there, unconscious in a way, just full of, yes, what exactly, yes there are so many faces that they're about to merge together into a single face, I think, and then from Ales's face spreading out all over shines the light of care and tenderness on all that she's looking at, I think and now I need to sleep, I am so tired so tired and I'm just lying here thinking thoughts that I've thought so many times before, I think, but I can't sleep, lying here in my bed at The Country Inn, Room 407, the room I always stay in, as long as it's free, and if it isn't I rent an adjacent room, I stay in Room 409, or Room 405, and all those rooms are small and look out on the backyard, I think and I lie there and I can't sleep and tomorrow I'll take a taxi to The Hospital and look in on Asle and tell him that I went to get his dog, and ask him if I can bring him anything, buy him anything, I think and then I'll take a taxi to The Lane and then I'll pick up his dog and then I'll walk to my car parked in front of The Beyer Gallery and it's probably totally covered in snow by now, but obviously I have a good snow brush and a good scraper with me so I'll manage, I'll get the car ready to drive so that I can drive to Dylgja and get back home, because I so wish I was back home and lying in my own bed and not at The Country Inn, yes, even though I've spent so many nights here in this bed too, it just isn't my own bed, it's a bed where lots of other people have slept too, and where lots more people will sleep in the future, that's how it is, yes, in fact it's so obvious that why think about it? why think these thoughts? because sometimes I really like being at The Country Inn, after all that's why I've stayed here so many times, that's why I always stay here whenever I need to spend the night in Bjørgvin, and I can't count the number of times I've spent the night at The Country Inn, so obviously I'm comfortable here, but I just can't get to sleep tonight, it's impossible, I don't know why, but I'm too restless, I can't sleep, everything is like it's crumbling and falling apart and I see Asle lying in bed with The Nurse and The Doctor standing next to the bed and they're saying something about him needing an IV, something like that, and then The Doctor takes his pulse and I see Asle lying there asleep, his long grey hair hanging down past his shoulders and then his whole body jerks and shakes, while he's sleeping his whole body is shaking and The Doctor says they should give him even more of some kind of medicine or another that he says the name of and The Nurse says they've already given him as much as they can and The Doctor says yes well in that case they should probably just wait a little and then give him more later, he says, and Asle's long grey hair, the shaking, the jerking and then I see The Nurse and The Doctor leave the room and then Asle is lying there and he's asleep and his body is trembling the whole time, and it's wrong to be looking at this, I don't want to see it, and it was good that I found him, when he was lying outside the door of number 5, The Lane, covered in snow, I think and I can't sleep and I think it was good that I drove back to Bjørgvin, and now why did I do that? it makes sense that I would think of it but why did I actually do it? I don't totally understand, it was like something was forcing me to, or guiding me to do it, I think and I see Asle on Father's shoulder and he's sobbing and sobbing and the crying has taken on a kind of life of its own, and he's twisting and writhing, because it hurts, his stomach hurts and Father is walking back and forth carrying him and rocking him back and forth in his arms and Father has left the upstairs bedroom and Father said he'd take Asle out into the hall so that at least Mother and Sister could sleep, he said, and Father walks and carries Asle, holds him against his shoulder, rubs his back, and Asle cries and cries and his crying gets louder and sharper, he's gasping, he's crying in bursts, he's crying so loud that it almost sounds like shrieks and Father rubs and rubs his back and then Asle's body gradually relaxes and the crying gets weaker, it turns into breathing, and Father walks back and forth with him, and Father and Asle and the breathing and the stroking of Father's hand on Asle's back are like one and the same movement and then Asle goes away, he disappears from the pain, from the stabbing in his stomach, and Father walks back and forth with him across the upstairs hall and then Father opens the door to the bedroom with his free hand as carefully and quietly as he can and Father and Asle go into the darkness and he hears Father from far away whisper he's sleeping now, he's finally asleep and he hears Mother say that's good, he's been crying for such a long time, she says and he realizes that Father has put him down in his bed and spread the blanket over him and then Father has lightly stroked his hair and then Asle has disappeared from there into his calm breathing, and into his calm sleep, and with his face turned aside he lies there breathing evenly and Father goes and lies down next to Mother and she says softly that Father must be so tired, first a long day of work, from early in the morning until late at night he's been out gathering pears, and then now, at night, all the way up until now, late at night, Asle's been screaming and Father was walking back and forth carrying him, she says and Father says that he is tired and that he'll try to get to sleep and I see Asle lying there and his body is shaking, jerking up and down, he's trembling, and then I see Asle being held against someone's breast, he's a little boy, it's not Mother's breast, it's another breast, but he feels warmth from a breast against his cheek, he is almost pressing his cheek against the breast, yes, he's leaning all the weight of his little head against the woman's chest and I see that most of her chest is covered by a dress, a flower-patterned dress, it's green and there are white flowers on it and it goes down in a V at the neck and behind the V are two big breasts, like two O's pressed against each other and Asle puts his little little hands on one breast and the woman holding him in her arms laughs and smiles and she rocks him back and forth against her chest and he looks at her and he looks at her chest, and at the crack between her breasts, and he thinks it looks like a butt, is she holding him against her butt? he thinks, she can't be, can she? there's no butt up top is there? and he doesn't understand, so he needs to ask, Asle thinks and he asks if she has her bud up here, because he can't say his "t"s, and then he hears a sudden laugh burst against his ears and laughter fills the room and the woman holding him against her chest bends forward and laughs so hard that Asle is moved up and down and she holds him tight to her chest and he feels her movements, and he's sort of hanging in mid-air, but she's holding him tight, she's holding him even tighter to her chest than before, yes, she's sort of clutching him to her chest and she laughs and laughs and Asle sees Mother standing there and she's bent over with laughter and he sees Grandmother standing there and she too is laughing and laughing and he understands that he's said something strange, and he doesn't totally understand what was so strange about what he said, and then the woman holding him to her chest starts to walk across the room and he hears her say can you believe the things he says, really, she says, and just two years old too, Grandmother says, yes that was really something, what he just said, Mother says and then the three women laugh again, but less wildly now, not as loud

212

and sharp, more slow and kind, and Mother says well they should go sit down at the table, the coffee's ready, she says and Asle twists free and the woman who was holding him at her breast puts him down on the floor and then Asle stands there and he looks at his Grandmother who has sat down at a table and then he goes over to Grandmother and he hears the woman who'd held him against her chest and put him down say he's a good walker even though he's so little, and Mother says yes he's a toddler now, she says, and he goes to Grandmother and she says now come to Grandma my boy yes, she says and Grandmother holds her arms out towards him and he goes towards Grandmother's arms and he reaches them and she takes him under his arms and picks him up and puts him on her thigh and then she hugs him to her and all at once he is in her good warmth and she rocks him a little in her warmth and I see Asle lying there with his hands down by his sides and his whole body's jerking up and down and there are several tubes attached to his body running up to a metal stand and I see The Nurse standing next to him put her hand on his forehead and then The Doctor opens the door and walks in and The Nurse says it's bad, the spasms need to stop soon, she says and The Doctor nods and he says that they've given him what they can give him now, they can't give him any more, he says and they stand there without saying anything and then The Doctor says he doesn't know how this'll end, if he'll make it, and The Nurse says yes, yes it's bad, she says, and the question is whether he should be kept under constant observation now, she says, if he needs to be moved to a room where he can be kept under constant observation, she says and The Doctor says that would be best and I lie in bed at The Country Inn, in Room 407, and I can't get to sleep and I see Asle lying there, shaking, trembling, jerking, his long grey hair moving up and down and I hear The

Doctor say no it doesn't look good and The Nurse says the question is whether he'll make it, she says and The Doctor says it sure looks bad, but maybe these spasms will stop soon, or at least get weaker, he says and Asle needs somebody with him at all times, The Doctor says, maybe he's strong enough to pull through, he says, yes The Nurse says and I see someone come in and they wheel his bed and the metal stand with all the tubes attached to his body out to the hall and into a lift and they take the lift one floor up and then Asle is wheeled down a corridor and then he's wheeled into a room where there's already a man lying in a bed and a man in a white uniform sitting on a chair and I see that Asle's face is almost totally grey and the man sitting there stands up and goes over to the bed Asle's in and helps wheel that bed over to the wall opposite from where the other bed is and then Asle lies there and his whole body's shaking, trembling, the jerking is going through him the whole time and then Asle just lies there and he wakes up and he looks at the man sitting on a chair in the room and the man sitting there says Asle should just sleep, he needs to rest now, what you need now is rest, sleep, he says and Asle shuts his eyes and then he just lies there in his shaking and I lie in bed at The Country Inn, Room 407, and I see Asle standing next to Father and he's looking down at a hole in the ground and he knows that the box with the wreaths and flowers on it is going to be put down into the hole and his Grandfather is lying there in the box and he was big, tall, broad-shouldered, enormous, and then Asle feels tears coming into his eyes and people are standing around the open hole in the ground, lots of people, and they're all standing far enough away from the hole in the ground so that there'll be room for the people carrying the white box with his Grandfather inside and they'll be able to walk next to the hole in the ground and there's a mound of dirt past the end of the

hole and Asle stands there and he sees the pastor, in his black
pastor's robe, with his white pastor's collar around his neck,
come walking in the lead and behind him are the men carrying
the white box with his Grandfather inside and Asle looks at the
box and he feels a fear take hold of him and he sees the pastor
step aside a little and take his place and then he's standing there
in his black pastor's robe with the white pastor's collar and the
men with the box come closer and closer and Father steps back
a little and Asle steps back with him and everyone else steps
back a little too and then the men carrying the box with all the
wreaths and flowers walk past Asle and he sees that they're
walking bent to one side, because it's heavy, carrying
Grandfather, big as he was, Asle thinks, and they put something
like a frame with straps across it over the black hole in the
ground and the men lift the box over the hole in the dirt and
they carefully put the box down on the straps across the top of
the hole that are attached to a frame and then the pastor speaks
and he throws earth onto the box and he says from dust you
come and to dust you shall return and then the people standing
around the box start singing Nearer My God To Thee and then
one or the other of them starts lowering the box down into the
hole, down, down, and Asle puts his hand into Father's hand
and then they stand there, Asle and Father, and watch the box
with Grandfather in it being lowered farther and farther down
into the dirt and then the box is out of sight and now Asle can't
hold back his tears any more and the tears start running down
his cheeks and he holds Father's hand and all he feels now is
Father's hand and people start walking away from the hole in
the ground where the box with his Grandfather in it is now
down in the earth, surrounded by dirt, and it's a long way down
to the box, and to his Grandfather, and Father goes almost all
the way up to the edge of the hole in the dirt and then Asle

looks up at Father and he sees Father standing and looking down at the box and then he too looks down at the box and while everyone else walks away he and Father stay standing and looking at the box where his Grandfather is lying and eventually it's just Asle and Father there and Mother and Sister and Grandmother are behind them and then he hears Mother say

Should we go? she says

and Father nods and quietly says yes and then Father stays where he is

All right, let's go, Mother says

and he sees Mother and his sister Alida start walking behind the others but a long way behind them while Grandmother stays where she is, and then Father shakes his head and I'm lying in my bed at The Country Inn, Room 407, and I can't get to sleep I see Asle lying there and his body is trembling, shaking, jerking up and down, he's shaking all over and The Doctor says it's bad but they can't do anything more for him now, they've given him as much medicine as they can, they can't give him any more, The Doctor says, and then both The Doctor and The Nurse leave the room and I'm lying in bed at The Country Inn and I can't sleep and I see Father and Asle go over to Mother and Sister who are standing waiting for them and Asle thinks his sister's name is Alida, there aren't many other people named that, he tries to just think about that, his not knowing anyone else named Alida besides his sister, he thinks, his sister Alida, yes, Asle thinks and then his Grandmother puts her hand under Father's arm and then Father and Asle and Grandmother and Sister and Mother walk away together after the others and I think that I need to get to sleep now, I can't lie awake in bed at The Country Inn all night, I think and I see Asle sitting in an upstairs room in an outbuilding and he's reading a book, and he's sitting in a rowboat with Father and he's sitting on a bus and he's thinking that a friend of his is dead, he has just then heard the news, he's sitting there and reading a book, and he's lying in a bed and reading a book, he's drawing, he's painting, he's walking down a street, he's drinking beer and she's naked and she's lying there in bed and he doesn't know what to do he puts his hands on her and he realizes he wants to lie down on her and he does it and he doesn't dare enter her something is holding him back he doesn't dare because just when he's about to a fear comes over him and he pulls back and she just lies there and her name is Liv and he's lying on top of her and then he's sitting at a schooldesk and he's standing there smoking rolling a cigarette books a teacher is saying something he asks the class drawing painting the other eleven students painting class girls boys smoking beer painting drinking beer talking and then just going there and waiting and then, finally, finally, he was born, finally he came out into this world into the light and Asle has become a father he is young very young but he's become a father and his long brown hair and everyone else is so much better than him he's worthless she just wants to be with the others with all of them all of the others and it's over and he wants to lie down and sleep in the snow because it's so far to walk and he's so tired and so drunk he sees the stars shining clearly one star and then he and Father are in a rowboat his son they're fishing books drawings paintings reading painting just painting just that and beer vodka that good rush the best nothing much at first and then better and better and he drinks and she says he mustn't drink every night a little rush every night and he drinks paintings money no money sells pictures for money has no money exhibition exhibitions critics selling pictures tubes of oil paint canvas always oil paint and always canvas oil on canvas stretchers boards stretchers nails canvas her and the woman who comes and sits down at his table and they start talking and she's seen his exhibitions home to her place lying next to each other kissing the woman one of his sons kissing her they take off their clothes he holds her tight they lie next to each other they talk go home she's lying there his son is asleep go home she's lying there she's lying there on the floor she's almost not breathing ambulance boy crying and crying howling ambulance he and his son she writes him a letter they meet kiss eat together he's sitting and drinking and she comes and sits down exhibitions oil paint canvas stretchers need to find a place to live boards nowhere to stay pictures the others vodka feeling warm beer another pint talk about this and that laugh she comes and it's Christmas lamb ribs summer her parents' house the white house the silence and painting never stopping always continuing they can say whatever they want just continuing the dark eyes children several children paintings house he sits and drinks children paintings their house needs repainting pictures days nights can't get to sleep and he lies there and he shakes up and down jerks trembling shaking and the man sitting there gets up and I sit there and I look at the picture, those two lines that cross and I see Åsleik standing there looking at the picture and he says St Andrew's Cross, it's a St Andrew's Cross, Åsleik says, and that heavy stress he puts on the words, he's so proud of knowing the term that he stresses it, a provincial pride, *St Andrew's Cross*, this pride in knowing the term and there's nothing more to do with the picture so I'll just put it aside, but not yet, maybe I should paint over those two lines, maybe it can turn into a good picture if the cross disappears from the picture, if it becomes invisible, or almost invisible, if it's turned into something way back behind the rest and I get up and I go over to the picture and then I pick it up off the easel and I put it back down on the easel and I think that I probably don't actually want to put it in the stack of paintings leaning against the

wall between the bedroom door and the hall door, the stack of
pictures I'm still working on and am not yet done with, the one
that my brown leather shoulderbag is hanging above, and I step
a little bit away from the picture and I look at it, and it's not
totally terrible, but some paintings just aren't there yet, but
maybe this one can still get there? because it can take a long
time for me to finish a painting sometimes, if I can ever finish
it, because there's something missing, but what? and that's how
it almost always is, I think, or if not always then very often, the
picture is almost what it's supposed to be, I'm almost there, but
not quite, I'm close, so close, I think, but it's too early to put
the picture in the stack leaning against the wall with the stretchers facing out and I see the man sitting between the two beds
stand up and he goes over to the bed where the other man is
lying and he presses his fingers against his shoulder and the man
is just lying there and he holds his hand in front of the man's
mouth and he feels for his pulse and he leaves the room and
now I need to get to sleep soon, I don't want to know what
time it is, but I'm so restless, I don't know what's wrong, and
anyway it's a good thing I drove back into Bjørgvin and found
Asle, he's never sober now, actually for several years now he's
never been sober, not once, not really, in all these years, even if
he says he only starts drinking in the evening or maybe late afternoon it's been a long time since he wasn't drunk, I'm sure of
that, I think and I think that I'm going to get up soon and take
a taxi to The Hospital and see Asle, tell him I'll take care of his
dog, Bragi, and then maybe I'll buy something for him, or
bring him something from his apartment, anything he needs or
wants, maybe a book, and then I need to get his dog from
Guro's apartment, that was her name right? the woman who
lives on The Lane, and she told me what number it was and I
can't think of it at the moment but I'm sure it'll come to me,

yes, Bragi, his dog, is there at the apartment of the woman I ran into, who makes a living doing Hardanger embroidery, she took the dog with her and so I need to go get the dog from her, and she lived at number 3, The Lane, or was it number 5? it was on The Lane anyway, and it's probably morning now, I think, anyway I'm awake, and it was around ten o'clock that I was supposed to go pick up the dog but I could also go by earlier, or I could go by later, however it works out, yes, that's what we arranged, something like that, I don't remember it too clearly, but she did live in The Lane, I remember that much for sure, and first I need to take a taxi to The Hospital and see Asle and I need to tell him that I'm looking after his dog, Bragi, while he's in The Hospital, so he doesn't need to worry about the dog, I have to tell him that, I think, and I can bring him anything he might want, from his apartment, or go buy what he wants, because there, in The Hospital, he probably can't paint but he could sketch or draw, but he doesn't like to draw, he's always said that, drawing was never for him, he said, always that, he's always said that he's a painter, not a draughtsman, for him what matters is oil paint on canvas, nothing else, and he doesn't know why but that's how it has to be, oil on canvas, still he always keeps a sketch-pad and pencil with him in the brown leather shoulderbag he always carries with him, so he can sketch down something that might turn into a painting later, yes, I know that, I think, but I don't understand why I'm so restless, I can't get to sleep and I can't get up either, but why? what should I do? or is it tomorrow already? did I sleep at all? or just doze off in a kind of half-sleep and dream or half-dream? I think, and since this trip happened so suddenly I didn't bring anything with me, not even a toothbrush and toothpaste, no change of clothes of course, and even if I have a sketch-pad and pencil in my shoulderbag I don't feel like sketching anything

now, because what would it be? I think, and I didn't bring a
book, I read a lot, and recently I most often read around in The
Bible, a little of one part and then a little of another part, yes, I
used to read through the whole Bible but now I jump around
at random and read a little from whatever page I happen to
open to, but I don't feel like reading in the Bible that's sitting
on the nightstand there, if I'm going to read in The Bible I
want to read in my own Bible, for whatever reason, and I consider myself a believer, yes, a Christian, yes, I've even converted
to Catholicism, but I can't believe in a God as vengeful as the
God of the Old Testament, who had children put to death and
wiped out whole peoples, no, I can't understand that, but that's
exactly why Jesus Christ came to earth, as the New Testament
tells us, isn't it? he came to earth to proclaim that God is no
longer a vengeful God, but a God of love, a merciful God, yes,
to proclaim that God is now a benevolent God and not one of
vengeance and punishment and destruction, that now he is a
God of love for all people, and not just Israel's God, yes, that's
how it had to be, that the old vengeful God took his own life
in and with and through Jesus Christ's death on the cross? I
think, even if it's the same God, because it's only we human
beings who have long misunderstood his will, what his kingdom really is, I think, because there's also a lot that's beautiful
and wise in the Old Testament, it's not that, and things in the
Old Testament point ahead to what happens in the New
Testament, or at least it can be read that way, if you want to,
but, as they always say, what stands written in the Old Testament
has to be understood in the light of Jesus Christ, of God become man, who gave himself to mankind and let himself be
crucified and killed, yes, changing the human condition and
re-establishing the connection, the oneness between God and
humanity that had existed before the Fall, which separated

human beings from God, brought them into sin and death, yes, before the devil, Satan, came to rule over this world, as stands written, yes, before the great breaking point when humanity, or Adam, tempted by Eve, as stands written, abandoned their oneness with God and gave themselves over to sin which spread through the world more and more, yes, God still understands people who sin, he was human too and he took his own life, or let people take it, and then he was the good God he'd always been when he rose up from the dead as Jesus Christ and left this earth, as God and man, undivided and whole, so that it would be possible for all people to do the same thing, since sin and death rule this world, it's like it's in the devil's power, God became human and died and rose again so that everyone who died, or who had died, could afterwards live in God, because he, the Son of Man, made it so that humanity and God were joined together as one again, in God's kingdom, which already exists, God's kingdom exists in every moment, in the eternity that's in every now, but do I believe that? do I actually believe in its reality? is it even possible to believe something like this? in this foolishness we're proclaiming, as Paul wrote, yes, that stands written, no, I probably don't, no one can believe something like that, it goes against all wisdom and understanding, because either God is all-powerful and then there's no free will, or God isn't all-powerful and there is free will, within limits, but in that case God is not all-powerful, so ever since God gave humanity free will he gave up his omnipotence, something like that must be true, because without a will that's free there can't be love, and God is love, that's the only thing that is said of God in the New Testament, and that's why God lacks divine omnipotence, he has God's weakness, impotence even, but there's a lot of strength in weakness, yes, maybe the weakness is itself a strength? and it's possible that God is all-powerful in his weakness and that there is free will, even if it's impossible to think that, because there are so many things that a person can't think, for instance that space goes on forever, and the strange thing is that it's possible to believe in the Christian message anyway, in the gospels, strangely enough you can because as soon as you start to believe it you believe it, the belief comes by itself, yes, it's like God's wordless nearness, or maybe like your angel, I think, and I am one of the people who believe, or rather one of the people who know, without knowing why, no, I can't say why, not about the whole thing and not even partly, because belief, or insight, knowledge, yes knowing is what I'd prefer to call it, is something that a person suddenly and mysteriously understands is the truth, and this truth has never been said the way it is, and it can never be said because it isn't words, it's The Word, it's what's behind all words and what makes words, makes language, makes meaning possible, and maybe it can be shown but it can't be said, yes, that's how it is, and a faith like that, an insight, a knowing like that is a grace that some people receive, but the grace, the knowledge, that these people are given can extend to cover even the people who haven't themselves been given it, yes, or don't even know it exists, the mercy embraces all of humanity, I think and I think that even just that isn't a very clear thought, if you can even call it a thought at all, I think, it's like a thought in a dream, I think, and I don't want to go to mass any more, because it's all just lies, I think, and I don't want to read from the Bible any more, I've done it enough, and especially not the Bible sitting on the nightstand, it annoys me, it's sitting there like it's staring at me, like it wants something from me, and plus it's so ugly to look at, that cover with a bouquet of flowers, it's a totally undignified Bible, I've never understood why almost every single hotel has to have a Bible sitting on the nightstand in every room, I think and now I want to sleep, just sleep, I am so tired so tired and maybe I'm dozing off a little, maybe I'm not, and I think that the first thing I'll do in the morning is eat a nice big breakfast, because they always have such good breakfast at The Country Inn, fresh-baked bread, the most wonderful scrambled eggs in a big bowl, and thin slices of bacon in a big tray with a curved metal lid, and you slide the lid back and out comes the most wonderful bacon, some pieces are crispy, some are just warm and soft, it all tastes amazing and I always take a lot of bacon and a lot of scrambled eggs and then I cut one or two thick soft fresh slices of bread for myself and find a table by a window, as long as there's one free, because I like to sit by the window and look out at The Wharf and down to The Bay, at the boats lying moored there, and then I get two glasses of water and then a big mug of coffee with milk and then I sit there and enjoy the best meal of the day, and maybe I get a newspaper, I often do, but not always, because more often than not reading what's in the paper only annoys me, and that's why I don't subscribe to any newspapers because I disagree with almost everything they say, yes, almost always, and especially what they say about art, for instance the man who writes about art for *The Bjørgvin Times* doesn't understand a thing about art, it's hardly possible to have any less understanding for art than he has, and yet a newspaper for some incomprehensible reason has him write about art, it's a mystery, he has hardly a single nice word to say about my shows, that is if they're discussed or mentioned at all, usually they're not even given a single word and now breakfast might be starting already, I think and I look at the clock and I see that it's almost six and that's when breakfast starts and I lie there in the bed and I've hardly slept a wink all night, or I guess I have been kind of asleep, as much as I'm going to be, and I probably might as well just get up and have breakfast, I think, and if Asle is better then maybe I can get him from The Hospital and then we can walk together to my car that's parked in front of The Beyer Gallery, because Asle knows the way so we can go there, and then pick up the dog, Bragi, from The Lane, before I drive Asle and the dog back home to his apartment, yes, it was quite a coincidence wasn't it, that the woman who makes her living sewing Hardanger embroidery and decorative bodices for folk costumes took Asle's dog home with her and she lives on The Lane, at number 5 The Lane, or was it number 3? and it was outside number 3, The Lane, that I found Asle lying on a step covered in snow, wasn't it? yes it was, and why just there? maybe he was going to see the woman who lives there? yes, Guro as she's apparently called, yes, that might well be, because Asle was lying sort of up on the step and turned to face a front door, so maybe it was her, Guro, that he was going to see? no he was just on his way to The Alehouse, and then he just happened to slip and fall there, because anyway that's where I was going, I think, but it's probably better if I get his dog from The Lane first before heading to The Hospital, I think and I can't get to sleep so I might as well get up, I think and did I sleep at all or just doze off? just lie there in a half-sleep? but I was gone a little, off in a sleep a little, a little in a dream, I think and then I realize that Ales is lying next to me and she's lying there with her arms around me and I take the brown wooden cross that's hanging at the bottom of the rosary, that I got from Ales once, I hold the cross between my thumb and index finger, and I think that maybe God doesn't exist, no, obviously He doesn't exist, He is, and if I were not then God wouldn't exist, I think and I see before me what Meister Eckhart has written, that if humanity didn't exist so wäre auch "Gott" nicht, daß Gott "Gott" ist, dafür bin ich die Ursache and wäre ich nicht, so wäre Gott nicht "Gott" and of course it's like that, I think, and I see in my mind Pater noster Qui es in cælis Sanctificetur nomen tuum Adveniat regnum tuum Fiat voluntas tua sicut in cælo et in terra Panem nostrum cotidianum da nobis hodie et dimitte nobis debita nostra sicut et nos dimittimus debitoribus nostris Et ne nos inducas in tentationem sed libera nos a malo and I move my thumb and index finger up to the first bead which is between the cross and the set of three beads on the rosary and I say to myself Our Father Who art in heaven Hallowed be thy name Thy kingdom come Thy will be done on earth as it is in heaven Give us this day our daily bread and forgive us our trespasses as we forgive those who trespass against us And lead us not into temptation but deliver us from evil and I move my thumb and finger up to the first bead in the set and I think I usually sleep if I either say the Jesus prayer or Ave Maria and then I see the words before me and I say I say inside me Ave Maria Gratia plena Dominus tecum Benedicta tu in mulieribus et benedictus fructus ventris tui Iesus Sancta Maria Mater Dei Ora pro nobis peccatoribus nunc et in hora mortis nostræ and I move my thumb and finger up to the second bead and I say inside myself Hail Mary Full of grace The Lord is with thee Blessed art thou among women and blessed is the fruit of thy womb Jesus Holy Mary Mother of God Pray for us sinners now and in the hour of our death and I move my thumb and finger up to the third bead and I say inside myself Ave Maria Gratia plena Dominus tecum Benedicta tu in mulieribus et benedictus fructus ventris tui Iesus Sancta Maria Mater Dei ora pro nobis peccatoribus nunc et in hora mortis nostræ

II

AND I SEE MYSELF STANDING and looking at two lines that cross, one brown, one purple, and I see how I've painted the lines slowly, with a lot of paint, thick paint, two long wide lines, and they've dripped, and where the lines cross the colours blend beautifully and drip and I'm thinking that this isn't a picture but suddenly the picture is the way it's supposed to be, it's done, and then I step a little way back from the picture and I stand and look at it and then I see myself lying in the bed at The Country Inn and I think it's Tuesday today, only Tuesday, and I might as well get up, or in any case get dressed, I think and I sit up on the edge of the bed and I think well now, that was quite a night, I think and I get up and go get my trousers from where they're lying on the floor and I put them on and I pull my black pullover over my head and I put on my black velvet jacket and then I sit down on the edge of the bed and untie my shoelaces, pull my shoes on, tie the laces again, and I see my black overcoat hung on the chair and I think that I hardly slept at all even though I was so tired when I lay down, or actually, I must have slept, but maybe I just didn't realize it? I think, and strangely enough I'm not as tired as I was before, I think and I get up and go into the bathroom and splash cold water on my face, once, several times, and I take off the hairband and run my fingers through my long grey hair and and gather up my hair again and tie it in the black hairband and then I rinse out my mouth with cold water, gurgle, spit it out, I do that several times and now I'm ready to go get breakfast, as ready as I'll ever be, I think, they start serving breakfast at six o'clock, I remember that, yes, I haven't started forgetting everything even if my hair has turned grey, I usually go to bed early and get up early, around nine o'clock I go to bed and I usually fall asleep right away and I wake up at around four and get up and I'm usually painting by five, that's how it goes, I think, and I think that breakfast'll be good and then I drape the long black coat over my arm and I put the brown shoulderbag on and then I unlock the door and turn off the light and I shut the door and I put the key in the pocket of my velvet jacket and I walk over to the lift and I make the sign of the cross while I'm in the lift, I do that every morning, either I just make the sign of the cross or I both make the sign of the cross and say a Pater Noster or Our Father and make another sign of the cross after the prayer, I think and the lift stops with a shudder or two and I go out into the dining room, into The Coffeehouse, because in the morning The Coffeehouse is the breakfast room for the guests at The Country Inn who are eating there, and it's good to have left the room, I always sleep so well there, in Room 407, but last night I had an uneasy sleep, if I slept at all, but it's strange, I don't feel tired, I think, and there's no one else in the breakfast room, it's probably too early, I think and I take a big portion of food and go to a table by a window with a view of

The Bay and The Wharf and I sit down and then I eat but the food doesn't taste as good as it usually does because the whole time I'm thinking about Asle, how he's doing, has he recovered? or is he doing a little bit better at least? will he be discharged today? and if not, then maybe The Handyman can get his apartment keys and then he and I can go get Asle anything he might want, because I can't take the keys myself, no, to get into his apartment I need to go with The Handyman so he can let me in and then lock up behind me, that's how it was when I went to get the dog last night, I think, yes, I was so confused by everything going on that I don't remember some things, I think and I look around and I'm still the only one in the breakfast room and I think that there must not be many guests at The Country Inn at this time of year, plus I'm up early, they've just started serving breakfast, and I haven't seen a single person out walking on The Wharf, I think, and there are no boats moored in The Bay, and everything's covered in snow, everything's white, and it's pretty, I think, but the food doesn't taste as good as usual and I only manage to eat a little scrambled eggs and a little bacon and a little coffee and even though it's a shame to leave so much good food behind I get up and go over to the reception and say good morning and the night attendant, someone I've never seen before, looks sleepily up at me and I say I'd like to pay for one night and she draws up a bill and I pay it and I hand her the key and I leave and it's not that dark out, because the moon, it's a full moon, is shining and the snow is shining white and it's cold and clear, yes, pretty, definitely, and the stars are shining and the snow has already been shovelled outside the entrance to The Country Inn, yes, the whole pavement's been shovelled, and now? what should I do now? I think, it's early, it's probably too early to go get the dog, because the woman who took him is probably still asleep,

the woman who'd lived with a fiddler who eventually just
drank all the time and she told him to leave and he did which
she's really regretted since then, but now what was her name?
and where was it that she lived? oh, I remember, her name's
Guro and she lives in The Lane, number 3, yes of course, but
I'm sure she's not up yet, or maybe she's also someone who
wakes up early? anyway I can just go to my car first, it must be
totally covered in snow but I have a snow brush and scraper in
the car, of course, so I'll go to the car and get the snow off it, I
think, and now, yes, now I feel confident about the way, I
think and I almost have to laugh at myself, because the way
from The Country Inn to the space where I always park my car
when I'm in Bjørgvin, in front of The Beyer Gallery, yes, in the
place to park that Beyer so to speak assigned me at one point,
yes, I know the way backwards and forwards, even if I somehow, unbelievably, managed to get lost on it last night, but that
was because I couldn't see because the snow was so thick, it was
practically a blizzard, I think, but now I'll just walk away from
The Country Inn up the street and then take a right and walk a
little bit and take a left and take The Lane up to High Street,
and go down the pavement a little more, and then The Beyer
Gallery will be right there in all its glory, The Beyer Gallery's
address is 1 High Street, and there's plenty of space to park in
front of the gallery, so I'll just go there first and brush the snow
off the car and scrape the ice off the windows and then maybe
I can take a walk, or, darn it, yes, after I've brushed and scraped
the car and maybe started the engine to warm the car up, then
I'll go and ring her doorbell, the woman who lives in The
Lane, named Guro, yes, Guro, in The Lane, at number 3 The
Lane, and since I've got that right I'll ring the right door at
least, I think and I walk down the pavement and then I walk up
The Lane and there's just a narrow opening, no more than six

feet wide or so, and then it gets even narrower until it's just about three or four feet wide, and then it gets a little wider, I think, and now I should look for number 3, and I stop, and I see in the half-darkness, it would have been so dark if it hadn't been for the full moon, that the number 3 is above my head by the nearest door, and I go to the door and I look at the name-plates next to the doorbells and they say Hansen and Nilsen and Berge and Nikolausen, but there's no Guro on any label, but since she lives in number 3 her name must be Berge, probably, that must be it maybe, since Hansen is a more common name but not for people from the country, I think, and I look up, and all the windows are dark, and then I turn around and I look at the other side of The Lane and there's the step that Asle was lying on covered in snow, I'm almost sure of that anyway, and there's a sign with the number 5 there on the wall next to the door and I go over and look at the nameplates there and they say Hansen, Olsen, and Pedersen and then, thank god, one of the doorbells actually says Guro, but didn't the woman apparently named Guro say that she actually lived in number 3, The Lane? but I guess I misremembered that too? I must have gone around thinking of the wrong number, I guess the surprising thing would've been if I'd actually got it right, and it's dark in all the windows of number 5 The Lane too, but this must be where she lives? because she's exactly the kind of person who would write just her first name on the doorbell, I think, so now I know where she lives at least, and I know that she wrote her first name and not her last name, and that I've once again messed up some numbers, I think, and it really was a stroke of luck that she wrote Guro on the door, I think, since I don't know her last name, but it's about time I had a little good luck, I think and I say out loud to myself that she's still asleep, Guro's still asleep, and I think that I can't ring the bell and wake her up

now, maybe a little later, I think, so first I'll go brush and scrape
the car, start the engine, warm up the car, the whole car, and
then I can wake her up, I think and then I think that it was on
those steps outside the front door of number 5 The Lane that I
found Asle last night, with his body on the little steps in front
of the door, outside the front door of number 5 The Lane, so
maybe he was going to see the woman named Guro? maybe,
because he did have girlfriends he liked to go see, maybe Guro
was one of them? and now she has his dog, if there's not another Guro who lives in the building across the lane? since I
thought the woman who took the dog with her said she lived
in number 3 The Lane, because that is what she told me, isn't
it? that she lived in number 3 The Lane? so maybe it really is
the woman whose last name is Berge who has the dog? and
she's not named Guro? because at first she did say her name was
something else, didn't she? now what was it? it was Silje or
something, so maybe Guro isn't really her name? I think, but
what was that other name? the one she said at first that she was
called? back at Food and Drink? I think, yes, Silje, that was it, I
think and I keep walking up to High Street and when I get
there I see The Beyer Gallery up the street, the building con-
taining The Beyer Gallery is there in all its white glory, the
gallery is downstairs, Beyer's apartment is up on the second
floor, and I see my car, it's parked next to Beyer's car, totally
covered in snow, and it's still a little dark out but the light of
the full moon and the streetlamps and the white snow make it
bright enough to see pretty well, so now let's see, I think, and
I think that when I saw my car again something like a little flash
of joy went through me, that's how childish I am, I think and I
go over to the car and unlock it and get in, so now let's see if
the car starts the way it should, and it will, because it's a
well-maintained car and the battery's in good shape, I think and

I put the key in and turn it and the car starts right away and I turn the heater all the way up because it's cold in the car, then I get out and go around to the back and open the door and I take out the brush and shut the door and then I start brushing the snow off the car, and it's snowed a lot, there's about a foot of snow on the roof of the car, about a foot, yes, I think and I sweep off the snow and I think that when I've got most of the snow off the car and scraped the windows I'll go ring the bell where it says Guro, yes, definitely, and I'll probably wake her up, but that's not so bad, she can just give me the dog and then go back to bed and sleep some more, but, yes, I was thinking this whole time that she lived in number 3 The Lane, not number 5, so maybe I should ring the bell where it says Berge instead? because she did say at first that her name was something other than Guro, back at Food and Drink, yes, Silje, or maybe Silja or something else like that? and she said that we knew each other, very well, yes, didn't she even say that we knew each other in the biblical sense? can she have said that? or maybe something like that? yes, it could be, it's not totally unthinkable, no, I think and I brush and brush and the car gradually starts to look more or less good, I won't get all the snow off it obviously but I'll get most of it off, I think, and now I need to scrape the windows, I think and I open the door to the back of the car and put the brush back in and take the scraper out and shut the door and then I start scraping the windows and both the front windshield and the back windshield have already warmed up a little so it's pretty easy to scrape the ice off them, then I scrape off the side windows as best I can and then I say to myself okay enough scraping and I put the scraper back in the back of the car and then I get into the car and it's a little bit warm inside and I sit there and I look straight ahead and I'm both wide awake and very tired, I realize, and now I need to go get the dog, Bragi, yes, that's the first thing I need to do, I think and I look at the clock and it's after seven, yes well then I can just go ring the bell at the woman named Guro's building, she still has the dog, because that's what the woman who took the dog was called, yes, she was kind of just playing around with that other name back at Food and Drink, I think, and if I'm wrong then that'll just be one more person mad at me, I think and I turn off the engine and I get out of the car and I lock it and now, I think, I should go straight down to number 3 The Lane and ring the doorbell next to the name Berge, I think, be-cause she said she lived in number 3 The Lane, I'm sure of that, whereas she said both different names were her name, so I'll ring the bell there, at Berge's apartment, I think and I walk down the pavement, down High Street, and then yes, yes, I take a left and I'm already in The Lane and I walk down The Lane and then I see the sign saying 3 and I see that all the win-dows in the building are dark and I go over to the front door and I push the button for the doorbell next to the name Berge and I hear a bell ringing inside, not loud, it's soft, a faraway ringing sound and so now I just need to wait, I think, because maybe she's still asleep? maybe nothing's happening? maybe I need to ring the bell again? after all, I gave a short ring just then, I pushed the button as little as I could since I didn't want to make too much noise, so now maybe I should ring the bell again? I think and I push the button again and hold it down for longer this time and then I see a light come on in the window right next to me, so she does live on the ground floor, unless I've woken up somebody else, but she said she lived on the ground floor, didn't she? yes, I believe she did, I think and then I stand there and I think that I don't like this, I'm waking up Guro or whatever her name is now, or maybe even someone else, whoever that might be, and it's too early, I think, but I can't just walk up and down the street either, or sit waiting in my car forever, I think and then I see a face appear in the window and it's a middle-aged woman, no, the face I see is the face of a women well on in years and she comes and opens the window

Yes what do you want? she says

and she peers at me, either angry or crabby somehow, or else just indifferent, and no oh no, I think, so I did get the number wrong, I screwed up yet again

I was sleeping you know, she says

and I think I probably need to say something, but what should I say?

Well? she says

and I say I'm so sorry, she should please forgive me, I am so very sorry, because I made a mistake, I rang the wrong doorbell, which is bad in any case, I say, but especially bad so early in the morning, that doesn't make it any better, going around waking people up

You didn't wake me up, the old woman says

I'm glad to hear that at least, I say

I almost never sleep any more, she says

and I don't know what to say

I almost never sleep any more, I'm just waiting until I fall asleep forever, for eternity, she says

and I just stand there and again I say that I'm very very sorry and I say that I was trying to ring the bell of a woman who I think is named Guro

You think? the old woman says

Yes, ha, her, she says

Yes there are men coming round and ringing her doorbell at all hours, she says

So you go right ahead and ring there, she says

She should be ashamed of herself, she says

But she doesn't know the meaning of the word shame, she says

And she had a good husband too, then she kicked him out, she says

and she shakes her head and she says it doesn't make any sense, she herself never kicked her husband out even though she had every reason to, he went around with other women, yes, it wouldn't surprise her if he was going around with that Guro woman too, even though she's so much younger, but she stuck it out with her husband, she did, she didn't go running around after men, and after he died she really missed him, she did, he was a good man despite everything, he did the best he could, he worked and toiled and supported himself and his family the way a man should, he did, but then, and I see her wipe her eyes with the back of her hand, yes one morning he was just lying there, he was dead and stiff, it was some years ago but it still brings tears to her eyes just thinking about it, she says and I say yes I truly am sorry I bothered her and she says I should just hurry on down the street and ring that hussy's doorbell in that case, since that's what I want to do so badly, the old woman says and I say no and sorry and she shuts her window and then I see the light go out and I think so I got the number wrong again, same as always, it wasn't number 3 The Lane where she lives after all, I guess, and so I really hope she's at number 5 The Lane, where it says Guro next to the doorbell, if she isn't there I have no idea where to go get the dog, Bragi, and if Asle doesn't get his dog back, no, what'll that do to him? I think, but the woman who took the dog with her did say The Lane, I'm sure of that, because words I remember, yes, I'm good with words, that's why I can read and reread books, too, several times even, I think and then I turn and cross The Lane and I see the sign saying 5 and I see that it's dark in all the windows there too

and then I push the doorbell next to where it says Guro and I
see a window open in front of me on the right and the woman
named Guro, yes, it's her, thank god it's her, sticks her head out
and says in a sleepy voice yes who's there?

It's me, I say

Aha, she says

and her voice doesn't sound exactly nice and then I hear
a dog start yapping and I go over to stand under the window

Oh it's you, she says

I, I thought it was somebody else, she says

Ah, I say

Just someone, she says

and she laughs a little and it seems like she's awake now

Yes, you know, she says

I was asleep, I, she says

Ah, I say

Yes well, you know how it is for a single girl, she says

and I just stand there and can't get a single word out

But won't you come in? she says

and I don't say anything

You can't just stay out there in the cold, it's nice and warm
inside, she says

and she says I need to come in, she'll come open the door
for me, she says and I realize that I don't want to go into her
house, I've never liked going into people's houses, it's like I'm
getting too close to them or something

You've been here before, after all, she says

Lots of times, she says

and she laughs

But I guess you don't remember? she says

You didn't even recognize me last night, she says

I would've thought you would, she says

and she says she's thought about me a lot, because I did used to come looking for her, yes she says come looking for her, lots of times, but I must've been too drunk to remember anything, yes, clearly, she says, clearly I was too drunk, she says, and anyway she's definitely wide awake now, I think and I say yes I was just, the dog, I

You woke up early? she says

Yes, I say

You couldn't sleep? she says

No, I say

You were lying in bed thinking about him? she says

and I say yes that's true I was lying in bed thinking about how Asle was doing, yes, and now I want to go home, drive home, and take his dog, Bragi, well she knows that's his name, I say, with me, of course, yes, as I'd planned, I say

Yes, yes, she says

And I know, I remember you live in Dylgja, she says

and she gives a short laugh and I nod and she says that as she's already told me she's gone to see every one of the shows I've had in Bjørgvin, at The Beyer Gallery, up on High Street, she says and she nods in that direction and she emphasizes the words *The Beyer Gallery*, as if it was something big and special, and she emphasizes *High Street*, just like how Åsleik emphasizes the words St Andrew's Cross, yes, exactly the same way, identically, with the same provincial pride, I think and she asks yet again if I won't come in and I say no and then she says well now I know where she lives anyway, because I'd probably forgotten? so the next time I'm in Bjørgvin I should drop by and see her, she says, but it would probably be a good idea if I called beforehand, she says, since, she says and she stops and she gives another short laugh and I ask if I can have the dog and she says yes of course of course and her voice sounds a little annoyed and then she's gone and then I hear footsteps and the front door opens and there she is in a yellow bathrobe holding the dog against her chest and she hands me the dog and I take him and hold him against my chest and I rub his back and I say thank you thank you so much for your help, I say and she says it was nothing, of course she had to help in a situation like that, she says and I start to put the dog down and I realize that the leash isn't there and I ask about the leash and she says wait, wait here, she'll go get it, she says and she shuts the front door and goes back inside and I stand there rubbing and rubbing Bragi's back and I think it's good to have you back, Bragi, it's good I got you back, I think, and I wait and wait and isn't she coming back? what's happened to her? she was standing there in the doorway and then she was just gone, I think, because it shouldn't take that long to find a leash, should it? I think and then the window to the right opens again and she sticks her head out and she says she can't find the leash, of course, isn't that always the way, she must have put it somewhere or another, she says, but if I come back a little later I'll get it back, because it has to be somewhere, she'll find it, it'll turn up, she says, and it'd be nice if I came by again anyway, she says and I say thank you, thank you, and I apologize for waking her up, but now she can just go back to sleep, I say and she says well then she'll expect me later, to come back to get the leash, and she'll make me a cup of coffee and a bite to eat, she says, yes, maybe she could even make me dinner? she says and I say thank you, thank you, but I need to get going back to Dylgja right away, it's a long drive, I say and she says to have a nice day anyway and it was nice to see me again and I say thank you, same to you, and then she shuts the window and she turns out the light and I start walking up The Lane with the dog held tight against my chest and it does me good to feel the warmth from the dog against my chest, it feels comforting and good and I walk up The Lane and I tell Bragi how nice it is to see him again and that we're going to my car now, I say, and then we get up to High Street and I go straight to my car and I unlock it and I see myself putting Bragi into the backseat and then I sit down properly in the front seat, take off my shoulderbag and lay it on the passenger seat, start the engine, and it's already cold again in the car but the heater is on full strength so it'll be warm again soon, I think and I pull out onto High Street and I think there's probably no reason to drop by The Hospital first, I probably won't be able to talk to Asle, it's too early, or else he'll be too sick to see me, I can feel it, I know that, I think, Asle needs to just rest, he needs to sleep, I think and I'm afraid, what if Asle just sleeps and sleeps and never wakes up? I think, and I think now, now I should drive back home to my house in Dylgja and then I'll rest too, get back to normal, and then I should paint, I think and I think that when I get home I can call The Hospital and ask if I can see Asle and if I can stop by today then there's no reason I can't drive back into Bjørgvin, at least if there's anything I can do to help him, I think and I drive confidently up High Street and I quickly turn around and see Bragi lying there on the back seat sleeping and I look forwards again and I see Åsleik standing and looking at the picture with those two lines crossing each other and then he says St Andrew's Cross, and it's like he's proud of knowing the term, and I think that I'm sure he teaches himself new words every now and then, studies them, yes, and once he's learned a term he has to say it whenever he can, like St Andrew's Cross for example, it's like he needs to show that he's someone who can do something too, the way he emphasizes the word shows that yes, he can use it, him too, even though he has just a middle-school education, he only did what was mandatory, nothing more, but that doesn't mean he's stupid, oh no, not Åsleik, even if he says for instance St Andrew's Cross with provincial pride, I think, no, he's a sharp one, Åsleik, he can say the smartest most insightful things and make someone understand something in a way they hadn't understood it before, see something in a way they hadn't seen it before, and that's exactly what you're trying to do when you paint too, yes, see something you've seen before in a new way, see something as if for the first time, no, not just that, but both see it afresh and understand it, and that's the same thing in a way, I think and I see that the two lines are Asle lying on his sofa unable to think anything except one single thought, the only thing he can think is that now he needs to get up and then he'll go down to the sea and then out into the water and then he'll wade out into the sea and the waves will wash over him and he'll just be gone, gone forever, because the pain now is unbearable, the suffering, yes, the despair, whatever you'd call it, yes, the pain was so unbearable and heavy that he couldn't even lift a hand, and plus he was shaking so much, his hands, his whole body was shaking, so he had to stand up, had to get himself something to drink, at least that, first I'll have a little drink and then I'll go down to the sea, wade out into the sea, Asle thinks, lying there on his sofa, thinking, and at the same time I was standing there in my living room or studio or whatever you'd call it and painting him as two lines of paint, one purple, one brown, I think, and I look at the road ahead and I feel happy, I'm so happy, so happy, and I don't understand how I can feel such joy just from driving away from Bjørgvin, I think and I think that maybe it's because I have a dog with me now, Bragi's with me, I think and when I get home I'll call The Hospital and ask when I can come see Asle and if I can bring him anything and I'll ask them to tell him that his dog, Bragi, is all right, I have him at home with me now, so he doesn't need to worry about that at all, I think and now I'm already out of Bjørgvin, I think and I'm driving north and I turn around and see the dog, Bragi, lying asleep on the backseat there and I feel both great joy and also worried, I realize, I have such a strong feeling of being worried that it's like something's breaking inside me, and I keep driving steadily north and I think that I just drove past Sailor's Cove, I didn't even look down at the building where Asle's apartment is, I think and I'm driving north and I'll be home soon, I think, and the first thing I'll do is go to sleep, because I feel so tired, so tired, and I fall into a kind of stupor and time just passes and I approach the turnoff and the playground and I think that even though I feel so tired I shouldn't stop at the turnoff and I shouldn't look at the playground and I shouldn't look at the old brown house where Ales and I used to live, because it's so hard to look at that house, when I do the loss of Ales overwhelms me and I drive past the brown house and I see a young man with medium-length brown hair, and he's wearing a long black coat, and a girl with long dark hair, I see them go up towards the brown house, hand in hand they walk up to the brown house and I look straight ahead and I keep driving north and I see Asle standing holding Sister's hand, his sister Alida, the two of them are standing by the side of the road, and it looks like maybe they were thinking about crossing the country road but they're so little, and why are they there alone? where are their parents? and do they live in one of the two white houses visible behind them, two houses next to each other on a not so steep hill? I think and I see Sister turn around and she says look, look at the houses behind us, she says

That's where we live, she says

Yes, says Asle

What about the houses? he says

That's where we live, Sister says

We live in one of those houses, and Grandmother and Grandfather live in the other, she says

I know, Asle says

Yes yes but I just realized something, Sister says

That we live there, in the taller house, she says

The house we live in is called The New House, and the house Grandmother and Grandfather live in is called The Old House, Asle says

It looks like the houses are holding hands, Sister says

Sort of, he says

The same way you and me are holding hands, the houses are holding hands like that, Sister says

You're right it does look like that, Asle says

and then they look at the houses and there are no grown-ups in sight, neither Mother nor Father, and not Grandma or Grandpa, just the houses, both white, one old and long and the other newer and taller, and both stand out so clearly against the green, the green fields with all the fruit trees, and the green leaves on the trees, and against the black hill rising steeply up that looks so massive like a black wall behind the meadows that slope up the hillside, and then the red barn behind the white houses

And that black hill, Sister says

Yes, Asle says

I think the houses are holding hands because they're scared of that big black hill, she says

and Asle says he's never thought that before, but that's exactly how it is, now he can see it too, the two houses are holding hands because they're scared of the black hill, yes, that's really how it is, Asle says and Sister says that the black hill is really scary, because it's so steep, and because it's always wet, water comes out from springs in the hillside, she says and she asks if Asle has heard of the princesses in the mountain blue, and he says yes he has

The mountain blue, Asle says

and Sister says that this one really ought to be called the mountain black because it's so black and Asle says that it is more of a black mountain yes and then they turn around again and stand looking at the road and I drive north and I think why are those children there alone? why aren't there any grown-ups with them? why isn't anyone watching them? I think and I see the children standing by the side of the road, along a small country road, and on the other, downhill side of the road directly above The Beach, a little ways off from the children, there's a little blue house, and a little farther down the road, a little ways past the blue house, there's a bend in the road, around Old Mound, and cars come driving fast around that bend in the road, I think, and those two kids aren't walking out onto the road are they? I think and I see that there's a mud puddle in the middle of the road and then Sister lets go of Asle's hand and runs out onto the road, into the mud puddle, and then she starts stomping her feet and the muddy water splashes up her legs, and onto her dress, and it's a good thing they have boots on, Asle thinks, and he says she can't do that and Sister says it's so fun, he should come splash around too, she says and Asle says she's getting all dirty, she mustn't do that, what is Mother going to say? she'll be so mad, she'll start yelling, Asle says but Sister acts like she doesn't hear him and just splashes away and now her dress is almost entirely muddy, almost covered in grey splotches, Asle sees and he just stands there watching and then he says she needs to stop now, it's not just that Sister's getting all dirty but it's dangerous to be in the middle of the road, a car might come, cars come driving by all the time, and the person

driving the car might not see Sister and as soon as he thinks that
he runs out onto the road and grabs Sister's arm and she shrieks
and he drags her over to the other side of the road and she's
screaming and saying she wants to splash some more and Asle
says she can't, just look at that dress, how filthy it is, he says and
Sister looks at her dress

Yeah, she says

and it's like she's about to start crying

It was so nice, so nice and blue, she says

And look at it now, Asle says

and he sees Sister start crying and he says she mustn't cry,
a dress getting dirty isn't so bad, it can be washed, and Mother
won't be that mad, and he'll say it was his fault, he'll say he
asked her to go out into the mud puddle and then she'll yell at
him not her, he says, because Mother always yells at him anyway, whatever he says and whatever he does, he says and Sister
wipes her tears away and Asle says no, he doesn't care if he gets
yelled at, not him, and he thinks that he's showing off a bit now
isn't he, he thinks

But my dress is all dirty, Sister says

and she starts crying again

Well if you're going to be so stupid about it, Asle says

and when he says that Sister really starts crying hard

I'm sorry, I shouldn't have said that, Asle says

I didn't mean it, he says

You're not stupid, really you're not, you're nice and sweet
and bright and clever, he says

and then Sister's just sniffling a little and Asle says it'll all
work out, it'll be fine, he says, but, he says, now she knows
she shouldn't do things like that, not with a nice dress on, he
says and Sister doesn't say anything and they just stand there
and then he takes Sister's hand and they stand there not sure

what to do and Asle thinks that they are going to get yelled at, he's going to get yelled at, Mother's going to get really angry when she sees how Sister got her dress all dirty, and on purpose too, Asle thinks, and he's promised Sister that he'll say it was him who told her to do it, told her to stand in the mud and stomp and jump, he's promised her that, yes, so now he has to keep his promise, Asle thinks, and even though he doesn't care that much if he gets yelled at he still doesn't exactly like it, he thinks, but anyway they shouldn't go straight home, he thinks, maybe they can come up with some other idea

Maybe we should go over to Old Mound, maybe the blue-berries are ripe there? he says

and Sister just stands there, still not sure, saying nothing

Don't you want to? Asle says

and Sister is still just standing there and she doesn't say anything and Asle realizes he's getting impatient, getting bored almost, he thinks, they can't just stay here on the side of the road like this, it'd be better to keep going to Old Mound, but if they want to do that they'll have to cross the road again, and if they do that they'll need to look carefully first, to make sure no cars are coming around the bend there before Old Mound, he thinks

You don't want to keep going to Old Mound? Asle says

and Sister just shakes her head and Asle asks what do you want to do then and she doesn't answer, and then he asks her if they should go to the smaller blue house, on the downhill side of the road, they've never done that before, and he's often thought about how he wanted to go see that house, Asle says and Sister shakes her head again and then he asks if they should go down to The Beach, down to The Boathouse, out onto The Dock, down to look at The Rowboat, as Father so often says, well I better go down and take a look at The Rowboat, Father says, either he says I better go down and bail out The Rowboat, and Mother tells him he needs to be careful and Father says he always is, he's always careful, he says, or else he says he'll go out on the water for a bit and try to catch a few fish and then Mother says the same thing, that he needs to be careful, Asle thinks, and both Mother and Father have said that they, he and Sister, must never ever go down to the water alone, it's dangerous, if they fell in the water they might drown, she said, and then she would tell them about the boy she went to school with, in the same class as her, who fell in the water, he was alone in a fishing boat and he tried to climb up out of the water and the water was cold and it's hard to get back on board a boat out of the water, it's almost impossible, Mother says, and he couldn't do it, and they found the boat empty in the water, it was just floating there, and the boy, the one she'd gone to school with, they couldn't find him anywhere, until a week later, maybe even longer, some men were out in a boat and saw something floating down in the water that looked like a person and they hooked the body and pulled it on board and it was him, yes, the boy she used to go to school with, and he didn't look too good, the men said, no, she can't think about it, it's too horrible, Mother says, and then they brought him back to land and then there was a funeral and she and all the other kids who went to the school were at the funeral and she remembers how sad it was, how the boy's parents and siblings cried and cried, it was like the tears would never stop running down their faces, and the pastor had said something about God's inscrutable ways, incomprehensible, yes, but there is meaning in everything that happens, the pastor said, and he said that God writes straight on crooked lines, or maybe it was the other way around, or maybe it was slanted lines, she can't remember exactly but she remembers it, Mother says, and she couldn't understand what meaning it could possibly have for a boy to get drowned, and the pastor said that too, that it was impossible to understand, it lay beyond human comprehension, he said, but even if he couldn't understand what the meaning was and no one else could either it still had meaning, that was certain, the pastor said, Mother said, because ever since Jesus Christ, who was God, part of the Trinity of God, had died and risen up again, yes, ever since God had become human and lived as people are fated to live, birth and then life and then death, ever since then death has been turned into life for us, the pastor had said, for all humankind, yes, for those who lived before Christ and those who lived at the same time as him and those who lived after him, death, yes, death had been turned into life, into eternity, the pastor had said, Mother said, and now the boy was with God, yes, he had come home, come home to where he had set out from, the pastor had said, and God had been with him when he drowned, and had taken as good care of him as he could, he was certain of that, the pastor had said, and Mother said she couldn't understand how that was any consolation because the boy was gone, he would never come back home, he was gone forever now, the sea had taken him, taken his life, and his body had been laid in the ground, Mother said, so they never, Mother said, they must never ever ever go down to the water, The Beach, The Fjord, alone, Mother said, only when she or Father or another grown-up was with them, only then could they go down to The Beach, to The Fjord, and they must absolutely never go out onto The Dock, because out past The Dock the water was very deep, she said, so they must never, never go out onto The Dock, she said and Asle stands there holding Sister's hand and he thinks that now they'll go down onto The Beach, yes, then they'll be able to wash all the dirt off Sister's dress, so it'll be clean and nice again, and then, once they'd washed her dress, yes, Mother couldn't be mad at them, she'd have to be happy, yes, because she wouldn't have to wash the dress herself if they'd already done it, Asle thinks, and plus there's probably nowhere he likes being more than down by the water, there's so much to see there, little crabs scuttling around between the stones on the beach, and there's seaweed, with bubbles you can squeeze or step on and then they crack, and tiny little fish swimming back and forth near the land, and then there are all the seashells, blue and white, some almost yellow, and it's so nice to sit on the rocks and just look at the water, at The Dock, at The Rowboat floating there nice and brown, moored with a buoy and floating on the water, and then there are all sorts of things that can wash up on The Beach, branches, broken oars, buoys, yes, maybe there'll even be a message, a scrap of paper in a bottle with something written on it, but he's never found a message in a bottle, not yet, even when he walked slowly along The Beach, he's walked all the way in to The Dairy and back again and seen so many things lying on The Beach but never a message in a bottle, although he's seen lots of bottles washed ashore, that's normal, so now if they walk slowly along The Beach in towards The Dairy they'll definitely find a bottle somewhere or other, and anyway down below The Bakery there's a huge pile of bottles, there must be hundreds, but that, he knows, is because they drink, both The Baker and his wife, The Baker's Wife, they live there and after they've drunk a whole bottle they take it down to The Beach and put it in a pile, not quite on The Beach, but the hill down from The Bakery goes down to The Beach, yes, it's really un-believable how many bottles there are there, Asle thinks, and he's often found bottles on The Beach, and he always finds driftwood, and twice he's found balls on The Beach and he still has them both, there was hardly any air in either one but then

Father inflated them so they were good to use, and they've played with those balls a lot, him and Sister, Asle thinks, and he's gone down to The Beach so many times, even though Mother said he's not allowed to, but Father never said that, and of course that's because he went to The Beach so much when he was little, when he was a boy like Asle is now, yes, because Father has always lived on the farm where they live now, he was born in the long white old house where Grandmother and Grandfather live, and Grandmother is Father's mother, and Grandfather is his father, yes, Father was born in that house and he's lived there ever since, and maybe he will too, Asle thinks, or maybe he won't, there are so many other places a person can live, he knows that because Mother was born in a town called Haugaland and grew up on the island there, Hisøy, and he's visited there lots of times, and he was born in the hospital in Haugaland, so that, yes, that's somewhere he could live too, he thinks, there or lots of other places, they don't need to live on the farm where they live now, the way Father always has

What should we do now? Sister says

It's so boring just standing here, she says

We need to think of something to do, she says

Maybe we can finally go to the blue house? Asle says

I've always wanted to go there but I've never done it, he says

But what if the people who live there come outside, I'm so dirty, my dress is all dirty, Sister says

and Asle says that her dress isn't totally clean but it's not that bad, they should just go over to the house, and no one will see them, or see that her dress is dirty, he says, and since she was stupid enough to go splash around in a mud puddle then of course her dress'll be dirty, even she must understand that, he says, but maybe they can go to the blue house anyway, Asle says and then Sister says well all right and they go down the side of the road and when they get to the blue house they stop and stand there looking down at the house

It's a nice old house, Asle says

Yes, Sister says

It's a really pretty blue, he says

and Sister nods

I'm sure it wasn't that pretty when it was new, but now it's prettier, the rain and the wind and the snow made it pretty, Asle says

and he says that the paint is flaking off in some places and that just makes the blue even prettier and Sister says she can't see it, that the colour is prettier, but she does see that the house is blue anyway, she says

You know the names of the colours? Asle says

Yes, Sister says

Because there aren't so many, he says

There are lots more colours than there are names for, or at least that I know any names for, he says

Yes, you're right, Sister says

Yellow, blue, white, Asle says

Red, brown, black, she says

And purple, he says

Yeah and a lot more, Sister says

and Asle says that's right, the colour of the blue house is totally different from the blue of the sky or the blue of the water or the blue of her dress, he says, she can just look

Yes, look how different the house blue is from your dress's blue, he says

and he says that colours are never exactly the same as one another and plus they're always changing, it has to do with the light, he says, so it's impossible to have names for all the colours there are, there'd be so many names that no one could ever learn them all, he says and Sister says still, blue is blue, she says, and yellow is yellow, she says

Yes, yes, you're right, Asle says

Of course that's right, he says

and then they stand there, holding hands, and Sister says that they've done something they're not allowed to do, hasn't Mother said over and over that they mustn't walk down the country road, she says, and Asle says yes well and he says if they listened to everything Mother says then they'd never be able to do anything at all practically, he says and then they just stand there and then they see the front door of the blue house open and someone comes out and it's a man and he has a big belly and a hat on and he turns around and shuts the door and then he walks on the gravel path to the road and there's a crunching sound when he walks and Sister whispers they need to leave, her dress is so dirty, she says and the man looks at them and stops and bends down

Well now, look who we have here, he says

What a long journey you two have been on, he says

You've walked all the way to The Knoll, he says

I didn't think your mother let you go such a long way by yourselves, he says

and both Sister and Asle look down

But it's nice to see you, the man says

And now what are your names? he says

My name's Asle, Asle says

And my name's Alida, Sister says

Asle and Alida, the man says

My name is Gudleiv, he says

And I knew your names already, but still I had to ask you, he says

and then Gudleiv holds his hand out to Asle, and then Gudleiv and Asle say Asle, and then Gudleiv holds his hand out to Sister and Gudleiv and Alida say Alida, and Gudleiv says well now they've finally been properly introduced, the way good neighbours should be, and it's about time, such close neighbours as they are, and now wouldn't they like to come inside their house? because his wife, her name's Gunvor, yes, she'd certainly like to be introduced too, actually he needs to go to The Co-op Store to buy a few things but there's no rush, now that he and his wife have received such fine visitors the shopping can always wait, neither The Co-op Store nor the things for sale there are going anywhere, he says, so why don't they just come inside for a bit? Gudleiv says and Sister looks at Asle and whispers in his ear that they really need to go home, Mother doesn't know where they are, and she's told them so many times that they're not allowed to go down the country road, she says and Asle looks at the man, at Gudleiv

Just step inside and say hello to Gunvor, she'll be so glad to see you two, he says

and Gudleiv turns around and starts up the gravel path and it crunches as he walks and Asle holds Sister's hand tight and almost drags her with him up the path after Gudleiv who's walking ahead of them with his hat

Yes, it's so nice to see you, he says

It's certainly a surprise, he says

But it's always nice to get unexpected visitors, he says

and he opens the front door and he says

Yes, welcome, he says

Welcome to our home, he says

and then he calls inside to Gunvor, come here, we have some surprise guests, he calls and he says that Asle and Sister should come inside and Asle goes in and he's holding Sister's hand and he almost drags her in after him and then he sees Gunvor walking over to them, and she's leaning on a cane

No, how nice, she says

If it isn't Asle and Alida come to visit, she says

You two have never been to The Knoll before, she says

But do come in, she says

and Gunvor turns and goes into the living room and Gudleiv shuts the front door and says they should go in and Asle says that Sister's dress isn't entirely clean and Gudleiv says yes he can see that, yes, even if his sight is pretty bad he can still see that well enough, he says and Asle says Sister just had to go stand in a mud puddle on the country road and splash around even though he said she shouldn't because her dress would get dirty, but still she kept doing it, he says

Little kids are like that, Gunvor says

But I can wipe off the worst of it, she says

and Sister looks down and she tugs a little at Asle's hand, as if she wanted them to leave, and he squeezes her hand and she says ow and Gudleiv asks if something is wrong? and both Asle and Sister shake their heads and she says no no nothing's wrong

It's nothing, Asle says

and Gudleiv says they should take their boots off and come in and Asle lets go of Sister's hand and they pull off their boots and put the two pairs of boots down next to each other

It's always a good idea to wear boots in weather like this, Gudleiv says

and Asle sees Gudleiv take his shoes off and then he puts on a pair of slippers

Come here little girl, Gunvor says

and Sister goes over to Gunvor and Gunvor holds her hand out to Sister and says her name is Gunvor and Sister says her name is Alida

Nice to meet you, Gunvor says

You too, Sister says

and Asle goes over to Sister and he sees that Gunvor is holding her cane with one hand and Sister's hand with her other hand, and she pushes open a door with the cane and then Gunvor and Sister walk through it and Asle sees Gunvor run some water into the sink and pick up a washcloth and wet it and then she starts wiping the dirt off Sister's dress and Gunvor says it's not so easy, is it, she says, but she should be able to clean off the worst of it, down by the hem, Gunvor says and Gudleiv tells Asle they should go into the living room and then Gudleiv opens the living room door and says come in come in and Asle goes in and Gudleiv says he should have a seat on the sofa and Asle goes and sits down on one end of the sofa, and then he sees Gunvor come in with Sister and Gunvor is holding her hand and she says Sister should have a seat on the sofa, next to Asle, and now they'll go see if they have something to offer their guests, Gunvor says and she looks at Gudleiv

Yes, maybe you two would like something to drink? Gudleiv says

Do you like soft drinks? he says

and both Sister and Asle nod

Yes, that'd be great, Asle says

and Sister nods and she says yes and Gudleiv says he didn't think they'd like soft drinks

Really, are you sure you like soft drinks? Gunvor says

Yes, Asle says

Yes, Sister says

Well I'll go see what we have, Gudleiv says

and then he opens a door and disappears from the living room

He's checking to see if we have any in the kitchen, Gunvor says

I think we have a bottle, she says

and Gunvor sits down in an easy chair and leans her cane

against the chair and Asle sees that there's a huge loom in the living room, it takes up almost half the room, and it looks like a double loom, like two looms facing opposite directions pushed together

Yes, there are our looms, Gunvor says

We sit there and weave, one on each side, Gudleiv and me, she says

We weave the ribbons on folk costumes, the ones that hang down from the belt in the front of the apron, they're called lap bands, Gunvor says

Yes, Asle says

Lap bands, Sister says

You two have probably never really noticed those bands, have you? she says

and both Asle and Sister shake their heads

Folk costumes, Sister says

Yes, the kind women wear when they're really trying to look nice, Gunvor says

and then they don't say anything and then Gudleiv comes in and he's shaking his head and he says he was so sure there was some soda in the kitchen, two bottles at least, but no, there wasn't even one, he says and Gunvor says that's strange and then Gudleiv says he'll go down to the cellar and look there, maybe there's some soda there, he's almost sure there is, he says

There must be some soda in the cellar, Gunvor says

and then Gudleiv opens a door and leaves the room and Gunvor points at the door and says that behind that door there are stairs going down to the cellar and she says yes, she and Gudleiv weave those ribbons for the folk costumes, she says, and that's how they make the money they need, she says, and when Gudleiv comes back upstairs he can look for a finished lap band so that they can see how it looks, Gunvor says and

Asle says that would be great and then Gudleiv is standing in the door holding a bottle of fizzy lemonade in his hand and he goes and puts the bottle down on the coffee table in front of Asle and Sister, right between them, and then he goes and shuts the door they use to get to the cellar and then he goes out to the kitchen and comes back in with two glasses and he puts one in front of each of them and then takes a bottle opener and takes the cap off and Asle thinks where did that bottle opener come from? the man named Gudleiv must have been holding it in his fist? he thinks and then Gudleiv pours a little soda into each glass and says enjoy and both Asle and Sister say thank you and then Gunvor says she hopes they like it and then Asle and Sister raise their glasses and drink and Asle thinks it tastes unbelievably good, he must have been really thirsty, and he drinks up all the soda in the glass and he puts the glass down and Gunvor tells Gudleiv that she told them they could see a lap band and then Gudleiv goes and gets one and hands it to Gunvor and she lays it out on the coffee table and Gudleiv smooths it down on the table and Gunvor says so that's what it looks like, a lap band for folk costumes, she says and Asle looks at the colours and the pattern and he has no words for what he is seeing and the colours and pattern lodge in his mind at once and no, he never knew, he never would have believed it possible that a piece of weaving could be so beautiful, he'd seen Mother or Grandmother in folk costumes probably lots of times and he never really thought the costume was especially nice but now that he's seen the lap band laid out in front of him, now that he's seen the colours, and seen the pattern, yes, he's seeing something he's never seen before, one of the most beautiful things he's ever seen, Asle thinks and Gunvor asks if he thinks it looks nice and Asle says it's one of the most beautiful things he's ever seen, yes, and he can't believe they made it, it must be really hard to make that, Asle says and Sister says she thinks it's beautiful too and she's also drunk her whole glass of soda and she puts her glass down on the table and then Gudleiv asks if they want a little more soda and both of them nod and then he pours the rest of the soda into the glasses, first Sister's, then Asle's

And that's the end of the soda, Gudleiv says

But it was good while it lasted, right? Gunvor says

It tasted really good, Asle says

Yes, Sister says

and she picks up the glass right away and drinks

I guess you do like soft drinks, don't you, Gudleiv says

and Sister drinks the whole glass and then she says yes quietly and puts the glass down on the table

You can have more the next time you come see us, Gudleiv says

and Asle drinks a little soda too and then he looks at Gunvor and he says again that the lap band is really beautiful and Gunvor says it made her swell up inside when he said it was the most beautiful thing he's seen in his whole life, she says and Gudleiv says you have a good eye, Asle my boy, a good sense of things, he says and then there's a knock at the door and Gudleiv says he'll go open it

Your mother must have seen that you'd come down here and now she wants to fetch you, Gunvor says then

and both Asle and Sister look down at the ground

She doesn't know you're here? Gunvor says

No, Asle says

But she must be worried about you? Gunvor says

and neither Asle nor Sister say anything

You just came? Gunvor says

Without permission? she says

and there's no answer

Then you need to go home right away, she says

Your mother must be wondering where you are, she says

I bet she's worried about you, Gunvor says

Maybe, Asle says

Yes, Gunvor says

But it was nice of you to come, and you'll have to come see us again soon, and when you do you need to tell your mother or father where you're going, she says

Yes, Asle says

and Asle sees Gudleiv come in and next to him is a big tall man with a giant belly and he's totally bald and Asle thinks he's The Bald Man that children need to watch out for, both Mother and Father have said that, and they've said that Asle must never go with him, either in his car or into his house, Asle thinks and Gunvor tells Gudleiv that their mother doesn't know where they are, they just came here, so it would be best if they went home right away, Gunvor says and Gudleiv says no, no, that's not what he thought

In that case they need to go home right away, Gudleiv says

Promise me you will, Gunvor says

and Asle and Sister get up and The Bald Man sits down on the sofa

And I also have to thank you for dropping by to see us and I hope I'll see you again soon, Gunvor says

Thank you for the soda, Asle says

Yes, thank you, Sister says

It was nothing, Gunvor says

and then Gudleiv says yes, they must come by again, it was so nice to have such nice children over for a visit, but when they do they must must promise to tell their mother where they're going, he says and then Gudleiv takes them out into the hall and they put their boots on

Thank you for the soda, Asle says

There's no need to thank us, it was nothing, Gudleiv says

Thank you for the soda, Sister says

There'll be more for you the next time you drop by, Gudleiv says

and then Sister puts her hand in Asle's hand

We hope to see you again soon, Gudleiv says

Yes, please do come and visit us, he says

But only if you've told your parents first, Mother or Father, he says

and he opens the front door and Asle and Sister go outside

Bye, Asle says

Bye, Sister says

Goodbye, Gudleiv says

and then he shuts the door and then Asle and Sister stand there outside the little blue house and Asle says that the tall fat bald man who came over is the one they call The Bald Man, yes, he's heard that many times

The Bald Man? Sister says

and both Mother and Father said that children have to watch out for him, he says

Watch out for him? Sister says

Yes, Asle says

Never get into a car with him, or go home with him if he asks you to, he says

and Sister doesn't say anything and then she and Asle go up the path with the gravel and they get to the country road

I want to go home now, Sister says

and they start walking along the side of the road and then they hear a car and they turn around and then they see a car coming up from Old Mound and they stop and stay perfectly still and the car drives past them

Or maybe we could go down to The Beach? Asle says

But we're not allowed to, Sister says

I know, Asle says

We need to go home, Sister says

No we'll go down to the water, Asle says

Why should we go right home? he says

There's nothing to do there, he says

I can play with my dolls, Sister says

and then they stay there standing at the side of the road

No let's go down to The Beach, he says

and Asle thinks that he's done it so many times but Sister's never once been to The Beach with him ever, she's never stood right at the edge of The Fjord and looked out at the water, and she's never seen The Boathouse, or The Rowboat, he thinks, and it'll be nice for Sister to see those things, he thinks, he himself has seen them so many times because he's constantly going down to the water, even if Mother tells him he's not allowed to, yes, maybe he doesn't go down to The Beach every day but he does go pretty often, and Mother doesn't notice, she probably thinks he's playing somewhere or other around the farm, maybe in The Barn, and that's why Mother hasn't yelled at him, but Sister has probably never been down to the water with him? no, it's never happened, and she's too little, Sister, and plus he knows she won't like being on The Beach, but maybe she would like it? maybe she would think it's beautiful to stand by The Fjord and look out at the water? and maybe they can go out onto The Dock and look at The Rowboat? he thinks

But Mother says we can't, Sister says

I know, Asle says

So we can't go down to The Beach? she says

But I go down to the water all the time, Asle says

and then they just stand there and then Sister says she wants to go home and then Asle says no they're going down to The Beach, no matter what Mother says, because Sister's never once been there, has she? he says and Sister says can they really just do that? and Asle says they can do whatever they want and then they go over to the path leading down the hill to The Boathouse

It's exciting inside The Boathouse, Asle says

Do you want to go inside it? he says

It's scary, Sister says

No it's not, Asle says

and he holds Sister's hand tight and they start down the path to The Boathouse and Asle thinks he really hopes Mother doesn't see them now, because then she'd come running after them and then they'd be yelled at double, both for Sister getting her dress dirty and for doing something they're absolutely not allowed to do, going down to the water, to The Boathouse, The Beach, The Fjord, The Dock, The Rowboat, they're going to see everything they're not allowed to go see, Asle thinks and Sister says no she doesn't want to she doesn't dare and she stops and Asle tugs at her hand and she says he needs to stop

Let go, let go of my hand, Sister says

and Asle lets go of her hand and then they stand there on the path leading down to The Boathouse and Asle looks at the roof of The Boathouse with the grey stones and he knows they're called slate, Father told him, slate, and one stone is laid on the roof against another with a little of each one on top of another one, and the roof of The Boathouse is a play of grey colours, he thinks, it's almost unbelievable that there are so many different greys, Asle thinks, and plus they look so different depending on what the weather's like, when the sun is shining it almost looks like there are just two grey colours but the shadows are lots of different grey tones, because the colours are always sort of moving and at the same time it's like they're resting, yes, the colours are moving at rest and resting in motion, Asle thinks and that's not to mention the walls of The Boathouse, the siding has turned totally grey and the cracks in the wood give it so many different grey colours, Asle thinks and he says that The Boathouse is grey but it's also so many different colours of grey that don't have names and Sister says yes and he holds her hand tight because it's almost enough to scare you that there are so many different kinds of grey, and so many kinds of the other colours, like the ones called blue, just blue, but there must be thousands of different blue colours, thousands, at least, no there are so many that you can't even count them, Asle thinks

And blue, you know, there are so many blues that you can't even count them, he says

Yes, Sister says

Blue, she says

The sky is blue, she says

Sometimes, Asle says

But today it's grey too, he says

And it almost always is, he says

Yes grey, Sister says

The sky is grey and The Boathouse is grey, the stones on the roof are grey and the walls of The Boathouse are grey, but you see how they're such different greys? he says

and Sister nods

You see that? he says

Yes, Sister says

But it doesn't bother you, he says

No, she says

We can go into The Boathouse if you want? he says

But isn't it scary? Sister says

It must be so dark in there? she says

and Asle says does she see the hatch there in the side of The Boathouse? the side right in front of them? and does she see that rusty hook there? it's so they can open the hatch and go into The Boathouse, he says and Sister says she doesn't want to go into The Boathouse

No, all right, Asle says

and then they go around the corner of The Boathouse and they go down the path around the boathouse to the front corner of the building and then Sister says it's scary, she doesn't know if she's brave enough to do it and Asle says that if they just go a little farther then Mother won't be able to see them from home but then they can see The Beach and The Fjord and The Dock and The Rowboat and Sister stops, and then Asle stops too, so now they're both standing there, he and Sister, and she's in her dress all covered with mud

They were nice, Gunvor and Gudleiv, Sister says

Yeah, Asle says

They gave us soda and everything, she says

But Gunvor didn't get much dirt off your dress, Asle says

We need to wash it or else Mother'll be mad, he says

Yeah, Sister says

We can wash it in the seawater, he says

That works? she says

Yes, it works fine, Asle says

And then Mother won't be mad? Sister says

No, no, not if the dress is clean, he says

Well okay, she says

and then they start moving again, going to the corner of The Boathouse and now they're far enough that Mother can't see them from home, not from the living room window and not from out front, Asle thinks, so now they're safe, he thinks and then Sister stops and she stands still and she says look, the path in front of them is, yes, it's full of tall burning nettle plants, doesn't he see them? she says and Asle doesn't answer and he sees that some of the burning nettle is taller than he is, and the leaves are jagged and pointing their teeth at them, and Asle tells Sister to walk as close to the wall as she can, behind him, and then he walks towards the burning nettle and pulls the plants down and Sister says she doesn't like this, it's scary, she says

Can we go back? Sister says

But it'll be fine as soon as we get around the corner, then we'll see the water, Asle says

I don't think I want to, Sister says

And anyway Mother said we can't ever go down to the water, she says

And now we're doing it anyway, Sister says

and then Asle starts walking again, slowly, and he moves ahead and Sister follows him holding onto his pullover and Asle looks ahead and he sees that lots of burning nettle plants are reaching their big jagged leaves across the path, big green jagged leaves, there are some farther downhill and others uphill, some of the leaves reach high above his head and are swaying a little, even when there's almost no wind the leaves are swaying, and now he sees a burning nettle leaf coming right at his face and he stops and lifts his leg and pushes the nettle down with his foot and then they go farther and Asle sees a burning nettle leaf sticking out like it's poking his legs and he lifts his foot and pushes that one down and then he sees a nettle with its leaves sticking almost halfway across the path, lots of leaves, so many leaves, and he needs to push those down too, Asle thinks and he lifts his foot up and pushes the nettle down and Sister says it's so scary, she's so scared, she says and she holds Asle's pullover tight and he walks carefully and as close to the wall as he can and Sister says don't go so fast and Asle starts to go slower and then he lifts a foot and pushes another nettle down and now there aren't many burning nettles reaching across the path and the corner is just up ahead and they go towards it, him first, then Sister, and Asle goes around the corner and Sister comes after him and then they're around the corner and Asle takes Sister's hand and he can't understand why it feels so good to see the water but it does, he thinks

I see the water, Asle says

Me too, Sister says

It's so nice looking at the water, he says

Yes, she says

and they are out on the big rocks and up ahead is The Dock, the beautiful stone Dock, and there's The Rowboat and The Fjord and everything, Asle thinks and Sister stops

But, she says

Yes, he says

Mother says, she says

and Asle interrupts her and he says that Mother says that they can't ever go down to the water but now they've done it anyway, he says

Right, Sister says

and she grips his hand tight

We did what we wanted and not what Mother wanted, she says

and she says it with something that sounds a bit like pride in her voice, Asle thinks, as if now they've really done something big, they must be pretty grown-up to do what they did, they did what they wanted to do and not what Mother wanted and told them to do, Asle thinks and he lets go of Sister's hand and then he walks up ahead on the rocks and he sits down and then he sits there looking out at The Dock and at The Rowboat while Sister stays standing, and then she's standing there, Sister, and he's sitting there, Asle, and he thinks that it's so beautiful seeing The Rowboat floating out there almost totally motionless in the water, moored to the buoy by The Dock, and then The Fjord, it's almost totally still today, the wind is making just a few small waves, and The Rowboat is just barely moving, a little up, a little down, a little to one side, a little back, and The Rowboat is brown and beautiful and there are so many brown colours to look at on The Rowboat that it can be totally bewildering to look at them but it's beautiful to see how the brown Rowboat is brown in so many ways, that it has so many different hues of brown even if it's just brown, and Asle sees before his eyes like in a vision all these brown colours as exactly what they are, brown colours, not as brown colours on a boat but as separate colours, just colours, and he sees how the different hues slip into one another and how each brown colour changes the next, in fact all of the others, and makes them something different from what they were before, and it's unbelievable that they're all called brown, just brown, because The Rowboat is brown, no doubt about that, and caramelized cheese, brown cheese, is brown, and Mother's handbag is brown, he thinks, even though they're colours that are almost completely different

Isn't it weird that people just say The Rowboat's brown? Asle says

What else should they say? Sister says

I mean, The Rowboat is brown, she says

Yes, Asle says

But there are so many brown colours and they just say The Rowboat's brown, he says

The Rowboat is brown, Sister says

I know it's brown, Asle says

But so is brown cheese, and Mother's handbag, he says

and Asle hears in his voice that he's a little angry, and he doesn't know why

Is that anything to get mad about? Sister says

A brown boat is a brown boat, she says

Yes, Asle says

But, he says

and he falls silent

I don't know what you're talking about, Sister says

If we had to say that The Rowboat is this brown and the cheese is that brown and that other thing's this other brown then we'd never stop talking, she says

Yes, Asle says

But you do see that The Rowboat is a lot of different browns? he says

Yes, in a way, Sister says

But it doesn't matter, she says

and she says that even if The Rowboat's brown colour isn't the same all over it's still brown and so The Rowboat is brown, she says

Yes, Asle says

And you don't feel how beautiful it is to see all the different browns? he says

They're not different, Sister says

They're the same really, she says

And I don't think brown's a very pretty colour anyway, she says

and Asle doesn't say anything and then Sister sits down next to him and then they sit there for a while and Asle looks at what's in front of his eyes, the browns of The Rowboat pulling away from The Rowboat, he sees the brown colours as if they're all gathered on a single surface and he sees how everything changes if he moves any of them slightly, how all the other browns turn different

Aren't we going to do anything? Sister says

All right, Asle says

Maybe we can pull The Rowboat in towards The Dock, I know how to do that, he says

and Sister says no, they, no they can't do that, because then not just Mother will get mad but Father too, she says and Asle says that maybe they should just leave The Rowboat there but they can go out onto The Dock anyway and Sister says Mother says they mustn't ever do that, go out onto The Dock, never ever, Mother said that too, Sister says and Asle says he doesn't remember her saying that, she just said that they must never go down to the water, to The Beach, he says and then Sister says yes she did, she did say it, she's definitely said it lots of times and now they've done exactly what Mother said they must never do and Asle says yes, exactly, yes, now they've done what they wanted to do and Sister says she didn't want to do it, it was he who wanted to, she says and Asle says yes yes and he says that that's true enough but he wanted to go down to the water, at least he did, and isn't it beautiful here? he says, it's so beautiful with The Dock and The Rowboat and The Fjord and all the rest of it, he says and Sister says well it's not bad but that burning nettle was horrible, and if she'd known that it was growing across the path then she would never have come down to the water, she says and Asle says he doesn't remember the burning nettle from before, it was there of course but the plants had never been so big before

Burning nettles, Sister says

They were giant burning nettles, Asle says

and he spreads his arms as wide as he can and Sister says they were so big, that big, she says, and then she says that it's boring just sitting here like this and Asle says they could go down onto The Beach, because there's always something to see there, crabs, tiny fish, and plus there's always stuff that's drifted onto land, flotsam and jetsam, he says

Flotsam and jetsam, Sister says

Yes it's called flotsam and jetsam, Asle says

Flotsam and jetsam, okay, Sister says

and Asle stands up and Sister stays sitting and then he goes out onto The Dock and he says come on and he unties the mooring and Sister says what are you doing? and Asle says he just wants to pull The Rowboat in and then get on board and be on The Rowboat for a little bit, he says, and he pulls The Rowboat in towards The Dock and he climbs on board The Rowboat

Be careful, Sister shouts

Okay, Asle says

and then he's on board The Rowboat and then he starts to pull the rope to the buoy and The Rowboat moves out onto the water

You can't do that, Sister shouts

It's dangerous, she shouts

No it's not, Asle says

and he thinks he'll show Sister how safe it is, and he climbs up onto the middle seat and stands on the plank

Sit down! Sister shouts

and Asle sits down on the plank and starts rocking from side to side and The Rowboat rocks from side to side with him and he calls to Sister look how beautifully The Rowboat's rocking, what beautiful waves it's leaving in the water, and Sister doesn't answer and Asle thinks he should probably get back onto land and he stands up and walks forward in The Rowboat and he pulls The Rowboat in towards The Dock, climbs out onto The Dock, and then pulls the rope to move The Rowboat out again and it floats there so beautifully bobbing up and down in

The Fjord and he moors The Rowboat and then he walks over to Sister who's still sitting where she was sitting before and she says can't they go home now? she doesn't like being disobedient, and they're not allowed to go down to the country road, or to the water, she says and Asle says now they have to go down onto The Beach

Come on, he says

and Sister just stays sitting on the shore rocks

I don't know if I want to, she says

Don't be stupid, he says

I'm not stupid, she says

Why're you telling me I'm stupid? she says

You're the one who's stupid, she says

I didn't mean it like that, Asle says

You're stupid, I'm not stupid, Sister says

I didn't mean it like that, Asle says

and Sister says well then, if you didn't mean it, that's all right, she says and Asle says she's not stupid and she says he's not stupid and then he holds out his hand to her and she takes his hand and then he pulls her up onto her feet and then they walk on the shore rocks down The Beach, and it's high tide so there's almost nothing to see on The Beach, and the waves are coming up over the rocks with little splashes and Asle says the tide's so high now that there's almost nothing to look at on The Beach itself, but he always finds something or another that the sea has washed up onto land, far up onto the shore, somewhere between The Beach and where the hill starts, he says and she asks what and he says maybe a bottle, like he said before, and maybe there'll be a letter in one of the bottles, and that's called a message in a bottle, like he said before, he says, and Sister says okay and he says that even he has never found a bottle with a letter, a message, but he's found lots of bottles, and outside The

Bakery there's a pile of bottles, yes, like he said, he says, yeah she won't believe how big the pile is, it's like a mountain, he says, and they can go down The Beach past The Bakery, till they get to The Dairy, but no farther than that, he says

Should we go all the way to The Dairy? Sister says

We can, why not, Asle says

and they start walking hand in hand across the strip between the water and where the grass starts growing and back again and they don't say anything for a while and then Asle says look, look there, look, the sea has washed a whole log up onto land, he says and Sister doesn't say anything and they keep walking and then there's a screeching sound and they walk farther without saying anything

What do you think that noise was? Sister says

I don't know, Asle says

and they keep walking

It was a really loud screeching noise, Sister says

Yeah, and like something's grinding, Asle says

A grinding noise, Sister says

It's kind of strange, but the sound seems to be coming from the country road, so it's probably an old tractor, Asle says

and they've walked as far as Boathouse Hill and they keep walking and past Boathouse Hill they get to The Headland and then they see the beautiful rowboat that the people who live at The Headland Farm have moored to a pier there in Hardangerfjord, and up there, in the white house, that's where Bård lives, Asle thinks, and from there, from The Headland, they can see all the way to The Dairy at the end of The Beach, below The Bakery and before The Co-op Store, but they can't see The Co-op Store because The Dairy blocks it so that they can't see it, and next to The Dairy is the big yellow house where The Bald Man lives, but they can't see that either, Asle thinks and Sister says it looks really far to walk, all the way to The Dairy, and Asle says it looks like a long walk but it isn't as far as it looks, he says

It's a lot closer than it looks, he says

Yeah, it's a long way, she says

and Asle grips Sister's hand harder and then he looks up at The Headland Farm and now he sees Bård standing there in front of the house looking down at them and he doesn't like talking to Bård because he's always so rude, he's always saying that their farm is bigger, their rowboat is nicer, his father is stronger than Asle's father, stupid things like that, Asle thinks and they start walking to The Dairy

That noise must be coming from an old tractor, Asle says

But it's really loud, like it's coming from right next to us, or somewhere near us, Sister says

Yeah, Asle says

Can a tractor really make a noise like that? she says

A screeching grinding noise? she says

I think it can, an old one can, Asle says

and they walk on and they aren't saying anything but it's like an uncertainty has come over them, and they think without thinking it in words that they shouldn't have done this, now they're doing something they're not allowed to do, something Mother has said again and again that they shouldn't do, they're doing something forbidden, and maybe that's why they heard that screeching grinding sound? maybe it didn't come from a tractor but just because they were doing something wrong? that's why they suddenly heard that sound? Asle thinks, because the truth is an old tractor can't make a sound like that, he thinks and he doesn't like the sound, he thinks and they walk farther and then they stop and Asle turns around and he says now Bård is standing in the rowboat they just walked past, he's standing up on a seat, he says and Sister turns around

That looks dangerous, she says

He's just doing it because he saw us walk by, Asle says

That Bård's just trying to act tough, he says

and he says Bård's a big scaredy-cat and he must be scared to death standing on the seat there and he's doing it just to act tough for them, there's no other reason, so they shouldn't look at him any more, they should just keep walking, Asle says and he and Sister turn around to face forward and they walk carefully on and Asle says that when they get past where The Beach kind of bends away they won't be able to see Bård any more, and that's good, he says and they keep walking and they're holding each other's hand and they go past the bend in The Beach and now they can't see The Headland any more and they walk towards The Dairy and Asle lets go of Sister's hand and points

Look, there's an oar there, he says

and Asle runs over to where the hill meets the beach and Sister stops and then Asle lifts up the oar

Look, he shouts

What's that, Sister says

It's an oar, Asle says

Yeah, Sister says

I found an oar, Asle says

A whole oar, perfect for using, he says

and Asle swings the oar back and forth in the air and he says maybe there's another oar farther up The Beach, closer to The Dairy, oars come in pairs, he says and Sister says she wants to go home

I don't like that noise, she says

No, Asle says

But we can just go to The Dairy can't we, he says

I don't like that noise, Sister says

We'll go as far as The Dairy and then turn around and go home, Asle says

Well all right, Sister says

and then they stay standing there and Asle puts the oar back down on the hill and then he gives Sister a big hug and then he says well they can just go to The Dairy, and then go look at all the bottles out behind The Bakery, and then, yes, then maybe they can go to The Co-op Store, because there's lots to see in the shop windows there, Asle says and Sister says they can't do that, because Mother's told them they mustn't go on the country road, it's dangerous, the road's so narrow that there's hardly enough room for both a car and people, so they can never walk there by themselves, only with grown-ups, only with Mother or Father, she said, Sister says and Asle doesn't answer and they walk carefully down The Beach and Sister says she's tired of walking and Asle says in that case they can sit down and rest for a bit and then they sit down, each on their own round stone, and they sit there and don't say anything and Asle thinks that it's boring just sitting like that, and it feels like they've been sitting there a long time, he thinks

Can't we keep going? he says

Okay, Sister says

You're not tired any more, he says

No, my feet are a little less tired, Sister says

and then they get up and Sister takes Asle's hand and they walk on and they see The Bakery up ahead and then The Dairy, Asle thinks, and they'll have to go up the path to The Bakery to get to The Co-op Store, past all the bottles, past the pile, yes, mountain of bottles, and then up to the country road, and once they're up there they'll be able to see The Co-op Store, and it's not so far to walk from The Bakery to The Co-op Store

Can't we turn around and go back now? Sister says

No, Asle says

I'm scared, she says

There's nothing to be scared of, Asle says

Yes there is, Sister says

What? Asle says

If we go to The Co-op Store we'll have to walk past the big yellow house, the one next to The Dairy, Sister says

And that's where The Bald Man lives, without a single hair on his head, in the big yellow house, she says

He looks so scary, she says

Yeah, Asle says

And he's the one children have to watch out for, you said so yourself, Sister says

Yeah, Asle says

and they walk carefully, step by step, up the path towards The Bakery

That bad noise is gone now, Asle says

and Sister nods

And there's the mountain of bottles, Asle says

and he points

Yeah, Sister says

and then she says that it's really not worth looking at, a mountain of empty bottles, she says and Asle says maybe not but they're empty bottles of alcohol, he says, because The Baker and The Baker's Wife both drink, and when they drink they don't stop, and then they bake lopsided bread but they bake even when they've been drinking and are drunk, because when people drink alcohol they get drunk, and then they're not always steady on their feet when they walk and sometimes they shake and anyway the bread that The Baker and The Baker's Wife bake then always comes out lopsided but what they bake when they haven't been drinking is straight and nice, he says and Sister nods and then she says that she wants to go home, now they're almost at the country road where Mother has said so many times that they can't walk by themselves and the hill is so steep and she's so tired, she says, and she sits down on the grass and then Asle sits down too next to her and they just sit there and they don't say anything and then Sister says that she can hear a voice and Asle says he can't hear anything and Sister says okay I guess not and Asle thinks that they need to keep going, it's boring just sitting like this, he thinks and he gets up and then he holds his hand out to Sister and she takes his hand and he almost yanks her onto her feet and then she stands there and she says she can hear voices, but they're far away, and Asle says he can't hear anything and then he almost drags Sister after him up to The Bakery and up to the country road and Sister says they're not allowed to walk on the country road here, both Mother and Father have told them that over and over again, she says and Asle says that's true and then someone behind them says look at that, two kids out for a walk and they turn around

Look who's here, The Baker says

Maybe your mother sent you to buy some bread? he says

Maybe you're big enough now to run errands for your mother and buy some bread? he says

What clever children, The Baker says

and they just stand there

Or maybe you've just gone out for a walk? he says

and the door to The Bakery opens and The Baker's Wife comes out

Well I never, look who's here, she says

They're probably out for a walk, The Baker says

But their mother doesn't let them walk here, The Baker's Wife says

No, The Baker says

Probably not, he says

and he goes over to them and then he puts one hand on Asle's shoulder and one on Sister's shoulder and then he says that the two of them need to go straight home to their mother right now, she must be worried about them by now, she must be scared, The Baker says

I'm sure she is, The Baker's Wife says

and then she says wait a second and she goes inside and comes back out almost right away and she comes walking up to them and she holds out her hands to them with a roll in each hand

Nice children like you deserve a roll, The Baker's Wife says

But only if you go right home to your mother, she says

Thank you, thank you very much, Asle says

Yes, thank you, thank you, Sister says

Don't mention it, nice children like you, The Baker's Wife says

Nice children, yes, The Baker says

But now you need to go home to your mother, really, The Baker's Wife says

I'm sure she's scared and worried about you, she says

And maybe she's already gone looking for you, she says

Because I'm sure you're not allowed to walk on the road alone, The Baker's Wife says

We went along The Shore, Sister says

And you definitely aren't allowed to do that, The Baker's Wife says

To go down to the water, she says

I'm sure you're not, she says

and Asle and Sister both start eating their rolls and they must have been hungry because they bite and chew and The Baker's Wife asks if the rolls taste good and Asle and Sister say yes at the same time and with their mouths full and The Baker says he's glad they taste good and Asle thinks that as long as The Baker and The Baker's Wife are there they can't go to The Co-op Store, because both of them, The Baker and The Baker's Wife, said they have to go back home to Mother, that she's worried about them, and that she doesn't let them walk alone like this, and that's true, but they haven't done anything wrong, it's just Mother who thinks they have, and it's only because she's always so scared about them, she gets scared and worried about everything in the world, they're not allowed to do anything, not walk down to the country road, down to The Boathouse or The Shore, nothing, they're not allowed to do anything, all they can do is stay home, inside or out in front of the house, nowhere else, ever, Asle thinks, and it's only because Mother's always so worried about everything, he thinks, and then he hears a voice inside himself, it's Mother telling Father that that's not true and then he says that it is true, they're not allowed to walk down to the road, or to the water, that's how it is, he says and Mother says you hear that, you hear that, Father is saying the same thing she is, Mother says, Asle thinks and there, over there, that can't be Mother running up to them, no, no, now they'll get caught and once they get home they'll be yelled at and he's the one who'll be yelled at and Mother comes running up towards them and she looks scared and it looks like she's been crying and she comes towards them and Asle doesn't understand, was she really that scared about them, he thinks, no, in that case they never should have done what they did, he thinks and then Mother puts her arms around him and Sister and hugs them both against her and then out of breath she says to The Baker and The Baker's Wife that, that, that, have they heard yet? have they heard that he drowned? that the boy from The Headland Farm, Bård, the boy the same age as Asle, was just found drowned, just now, she was going up The Beach, because she didn't know where Sister and Asle were and then she got scared that they'd gone down to the water and she went down to The Beach to look for them but they weren't there, then she went up along The Beach and when she got past Boathouse Hill and out by The Headland she saw a crowd of people on The Beach below The Headland Farm and she saw that The Doctor's car was parked up there in front of The Headland Farm and she went over to the people there and then she saw Bård lying on The Beach, no, she can see it now, it's too horrible, Mother says and she lets go of Asle and Sister and covers her eyes and then hugs them to her body again and then Mother says that a woman, she can't think of her name right now, it doesn't matter anyway, this woman, yes, said, said, this woman told her that as she was walking past The Headland Farm, on the road, over there, Mother says and she points, she looked down at The Fjord and saw something floating in the water next to the rowboat that belongs to The Headland Farm people and it looked like a little person, and then she ran and knocked at the door and the mother was home and then the two of them ran down to The Beach and when they got to The Beach the mother saw that it was her son Bård lying there floating in the water

It's Bård, she'd said

and then Bård's mother waded out into the cold water and started swimming until she got to Bård and somehow she got him onto land and then she picked him up and held him to her breast and she carried him onto the hill of The Beach and he wasn't breathing and he was lifeless and she, yes, she, when she saw the lifeless boy she thought she should go call The Doctor and she ran up to the house at The Headland Farm and looked up The Doctor's phone number and dialed it and he said he'd come right away and that they had to try to blow air into the boy, put your mouth against his mouth and blow air in, and when he's breathed it out blow more in, The Doctor had said, something like that, and she'd run back down to The Beach and then she'd taken a deep breath and blown it into Bård's mouth, again and again, she'd, she couldn't remember her name, she'd kept doing that with the breathing until The Doctor came and then The Doctor had done the same thing and pushed hard, both on Bård's stomach and on his heart, and he kept doing that for a long time but Bård was still lying there lifeless and eventually The Doctor looked up, yes, up at the sky, and he'd said Bård was dead, he'd drowned, that woman told Mother, and Mother saw Bård lying dead on the hill and she can see it now and it's too horrible, she says and Mother squeezes her eyes shut and then Mother says she'd started thinking where were her own two children? could they have drowned too? it'd been a while since she'd seen them and then she'd run towards home and out onto The Dock but nobody was there and she'd looked in the water around The Rowboat and she couldn't see anyone in the water and then she'd run back down along The Beach and then then she'd run up to the country road and she was running faster than she'd ever thought she could, Mother says, and now after running all over here they were, here were Asle and Alida, yes, both of them, and they were alive, they were alive, and she couldn't believe it, they were alive, they were alive, Mother says and she starts crying again and then she presses Asle and Sister hard against her, so hard that it hurts, Asle thinks, and he tries to get loose but then Mother just holds them even tighter, yes, she's holding them so tight, so hard, that they almost can't breathe, Asle thinks and he hears The Baker's Wife say she can't believe it, so young, just six or so and now he's drowned, he hadn't started school yet anyway, and now drowned, no, it's too terrible, The Baker's Wife says and Asle looks at The Baker just standing there staring and staring at nothing

Little Bård from The Headland Farm is drowned, he says

No, impossible, I don't believe it, he says

It's unbelievable, Mother says

He probably just wanted to go on their boat, The Baker says

and Mother says he'd pulled the rowboat in and got on board and then pulled the rowboat out and then he'd fallen into the water somehow, into the cold water, and he couldn't swim, and then he hadn't been able to get back on board the boat, that's how it must have happened, Mother says and she says that when she was a girl the same thing happened to a boy in her class, he was out fishing and he fell into the water and then they found him drowned, and after he'd been in the water so long, Mother says, and The Baker says it's too horrible he can't believe this has happened

It's unbelievable, The Baker's Wife says

There are no words for it, The Baker says

No, there aren't, Mother says

No, no, no, she says

and she hugs and hugs Asle and Sister to her and Mother says that when she couldn't find Asle or Sister she got so scared, more scared than she'd ever been in her life, because by that point she was sure they'd been out in the rowboat with Bård from The Headland Farm and they'd fallen into the water too and were lying on the bottom, on the shelf underwater, Mother says, and then here they both were, Asle and Alida, outside The Bakery, large as life, and never, no, nothing she had ever seen had made her happier than seeing her two children standing there large as life, each eating a roll, Mother says and the tears are pouring down her cheeks and she lets go of them and wipes the tears off her cheeks with her hands and away from her eyes with the backs of her hands

Yes, I gave them rolls, The Baker's Wife says

And then I said that they had to go home, because their mother doesn't let them go for walks alone like this, she says

and Mother says no of course not

These children don't do what they're told, she says

and then she laughs with pure joy between her tears and then she says it was probably Asle who decided to do it, but now, no, now she's so happy, so relieved, that she can't be angry, and anyway now, yes, now she just wants to go home, get her children back into the house, she says and The Baker's Wife says she can have a few more rolls to take with her and then The Baker's Wife goes into The Bakery

No, it's beyond belief, The Baker says

No, Mother says

It's just too terrible, The Baker says

Yes, Mother says

and then they just stand there and then The Baker's Wife comes out with a brown bag

Have some rolls, she says

and she hands the bag to Mother

Okay thanks thank you, she says

and then Mother takes the brown bag and Asle thinks that this bag is yet another brown colour and then Mother grabs Asle's hand with one hand, the one she's holding the brown bag of rolls with, and she grabs Sister's hand with her other hand and then Mother says now they're going to go home and get back inside safe and sound and they stand there not moving

What horrible news, The Baker's Wife says

Unbelievable, I can't believe it, The Baker's says

I don't understand it, he says

I can't believe it, The Baker's Wife says

How can God let something like that happen? The Baker says

How can a good God let something like that happen? he says

There is no God, The Baker's Wife says

Not a good God anyway, she says

Or not a God who's all-powerful anyway, The Baker says

I believe that the little boy is with God now, he's resting with God, Mother says

Yes, he is, The Baker says

He's at peace with God now, the boy is, he says

Bård, yes, The Baker's Wife says

and then they just stand there and Asle feels Mother gripping his hand so hard that it hurts and he shakes his hand a little and Mother loosens her grip a little

We have to believe that he's at peace with God now, Mother says

and then she turns around and they start to go up to the country road and after they get to the road they start walking up the road and they can see their house and Asle thinks that Bård, from The Headland Farm, is drowned, he's dead, he's gone forever, he'll never talk to him again, and he can't understand it, because it's only old people who die and are gone forever, not children, children don't die, Asle thinks, he didn't think they could, and dying, being gone forever, was something so far in the future that you couldn't even see it, Asle thinks and he hears Mother say that she has never been as happy as she was when she saw them, never ever in her whole life has she felt that happy, felt such joy, she says

I was so happy I could've jumped for joy, Mother says

and then she jumps and she starts laughing

When we get home I'm going to make hot chocolate for you two and then we'll eat these rolls and drink chocolate, she says

and Asle thinks that sure he can eat the rolls and drink the hot chocolate but he doesn't really like them, no, but he can't say something like that, he couldn't tell The Baker's Wife when she was trying to be nice and giving him and Sister a roll, all he could do was take it and eat it and say it tasted good, and now he'll probably have to do the same thing when they get home, even if Mother knows full well that he doesn't like hot chocolate, or rolls, but she's probably not remembering anything like that now, he thinks, because anyway she likes rolls and hot chocolate, Asle thinks and I sit here in my car and I look straight ahead and I'm already at Instefjord and I start driving slowly up Sygnefjord and I drive carefully and I think that actually I didn't want a driving licence or a car and now I like driving, I think, and Father was the same way, he didn't want a car, but Mother kept bringing it up, again and again, she said how great it would be to have a car and then Father says yes and Mother says in that case they should do it soon and actually buy a car and Father nods

Can't you get a driving licence? Mother says

and Father says he supposes he could, but he doesn't know if he can afford to buy a car, he's just about getting by with his orchard and his boatbuilding out in The Shed, and it'll be expensive to get a driving licence, and even more expensive to buy a car, and however good the fruit harvest is, however many kroner it brings in, and however many boats he builds and however good and beautiful they are, no, it doesn't add up to all that many kroner, he said, they managed, yes, they got by, but was there really any way to lay out all that money and buy a car? no, he really doesn't know, Father said and Mother said they had to be able to manage it the same as everybody else, they weren't any worse off than other folks, she said and Father said that he wasn't sure he could afford to buy a car, he just wasn't, and Mother said she was sure he could do it and Father said yes well and then he'd have to find the time, he was so busy, he had so much to do, he'd have to build quite a lot of boats that winter for them to manage it and then in the spring the fruit trees'd have to be tended to and trimmed and fertilized, and sprayed, and the summer is when it's easiest to sell boats, because everyone with a cabin by the water needs a boat, and then comes fall and all the fruit needs to be picked and sorted and packed and sold, Father says, and he doesn't know how he's been able to do it, he says and Mother says yes, it's a lot to do, you work hard, but it would really be great to have a car, and more and more people in Barmen have cars now, yes, half the families their age in Barmen have bought cars, or almost half anyway, yes, she says

Soon there'll be more people driving to The Co-op Store to do their shopping than walking, Father says

Just about, Mother says

Plus we could take car trips, she says

We could drive out to Haugaland, and Vika on Hisøy, to visit my parents, she says

And my brothers and sisters, and nieces and nephews, she says

Yes, Father says

and then he doesn't say anything else

A car's expensive, he says then

You work all the time, you must make some money, and if other people can buy a car why can't we? she says

But people are paying less and less for boats, most people want plastic boats now, and there's less work to do on a plastic boat, so it's harder and harder to sell wooden boats, for a good price anyway, and I don't get paid as much for the fruit either, that gets lower prices too now that there's so much imported fruit, Father says

But you work so hard, you're always busy doing something, Mother says

and then she says that other people, other people who work a lot less than he does, they have driving licences and cars, she says

A driving licence isn't free either, Father says

and then they don't say anything else

But yes, we'll get a car sooner or later, Father says

Well I'm really looking forward to it, Mother says

It would be nice, Father says

and I've driven past Åsleik's farm, and the roads are well cleared, like always, because as soon as any snow falls there's Åsleik with his tractor, I think, and it'll sure be nice to get back home, I think and I turn off of the country road and I drive up my driveway, and Åsleik has cleared that too, I think, as soon as it snows up comes Åsleik clearing the snow with his old tractor, I think and I stop in front of the door and I stay sitting in the car and I breathe slowly out and I think that it feels so good to be back home, back home in Dylgja, back to my good old house, I think and I get out of the car and then open the passenger door and pick up Bragi and then put him down in the snow and he runs around in the snow and jumps here and there and then he lifts his leg and lets out a yellow stream and he makes what looks like a black hole in the snow but there's yellow and when he's done he starts running around and around in the powdery snow and I call him and Bragi stops and he stands there and looks stubbornly at me and I think so I finally got myself a dog, I think and then I say come on Bragi and then he comes trotting over to me and I go into my house with Bragi at my heels, and then I go into the main room and then out to the kitchen, still with Bragi at my heels, and I run some water into a bowl and I put the bowl down in the corner behind the hall door and Bragi is there in a flash and he drinks and drinks and then I get another bowl and I slice a piece of bread and tear it into pieces and then I put the bowl of bread pieces down next to the other bowl and Bragi is there in a flash and he eats and eats, so he must have been really thirsty and hungry too, yes, I think, standing there looking at the water bowl and I see that Bragi has drunk up all the water and I refill the bowl and I put it back down and then I see that the food bowl is empty too and I slice another piece of bread and tear it into pieces and put them in the bowl, but now Bragi just sniffs at the bread and water a bit, he doesn't touch it and then I go back into the main room with Bragi at my heels and I go and stand where I can look at the painting with the two lines crossing and even now, well into the daytime hours, it's only half-light, or half-darkness, whatever you'd call it, I think and I see that the picture is shining, yes, even in the half-dark it's now like there's a light shining from almost the whole picture, and it's impossible to understand, and yet I do understand, at the same time, that with these two lines I've made something, I've actually painted a good picture, in its way, in its own way, and I know that I won't do anything more with this picture, and I think that I can sell this picture, but for a low price, for much too low a price, even though this might be one of the best paintings I've ever managed to paint, I think, one of the paintings with the most light in it, I think and I think I should keep this painting for myself, because if I sell it it'll go away somewhere and then it'll be gone, and then maybe it'll be sold or given to someone else in turn, and I know I wouldn't get much for this picture anyway, no one wants to pay much for a picture like this, not one painted by me anyway, I know that, so I should keep this picture for myself, because really, yes, even if this picture may be a failure in others' eyes, and for all I know may actually be a bad picture, still it's one where I've truly painted some of what I try to get into all of my pictures, I think, that something, that, that, yes, it can't be said but maybe it can be shown, or almost shown, yes, whatever it is that can be captured in a picture somehow and shown rather than said, but not only in a painting, it can be shown at least as well in writing, in literature, I think, and this picture isn't like the others I've painted, you can tell just from the canvas, because I usually like to paint the whole canvas white first instead of letting the canvas show through, that's why I use so much white oil paint, I think and I think that I'm so tired now that the only thing to do, the only thing I want to do, is get a little sleep, I think and I hang up my brown shoulderbag on its hook between the bedroom door and the hall door and then I go out into the hall and hang up my black coat and I take off my shoes and then I go back into the main room and I take off my black velvet jacket and I hang it on the back of the chair to the left of the round table and then I go over to the bench that I have in a corner and I lie down, and even though it's cold in the room, despite the electric heater that's been on full-strength while I was gone, and even though I should light the stove I just lie on the bench and drape the grey wool blanket over me, the one Grandmother had when she was lying sick at home in The Old House and that she handed to me when they came to get her and drive her to The Hospice and that I took with me when I left home to go to The Academic High School and that's stayed with me ever since, wherever I lived the blanket came with me, I think and I see Bragi come padding over and he hops up onto the bench with me and he lies down next to me and I spread the blanket over him too and then I stroke and stroke his fur, up and down, and Bragi presses against me and he's good and warm and then I think well then I've got myself a dog and it really was good that Åsleik cleared the roads, yes, the main road and the driveway too, yes, how would I ever get by without Åsleik? without him and his old tractor? who else would clear the road up to my house? yes, I'd probably have to do what I did before, before I had the driveway built, park my car down on the main road and walk up, but it's steep and it feels like a long walk especially when I'm carrying something so it was a real slog to carry everything up to the house, yes, a real slog, but it was all right, I managed that too, one way or another, before I had the driveway built, I think, but now as soon as any snow falls there's Åsleik with his tractor, and he's always home, except for the two days a year when he goes to see Sister in Øygna, right by Instefjord, for Christmas, I think and I tuck the blanket around me better and I lie there on the bench with Bragi tucked against me and I close my eyes and suddenly I start in fright, because I can clearly hear a screeching sound, the same sound, I think, and it sounds like it's coming from somewhere right near me, right next to me, a screeching grinding sound, and it has to be coming from an old tractor, I think and I think that I don't feel so tired any more, so I must have nodded off, I think, and now I need to get up and get some things done, I think, and now the screeching grinding noise is very near me, I think and I get up and Bragi gets up and he stands on the bench and looks at me, so, I have a dog now, yes, I think, and I've thought so many times about getting a dog but never done it, I think and I look at the chair I always sit in, on the left next to the round table, and I go and sit down in the chair and Bragi comes and jumps up and lies in my lap and I take my bearings, the top of the pine trees outside my house have to be exactly in the middle of the middle right pane of glass in the window, and then I look at the landmark I always look at, near the middle of the Sygne Sea, and I see waves and it makes me feel calm in a way to look at the same place, at my landmark, at the waves there, every time I fall into a kind of light doze that's a bit like sleep but isn't, maybe, I think, and then I notice that the room is cold, so I need to light a fire in the stove, but it's always so sad and painful to do that, I usually put it off as long as I can until it's so cold that I absolutely have to light the stove, I think, and now, yes, now the room's cold enough that I really do have to light the stove, I think and then I pet and pet Bragi's fur and I think now I'll go light the stove, I think, and then there's that noise, that screeching sound, that grinding, I think, but how can I just sit here like this so sluggish that I can't even light the stove no matter how cold it gets in the room, I think and then I listen to that screeching grinding noise, and now it's very close, and it's unmistakable, that screeching grinding noise must be coming from Åsleik's old tractor, I think, so now Åsleik'll probably be standing outside the door any minute and knocking, I think, and that means it must have snowed more, I think and I look at the waves and I see Asle and Sister walking over to The Dairy, they're walking hand in hand, and they've started walking so fast that they seem to want to get to The Dairy quickly and then right back home, I think and now I really need to stand up and light the stove, I think and then I hear that it's fallen quiet, so Åsleik's probably standing in front of the house now, I think and I hear Sister say that now that screeching grinding noise has disappeared and Asle says yes and Sister says that it was a terrible noise and I hear a knock at the door and I get up and I'd forgotten I had Bragi on my lap and he falls onto the floor when I stand up and he starts yelping loudly

Hush, I say

and Bragi just keeps yelping

Hush, I say

and now he's barking in a loud and strong voice and so I pick Bragi up and I hold him in my arms and Bragi stops barking and I think that it was probably Åsleik at the door, my neighbour and friend, I think and I go out into the hall and I open the front door and I see that it's snowed a lot since I got home and I see Åsleik standing there in his brown snowsuit with the brown fur hat with flaps over the ears down to his long grey beard

Did you get a dog? Åsleik says

That's a surprise, he says

Is it a puppy? he says

and I say that I'm just watching the dog for someone I know in Bjørgvin, and he's not a puppy, just a small dog, I say and Åsleik asks if I'm watching the dog for my Namesake and I say yes and Åsleik says that I've talked about getting a dog so many times that he thought I'd finally gone and done it

No, I say

and I put Bragi down and he barks a couple times at Åsleik who is holding out his fist to him and then the dog sniffs his hand and then he relaxes

His name's Bragi, I say

That's a good name for a dog, Åsleik says

and I see Bragi run out across the snow and he lifts his leg and then he stands there and pees

I cleared your driveway earlier today, Åsleik says

But then it started snowing again, he says

We don't usually get so much snow in Dylgja, I say

Sometimes it's years between snowfalls, he says

and then we stand there and I feel tired but I can tell that Åsleik's in the mood to talk and I can't very well not ask him in

You should come inside, I say

You don't mind? he says

No, come in, I say

You waited a long time before inviting me in, he says

Please, you're always welcome, I say

Well, he says

It's cold standing in the door, I say

All right, Åsleik says

and then he says he has something for me and then he goes over to his tractor and he takes two shopping bags out of the driver's cabin and he comes walking over to me holding up the bags

I have something here for you, he says

And I bet you can guess what it is, he says

and he hands me the bags and they give off a powerful smell of the best smoked lamb ribs and I see that one bag is almost full of sliced Christmas lamb ribs and in the other are lots of big pieces of lutefisk packed up well in their own plastic bags

Thank you, I say

Just the way it should be, Åsleik says

Glad to help, he says

Yes, thank you, I say

and then I stand there with a bag in each hand, and the weight feels heavy on both arms so Åsleik really must have filled the bags up, I think

I brought a lot this year, Åsleik says

Can you tell? he says

More than usual, he says

Yes, I can tell, I say

And I did it for a reason, Åsleik says

Yes, I say

and then there's silence

And that is, Åsleik says

Yes, I say

It's because this year I want a bigger picture to give Sister as a Christmas present, he says

She has enough small ones, he says

You've always given me one of the small ones, he says

I was almost starting to think you'd paint a bunch of small pictures just to make sure you could give me one, Åsleik says

and I hear what he's saying and now that I think about it maybe he's right? could I maybe have been doing that? but I've painted hardly any small pictures recently, I have just a few, four or five maybe, so it's fine to give Åsleik one of the bigger pictures, but the newest one, the one with the St Andrew's Cross, no, he can't have that one, that's for sure, I'd rather he just take all his lamb and fish and go right back home, but no, that's a bad idea, because Åsleik makes exceptionally good Christmas lamb ribs every year and his lutefisk tastes exceptionally good too, not to mention the dry-cured mutton he makes, but we still need to come to an agreement about which picture he'll get, it's just that Åsleik really understands pictures, he can see pretty much right away if it's a good picture or a bad one, and he's always picked out the best one, yes, the best of the small pictures he's been choosing up until now, I think and then Åsleik says Sister has pictures of mine all over the house by now, in the hall, in the living room, in the stairwell, yes, he can't think of anywhere she doesn't have pictures I've painted, and she has three small pictures hanging over her sofa, but it would look nicer there with one big one, he says, so this year he would really like one of my bigger pictures, and I say that's, that's fine, because it's true what he says, he's always taken one of the smaller pictures, but I'd never thought about it before, even if what he's saying is totally right, I say

Yes you can pick one of the big pictures this year, I say

and Åsleik says that he doesn't want to be pushy, or rude, but he'd be grateful if he could take the picture with him to-day, because Christmas is coming soon and he has to wrap the painting in proper wrapping paper with pixies and angels and such, and he needs to put the nicest red ribbon he can around the package, and a little card that says For my dear sister Guro, he says, and, yes, well, he knows he's asked me about this every year recently but it really would be great if I'd come with him to Sister's to celebrate Christmas, it's just the two of them so it would be nice for them if I came along, and of course it's also always much nicer and safer to have two people in a boat than just one, he says, so it would be a great help to him as well as making him very happy if I'd come with and celebrate Christmas with Sister, way up in Sygnefjord, yes, it takes a whole short day to go to Øygna in The Boat, he says, but that's what he's done every year now for quite a few years, rowed there and rowed back, he says

You call her just Sister? I say

and I think why am I asking him that now

I guess I do, Åsleik says

Yes, I guess I've always called her just Sister, it's true, Åsleik says

Yes, I say

But her name's Guro, Åsleik says

Yes, I say

Guro, yes, he says

and then we stay standing silently

But, please, come in, I say

and Åsleik says thank you and he comes into the hall and I call Bragi and he comes running right into the hall and then he stands there on the floor and shakes the snow off himself and snow flies in all directions and I shut the front door and Åsleik says he can't go tracking snow into my living room, or studio, as it's called, or whatever it is, in his boots, so if it's all right he'll just take off his boots and pick out a picture today, yes, that would be great and I say yes, yes of course, he should just come right in, he's always welcome, I say and Åsleik says then in that case he should probably take off his snowsuit too, even though it's a bit of a hassle, he says and then he takes off his boots and fur hat and then unzips the front of his snowsuit and starts twisting and turning and he says this coat is a real pain but it always keeps you warm, it really does, he says

My sister's name is Guro, yes, Åsleik says

Yes, I say

and I think that that's strange too, because the woman I ran into in Bjørgvin who kept Bragi for the night at her place was named Guro as well, and it's not such a common name, but maybe it was a common name in the countryside at one point, I think

And the dog's name is Bragi, yes, I say

What a nice little scamp, Åsleik says

and again he holds out his hand to Bragi, who goes over to Åsleik and licks his hand a couple of times and then Åsleik clutches Bragi's fur and tugs a little and now they're good friends, I think

Bragi, yes you are, Åsleik says

and he says if I need someone to watch the dog for me I should just call him, he says and I think that actually it's kind of strange that in all these years Åsleik has only ever talked about Sister and almost never called her Guro, I think and we go into the main room and Åsleik says I keep it so cold in the room that he should probably go back out to the hall and put his snowsuit back on, he says, don't I have a fire in the stove? I have plenty of wood in The Shed, last summer he drove a giant load of wood to my house and we stacked it all in The Shed, good dry birchwood, and a generous amount of kindling, and wood chips, he says, and now here I was without a fire in the stove, and not only do I have more than enough wood in The Shed, there's also lots of wood in the woodbox, he can see that, and kindling, and wood chips, yes, so now things with me have reached the point that I'd rather sit there freezing instead of lighting a good fire in the stove, he just doesn't know, Åsleik says and I don't know quite what to say, because I do probably need to defend myself or explain myself somehow but what should I say? and why haven't I lit the stove? yes well it's probably just that I was too tired or something, I think, and that's something I can say

I was so tired that I just lay right down, I say

Yes, well, that makes sense, Åsleik says

Back and forth to Bjørgvin three times in the same day and then again the next day to get back home, that'd tire you out, he says

Yes, I say

When I got home I lay down on the bench with the blanket over me and the dog was lying next to me, so I wasn't cold, I say

If you're wrapped in a good blanket it's true you don't get cold so easily, Åsleik says

and he says that your body heat stays trapped in the blanket somehow, and that's how it keeps you so warm, but since I'm tired he can light the stove for me, that's easy enough, he says and I see Åsleik go over to the stove and open the hatch and he starts putting wood in it and I go out to the kitchen and I see the six shopping bags I bought yesterday on the kitchen table, yes, I drove right back to Bjørgvin without even taking everything out of the bags, I think and I need to put the food away soon, there are already so many bags on the kitchen table that I need to put the lamb and fish Åsleik brought me in the pantry under the stairs to the attic right away, the same as I usually do, but it can wait, because both the lamb ribs and the lutefisk will be fine in the cold kitchen, I think and then I put the two shopping bags Åsleik brought me up on the table with the other bags that are already there and now there are no fewer than eight shopping bags there, I think, and I go back into the main room and I see the stove hatch standing open and Åsleik is there looking at the logs in the stove

It'll catch in a second, Åsleik says

So we'll be warmer soon, he says

and he holds out his hands to the stove and he says that the stove is already nice and warm

You're probably freezing, you should come over here and warm up, he says

and to tell the truth I do feel a little cold and I go over to Åsleik and I stand next to him by the stove and I hold my hands above the stove and it's good to feel the warmth coming up towards my hands, they really were quite cold, I feel

It'll start to warm up in your stove soon, Åsleik says

and then Bragi comes slinking in and he lies down in front of the stove and then I just stand there not saying anything

And now I can take a look at the pictures, and pick out one for Sister? Åsleik says

Yes, I say

and Åsleik turns around and he says that the stack of finished big paintings is big now, but the stack of smaller pictures isn't that big, he says, so I must not have been painting as many smaller pictures as I usually do, he says and I say that's right, and I don't know why, that's just how it is, I say and Åsleik says well that's usually how it goes, things turn out however they're going to turn out, he says and then we just stand there by the stove and I feel warmth spreading through my body and it feels good and Åsleik again says that this year he wants a big picture, I've always, for whatever reason, given him one of the small pictures every other year and that's fine, of course I need to be thrifty to get by, tubes of oil paint and canvases aren't free now are they, no, and of course I get more money for a big painting than I do for a smaller one, he understands all that, but he's been thinking for some years now that he really wanted to give Sister one of the bigger paintings, but I'd always taken him over to the stack of small paintings and shown him those and he'd decided among them and chosen a small picture, and if he hadn't been able to decide on one of those then I'd found some more pictures and put them on the living-room table, but always small ones, yes well what do I mean living-room table, it's been years since you could call it a living-room table strictly speaking, a table you could sit around, could eat at, because there've been tubes of paint and brushes and a hammer and nails and a saw and cloths and rags and other junk and he doesn't know how I can find what I need in that mess, but then again I do have that good long kitchen table, yes, it's been there all these years, since long before when Ales and I moved into the house, yes, it was there when old Alise lived in the house, Åsleik says, yes, and that goes for the living-room table too, of course, all the furniture, yes, we didn't change that much, because there's also the round table with the two chairs that's still in front of the window the same as it was when old Alise lived in the house, and the same bench in the same corner it used to be in, Åsleik says and then there's silence

Yes, you and Ales, he says

Ales and Asle, yes, he says

Yes, I say

It's so sad she got sick and passed away when she was so young, so young, and it was so sudden too, Åsleik says and then we just stand there and we don't say anything, it's like we're frozen in place and I see Ales the first time we walked into the kitchen together and she says she'd always thought they were so beautiful, old Alise's old kitchen table with the old chairs, she said, and then when we went into the living room she said the same thing about the furniture there, and she especially liked the round table with the two chairs in front of the window so that you could sit and look out at Sygne Sea, that in particular she'd always liked so much, she said and then she'd sat down in the chair on the right and I'd sat down in the chair on the left, and that's the way we always sat from then on, me in the chair on the left, where I still sit, and Ales in the chair on the right, I think and I turn around and I see Ales sitting in the chair on the right looking out at Sygne Sea, she's sitting there at the window without moving and her long dark hair is hanging loose down over her back and I don't want to see her and I don't want to think about her, because it's too terrible, the pain is too great, so I don't want to do it, I think and Åsleik says he's sorry, he shouldn't have mentioned Ales, and I don't say anything and then we just stand there by the stove and then Åsleik says the best thing would be, yes well, as he's already said, if he could pick out a picture today, or at least look through them today so he can think it over, think about which picture Sister would like best, if he didn't see it right away, he says and I say that's fine, of course he can look at the pictures today, and I think that actually there's no one besides Åsleik that I show my pictures to, before they're shown at The Beyer Gallery in Bjørgvin, and that it won't be long before I have a new exhibition there, but I have enough pictures for the show, so now I just need to, actually as soon as I can, drive the pictures to Bjørgvin, yes, the thirteen pictures I'm going to show, or at least it's going to be thirteen once Åsleik has taken one for himself, no more and no less, though that's fewer than usual, usually I have thirteen big pictures and six small pictures, nineteen all in all, I really believe in the number nine and I always want it to be in there one way or another, or else it can be a number where the digits add up to make nine, or something, I think, but the woman supposedly named Guro told me that the number that brings me luck, yes, my lucky number, is eight, or four times two, as she also said, because that was the number she got to by adding up the digits of my birthday, she said, but I've stuck with nine, and also three, I think, and so now I'm not sure about the number thirteen, because I think that thirteen can be both a good number and a bad number, the same with eight maybe, I think, no, anyway, eight is a good number, I think, but usually I've always had it be nineteen pictures, some of them small, because The Beyer Gallery isn't that big and Beyer told me that he doesn't want any more pictures than that so I've never had more than nineteen, but one time I brought nine pictures and Beyer said it wasn't enough, or barely enough, it couldn't be any fewer than that in future, he said, it didn't really matter much how big the pictures were of course, though the pictures I paint are never that big, they're just bigger or smaller, and almost no pictures are long and thin like the picture with the two lines crossing each other, which, obviously, there's no way around it, I think, I'll call it *St Andrew's Cross,* and I'll paint the title in thick black oil paint on the top of the stretcher today and then sign it with a large A in the right-hand corner of the picture itself, like I always do, and if I was alone I'd do it right now, but I'll sign the picture as soon as Åsleik leaves, I think, and then I'll need to drive the pictures down to Bjørgvin soon, just get it over with, I think, but now I've driven to Bjørgvin twice without bringing the paintings with me and I guess the reason why I haven't taken them to

Bjørgvin yet is that Åsleik hasn't chosen the picture he wants yet, even though I didn't realize it, without thinking about it that way that's what it was, I think, it's after Åsleik chooses his picture that I'll drive the paintings down to Bjørgvin, because Beyer always wants to hang the pictures himself, he says that it's so important to hang them right, the whole exhibition is like a painting of its own, he says, and that, yes, that's the painting that he paints, or assembles or however you'd put it, Beyer says, and really I have no opinions about how the pictures should be hung, which ones next to which other ones or anything like that, and before Beyer sees the pictures the truth is and has been ever since Ales has been gone that Åsleik is the only one who sees them, and he has an amazingly good eye for pictures, more often than not he sees the same thing that I see, and he almost always has the same opinion about a picture as I do, so he almost always picks one of the pictures that I would have picked myself if I had to choose one, so from one point of view Sister, this Guro woman, probably has the best collection of my pictures anywhere, limited to the small pictures, but truth be told I'm doing something different in the bigger ones, and she's only been given smaller ones, that's true

And you can take one of the big ones, of course, I say

Obviously, I say

I shouldn't have said that about always being given one of the small ones, Åsleik says

and I think that it's true, I've always offered him one of the small pictures, but it wasn't on purpose and I feel a bit ashamed about it now, it's not that I think he doesn't deserve a bigger picture, or Sister for that matter, but for some reason I've acted like Åsleik would always prefer to give Sister a smaller picture and Sister would always prefer to get a smaller picture, yes, in a way I'd have felt like I was forcing it on her if he tried to take a big one, since she'd come to own a lot of paintings over the years, a new one every year, so I probably thought a big one would be too much, she wouldn't have enough space on the wall for them all

Sister's whole house is almost full of your paintings now, Åsleik says

And that's all well and good, it's not that, he says

and Åsleik says that Sister is still just as happy and just as grateful every year for the picture she gets, he says and then he goes over to the stack of the bigger paintings and I see him start to look through the stack and he looks closely at each picture, one by one, and I'm standing by the stove and looking in at the flames and I think that up in the attic, in one of the storage spaces, I have some pictures stored that I didn't want to sell, and two of them are among the first ones I painted when I started painting the way I wanted to paint and not just pictures of people's houses from photographs, and those two pictures are still two of the best I've ever painted, they're pictures where I felt like I'd really accomplished something, yes, more than I'm capable of actually, more of something that's bigger than life is, maybe you could put it that way? yes, even if that's kind of a grand way to put it and it feels too big and grand, still, yes, but, in some of the pictures I've done what I wanted to do, I can see that, I know that, and obviously the picture can say what can't be said in any other way except precisely how that picture is saying it, and I don't want to sell these pictures, my very best ones, because I know that most likely no one else wants to see what's in these pictures, but I almost always have one on display up in the attic room I don't use for storage, and for a long time now it's been a portrait I painted of Ales, I think, because there are two rooms up in the attic, with two storage areas, and I use one room for storage too, I keep a lot of wood I can make stretchers from up there and a lot of canvas and more than a few tubes of oil paint and a whole lot of turpentine, but in the other attic room, on the left, I have only a chair in the middle of the room between the two small windows in the gable and I always have one of the paintings I don't want to sell sitting on that chair, and I don't want to sell it because the ones I sell just go away to someone else and then they're gone, like the two stacks of pictures leaning against the wall by the kitchen door are about to do, because even if Beyer carefully notes down the name and the address of the buyer of this or that picture, yes, he's photographed every single picture since the very first exhibition and numbered them and written down the buyer's name, even then no one knows what happened to the painting after that, if the buyer gave it away or sold it to someone else, yes, strictly speaking the picture vanishes into the unknown and there's no way to find it again, yes, there are pictures I've sold and regretted selling, especially the ones I painted when I was going to The Art School before I realized that there are some pictures I'm just not willing to sell, and those are the ones up in the attic, I keep the pictures I don't want to sell in the storage space in the room on the left, and then I put a new one out, in place of the one I have sitting on the chair, and sometimes, especially when I sort of haven't been painting for a while, when it's stopped, I've gone up to the attic to look at the picture I have on display on the chair or else taken one of the other pictures out of the storage space and put it on the chair and then I also have a chair a few paces back from the chair with the picture on it and I sit down on it and then sit and look and look at the picture, yes, I can stay there for a long time, I don't know how long, and I try to see why I actually keep painting pictures, and I sit and silently fall deeper and deeper into what I'm seeing, into what's bigger than life, maybe, but that's not the right

way to say it, because what it is is, yes, a kind of light, a kind of
shining darkness, an invisible light in these pictures that speak
in silence, and that speak the truth, and then, once I've entered
into this vision, or way of seeing, so that it's not me who's seeing but something else seeing through me, sort of, then I always
find a way I can get farther with the picture I'm struggling
with, and that's how it also is with all the paintings by other
people that mean anything to me, it's like it's not the painter
who sees, it's something else seeing through the painter, and it's
like this something is trapped in the picture and speaks silently
from it, and it might be one single brushstroke that makes the
picture able to speak like that, and it's impossible to understand,
I think, and, I think, it's the same with the writing I like to
read, what matters isn't what it literally says about this or that,
it's something else, something that silently speaks in and behind
the lines and sentences, but, yes, this is what happened, the
pitctures I keep in the attic are only some of the bigger pictures
because Åsleik chose all of the truly good smaller pictures and
took them to give to Sister, yes, it's a bit ridiculous, but he must
see the same way I do, or pretty close, anyway there are lots of
pictures Åsleik picked out and gave to Sister that I really wish I
had in my own collection up in the attic, not all the ones he's
bought, or rather traded for lamb and fish and wood and clearing the snow, there aren't many of the ones he took that I wish
I still had, but all the small pictures I might have imagined
keeping in my collection up in the attic are ones Åsleik took
and gave to Sister for Christmas, yes, it's almost unbelievable
but it's true, her collection of my smaller paintings is a collection of the best smaller paintings I've ever painted, or even the
best pictures I've ever painted altogether, that's how I see it, not
counting the paintings I have up in the attic, and the one I've
had out on the chair up there for quite some time, I don't

remember exactly how long, is the portrait I painted of Ales, and I can't bring myself to put it away, to swap it out for one of the other pictures in the storage spaces there, I think, and it would be nice to see the best smaller paintings I've ever painted again, just once, and anyway it's a good thing that I know where they are, because it doesn't matter so much whether I have them here in my house as long as I know where I could go see them, I think, but I've never gone with Åsleik to visit Sister, the truth is I've never even met her, even though I've driven past her house every single time I drove to or back from Bjørgvin, and it's a pretty, old, small house, even if it does need a little paint, a grey house, but a bit rundown, it's true, and obviously it's never occurred to me to go knock at that woman named Guro's door and ask if I could take a look at the pictures, but still, it really is a bit strange that I've never met Åsleik's sister, because she drops by to see Åsleik now and then, to come see her childhood home, as they say, but she's never spent the night there, Åsleik has said, she takes the bus round-trip the same day, yes, because there's a bus connection once a day between Dylgja and Bjørgvin, to Dylgja in the morning, from Dylgja in the afternoon, it's a small bus, because there aren't many people who take it, I think, it's basically empty past Dylgja more often than not, but some people do travel to or from Bjørgvin, I think and I think that Åsleik said that Sister doesn't want to spend the night in her childhood home, he says, and he doesn't understand why she doesn't want to but anyway it's high time we met, what with all the paintings of mine she has hanging in her house, I think, so maybe I will go with Åsleik for Christmas at Sister's house this year? after all, Åsleik asks me every year if I can't go with him to celebrate Christmas with her, and he says why can't I come? because it would have to be much nicer for me than spending Christmas alone in Dylgja? he says and I always say no, I'd rather be alone, I say, but now, this year, maybe this year I can go with Åsleik and celebrate Christmas at Sister's? because then I'd get to see all the good smaller paintings I've painted, if nothing else? and Åsleik said it'd be easier for him, too, if I came along, because then he wouldn't have to go to Øygna alone in The Boat, and it's always so much safer in a boat when there are two of you on board, but he's always alone, Åsleik said, and I see that he's pulled a picture out of the stack and now he's looking at it and he's not saying anything

Maybe I can come for Christmas with you and Sister this year, I say

and I look at Åsleik and there's silence for a moment

You think you might come to Sister's for Christmas? Åsleik says

and it's like he can't believe his ears

Yes, maybe, I say

That's a surprise, Åsleik says

Well there are a lot of paintings Sister has that I'd like to see again, I say

Yes I suppose there are, Åsleik says

and we stand there silently

I'm having a new show at The Beyer Gallery soon, I say

Yes, Åsleik says

But I have enough pictures, more than enough, of the big ones too, so you should take whichever one you want to give Sister today, I say

Since I need to drive the paintings down to Bjørgvin soon, I say

Is that why you didn't take them with you when you kept driving to Bjørgvin, because I still had to pick out a picture? Åsleik says

and I say maybe, yes, maybe that's part of the reason, but it was probably mostly that I wasn't paying attention to the date and I realized only recently that the show is coming up soon

So it's fine if you pick out a picture today, I say

Thanks, Åsleik says

I just realized, I say

Realized what? Åsleik says

That I have a show soon, I say

So I need to drive the paintings down to Bjørgvin in the next few days, I say

and I think that then I can also check on Asle in The Hospital, because there's no way I'll be able to visit him today, but maybe I can tomorrow? or the day after? I think and I say yes I'll probably drive down as soon as tomorrow, or the day after, down to Bjørgvin with the picture, even if that means a lot of driving, I don't think I've ever driven to Bjørgvin so many times so close together before, I say

You could have taken the pictures with you yesterday, Åsleik says

Yes, I say

But you didn't think of it? he says

No, to tell you the truth I didn't, I say

and there's silence

Because I could have chosen the painting I want yesterday, or a few days ago, Åsleik says

Yes, I say

You've probably never driven to Bjørgvin twice in the same day before, you're right, he says

No, I say

and we stand there not saying anything

You usually never drive to Bjørgvin to go shopping more than once a month, do you? Åsleik says

and I say he's probably right, anyway it's no more than that, I say

And then you do go almost every Sunday, papist that you are, to mass at St Paul Church, he says

and I nod and I think will he never stop using that word? it's like with St Andrew's Cross, it's like he's proud that he can say this word too, can say papist, I think

It takes you all day, he says

Yes I often do, I say

No, I really don't understand you, Åsleik says

Plus you're practically a Communist, he says

No, I don't get it, Åsleik says

A Catholic and a Communist at the same time, he says

and Åsleik shakes his head and then we just stand there and then I say that Christmas is coming up soon and I need to drive the pictures down to Bjørgvin this year same as every year, because every year I have an exhibition at The Beyer Gallery before Christmas, as he knows of course, I say

During Advent, yes, he says

But you should pick out a painting first, I say

and then I say that it's good he wants to do it today

I'll pick out a painting today and just take it with me, Åsleik says

and I realize that I'm kind of hungry, after all I haven't eaten anything since breakfast at The Country Inn this morning, and I didn't eat much then either, I think, but I don't feel like cooking a big meal, I'm too tired, but I can always fry an egg with some bacon and onions, I have good fresh bread, yesterday I bought bacon and onions I can fry up, and I ask Åsleik if he'd like some fried eggs with bacon and onions and he says he wouldn't say no to that, it sounds delicious, Åsleik says, and I see him looking at one of the big paintings and then Åsleik says he'll just look at the pictures a little more so maybe he can choose one while I'm frying the bacon and eggs and onions and I say that's fine and I see that there's a good fire in the stove and then I put a log in the stove and I shut the hatch and then I go out to the kitchen and I see all the shopping bags on the kitchen table, yes, I didn't even unpack what I bought before I drove back to Bjørgvin yesterday, I think, and now, yes, now I'll unpack them and put all the food away because there's eggs and bacon and onions and bread somewhere in one of the bags, I bought a lot of bacon, and lots of bread, and I need to wrap them in plastic bags and put them in the freezer out in the hall, because there are two main rooms in the house, and the one next to the kitchen is where I paint, and where I read, it's where I spend my time, and then there's a little room off the side of the main room with a double bed where I sleep, and that was where Ales and I slept too in the years we shared, the years we were together, and then there's the hall, and off the hall there's one more room, yes, The Parlour as old Alise used to call it, and that's what Ales always called it too and so that's what I still call it, The Parlour, because the room was thought to be especially nice somehow, it had the ugliest wallpaper I've ever seen, yes, red and white roses twined together from floor to ceiling, and old Alise was so proud of the room that she practically never used it, and the first thing Ales and I did when we moved into the house was paint over the wallpaper, we painted the room white, but other than that we didn't change too much in the house, I think, we took it over just the way it was, plates and bowls, knives and forks, I think, but we did paint The Parlour white over that wallpaper with roses on it and after a while it was there, in The Parlour, that Ales painted her paintings, and it comes back to me that it was then, while we were painting The Parlour, that I stopped smoking, yes, Ales thought that when we were moving to Dylgja was a good opportunity to stop smoking, the same way I'd stopped drinking when we moved into the brown house, yes, she said, and that's what I did, yes, I stopped smoking and started taking snuff and even though Ales didn't exactly love that I took snuff she accepted it, I who had smoked almost constantly, rolling a cigarette and lighting it while I was still smoking the last one, I had stopped, but I did start taking snuff at the same time, and now why am I starting to think about that? I think, and I think that at first after Ales was gone, after she'd gone to her rest with God, I'd left everything how it was, but it was too sad to keep the room the way she'd left it so after a while I moved the tubes of oil paint and brushes and such out of The Parlour, yes, everything she'd used for her painting I took and used myself, except what she'd used to paint icons, because in the last few years she'd painted nothing but icons, and everything that had to do with icon painting was still where it was when she'd died, on the big bookshelf I made myself to cover the whole long wall there are her books, but also my books, and I've put the ones I've bought more recently on the bookshelf there in The Parlour too, it's turned into a real library, not least because of the many books Ales bought about icons and icon painting, and when Ales was gone I hung all her icons up in The Parlour, including the ones that weren't totally finished, and then I hung up the few paintings she'd left behind, because she'd painted over almost all her paintings with white and some of the best paintings I ever managed to paint were on canvases where Ales had painted over her own pictures in white, I think and I think I can't just keep standing here like this not doing anything and so I go over to the kitchen table and I start to unpack a bag of groceries, I put the groceries on the table and I take the groceries out of all the other bags and then the table is covered with all kinds of things, meat, bacon, potatoes and vegetables, butter and margarine, flour, soap and shampoo and I don't know what else, and then the two bags I got from Åsleik are left, one with lamb ribs and one with lutefisk, and I think I'll carry them out right now to the pantry under the stairs up to the attic, and I take the bags and leave the kitchen and I put them in the pantry and I think now I need to get everything that needs freezing into the freezer, I think, I have a large freezer in the hall, yes, so big that when I bought it and had it delivered it barely fit through the front door, because I wanted a big freezer since I can sometimes go quite a while between shopping trips, and since I really go shopping only when I go to Bjørgvin, because I don't like spending money, I think, and I think another reason it's good to have a big freezer is that I can get more fish from Åsleik now, I don't only get lamb ribs and lutefisk from him, no, I get dried fish and smoked herring and dry-cured herring and fresh cod and I don't know what else, I think, and now I need to fit all the food into the freezer, I think and then after that I need to make some fried eggs and bacon and onions, I think and I go into the kitchen and I put the bread and the packages of pork cutlets and the ground beef and frozen vegetables into two bags and the frozen things have thawed but I'm sure they'll be all right to eat even if they've thawed once, I obviously should have put them in the freezer yesterday, and I can't believe I was so forgetful that I didn't, I think and I go out into the hall and I hear Åsleik call what are you doing? and I say I just need to get the groceries into the freezer and I hear him answer yes it's certainly time you did that, if I was in such a hurry to get back to Bjørgvin that I didn't even unpack the groceries and put them in the freezer, no, I'm really something, I hear Åsleik say, and I put the two bags in the freezer and I think I should have put the groceries in the freezer properly, item by item, because I keep the freezer neat and organized, everything in its proper place, in the freezer like everywhere else, and what Åsleik calls the mess on the table in the main room is actually very organized,

I think, but I'll have to organize the food in the freezer some other time, because now I'm really hungry, I think and I go back into the kitchen and there's Åsleik

Yes you sure did some shopping, he says

Yes, I say

and I know Åsleik is thinking about whether I've bought anything for him, because I usually do since it's cheaper to buy things in Bjørgvin than at The Country Store in Vik, everything's expensive there, which makes sense, The Shopkeeper has to mark it up more to make enough to live on, and there isn't much choice there, because there aren't that many customers in Vik or Dylgja, so I always tend to buy something for Åsleik when I go shopping in Bjørgvin, I think and I don't want to take any money from Åsleik for the things, because he has so little money, he's just barely getting by, I think, and when I try to give him what I've bought he never wants to take it at first, because he gets by just fine on his own, he doesn't need help from anyone, he doesn't need anything from the city, no, he doesn't need charity, no he always says something like that and I always say yes yes I know and then I say that it's payment for everything he's done for me and eventually he takes the bags of groceries kind of like he doesn't realize it, but he absolutely refuses to take any money, even if I sometimes do slip him a few kroner when I notice that he's in bad shape, and then we both pretend that neither of us notices what we're doing, kind of

Did you decide on a picture? I say

Yes well, Åsleik says

and then he goes back into the main room and I start putting various things into one of the bags and I go out into the hall with the bag and I put it under the hook all my scarves are hanging on and Åsleik will get it from there, I think and then I go back into the kitchen and then I start putting the fresh

vegetables and other things into the big refrigerator, because I
have a big refrigerator too, and both the fridge and the freezer
were bought when Ales was still alive, I think and I can't start
thinking about Ales again now, I think and then I start putting
the dry goods away in the cupboard in the corner and I put the
cans and soup and bags of flour and sugar and salt and various
bags of pepper and whatever else away and then I take the one
piece of bacon I have out, I've put the rest in the freezer except
for two pieces in the bag for Åsleik, and the egg carton and an
onion and a chunk of bread, and I put it on the kitchen counter
and then Åsleik comes back into the kitchen

Yes you sure did buy a lot of groceries, he says

You know I don't really like going shopping, so I buy a lot
when I do go, I say

I know, Åsleik says

and I look at the frying pan sitting on the stove where it
usually is, and it's an old stove, it was there in the kitchen when
we moved in, we inherited both the range and the frying pan
from old Alise, but every burner on the stove works, and the
oven too, so I imagine I'll be able to keep this range as long as
I live, I think and I turn on the burner with the frying pan on
it all the way and I cut a thick slice of bacon, enough to fill the
whole pan, and I lay it in the pan and it starts sizzling right away
and I turn down the heat and then I cut some slices of bread,
two for Åsleik, two for me

You're such a good cook, really, Åsleik says

Well now, I don't know about that, I say

and the good smell of bacon starts filling the kitchen and I
go turn the meat, because one side is all cooked, and then I get
two plates and knives and forks and Åsleik says those are old
plates, he remembers them from when he was a boy, from old
Alise's time, he says

That smells great, Åsleik says

and I stand by the stove, and I look at the bacon sizzling in the old pan and the pan is so heavy that Ales said it was too heavy for her, she complained about the pan constantly, and she also thought it smoked too much, so that's why we bought a new frying pan that Ales always used while I always used the old cast-iron pan, and the one Ales used was in the pots and pans cupboard next to the stove and it's almost like I can feel the tears coming just from thinking about the other frying pan, I put that pan way back in the back of the cupboard so that it would be hard to see, because that pan always reminds me of Ales and it hurts so much every time I see that pan, yes, tears come to my eyes, to tell the truth, but I don't want to think about that now, about when Ales and I bought a new frying pan, that's another thing I can go around remembering, I can remember it like it was yesterday and go around in circles remembering it, I who have such a bad memory about other things, yes, except for the store of pictures in my head, all the pictures that fill my head, yes, those I remember all the time, but other things, like when Ales and I bought a frying pan, things like that, yes, well, I remember those things too, as clearly as anyone can remember anything

Don't forget about the bacon, Åsleik says

and I give a little start and realize right away that it's starting to smell burnt and in one movement I take the pan off the stove and turn off the burner and I turn over the bacon and it has burned a little but there's such a smell of burnt bacon in the kitchen that most people would think the bacon was totally burnt black but it isn't, it's just cooked well on one side, you might say

I came here a lot to see old Alise, Åsleik says

And she cooked for me a lot, he says

and he says that he has a feeling she used to think that they were practically starving back at their house and then he says well it's certainly true they were in a bad way when he was growing up, but it was just him and Sister, there wasn't a big flock of kids with mouths to feed, the way it was in a lot of families in those days, for whatever reason there was just him and Sister, yes, but, well, after his father never came back from the sea, yes, well, Åsleik says and he breaks off and I put the bacon on the two plates, and I'll put the bacon that's less burnt on the plate for Åsleik, I think and then I put the four slices of bread in the pan and fry them in the bacon fat a little before putting them on the plates and then I take a big onion out of the cupboard and I peel it and slice it and chop the slices into smaller pieces and then put it in the pan and then stand there stirring the onions and I see that they quickly turn slightly yellow, and I like onions best when they're only lightly fried, yes, just soft and barely cooked, and then I get four eggs from the cupboard and I crack one after another against the side of the frying pan and empty them over the onions and then I stand there looking at the pan and not thinking anything and Åsleik doesn't say anything

Food'll be ready soon, I say then

and I say it kind of to break the silence and I think that I almost never do that usually

And I sure am hungry, Åsleik says

Those onions are going to make it taste really good, he says

Onions kind of make everything taste different, he says

and Åsleik says that bacon and fried eggs are always good but they're especially good when you make them with onions, he says

and I think it'll be good to have something to eat because it's nighttime and I've had almost nothing to eat all day, I think,

yes, my stomach's grumbling, so it'll be good to have something to eat, yes, I think and Åsleik says that this is a real meal
fit for a king, he says, and he says it again, a meal fit for a king,
yes, fit for a king, he says and again it's like Åsleik is proud that
he knows the idiom, because that's how he is, there are words
he has to emphasize, give weight to, and sometimes that's fine,
with a term like St Andrew's Cross, because there aren't actually that many people who know what that means, but fit for
a king, such an ordinary phrase, old-fashioned even, yes, why
would anyone be proud of knowing that? I think, and I say that
the eggs are done and then I put them and the onions on the
two plates and then I take one plate, the one with the bacon
that's less burnt, and put it down in front of Åsleik and then I
get a knife and fork and give those to him

Looks good, Åsleik says

and then I go get the other plate and knife and fork and I
put them down at the end of the table where I've always sat,
right here at the head of the table, is where I sit, and Ales always sat to my left, that's where the two chairs are, and when
Åsleik ate with us he always sat on the right side, on a bench
that's along the wall so a person sitting there could lean his back
against the wall, and that's where Åsleik is sitting now, where
he's always sat, I think and I sit down and I say bless this food
and then we start eating and we eat without saying a word,
and it tastes good, yes, it's unbelievable how good simple food
can taste, the eggs are just eggs, the onions are just onions, and
the bread I buy is just bread I pick out at random, whatever's
cheapest, so the bread usually tastes the same but sometimes a
little different, while that's not true of the bacon, there can be a
big difference there, sometimes it shrivels up into almost nothing and sometimes the fully cooked slices are practically as big
as they were raw, and the taste is different too, yes, I think, but

today, today everything tastes unbelievably good, and maybe it's because I'm so hungry, I think and then Åsleik says it tastes good, yes, I always cook bacon and eggs and onions in the best way but even so today it tastes even better than usual, he says and I want to say something to him but I agree so I don't say anything and then Åsleik puts the knife and fork down next to each other on the plate and says yeah that tasted great and I finish and then put my knife and fork down on my plate too and Åsleik says thank you so much for the food, but now he really should be getting home, because I must be tired after all that driving, two round trips to Bjørgvin, one after the other, he says and I say yes you really start to feel it after you've eaten and Åsleik says yes well he's looked at the pictures but he isn't totally sure which one he wants, so maybe he can come back tomorrow and take a painting then? he says

But if you still want to drive the paintings to Bjørgvin tomorrow maybe it's better if I just pick one now, he says

You can if you want, sure, I say

But I'll have to drop by tomorrow anyway, because it's supposed to snow so much tonight that I'll have to clear your driveway tomorrow too, he says

and then Åsleik says that he'll stop by tomorrow, early tomorrow, both he and I get up early, so he can probably pick out a picture for Sister tomorrow, that way he'll have time to sleep on it too, because he's deciding between two pictures, he says, so if it's all right with me he'll come over tomorrow morning, and then he can help me load the pictures I'm taking to The Beyer Gallery into the car too, he says

Yes, you usually do that, I say

Well it needs doing, Åsleik says

Yes, I say

You need to be careful handling pictures, he says

And every one of them needs to get wrapped in a blanket, he says

Yes, I say

That's how I do it, yes, I say

I use a whole blanket for each big picture, and half a blanket for the smaller ones, as you know, I say

That's right, Åsleik says

Yes, I've often wondered where you got so many blankets, he says

and I knew he was going to say that, because he says it every time, and I've sworn to myself that I'm never going to tell him, he will never know, I need to keep some things to myself, I think, even though it's nothing, the answer is totally normal and boring, I just bought the blankets at The Thrift Shop in Sailor's Cove, a little north of the centre of Bjørgvin, in fact on the block where Asle lives, and obviously I didn't buy them all at once but I've been to The Thrift Shop lots of times and sometimes there'd be a blanket or two there and I'd buy them, and that's how after a while I got to have so many blankets

So, see you tomorrow morning, Åsleik says

See you then, I say

and Åsleik gets up and picks up his plate and knife and fork and Bragi is already at the ready next to the table wagging his tail and Åsleik puts the plate down on the floor and Bragi licks it and then Åsleik puts the plate and knife and fork into the sink and I fill Bragi's bowl with water and put it where it goes in the corner behind the hall door and Bragi runs over to the bowl and slurps up the water and I pick up my plate and put it in the sink and I see Åsleik standing in the door to the hall and he says yes Bragi needs his too, he says and then he says see you tomorrow morning and he'll pick out a painting for Sister then and I can think some more about whether I want to come with him this year to celebrate Christmas in Øygna, since I think maybe I can this year, because then, well, then we could probably just drive there together? he says, since I have a car, and a driver's licence? but no, that wouldn't be right, in all these years he's always gone to Øygna in The Boat for Christmas, there's a good landing there in a small bay, so that's how he'll go this year too, he says, but no one's getting any younger, so if I start coming regularly to celebrate Christmas with Sister, with Guro, then maybe some other year, when it gets too rough to go in The Boat, maybe we can take my car to Øygna? he says, well I should think about it, he says, because Sister's hardly some kind of a monster, maybe I'll even be glad I met her, and talked to her, yes, there's aren't that many people I talk to during the year, no, there can't be many, there's him, Åsleik, and then Beyer, the gallerist, and then I probably talk every now and then to the man with my Name, Åsleik says

But there's something I wanted to ask you about, Åsleik says

and I look straight at him standing in the doorway

Yes, I say

Yes, I've thought about asking you lots of times, but I've never done it, he says

But now, well, now that you're maybe thinking about coming to spend Christmas with me and Sister, since this might be happening for the first time, yes, well, I feel like I can ask you, he says

Go ahead, I say

Why is your hair so long? Åsleik asks

and I realize I'm about to start laughing but I manage not to

Beats me, I don't know, I say

Yeah? Åsleik says

I've had long hair almost since I was a kid, I say

Yeah, Åsleik says

and I say that one time when I was young I decided I wanted long hair, and so I grew my hair out, and then my mother dragged me to a hairdresser's, because even in Barmen where I grew up there were places where ladies would cut your hair, and now that she was getting her first chance to cut my hair she really went at it, I was left almost bald, it was a disaster, and since then I've never let any lady at a hairdresser's touch my hair, any barber either, and all my mother had to do was mention that I needed a haircut and I'd almost go after her with my fists, I say, even though I'm not a violent person, I've never hit anyone, but Mother eventually realized she had to give up on getting me to cut my hair and she let it just grow, and when it did get too long I would cut it myself, the way I still do, I just need two mirrors and a pair of scissors, I say

But now, well, now that it's gone all grey? Åsleik says

And so thin too, he says

That doesn't matter, I say

And with that bald spot you've got, too, it's pretty big, he says and there's silence

When my hair started thinning out, I started tying it back with a black hairband, I say

Yes, a ponytail they call it, Åsleik says

The name says it all, he says

and I say I don't know how many years I've been doing it, wearing my hair in a ponytail, but yes, it's been a long time, because my hair turned grey early, I say, and I think I should have asked Åsleik why he has such a long grey beard, but I know what he'll answer if I do, I think

So it's because your mother made you get a horrible haircut once that you still have long hair? Åsleik says

If you want to put it that way, he says

Yes it's partly that, I say

I also just like having long hair, it's like it helps me in a way, it gives me a kind of protection, I say

Protection? Åsleik says

Helps you? he says

Yes, it helps me, helps me paint well, kind of, I say

and Åsleik says that he can't understand a thing like that and he says I look tired and I say that I am tired

I'm going to go right to bed, I say

When you're tired that's the best thing, Åsleik says

Even if it's early, he says

Yes, I say

So then it's probably time for me to go, he says

and Åsleik goes out into the hall and I follow him with Bragi at my heels and I open the front door and Bragi runs out and I see Åsleik standing there pulling his brown snowsuit on

He was sure in a hurry, Åsleik says

and I see him put on his boots and the brown fur cap with the earflaps

He must've needed some fresh air, I say

Yes, probably had to get some fresh air too before he lay down, Åsleik says

No big difference between dogs and people there, I say

Good point, Åsleik says

and he goes outside and I think now he's going to start talking about why he doesn't have a dog and I can certainly listen to all that, I've heard it so many times already, but I'm too tired now and I say goodnight to him and he says see you tomorrow, because he wants to come pick out a picture for Sister, yes, before I take the pictures to Bjørgvin, of course, yes, he says and I think that he's already said that and I say yes yes see you tomorrow and then I call Bragi and he comes running over and into the hall covered with snow and then he stands there and shakes off the snow and I see Åsleik climb up to the cabin of his tractor and I remember the bags of groceries I bought in Bjørgvin to give to Åsleik, they're still under the hook with the scarves, and I pick up the bags and I step into my boots and I hurry over to the tractor with Bragi at my heels

Wait a second, I shout

What is it now? Åsleik says

and I know perfectly well that he knows why I'm asking him to wait

Just wait, I say

I was just leaving, Åsleik says

and I hear Åsleik start the tractor, with a grinding sound from the engine, and I hold up the bags of groceries

Here, I say

You know I don't need anything, Åsleik says

I don't need any charity, he says

It's payment, for clearing the roads, I say

I don't need to get paid for that, he says

and I put the bags down at his feet and he just barely audibly mumbles thank you and then he starts carefully driving off and I go back to the front door with Bragi at my heels and I see him run into the hall and then I shut the front door behind me and then I go and make sure the burners on the stove are off and then I turn off the light in the kitchen and go into the main room and I stop in the middle of the room and I think that before I lie down I want to take a little look at the picture I'm working on, the one with the two lines that cross in the middle, and I think that maybe I should shut the curtains, I usually do, but now it's so dark out that I can look at the picture in the dark just fine without closing the curtains like I usually do, maybe it's a strange habit, always wanting to look at my paintings in the dark, yes, I can even paint in the dark, because something happens to a picture in the dark, yes, the colours disappear in a way but in another way they become clearer, the shining darkness that I'm always trying to paint is visible in the darkness, yes, the darker it is the clearer whatever invisibly shines in a picture is, and it can shine from so many kinds of colour but it's usually from the dark colours, yes, especially from black, I think and I think that when I went to The Art School they said you should never paint with black because it's not a colour, they said, but black, yes, how could I ever have painted my pictures without black? no, I don't understand it, because it's in the darkness that God lives, yes, God is darkness, and that darkness, God's darkness, yes, that nothingness, yes, it shines, yes, it's from God's darkness that the light comes, the invisible light, I think and I think that this is all just something I've thought up, yes, obviously, I think and I think that at the same time this light is like a fog, because a fog can shine too, yes, if it's a good picture then there's something like a shining darkness or a shining fog either in it, in the picture, or coming from the picture, yes, that's what it's like, I think, and without this light, yes, then it's a bad picture, but actually there's no light you can see, maybe, or is it that only I can see it, no one else can? or maybe some other people can too? but most other people don't see it, or even if they do sort of see it it's without knowing it, yes, I'm completely sure about that, they see it but they don't realize that it's a shining darkness they're seeing and they think that it's something else, that's how it is, and even though I don't understand why it's at night, in the darkness, that God shows himself, yes well maybe it's not so strange, not when you think about it, but there are people who see God better in the daylight, in flowers and trees, in clouds, in wind and rain, yes, in animals, in birds, in insects, in ants, in mice, in rats, in everything that exists, in everything that is, yes, there's something of God in everything, that's how they think, yes, they think God is the reason why anything exists at all, and that's true, yes, there are skies so beautiful that no painter can match them, and clouds, yes, in their endless movements, always the same and always different, and the sun and the moon and the stars, yes, but there are also corpses, decay, stenches, things that are withered and rotten and foul, and everything visible is just visible, whether it's good or bad, whether it's beautiful or ugly, but whatever is worth anything, what shines, the shining darkness, yes, is the invisible in the visible, whether it's in the most beautiful clouds in the sky or in what dies and rots, because the invisible is present in both what dies and what doesn't die, the invisible is present in both what rots and what doesn't rot, yes, the world is both good and evil, beautiful and ugly, but in everything, yes, even in the worst evil, there is also the opposite, goodness, love, yes, God is invisibly present there too, because God does not exist, He is, and God is in everything that exists, not like something that exists but as something that exists, that has being, they say, I think, even if good and evil, beauty and ugliness are in conflict, the good is always there and the evil is just trying to be there, sort of, I think and I can't think clearly and I understand so little and these thoughts don't go anywhere, I think and I look at Bragi and I see life shining in his eyes and I think I understand so little while it's like these dog eyes looking at me understand everything, but they will rot too, will pass away, the same as all human eyes, they'll rot, they'll pass away, or else flames will consume them, once it would have been on a bonfire and now it's in an oven, for an hour or two or however long it takes now in an oven and then the whole visible human being, the body, is gone, but the invisible human being is still there, because that is never born and so it can never die, I think, yes, the invisible eye is still there after the visible one is gone, because what's inside the eye, inside the person, doesn't go away, because there's God inside the person, it's the kingdom of God there, yes, as stands written, and yes, yes, that's how it is, in there, there inside the person is what will pass away and become one with what is invisible in everything, and it's like it's tied to the visible but it isn't the visible, yes, it's like the invisible inside the visible, and it's what makes the visible exist, but out of everything that exists it's only people in whom the invisible in the visible is so closely related to what's invisibly visible in everything else, but different from everything that exists because it belongs to everything that exists, even though it doesn't exist itself, not in space, not in time, it is not a thing, it's nothing, yes a nothing, I think, and only while the person is alive does it exist in space, in time, and then it leaves time, goes out of space, and then it's united with, yes, with what I call God, and that, yes, invisible thing in the visible, which acts within it, which sustains it, yes, it shows itself in time and space as shining darkness, I think, and it's that and nothing else that my pictures have always tried to show and once my eyes get used to the darkness so that I can see a little, yes, then I can see if there's any of the shining darkness in the picture, and if there isn't then I'll usually always paint a thin coat of white or black, either one coat or a few thin coats of white or black, in some place or another, a glaze, they call it, and then I keep doing it, sometimes with just white, sometimes with just black, but always with a thin coat of oil paint, I keep doing it until the picture shines darkly, I paint with white or black in the darkness and then the darkness starts to shine, yes always, yes, yes, sooner or later the darkness starts to shine, I think, but now I'm so tired that I just want to go lie down, I think, but first I have to look at the picture with the two lines crossing in the middle in the dark, because maybe there's the shining darkness in the picture and maybe there isn't, and I have to see if it's there before I lie down, I think, and I turn off the light and I can't see anything in the room and then I stay standing up to get used to the darkness, until I can see a little, because I do need to be able to see a little even if I'm painting in the dark, of course, and it doesn't take long before my eyes get used to the dark so that I can see a little and then I go stand a few steps back from the easel and I look at the picture, step closer, step back a little, and I see that the black darkness is shining from the picture, from almost the whole picture, the black darkness is shining, yes, I've hardly ever seen the black darkness shine like that from any other picture, I think and I stand there looking at the picture and I think that this picture is done, I won't do anything else to this painting, and I won't sell this painting, I'll put it up in the attic with the other pictures I want to keep for myself and not sell, the pictures I go look at every now and then when it sort of stops for me, when I sort of can't start painting any more, my best pictures, and the ones I think no one else would get anything from anyway and wouldn't want to pay anything for, like this picture with the two lines crossing, and I stand there and I look at the picture, I step a little to one side, I look at the picture from that side, then from the other side, from below, from above, and it's the same however I look at it, yes, the picture has its shining darkness and I think that tomorrow the first thing I'll do when I wake up is take this painting up to the attic and put it in the stack in the storage space with the other pictures I don't want to sell, because this picture, yes, it's finished, and I don't want to sell it, and if someone did want to buy it I'd get paid barely enough money to cover the cost of the stretcher, the canvas, and the oil paint, at least after Beyer takes his cut, because he takes half of whatever a picture sells for, I think and

I am so tired so tired, I think and now I'll lie down, I think, but first I have to sign the picture and I turn on the light and I pick up a tube of black oil paint and a brush and then I paint *St Andrew's Cross* on the back, on the top of the stretcher, and then in the lower right-hand corner on the painting itself I paint a large A and then I wipe the brush off with turpentine and put it back where it goes and then I open the door to the side room where I sleep and I feel a rush of cold hit me, because I've always slept in cold rooms, but now the open door will let a little warmth into the side room and I turn on the light in there and go back into the main room and turn off the light there and go back into the side room and I get undressed and hang my clothes on a chair and then I'm standing there naked and shivering a lot and then I turn off the light and lie down in the bed and I tuck the duvet around me and I think I'm too tired to go brush my teeth and then I call Bragi and he comes right away and he jumps up onto the bed and crawls in under the duvet and I tuck the duvet well around both of us and Bragi lies down against my side, all the way under the duvet, and I press the duvet against his body and I feel so tired so tired and then I feel Ales lying there next to me in bed and we're holding each other tight and giving each other warmth and I can't think about Ales, not now, and then I say I'm so tired and I want to sleep now and so she should have a good rest and it won't be long before we see each other again, I say, and I feel how close Ales is, because even if it's been many years since she died she is lying next to me in bed and I say I don't want to talk any more now, I can't talk with you tonight, Ales, I say, because then I'll start just missing you so much, so terribly much, I say, and I have my arms around Ales and I hold her and she holds me then I say that it won't be long before we're together again, she and I, and actually we are always together, now too,

I think, but now I want to sleep, there's been too much today, and yesterday, I say, and then Ales strokes my hair and then I take the cross on my brown rosary that I got from Ales once and I place the cross down on my belly, and I'm lying there, and I realize I'm so tired, so tired, and I think even so I need to say a Pater Noster before I go to sleep and so I make the sign of the cross and then I take the cross between my thumb and index finger and hold it tight and I say to myself Pater noster Qui es in cælis and I pause after those words and already I'm starting to drift off into the fog of sleep and I say Sanctificetur nomen tuum Adveniat regnum tuum and I think yes Hallowed be thy name Thy kingdom come, yes, God's kingdom must come, your kingdom, come, I think and I breathe deeply in and I say to myself Kyrie and I breathe slowly out and I say eleison and I breathe deeply in and I say to myself Christe and I breathe slowly out and I say eleison and I breathe deeply in and slowly out and then I see Asle standing at the side of the road, with a tin milk canister in his hand, and he sees a white car come driving up, and it's The Bald Man's white car, the man who lives in the big yellow house, on the downhill side of the road by The Dairy, and it's a big car, a wide car, taking up the whole road, and so Asle is standing a good ways back on the hill with a tin milk canister in his hand, because Mother has asked him to go shopping by himself, so he's going to go to The Bakery to buy bread and then to The Dairy to buy milk, and then he'll go to The Co-op Store to buy what Mother has written down in a shopping list, and the person at the cash register in The Co-op Store will write down what it costs in a little notebook, and Asle thought he would go to The Co-op Store first, since it's farthest, and then to The Dairy, and then up the hill to The Bakery, and then he'll go home to Mother with the things, he thought, and Asle sees the white car stop and The Bald Man rolls down his car window and asks Asle if he wants to come with him and take a drive with him and why not, Asle thinks, he could do that, even though both Mother and Father have told both him and Sister that they must never get into a car with The Bald Man and never go into his house if he asks them to, Asle thinks, but he's never entirely understood what's so dangerous about sitting in The Bald Man's car, and it might be nice to take a little drive, Asle thinks and The Bald Man looks at Asle and he's obviously waiting for an answer and it might really be nice to take a drive, Asle thinks as he stands there at the side of the road with the tin milk canister in his hand and he asks where they'd drive to and The Bald Man says he needs to go see a man at Innstranda to discuss something with him and Asle thinks yes sure he could always go for a little drive with The Bald Man, yes, as long as his parents don't find out, he thinks, because he's not that busy, after all, there's no big hurry to buy what Mother said to buy for her, and he thought he'd go to The Co-op Store first so this way The Bald Man can drop him off at The Co-op Store after they come back, Asle thinks

I'm going shopping for my mother, he says

At The Co-op Store? The Bald Man says

Yes, Asle says

And then at The Dairy and The Bakery too, he says

and Asle holds up the tin milk canister and The Bald Man says he can see that Asle is carrying a tin milk canister, isn't he, and it must be his mother who asked him to go shopping for her, he says and Asle says yes it was and The Bald Man says he can get in and sit with him if he feels like coming along on a drive, and then they'll drive on over to Innstranda, because he needs to talk to a man there, The Bald Man says and then he asks Asle to get into the car and The Bald Man rolls up the window and then opens the front door and Asle gets in and sits in the passenger seat with the tin milk canister between his legs and he slams the door shut and then The Bald Man starts driving and he doesn't say anything he just sits there and grips the wheel and looks straight ahead and then Asle sits there in the front of the car and they drive past The Bakery and past The Dairy and past the big yellow house where The Bald Man lives and then they drive past The Co-op Store and around a bend and once they've taken that turn they can see a long way up The Fjord, up Hardangerfjord, all the way to where The Fjord ends, they can see to The Bottom Of The Fjord and then they drive in along Hardangerfjord towards Innstranda and The Bald Man says he needs to have a little talk with a man at Innstranda, yes, and Asle hears that The Bald Man's voice is a little shaky and he thinks it must be lonely living by yourself in such a big house like The Bald Man does and then The Bald Man puts a hand on Asle's leg and Asle pushes his hand away and he thinks why did The Bald Man put his hand on his leg? and then they drive farther and neither of them says anything and then The Bald Man puts a hand on his leg again, and he runs his hand up and down Asle's leg and Asle pushes his hand away and then he asks The Bald Man why he's doing that and he doesn't answer

You mustn't tell anyone, The Bald Man says

and his voice is shaky and he's looking straight ahead and he keeps driving

It would be best if you didn't tell anyone that you came for a drive with me at all, The Bald Man says

Especially don't tell your parents, he says

and The Bald Man says that if Asle comes home with him he has both soft drinks and hot chocolate, if not today then maybe some other day, he says and Asle doesn't say anything and then The Bald Man turns off the country road and drives up a driveway and he stops the car and turns off the engine and then he gets out and knocks on a door and a man comes out and he and The Bald Man stand in front of the house and the man looks at Asle and The Bald Man talks to the man who's come out of the house and who's looking at Asle, and why did The Bald Man put his hand on his leg? Asle thinks and then The Bald Man comes back and gets into the car and he starts the car and he puts his left hand on the wheel and drives down the drive-way and Asle looks a little off to the side and then The Bald Man puts his hand on Asle's leg and then puts his hand on his fly and unzips his fly and takes his penis in his hand and moves his hand up and down on Asle's penis and it tickles and Asle pushes his hand away and he hears The Bald Man breathing as if he's out of breath and Asle turns and turns and looks at The Bald Man and sees that he's pulling up and down on his own penis, and The Bald Man's penis is big and long like a stick and Asle looks straight ahead again and he hears The Bald Man groan and then The Bald Man puts his right hand on the steering wheel too and he looks straight ahead and again The Bald Man says that Asle mustn't tell anyone that he's been on a drive with him, he says and Asle sits there with the tin milk canister between his legs and he says he won't tell anyone and he thinks that he'll nev-er tell anyone, never, because this, he knows, is something you don't talk about, you can't tell anyone about something like this, and especially not Mother or Father, Asle thinks and The Bald Man asks shouldn't he do his shopping at The Co-op Store now and Asle says yes he should and The Bald Man says he can give him a few kroner so that he can buy something nice for himself and then Asle can come over to his house someday and get ice cream and hot chocolate, he says, but yes the best thing to do would be to drop Asle off a little before The Co-op Store, he says and Asle says that's fine with him and then they drive out along Hardangerfjord without saying anything

You musn't tell anyone, The Bald Man says

I'll give you a few kroner if you promise not to tell anyone, he says

and Asle says he won't tell anyone and The Bald Man pulls over and stops and then he takes out his wallet and gets three kroner out and he gives them to Asle and he puts them right into his trouser pocket and at the same time he zips up his fly and then The Bald Man says that it would be best if he stops here, because it's not far to The Co-op Store, he says and Asle says yes and he puts his hand down into his pocket and he feels the three kroner he's been given, that's money for three ice creams right there, he thinks and The Bald Man bends down over Asle and his belly is covering Asle's whole body and then The Bald Man opens the door on Asle's side and he gets out of the car and then Asle is standing here holding the tin milk canister and then The Bald Man drives on and Asle goes to The Co-op Store and I lie there in bed, and did I doze off? or maybe I've been awake the whole time? I, Asle, I think and I'm probably too tired to fall asleep, overtired they call it, I think and then I stroke Bragi's fur as he lies stretched out next to me, and a dog gives off a good warmth, I think and now I can't start thinking about how I found Asle there in the snow, almost covered with snow, I think, because then there'll be no way I can get to sleep tonight, and I'm so tired, so tired and I see Asle lying there and his whole body's shaking, jerking up and down and The Doctor is standing there looking at Asle and he says it's bad and I hold between my thumb and index finger the brown wooden cross on the rosary I got from Ales once and I say inside myself Pater noster Qui es in cælis Sanctificetur nomen tuum Adveniat regnum tuum Fiat voluntas tua sicut in cælo et in terra Panem nostrum quotidianum da nobis hodie et dimitte nobis debita nostra sicut et nos dimittimus debitoribus nostris Et ne nos inducas in tentationem sed libera nos a malo and I move my thumb and finger to the first bead and I say inside myself Our Father Who art in heaven Hallowed be thy name Thy kingdom come Thy will be done on earth as it is in heaven Give us this day our daily bread and forgive us our trespasses, as we forgive those who trespass against us And lead us not into temptation, but deliver us from evil and I think that I want to say a Salve Regina but I haven't managed to make a good enough Norwegian version of that so I can only say it in Latin, I think and I move my thumb and finger down again and I hold the cross and I say inside myself Salve Regina Mater misericordiæ Vita dulcedo et spes nostra salve Ad te clamamus Exsules filii Hevæ Ad te suspiramus Gementes et flentes In hac lacrimarum valle Eia ergo Advocata nostra Illos tuos misericordes oculos ad nos converte Et Iesum benedictum fructum ventris tui Nobis post hoc exsilium ostende O clemens O pia O dulcis Virgo Maria and I hold the brown wooden cross between my thumb and my finger and then I say, again and again, inside myself, as I breathe in deeply Lord and as I breathe out slowly Jesus and as I breathe in deeply Christ and as I breathe out slowly Have mercy and as I breathe in deeply On me

JON FOSSE was born in 1959 on the west coast of Norway and is the recipient of countless prestigious prizes, both in his native Norway and abroad. Since his 1983 fiction debut, *Raudt, svart* [*Red, Black*], Fosse has written prose, poetry, essays, short stories, children's books, and over forty plays, with more than a thousand productions performed and translations into fifty languages. *The Other Name* is the first volume in *Septology*, his latest prose work, to be published in three volumes by Transit Books.

DAMION SEARLS is a translator from German, Norwegian, French, and Dutch and a writer in English. He has translated many classic modern writers, including Proust, Rilke, Nietzsche, Walser, and Ingeborg Bachmann.

Transit Books is a nonprofit publisher of international and American literature, based in Oakland, California. Founded in 2015, Transit Books is committed to the discovery and promotion of enduring works that carry readers across borders and communities. Visit us online to learn more about our forthcoming titles, events, and opportunities to support our mission.

TRANSITBOOKS.ORG

Printed in the USA
CPSIA information can be obtained
at www.ICGtesting.com
JSHW022102010124
54629JS00005B/64

9 781945 492402